COMMAND OF THE BLOOD SERVICE

A SCI-FI ACTION ADVENTURE

THE CAPITAL ADVENTURES
BOOK 3

ALLEN IVERS

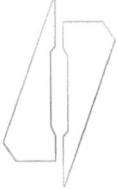

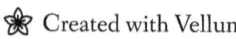

For my wife, Lyn—
I'd never have finished this without your love, support, and friendship.

FOREWORD

Welcome to Book Three of the Blood Service, a series in the Capital Adventures. If you haven't seen the beginning of Aaron's story, check out *The Blood Service*.

This book contains the following content matter:

- *Graphic Violence & Traumatic Injuries*
  - *Many people are shot, stabbed, and torn apart in war-like environments*
  - *Several deaths from energy weapons boiling and charring flesh.*
  - *Trauma surgery performed in less-than sanitary conditions with improvised tools.*
- *Frequent Foul Language*
  - *People swear under these conditions*
- *Sexual Activity*
  - *Referenced but not depicted.*

We're here to have a good time with characters we love. If any of this material distresses you, it's okay to grab another book instead.

Hope you enjoy!

CONTENTS

PART FOUR
TARTARUS

MAP & CHRONOLOGY

The Solar Imperium, also called the Gnostic Empire by the more faithful citizenry, stretches over a fifth of the Milky Way Galaxy. This map features the primary locations featured in the series thus far.

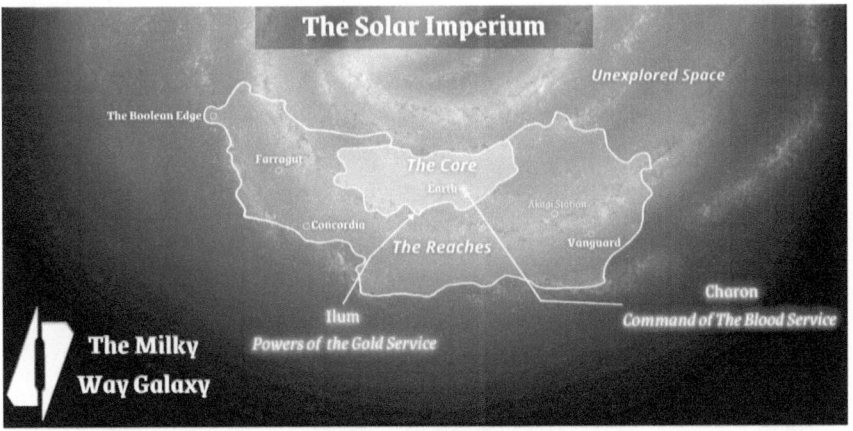

| Map of Solar Imperium controlled space, 2241 CE

The events of the Capital Adventures occur entirely within these borders. Events from one book may be mentioned in another, or characters may cross over from one trilogy to another. Think of it as a shared universe, with the individual stories having unique tones and flair, while building an overarching plot.

You may enjoy each trilogy independent of the others—and I've meticulously built them so that your enjoyment is not contingent on having read the others! But if you want the full experience of the Capital Adventures, I do encourage you to pick up the other books to get a full sense of the Imperium's reach. The official reading order would be to read the trilogies starting with The Blood Service, then The Gold Service, and finishing out with the upcoming Iron Service.

If you're like me, however, and you were looking to read the novels in chronological order, the events of all nine books are as follows:

————

1) THE GOLD SERVICE
2) THE BLOOD SERVICE
3) THE IRON SERVICE

4) RANKS OF THE BLOOD SERVICE
5) COST OF THE GOLD SERVICE
6) SWORDS OF THE IRON SERVICE (COMING SOON)

7) COMMAND OF THE BLOOD SERVICE
8) SHARDS OF THE IRON SERVICE (COMING SOON)
9) POWERS OF THE GOLD SERVICE

WITH EVEN MORE TO COME...

The Blood Service Trilogy has a darker tone than the other two members of this series, with frequent and graphic military violence and confronting concepts like slavery, child soldiers, and war crimes. If you're looking for some weight in your space opera, this trilogy is going to scratch that itch.

"It is easy to go down into Hell; night and day, the gates of dark Death stand wide; but to climb back again, to retrace one's steps to the upper air - there's the rub, the task."

VIRGIL

PART ONE
EREBUS

CHAPTER
ONE

FIONA

IT WAS a tragic bit of misinformation that space was quiet; there were all kinds of radio and electronic interference out in the black. But Fiona always liked to fill it with a bit of music.

Science told her there was no measurable difference between live performance and the pre-recorded compositions blaring through the Jump Deck speakers, but it always felt...wrong to her ear. Too tinny, brassy. It was missing that warmth, the personality that came from the real thing, the unctuous seduction between a listener and a singer. Through a speaker it just felt...isolating.

But maybe that was because it cost exponentially more to put five classically trained people in a large room and tell them to play two-hundred-year-old classics for public amusement. It certainly felt more satisfying, to feel the vibrations rolling up along her augmented hand, how the silksteel hummed against her elbow. The songs would pluck at dusty strings in her heart and give her a certain swagger that was hard to replace.

Now this noise—with its warbling trumpet and discordant piano —just felt staid. Bloodless. Fiona McCorty felt her throat clench and her heart sink into some previously unseen muck at the bottom of her chest.

That brass section in the vaulted halls back on Delta Boolean were so far from her crunchy captain's chair now. Three hundred meters of bulk freighter drifted around her, tumbling in space like it was riding some forgotten breeze. The KC-801B was three generations out of style and at least two since it stopped production, but that suited her just fine. Nobody would question space debris with that aged profile drifting far off the beaten path on lanes only walked by those keeping their heads down.

There was an odd politeness that far into the black, like a dark alley in a seedy city, as mutually ambivalent ships would 'lifelessly' pass each other in the night. Each would adhere to a gentlemen's agreement never to mention seeing one another as they went about their business. No idle conversation, no polite acknowledgement.

If she was this far off the beaten path, it's because she didn't want curious eyes. It actually meant *less* scavengers compared to other more law-abiding spaces; any ship lost out here better have the ability to defend itself from a pirate or two. She wasn't worried about getting mugged.

The fatted calves running on the primary lanes? Now, they were dependent on slow and ineffectual rule of law. Pirates busily scanned those thoroughfares for valuable cargo.

Now, if a team of junkers wanted her ship for scrap? *That* would be a problem.

Her ship drifted in the dark, engines off so as not to attract attention like one of the aforementioned calves that might have limped into the wrong neighborhood. Heat sinks were engaged to minimize her thermal footprint. With a little luck and some creative tumbling, she'd look like any old derelict, cold and forgotten.

That asinine trumpet whined in her ear, crackling out of that metal speaker, one time too many. She'd finally had enough. "Bosun? Can you please give me something with less dying animals in it?"

"One moment," came the strained baritone response as it pondered the question. Finally: "There was a lovely composition from a new Saturnian composer. He recently conducted at the Kennedy Center."

"Agh," she grunted, dismissive.

"The relative age of the piece is disqualifying?" the Bosun asked.

"The correct answer is 'yes ma'am.'"

"...Yes, ma'am. Perhaps a classic from the 21st century. A contemporary seasonal by one Jori de Marqul?"

She raised an approving thumb.

Either the orchestra on the recording had finally put the drowning cat out of its misery or the Bosun had gotten around to turning off that wretched song. What replaced it was soft strings and gentle reeds, like the coming of spring, bereft of virtuoso pretension. She closed her eyes and leaned back into her squeaking chair. It was like drifting off to sleep on the sea, carrying her off to somewhere new.

She waved a hand in the air, turning down the opacity of the cockpit walls. Her heads-up display came alive, hiding the thick steel bulkheads and revealing the glittering stars and rich violet nebulae around her ship.

It was like standing in a watercolor painting, all alone, draped in starlight.

She took a cooling breath as she stared at the majesty of it. Maybe she should've taken Osyen up on his offer. Because being at the helm of a ship, out in the dark...there really was something seductive about this. Like she never wanted to get up from her chair. Just have this moment forever, her and the glittering stars.

No distractions, no politics, no palmed blades or pocket pistols. All quiet. It reminded her of falling, flopping backwards onto a ratty but familiar mattress. It creaked and moaned just the way she liked.

Instead, she'd lost everything, standing on a mountain made of sand. The Imperial Navy had kicked her right off her feet—and they would've sent her screaming back to the hot boxes of Charon in a heartbeat.

She could still feel the sweat beading on her cheek, dribbling down to her chin, carving a path through the muck and salt now caked to her skin.

Keira Ladd stared back at her from the dark, the big Valkyrie reaching down, down into the hole and pulling on Fiona's collar. She was just about free...when something grabbed Keira, dual claws yanking her backward into the shadows—

"Excuse me, ma'am?"

She jerked awake. When had she fallen asleep? How long had she been out? "Ye-what? Bosun?"

"We are five minutes from event horizon, and I require your input at this time." She'd fallen asleep. That's great, that's just perfect! She could've drifted the freighter into an asteroid and all Bosun was authorized to do was record the time and place of her death.

She shook her head, trying to clear that thought—and that dream—from her skull. "What do you need?"

"Certain navigational processes appear to be hard-locked, and I cannot access them. I require user override."

Fiona pushed her right hand against her steel arm, cracking the knuckles loudly against the prosthetic. "Can do, Bosun." She set to work on her controls, quickly freeing up the necessary systems.

Her augment started to ache at the elbow, little tugs at the joint where the tech interfaced with her nerve endings. She needed to get the socket adjusted, maybe get a bur polished off. Fiona was unlikely to see a new model anytime soon, and it had to be suffering from age by now.

And its unique tricks and functions would not be cheap to replace.

She scratched at the spot, pressing her searing hot palm against the elbow—half steel, half skin under her fingers. She rotated the silk-steel attachment around, whirling it in impossibly wide circles once and twice through the air to loosen up whatever was binding it. Kept it from sticking to the skin, like a lip to an ice-cold glass.

Satisfied, she spread her metal hand wide over her console, five fingers stretching unsettlingly far apart and dancing across the keys like they were five separate members of a chorus line: barely associated and a little drunk.

"How we lookin', beautiful?" she asked the ship.

The night sky was just a holographic projection of what glittered outside the thick hull. It did make the resulting echo off of invisible bulkheads a little disquieting—the stars somehow speaking back.

Words muffled over her shoulder. It sounded like the Bosun's proverbial head was shoved into the wall and having to murmur back through the steel to her. "Nearly there, ma'am. This architecture is not the most refined."

"Don't mind me," she said, taking in the royal purples and rich blues of a nearby gas cloud. "It's just my ass twisting in the breeze."

"I keep seeing references to a 'Captain Harlowe'?"

Fiona raised an eyebrow, unable to keep herself from laughing soft, like a cat's purr. "He won't be lodging any complaints. Move around whatever you need to."

A glowing, pixelated head peeked into view, the image of a scarred middle-aged Colonial man. Fiona had picked the face for her AI from a lineup of the Harbormaster's favorites. There was something very debonair about some well-placed flaws, like someone had underlined the attractive features for additional focus. A good nick to the eyebrow interrupting the bushy line, or a knife scar to a chin.

The butler personality program was just for kicks. "Did you kill him, ma'am?"

She considered her answer with a playful tilt to her lip. "I didn't kill him. But he *is* dead."

"Charming." The head receded back into the bulkhead. Not that the AI had ever stopped its work, but it had some dedicated memory to present small moments of human companionship. She found it helped ward off her desire to climb the walls.

Somewhere ahead of her was a gravity well warping space and time. The Bosun's memory had stored its location well enough to find it again, despite celestial drift. And he could calculate the thousand variables needed to punch her, her ship, and anything aboard safely to the other side—given enough time to do the math.

It might have become a common enough event in modern life—Jumping a gravity well—but Fiona knew just enough advanced mathematics to know how far over her head it all was.

Her radio crackled: "Unidentified KC-801 Bravo, this is IPS 31. Stand by for inspection."

Fiona lifted her head. Authoritative tone, bit scratchy, some accent she didn't quite place. Now who the Hell was going to hail her with a demand like that?

She reached up, twisting her fingers to spin her view of the outside world. Her HUD highlighted a particular dart of light. Pinching her fingers, she spread it out to zoom in the view.

And her stomach flipped on itself. "Bosun, when were you going to warn me about the Imperial Corvette burning for intercept?"

"Apologies, ma'am," the AI babbled, "I have no access to the ship's detection suites. Please don't deactivate me."

She grumbled as she strapped herself into her seat. "What's the time to Jump?"

"Two minutes till event horizon."

The radio crackled again. "KC-801 Bravo, respond on open frequency or we will open fire."

Well, they weren't messing around today. Suppose the ammo was cheap, even if they were firing on space trash. Think fast.

She keyed her radio open: "Boy, am I glad to see you! I've lost primary power, and we drifted off the lanes."

A pause. "What is your operating number?"

She had that one memorized. "TYZ-555-KL11. I'm working with a solar capacitor right now. We were on a resupply run when, wouldn't ya know it, the reactor just gave up the ghost on us. Took my engineer right along with it. You do *not* want to see the inside of that manifold." It was a lot of pointless information, but panicked people talked a lot, trying to find calm in oversharing. She even cracked her voice once for good measure.

"Stabilize your spin, TYZ. Prepare for boarding."

Boarding? She had declared distress. They should tow her to a depot for repairs and maybe a fine for being off the approved flight lanes. Unless...

Did they know who they'd found? Did good old Captain Harlowe flag an old contact, tell the Imperials to come looking for his ship—and the rogue pirate lord wanted for about five thousand counts of treason?

"Negative, boys. With the reactor down, I have no lateral control. I'm dead stick." She clicked the radio off. "Bosun, fire up the reactor. I'm going to need every drop of juice you can spare."

The Bosun, of course, objected. "Ma'am, we have not yet reached event horizon."

"I'll get you to event horizon," she grumbled as she slid her command chair up to the navigation console. "You just get us through that Jump in one piece."

"Yes, ma'am."

"KC-801 Bravo, stabilize your vessel." The Imperial had one final leather-neck warning to give her. She'd manufactured a perfectly reasonable explanation for why she couldn't comply, but that deviated from their prepared script. They really didn't know what to do with that, so the Warrant Officer just tried to ram this little story back onto something resembling a familiar track.

Well, let's see if he was prepared for this.

"Oh no," she lamented into the radio, "the crew. They've mutinied!"

The Bosun knew his cue. The ship came alive around her, whistles and chirps and the gong of the reactor interfacing. It was like the whole great ship took a deep breath.

It was going to need it.

Fiona keyed the flight path, pulling the freighter up and firing the main engines. Lateral thrusters pushed, keeping the narrow side of the ship toward the pursuing Corvette. It was a gentle maneuver, to keep the smallest silhouette facing the threat.

"The Imperial Corvette is opening fire," Bosun warned. "Stern mounted mass driver. Bearing three five two, twelve degrees down."

"Let me see it."

A holographic display of the freighter popped up between her hands. It was a spindly thing when it wasn't laden with cargo containers, essentially one empty ribcage attached to an engine block.

And she saw the flickering dots of incoming metal slugs.

Every ship that flew fast enough in space required a deflector shield, because space was far from empty. Even a small speck traveling at half the speed of light would blast right through the thickest armor. But a weaponized kinetic shot into the side of her thin civilian vessel would likely have enough force to pierce that barrier, punch through the hull and back out the other side.

First, they wanted to board her, now they want to kill her. They were skipping some levels to go right to the bang-bang. Trigger happy goon squad.

She 'grabbed' the side of her holographic ship and twisted, peeling the colorful representation out of the way. She felt the RCS thrusters fire to match and the ship lurched—somewhere outside, a 102-millimeter kinetic shell breezed on by.

"That was *very* close, ma'am!"

Fiona chuckled. "Oh, it's going to get a whole lot worse in about five seconds."

More shots came streaking in, blinking in and out of sight. These were smaller, lost in the background radiation of the black. No heat signature to pick up—she was dependent on active scanning.

Fiona squinted, charting the geometry of each shot in her head as she gripped the ship between her fingers. It was like trying to make the strange wiry shape fit between all of the hostile screaming dots.

She was not successful, and she could hear the hollow bangs on steel behind her. Her hair pulled backward, a lock of bright red flashing across her face.

"Multiple ruptures," the Bosun reported, "eighty meters aft. Sealing the Jump Deck."

The doors behind her slammed shut and she swiped her bangs out of her face. "I screw up, you die too!"

"Not strictly true, ma'am," the Bosun said. "I would require exposure to extremes in solar radiation. Or experience a total loss of power for an extended period."

"I can arrange that!"

"Please refrain from drifting further off course."

"You want to drive?"

She was getting them away from the Jump point, drifting up and off the Corvette's firing line. And with every change in angle of approach, speed—and the condition of the ship—the Bosun had to adjust his calculations.

She tumbled the big fat hull as best as she could, grabbing and pulling the holographic model and threading through the hailstorm of incoming bullets on her scope.

Until she took one too many hits and the screen blinked out. The thrusters quieted and the ship settled around her. "That's it, Bosun. I'm driving by keyboard right now."

"Calculating..."

She tried to type out commands manually on her console. Thirty degrees down, thrust at 82%, mark & execute. It was such a cumbersome way to fly. And the ship drifted onto the course like it was being led along by a lazy farmhand.

They were going to get shredded loafing around like this.

"Bosun!"

Whatever salvo was inbound never landed.

Because time stood still, and space compressed to nothing and filled with everything. She could feel herself outside of herself, like she was touching every inch of her own skin, like it belonged to someone else and she was just borrowing it.

She could see herself, feel herself, sitting in that chair far away and close by—

And just as quickly, she lurched in her creaky captain's chair as the freighter's Jump drive wound down.

"Jump complete," Bosun said. "Opening thermal vents."

She took a deep breath, reminding her recently reconstructed body how to breathe. "Report?"

The Bosun's pleasant face slipped up from the ground, soft smile and bright eyes. "All systems nominal. Point oh one five placement drift. Planetary body detected."

"Did they follow us?" she asked.

The Bosun's head glitched for a second, as processor power struggled with the ailing freighter's hardware. "If they attempted the Jump, they were not successful."

That'll have to do. "Okay...if I give you navigational control, can you get us planetside in three pieces or less?"

"Of course, ma'am," the Bosun said. She heard the click of a hailing frequency and a hundred crickets worth of chirps passed in half a second as he interfaced with whatever limited computer operated the colony's air traffic control.

She slumped into her seat, the sweat on her back sticky and grimy. Somewhere below her was a savannah planet with a small industrial colony that had been the epicenter of some violence, whereupon lived a particular peculiar perplexing young man. By reputation, he was both dangerous and trustworthy, charismatic yet unsettling.

She had come halfway across the occupied galaxy to meet Aaron Havenes, bringing with her all that she had left in this damn universe.

Because he knew who killed Keira Ladd.

CHAPTER
TWO
AARON

HE WANTED nothing more than to lay down in a field of soft grass and stare up at the sky, trying to decipher what they were saying to him in their twinkling patterns. Had he done that this morning, he'd have seen Fiona's light freighter rattle its way through atmo to the landing pad, sprinkling bits of shrapnel all the way down. The ship looked like it had been through a messy divorce with a sentient alcoholic rail gun.

But who was he to judge? His city had been under siege, peppered with gunfire big and small, and hosted numerous crash sites packed with military hardware. There was more viscera and debris in Vanguard's streets than domesticity.

Still, he had expected Fiona would bring something more solid than the rusty cheese grater she dropped on the dirt outside of town. It would be a couple of long days before it was ready to take off, let alone carry his team on a suicide mission chasing a battleship a hundred times larger.

And it was currently being mobbed by a thousand desperate colonists, eager to trade anything they owned for a seat off-world. They battered the hull with their clenched fists, misting waters against a cliffside. Their money, their clothes; reports said some even offered to sell themselves.

They'd seen what happened when a single Eisenclad dreadnought had come into orbit over their pitiful mining colony. Whatever peculiarities awaited them in this regrettable junkpile would be preferable to righteous hellfire, locked and loaded from a vengeful and bloodied Imperial Navy looking for some payback.

Aaron pushed his monitor closed, flush with the desk, his eyes poring over the smooth, off-white surface. He could feel Talania and Aisling considering him from the other side of the office, trying to deduce what he might say next, predict his reaction so they could meter their own.

Talania's heart sank between her narrow shoulders, hoping that Aaron might provide some much-needed pep. And Aisling, well...Aisling was overly eager to launch herself back into the mix, perhaps more eager than her heart was ready for.

He could read it on them, see it etched in their flesh like blue fire.

If only he could turn this off. He had liked being nobody. Nobody looked at him with expectant hope back when he was just a number.

"Nobody gets on that ship without my say so," Aaron sighed.

Aisling bobbed her head at that, like she was tossing the idea about in her head, hearing it gong off the walls. "They're going to start pushing and shoving."

All he could think of was Eden's battered face, hanging from her wrists. The blood caked to her face, her head limp on her shoulders. There was only one way he was going to help her, and he couldn't do that if the panicking masses took his one ride out.

"We need to offer 'em something better then," he countered.

"You got a secret stash of ship captains I don't know about?" Talania asked, a touch more acidic than she meant to. She realized she'd come off harsh and masked her wince well, just a flutter of her eyes.

She really had become quite the politician.

But she wasn't wrong. No human being in their right mind would want to be associated with the Vanguard rebellion. They'd be ripped to pieces coming out of the Jump Point, and even if they weren't, the Navy would simply tag any vessel that came or went—and track them down later. There were no contradicting testimonies taken from a pile of debris, after all. The Empire would make sure no one could say what happened but the official line.

So...no one was even coming near them. Vanguard was very competently isolated.

Aaron cocked his head, jaw tight. "I'm working on that part."

"We can't promise them something we don't have," Aisling said.

"Make Nora do it then," Aaron offered. "She lives to pick fights."

Aisling grimaced. "I'm not arguing, Aaron, I'm jus'..."

Yes, she was. But deference was preventing her from fully committing to it. It made his head hurt. She was diametrically opposed to this idea, but she had too much respect, too much reverence, to just say what she meant.

Of course, she didn't have to and maybe that was why she didn't. He always knew what she meant—what they all meant—so she didn't have to heap being rude on top of that.

Some people could read a poker face, others had a natural empathy for the wants and needs of their fellows; Aaron could see Aisling's cards like she was splaying them out on a table. This power...made the most closely guarded secrets an open broadcast for his review.

Was this how the Queen saw the world? How she saw him?

He learned good and fast to shut his trap. People didn't respond all too kindly to being called out on their truth, no matter how accurate it wound up being.

Aisling wanted Eden back, free and safe, with a fair dose of revenge tucked in there. They all did. But they couldn't abandon the people of Vanguard to the whims of a vengeful armada.

And any delay might be the delay that cost Eden her...

No. Don't think like that. Whatever happens, happens, but it wasn't going to be *his* fault. It was going to be Admiral Deckard Tiberiet and the Imperial Navy. They brought Aaron to this point. And he was going to bring Eden out of it.

Aisling stared at him, expecting some magical solution. But none came.

Until Talania opened her mouth. "There's a reactor leak," she mused, throwing her hands in the air. "That ship's practically dismantled. So, there's a...reactor leak and we need time to lock it down."

"And if someone in the crowd takes a reading and says, 'you're lying?'" Aaron asked.

"I'm a politician," Talania said with a shrug. "I'm always lying."

"Let's go with the reactor leak. Have the engineers screw with the reactor, just enough to put off a signature. *And* we've just made contact with a smuggling cartel," Aaron said. "That should keep them from killing each other for at least another day."

Aisling shrugged. "We could always tell them nobody's coming, and distribute robes for the Bacchanalia."

"Go," Talania blurted.

"Bonfire, booze, clothing optional?"

Now it was Aaron's turn. "Go!"

He didn't need this new Eldritch power to notice the comical overarch of the sweeping salute Aisling snapped off. He could practically hear the whistle of the wind between her fingers. And with that, she pushed her maglev chair out of the door.

There wasn't so much as a mechanical moan as a thousand computers read the sliding ground underneath her, as electric current modified the maglev quotient to slide her softly around the corner. He could've sworn she actually tilted the chair a bit and bounced the magnet off of the wall—the show-off—pressing one palm against the bulkhead and shoving herself out of sight with speed and style.

She'd learned that one from Keeper.

The door hissed shut and Talania's heart rate spiked. She'd been holding back her mounting panic. "Forty thousand people aren't going to fit on that tugboat," Talania noted.

"They wouldn't want to get on if they knew where we were going," he mused.

"Y'know, I..." she started, pausing as she drew circles on her cheek with one finger. She was considering whether or not to even open her mouth again. "I never wanted to be a Governor."

"As a kid?" he asked.

"Yeah."

"What *did* you want to be?"

She shook her head, an embarrassed smirk. "You already know."

He did. It was on the tip of her tongue, which meant it was jammed into his skull with neon lights and a marching band. "What even is a 'Pathfinder-President?'" The combination explorer and archaic elected official made him crack a smile.

"I read a lot of books as a kid." Like that explained anything at all.

"Lot of history books, apparently."

Talania straightened up in her seat, looking at the wall out towards where the ship was docked. "Too much to hope she'd bring half a pirate fleet on her heels," Talania said, straightening up in her seat.

There was a thought. A host of angry criminals, notorious for violence and hostage taking, swooping in to rescue thousands upon thousands of people? Aaron shook his head. "Not sure I'd let her, to be honest."

Fiona was a noisy, cranky, impulsive woman drenched in crime and blood. It was hard to believe even half of the stories about her.

But then, he was equally unbelievable.

Don't make noise. Don't be quiet. Don't burn bright, but do not hide in the dark. Aaron had walked that line for a long time. This woman? She scuffed her heels on that line like it owed her money.

"You know, she has a proven history of making noise," Aaron noted.

"Yeah, that's what's got me worried." Talania raised an eyebrow, like a cautionary warning flag. "When she gets here, let me do the talking."

"Civilian authority." He remembered. They had to establish that Aaron might be a superhuman soothsayer with command of a legion of affectionate alien tanks, but Talania was the Governor, duly elected.

She was in charge, not him. Fiona respected power. They were going to have to project some.

"I was going to say because I know more words than you do," she said, with a wry grin.

"See, and I was..." Aaron stopped, chewing, brain grinding to a halt. And she just stared back at him, judging green eyes batting at him. "Nothing. I've got nothing."

"That's what I thought." Her father dies in a coup attempt, her city lies in ruins, and her sweetheart was in chains somewhere far away, but she was never going to lose that playful glee from a verbal duel fought and won. Parry, riposte, and gloat.

Being able to read her mind helped, but sometimes it just meant he knew he was going to lose before he got there.

Her hand drifted to a hip flask, fingers flicking across its cold tin. But then drifted away, skittering instead along the steel of the chair.

Eden. He didn't know why. But he could feel that whole motion had Eden stamped all over it.

Talania's Entiglas chirped with a call. She groaned, throwing the amber image up on the wall without so much as asking. At this point, she treated Aaron's office much like her own, and Aaron hadn't done anything to really dissuade her from that.

"If it isn't my favorite shoe leather," Talania greeted. "What's the news?"

Sergeant Bray loomed on the wall—as he was staring down into his own bracer. "Governor, I'd like to request permission again to restrain the prisoner. And possibly remove his teeth."

"Ulrich Wolcott is a guest," Aaron corrected, "not a prisoner."

"You know a whole lot of guests not allowed to leave their rooms and are fed through a slot in the door?"

Aaron shrugged. "I know an Imperial officer wouldn't last long on these streets." Maybe before the siege, there'd been some sympathy, but after the camps they built and the tactics they deployed...the colonists would rip him apart with farm tools.

"What did he do?" Talania asked, knowingly.

"Tried to overpower his guards," Bray summarized, cracking his neck to emphasize. "He did not succeed."

Aaron closed his eyes. Thirteen miles away at the Wall Prefecture, Wolcott's cell was dark. The young captain's head hurt. Dehydration, but also from a blow to the nape of his neck where a guard had to subdue him. His skin cracked and flaked, and his eyes were scratchy. His naval uniform and the Orchid flag, once a shining example of a young officer beloved by his commanders, were now sullied and stained by the grit of his accommodations.

"Get him some water," Aaron ordered. "And we should have a medic look at his head."

"I'll get it done."

Aaron could feel the Sergeant's gut quaking. He'd pulled the skin patch off the gunshot in his belly. "And you should get yourself to an AutoDoc."

"Yeah," Talania added, "you look like shit, Gunny."

"And you look like two kids in a trench coat, ma'am."

Aaron raised two fingers. "Doctor. Water."

Bray nodded and closed the call, plunging the room into cool brisk colors again. Talania eyed Aaron, draping an arm over her chairback. "You really think Deckard will trade Eden for Wolcott?"

No. He really didn't. Deckard had convinced himself he could kill Eden in public and still get Wolcott back safe. "I just think Wolcott is worth more alive than dead."

A knock on the door. A figure beyond. Soft-feet, coiled steel, over a dozen augments buried in the body. Body temperature idling hot with all that extra hardware.

"Come on in, Graccus," Aaron said.

The door slid aside—but there was a second face behind the retired spy.

Despite poor condition, her clothes were handmade, a waistcoat drawn tight to hide body armor. Her ruby-red bangs drifted over her right eye, curled but frayed at the tips from abuse and time. The undercut shave to the opposite side had started to grow in with a soft brown tint to her scalp. Her silk white blouse, now stained with dried blood and carbon scoring, still looked regal and puffy. Riding boots once polished to a shine were now scuffed and dim. She made oil stains and battle scars look like they belonged on a crown.

And he hadn't seen her. Well, he hadn't *Seen* her, no Sense of her presence. Nothing then, nothing now.

Aaron's brain might as well have thrown a rod.

He could feel Talania shift her weight in the chair, could hear the squeak of Graccus's heel like a trumpet in his ear; he could hear the concentrated panic of forty thousand souls down below him. But he couldn't See *her*, not one surface level emotion, no thought, no *nothing*.

And yet, he knew his squishy human eyes weren't lying to him. There stood the woman he had expected, tall in her leather boots and a focus behind her eyes that could cut through stone given enough time.

"Fiona McCorty, Pirate Master of the Boolean Edge," Graccus introduced, immediately tracking on Aaron's completely obvious panic.

Talania was out of her seat, her ponytail squishing against the roof as she moved to welcome her guest. She'd had her back to Aaron, missing out on the flash of wide-eyed gawking.

For Talania, this was time to turn on the signature charm. Left hand to chest, holding in her jacket lapel, as she reached with her right hand. "Thank you for coming, Fiona." When the recipient took the greeting with their own hand, that left hand would drop down and clasp the back, gently trapping them in the moment.

Fiona gave Talania a once over from head to toe, impossible to do so subtly—Talania was well over six feet. And when she took Talania's hand—the steel grip of her polished augment gave a firm test of Talania's pain threshold. "Uh-huh."

Her hand probably screamed, but Talania didn't let a thing through that iron mask. "Welcome to what's left of Vanguard."

Fiona's hair drifted, willowy like hanging silk, as her head turned. But Aaron might as well have been looking at an ice sculpture, all cold darkness. A void bereft of feeling, emotion, or intent.

A skilled liar might be able to control muscle twitches or even meter their heart rate. But Aaron wasn't tracking biometrics like some lie detector machine. He wasn't interpreting raw data looking for fluctuations.

He should be able to See an aura full of a life lived, memories and personality and intentions and dreams and ambitions and nightmares and *everything*. And instead, like a deep sea, he Saw nothing at all.

Graccus sidled up next to him, leaning in. "You need a system update or something?"

"I'll tell you later," Aaron whispered back. That was apparently good enough, as Graccus took his place at Aaron's shoulder.

Meanwhile, Talania had launched into full press briefing mode. "It's been a hard three months, and we're happy to have your support."

"Hey, I'm sorry—what was it? Your name? Never mind, I don't care." Fiona never intended to pursue that line of thought very far. "I know you stayed up late working on that speech, but let's skip the pageantry and the balloons."

"You had balloons?" Graccus chirped. And Talania glared a full second of murder at him.

"Consider it skipped," Aaron said, throwing up his hands. "What would you like to talk about?"

"I want to see her." That pulled the oxygen out of the room. And Fiona knew how to play with that empty air. She took a step forward, almost checking Talania with her shoulder. "You call me out of the blue, you tell me she's with you, that she got herself killed fightin' in your stupid revolution. If that's true...I want to see her."

Keira Ladd. She'd been cut down by an Oskie in full Warcom gear. And he hadn't been kind about it.

"It's not a pretty sight," Aaron warned.

"My delicate system will just have to find a way to soldier on."

Talania tried to draw focus. "We're a little pressed for time—"

"You waited two solid weeks for me, and it looks like you don't really have a plan to go anywhere *without* me, so why don't we save the next five minutes of fighting, and you just...take me to her."

Aaron couldn't tear his eyes from hers, colors like gemstones, radiant and wonderful. But it was like being deafened or blinded, an entire part of experiencing life suddenly absent. She was a gaping hole in his Sense, a blindspot. He couldn't read her.

Like she was already dead.

"I'll have to call for permission first," he hedged.

Fiona tilted her head, charmed by the very notion. "Permission? From who?"

CHAPTER
THREE
AARON

FIONA STOOD OVER THE BODY, considering what remained of the Valkyrie, Keira Ladd. Her two halves were laid on the slab, pallid and gray. Blackened flesh along the edge of her shoulder down across to her waist, where she'd been bisected.

Reports said she'd been alive for the last few seconds before she succumbed to shock and eventually suffocated. It was a morbid question that Aaron had immediately regretted asking.

The visiting pirate lord hadn't been the most animated of people to begin with. Not stoic, but purposeful, like a mural of a swordsman, waiting for their opponent to make a critical error, then lashing out with precise fury. But when Fiona finally laid eyes on Keira's dismembered form, she froze to her spot. And here is where she would remain, stuck to that ground until she thawed with the coming of spring.

Was it anger or simply denial? A failure to compute? Running the equation again? He couldn't tell. And every time he couldn't tell, Aaron locked up on her, this impossibility fracturing his new normal.

She was invisible to him, the sole living thing he'd ever encountered he could not Sense. And she blended in with all of the rest of the death like she belonged here.

There were hundreds of slabs in the building, each with a corpse laid out for the morticians. These four walls had been one of the Capitals' barracks in the last year, vaulted ceiling and dim lighting. A former warehouse, so it had made for a fine place to put 'munitions' like the Capitals.

But in present, it had taken on a new purpose; it had enough space and was temperature controlled, so the dead could be preserved before burial. It made Aaron's hands tingle, and his ears burn. This room was so full of nothing, an absurd lack of sound as to become distracting.

A year ago, this raw amount of death would've unsettled him, humbled him. Now, it made his jaw click and his skin crawl. He wanted to back away soft, lest he disturb whatever slumbered here. It was as though light entered this space—and was consumed.

In all of that drowning silence, he could still feel Graccus step right out of a children's nightmare. His active camouflage melted from the darkness into corporeal, like he was parting some extra-dimensional curtain, as he tiptoed up to Aaron's shoulder to—

"Nope."

And with just one word from Aaron, Graccus deflated. "Dammit."

Graccus always glowed brighter right before he got within striking distance. He was getting excited and he lit up like a bonfire.

The seasoned espionage agent propped his hands on his hips, shaking his head. "It's like you have a proximity alarm on ya."

"Graccus." Aaron looked over at him, scolding. "Time and a place."

He didn't say anything, but he nodded. They were, in every other respect, standing in a cemetery. Childish games like this should stay at the door.

A few seconds passed, heavy air and solemn silence. And Aaron could feel the question coming, swirling in the defector's mind, coalescing into nascent thoughts and tangible words. Watching someone compose a question was like tracking a stormfront building on the horizon, a cloud bank taking shape before it could swoop down on the plains.

And sure enough, Graccus leaned in to whisper. "What was bothering you? Before, in your office?"

Aaron nodded at Fiona as the pirate continued to absorb the sight of her dead friend. "What implants do you think she has?"

Graccus blinked, taking a scan of his own with his sophisticated suite of espionage augmentations. "Class two prosthetic on her left arm, amputation just below the elbow. *Big* capacitor in there too, maybe a personal shield. She's got a subdermal radio interface. Some cosmetics. Why?"

"I can't See her."

The officer processed that admission. He clearly could see her with his own two eyes so that must mean...

Graccus's voice was almost singsong in response. "Understood." And just like that, he melted back into the shadows.

Anyone that could hide their very life force from the all-Seeing eye might have more elaborate tricks up their sleeve, more than his soured cynical training could predict. So Graccus wasn't going to take any chances.

Suddenly, Fiona raised a hand, pointing. "What's *his* situation?"

Aaron followed her finger out to the periphery along the building's concave wall, where Solomon Lipkin lingered, arms crossed and pacing back and forth, slightly panting through an open mouth. And yellowed eyes never leaving Fiona.

Solomon was not a large man, emaciated and skeletal, but it was like looking at a caged predator, hungry for something beyond its bars.

"Solomon...he's..." How to explain that whole situation? Solomon and Keira weren't just partners in devilry, or companions in the dark. They were an institution, a force of nature, a cosmic truth. If one was near, so was the other, pulled to each other like gravity.

And now, after this...Solomon was a convicted serial killer without his one person, the one person he'd ever connected with.

"We needed *his* permission," Aaron summarized.

Fiona looked up at Solomon, his eyes peering back out from the shadows. Whatever haunting imagery that rolled through his head was almost drawing itself on the walls. He dared her to offend. Longed for it. He wanted an excuse to loose the ravager inside himself, that monster that Keira had somehow contained.

But Fiona didn't seem to register the present threat, or plain didn't care. She took two strong steps right toward him, and Aaron could swear, Solomon hissed at her. Or maybe that was just the sharp intake of breath.

He didn't want Fiona disrespecting the dead, defacing or stealing anything. If there was a possession she had that Fiona wanted to reclaim, or a debt she wanted payment over...she'd have to kill Solomon to take it. Keira's body was sacred ground.

But Fiona simply snickered right in his dark and brooding face. "I like this one."

Aaron blinked. "What?"

"Anybody this protective of Keira..." Fiona looked back at Solomon, appraising eyes and approving smirk. "You've racked up quite a body count."

"Forty-seven," was Solomon's simple answer.

Fiona warmed even more, impressed. "And you're not lying."

"You some kind of witch?" Solomon asked, trying to not look Aaron's way. He thought there was only one mind reader in the room. But were there two?

Fiona shook her head. "Some people just wear their whole lives on their sleeves. I'm Fiona."

"Solomon." That was not a pleasantry. It was the name of the person who would skin her alive should she step out of line.

Fiona giggled, rolling her shoulders to exaggerate the excited chill that rolled up her spine.

Solomon finally looked at Aaron, passing the torch off. Aaron drew in a breath, standing up straight. "There are only two men alive who have killed an Oskie in hand-to-hand combat," Aaron said.

Solomon's words were few, like thickened venom. "And you're looking at 'em."

Fiona held up three fingers, too close to his face. "There's one more."

That broke Solomon out of his brooding dramatic persona. And he just grunted like a farm animal: "Huh?"

Again, that giggle, a school girl with a secret—or a villain unchecked. Aaron wanted to know how much of that was a put-on, like his instincts guessed, but all he could See was her perfect chin, that singular emerald eye peeking out from behind her radioactive hair, and that wry twist of her lip. "There's actually three. That I know of, anyway."

Solomon and Aaron exchanged a look. Who the Hell was the third?

But Fiona blew right past that, pointing back at Keira's body. "I want a name."

"You'll get it," Aaron said. "But first I need—"

Fiona shut him down quick. "I get a name, or I go get it myself. I don't do anything for you until then."

Graccus melted out of thin air right next to Fiona, close enough to slip a dagger between the ceramic plates on her stomach. And he leaned in a bit closer, so that when he spoke at full volume, he'd have her full attention. "His name is Callum Remus."

His satisfied smirk positively screamed joy—just because Aaron could catch him didn't mean the others could. And he'd just proven that the new girl wasn't beyond his skill.

Maybe he expected her to twitch, lash out, so that he'd have an excuse to use his flashy training and expensive implants to break some pirate bones. But Fiona's eyes just went wide, and she craned her neck to stare at Graccus. He was well inside what she would consider comfortable. But she was more offended than threatened.

He just smiled, all dopey white teeth, daring her to try and move him. Aaron had seen what Graccus could do. He'd unscrew her

27

shoulder from its socket, rip her augment off, and beat her to death with it before she finished spitting in his face.

"He's Oskie, Aug-6," Graccus said, like that meant anything to anyone else in the room. "Specced for Combat Drop and Endurance. Top of his class at Holkstad in Flash & Burn operations."

"You know him?" she asked, as if the association was enough to kill him too.

He nodded, solemn, eyes drifting. His face suggested a deeper past, but his voice covered it with mock jealousy. "I was number two."

"Well then," she said, "seems like I found the right partners."

"We're after our friend," Aaron cautioned. "You jeopardize her safety, and you will find yourself abruptly in many small pieces. Are we clear?"

She didn't miss a beat. "I'm after a murderer. You get in my way, superman, and you will find what the unpleasant side of a knife feels like."

Solomon snickered at that. No need to respond. Everyone in that room had been shot, stabbed, repeatedly and often. Aaron had taken a Jergad claw clean through his leg. They couldn't be threatened with what basically amounted to a normal day at the office.

Graccus checked in with Aaron's state of mind with a glance. Was this pirate worth their time? Suppose they just take her ship. Did they really need *her*?

Fiona scanned the hall of bodies, a receding pattern of white sheets that could've stretched into oblivion. "You've fought a little war, even had some success. Cue applause, but only from the cheap seats, Mr. Havenes. You've lived far too long around people that tiptoe around you. I won't. I don't care about your revolution, I don't care about your politics, and there is not enough money in the world to make me care about your little friend. I have a debt to square up. Full stop."

She sauntered over to Aaron, savoring each step, holding the spotlight. "All I care about is if you can get me within arm's reach of Callum Remus."

Fiona was not a large woman, but she still looked down on Aaron's diminutive stature, and she knew how to use that height advantage to push him into a corner.

But Aaron had some experience with tall women trying to push him around. "I have forty thousand colonists here." Aaron matched her energy. "And I'm not leaving until we ensure their safety."

She tilted her head, that curtain of hair slipping aside to reveal her face. Confidence leaked off of those eyes, almost like he'd found the true source, where all confidence in the universe came from, like any other bravado was a cheap imitation of this purest form. "Well, let's consider that our first hurdle."

"Who's the third?" Aaron asked, curious.

She purred, pleasant memories rolling back. "Get me what I want, maybe I'll introduce you."

Tentative alliance made. Hold on, Eden. They were coming.

CHAPTER
FOUR
DECKARD

THE IMPERIAL NAVY, in its hundred-and-fifty-year history, had seen retreat a handful of times. Two were tactical maneuvers taught at the Academie Bellator, methods of luring an opponent into an over-leveraged stance. The others...the commanders involved were never seen publicly again, their names scraped from the histories, along with the incidents themselves.

So, Deckard was not in a strong position, even if he *had* followed his orders to the letter. Disobeying a Cabinet Minister during open hostilities with rebel forces? That was grounds for excommunication, in and of itself.

He only hoped that the gas bag Caldwell would keel over before he could log that report, take an express elevator to Hell's inner circle, where white-hot tongs were applied to his extremities on the daily. If Deckard had been allowed to run the operation without political interference, none of this would have happened!

And yet, he knew whose neck it would hang on now.

What a shitshow. A colony of Dusters, along with an alien race still struggling with the Stone Age, had successfully destroyed a Naval troop carrier and taken officers hostage. Deckard had likely saved young Wolcott from the scathing ire of history, by volunteering his own neck and turning Wolcott over to the enemy.

If Wolcott had been hurt...

Deckard's ship had suffered in the skies over Vanguard. Most of the breaches had been sealed, and those that couldn't be would have to wait for a proper drydock. Power had been diverted from non-essential systems to make their passage through the Reaches as swift as possible. Medical teams had been dispatched to all decks to triage the wounded and transport them for care as needed.

Deckard stopped outside the brig. The guard saluted, a touch more crisp than usual, with a whip at the wrist. "Admiral," he said, full and proud.

Admiral.

Everyone still called him that, like it was his birth name. And it felt wrong every time. Minister Caldwell had publicly rebuked him, stripped his title, and remanded him as a Capital offender. And yet, the entire crew spoke that title with treasonous glee. At this point, they knew what they were doing—and what it meant for them.

Deckard had stripped his Command Orchid off his lapel a week ago, shoving the brass insignia in his pocket. That way he could still feel it whenever he needed an adjustment to his attitude, remind himself that he did not deserve to wear it any longer.

"Haven't been an admiral for two weeks, so hold that salute for a man who deserves it. Captain Remus already arrived?"

"Yes, sir." He didn't wait for further instruction and turned to hand crank the door open. With auxiliary power down, all of the ship's doors were down to manual operation. Failing into the locked position was inconvenient, but if convenience was enough reason to melt down the rulebook, the Empire would've collapsed long ago.

The doors hushed open as the seal broke, before grinding out of the way. Deckard stalked through the opening like he was tilted downhill.

The observation deck of the brig had a clear view down into the solid white containment cells. Smart Bricks managed by the shipboard AI blared blinding white light at the occupant, but would part for any qualified officer, allowing free movement of anyone but the tenant. He could even have a seat and the bricks would rise up to cushion his back and legs, fabricating a chair where none had been before. Where a visitor might have complete ease, the prisoner would have absolute discomfort—without running afoul of civil liberties.

Of course, that only applied to citizens. She was a Capital.

Eden Neria hung from her wrists, silksteel cable dangling her from the roof of her cell. The metal had bruised and cut into her skin, sending dried trails of blood down her forearms, but she'd finally been allowed a small stool, barely able to touch her toes to it and take the weight off. If she fell asleep, lost her balance, or slumped, the metal would bite anew.

Pain could be tolerated, even embraced. But crush hope, and a prisoner would melt.

Callum glanced over at the door as Deckard entered, arms folded across his broad chest. His greeting was genial but brusque. "Morning."

"She said anything?" Deckard asked.

"Various elocutions on the many ways I can interface with my mother." Callum's voice dripped with derision. "In a few different languages."

"If only she knew you were found fully grown in a pool of human blood."

"Already full beard too." Callum might be smiling, enjoying the banter, but Deckard had meant every word.

Callum rubbed at a burn mark on his neck, charred black, crinkling under his fingers. Deckard had to contain his wretch. "For the love of—Doc Findley needs to take a look at that."

"I went by Meditech three days ago. He said he doesn't treat drunks, wife-beaters, or traitors."

"And which one of those are you?" Deckard asked.

Callum shrugged. "Could be I'm just unpleasant, sir."

No argument there. Deckard turned his eyes back to the cell.

The way the Capital dangled from the ceiling, the white light bleaching her flesh, almost to the point of burning...despite all sense, all Deckard could see in that room was Wolcott's face. The young boy hanging in a darkened room, as the Capitals tortured him, trying to dig out troop movements, technology, capabilities.

Worse still, he could be with those beasts. Perhaps the Capitals would simply turn him loose into the field and let the creatures hunt him for sport.

Or meat.

Deckard couldn't let that happen. "Let her down."

"I'm sorry?" The Oskie had enough enhancements in him to hear the footsteps two decks above him. He'd heard the old man just fine. He was objecting.

But Deckard did need a good enough reason. "If the Capital is harmed further, that may provoke our enemy into harming their own captives. Unless you see a further benefit to continuing this treatment?"

Callum considered the small woman, mentally sorting through the hundred or so interrogation scenarios filed away in that hard drive he generously called a human brain. "Her intelligence would be dated, at best. Useless at worst. Though sociological data implies that Havenes wouldn't harm a captive."

"He won't," Deckard concurred. "But not every Capital is as considerate. Let her down, give her water."

Callum nodded his begrudging assent, but then a thought occurred. "She may yet be more compliant with a friendlier face."

Deckard go and face her? Talk to her?

No. His entire body rejected that idea at the cellular level, like an autoimmune response. Looking at her from afar was almost more than he could bear. "Do you have family, Remus?"

Callum's shoulders squared and his head tilted, as though to study the abrupt change of topic from a safer distance. "My family is the Service, my service to the People."

"But you must have parents?"

"I do, patriots both."

"But not a family?"

"...Occupational hazard, Admiral," he said with a little salt.

It was a fair hit. Oskies didn't exactly have a retirement plan. And even if they did, he wouldn't be able to talk about much. He would have been given to the Academie at the tender age of six, and to Holkstad after that. His body belonged to the Navy, his soul to the Pilgrim, blessed be his steps.

No one to judge him for his deeds in the Empire's Service.

Deckard's lips tightened to a line. "I don't suppose I'll see mine again."

"You sound lost, Admiral," Callum whispered, cautious. "I think the chaplain would be a better person for this conversation."

The chaplain was servicing the dead and ushering them onto the Sojourn. And he didn't need her idiomatic dogma, all quotations and heavy breathing. "Well, I'm talking to you, Remus. I need wisdom, not platitudes."

Callum crossed his arms. "Sir...I can teach a man to storm a building, manufacture explosives, or field strip a Warcom. But I've no mind for...whatever it is you're asking."

That's precisely why he was perfect. Callum wasn't laden down with connections and bonds and...Deckard needed to be an island, cut off from it all, a monolith. Instead, he'd somehow slipped down into the sea, swallowed by it, just another raft tossed between the white caps and waiting to be battered against the rocks.

"I've been an officer for thirty years," Deckard began. "I've done things I'm not proud of, but I take pride in my Service."

Until Vanguard.

Now he wasn't so sure. Ministry orders had erected concentration camps, orbital bombardments, decimation tactics used against a compliant civilian population. It wasn't for them—it was for everyone watching across the Empire's domain. They committed undue atrocities.

As a deterrent, to quash other as-yet unseen uprising.

Callum didn't seem to pick up on the dangling thread. He took a breath of ice-cold patriotism, his chest swelling up. He actually smiled as he looked in on the prisoner, twisting on her chain. "Difficult jobs can only be done by exceptional men, Admiral. Have pride in *that*."

Deckard huffed. Maybe pride was the problem.

———

Deckard stared at the wall of his cabin for ten solid minutes. This call might decide the next twenty years of his life, if handled poorly. Of course, it might also simply serve to notify him of the decision already made by powers beyond. Minister Caldwell had cursed him as a Capital; this was his one chance to reverse that course.

And so, he hit the button. The signal would have to route through two Jump Points and lance across open space, all the way to a planetoid on the edges of the Kuiper belt in Sol.

The amber glow of the Entiglas projection filled his office like a shroud being pulled back, revealing a golden fireplace. A woman looked back at him, skin like fragile white porcelain—likely an aftermarket addition, because there wasn't a single human pore in that visage.

That mask articulated like a face well enough, probably ballistic protection of some kind. But everything about it was... wrong. A shard of inky green-black glass cupped along the jaw. He thought for a moment he could make out some kind of writing along that obsidian surface, but it seemed to smooth out on inspection.

Her jet-black hair was cut harshly along her jaw, like a picture frame boxing in some reputed piece of classical art. Over a flowing red tunic, she wore a square-shouldered longcoat, slung about her like a cape, with gold filigree sewn to the epaulets.

Cassandra Meilos: even her smile felt hollow. "Admiral Tiberiet. I haven't seen you in years. You look well, considering."

'Considering.' That was one extremely loaded word. "I take it you've heard the news, Ms. Meilos?"

Her eyes wandered far afield, playfully brushing off the apocalyptic circumstance. "Oh, well, you know how Caldwell likes his speeches. But he didn't speak of you by name."

He didn't have to. Every legal port in a five Jump radius would be closed to the *Tartarus* now. No one wanted to be caught servicing a rogue Imperial admiral and his crew of rebels.

But this didn't seem to bother Cassandra one bit. "It's politics, darling. Everything that's sold can also be bought."

Everything was always about the money. She was giving him an open door, so long as he paid the toll. "Is that painted on your mirror?"

"Temper, temper, Admiral," she warned him. "You're not in any position."

"You're a prison warden, Cassandra, governing unruly chattel. I'm the one with a battleship and very little to lose."

"Do you think an Empire grows from good soil, Admiral?" she repeated the words like they were from a children's rhyme. "Or from good stock?"

Deckard began his pitch. "I'm a patriot, Cassandra. I don't need you to teach me the philosophy. I just need your help getting this done."

"And what would that be?"

"Can you get word to Philippe dei Mogglin for me, quietly?"

She tilted her head, reptilian. "I'd be hard pressed to *keep* information from the Imperial Spymaster. What did you have in mind?"

"I still intend to complete the mission I was tasked with, and—with your permission—would like to utilize your station and resources in that pursuit."

Her head bowed forward, like a small curtsy. "Admiral, due respect, I do business with the Navy. I can't be seen cavorting with a wanted fugitive."

Fugitive, huh? Caldwell had throttled that language right to the

red line. All because Deckard refused to turn a colony full of innocent people into a glass marble. There was likely to be a small fleet
scouring the lanes for a rogue Naval dreadnought limping through
civilized space.

He was going to have to take them off the civilized roads then.

"I don't need a partner in crime," Deckard amended. "I intend to
follow this one by the letter of the law, and possibly even the spirit
of it."

"I'm listening."

Listening, and triangulating his location. He would have to be
quick.

"I plan to demonstrate my loyalty to the Consul, and to my
command. I will bring Aaron Havenes into captivity and I will do it
without a shot fired. If I fail, I will remand myself into your custody.
Either way, you win."

A cocktail of emotions rolled through her eyes, from confusion to
alarm to a kind of admiration. "Did I hear that name correctly, Admiral? Did you say 'Aaron Havenes?'"

"Thought that might pique your interest. His file says he spent
time in your keeping."

Her smile again, soft, lips curled. Her voice quiet as she shook her
head: "Two years, four months, sixteen days, and one hour. Approx-
imately."

My God, she was strange. "Two years with you before he went
berserk and took over an Imperial colony. That can't reflect well on
your professional reputation. Your product just blew up an Imperial
fleet, Ms. Meilos. I think you and I are in a position to help each
other."

That porcelain face looked aside, calculating the odds.

He had to seal the deal. Now. "It'd better if we spoke in person.
These aren't secure channels."

Her laugh could only be described as wicked. "Admiral Tiberiet,
I took this call out of an abundance of civility. But now you have my
anticipation. You know where to find me."

CHAPTER
FIVE
AARON

NORA AND BRAY were not happy about it, but Aaron wasn't going to leave Vanguard without him. They'd fought an enormous battle to rescue Captain Ulrich Wolcott from the wreckage of the *Pompeii*, specifically because Deckard would never risk harm befalling the young officer. Aaron was counting on that still being true.

Wolcott was the only way they were going to get Eden back safely.

He led Fiona and Talania down the narrow hall. Talania needed to sign off on his release. And Fiona didn't want Aaron out of her sight. Everyone was grumpy at her for about five minutes, and Fiona hadn't really cared. So, she came along, despite repeated instructions not to do so.

The security guard at the checkpoint had requested her identification; she'd instructed him briefly on the nuanced ways she could remove his fingers from his left hand. Turns out an order without adequate supporting logic wasn't going to have any effect on her. Something told Aaron that supporting logic wouldn't help the cause all that much, either. She did what she liked, and damn the rest.

The trio navigated past engineers working double-time, stripping

the insides of the building for anything of use. They were disman-
tling pipes, pulling electrical, cleaning the metal siding—anything
that might help the refugees. Some were pulling parts, while others
were organizing baskets of the stuff into automated wagons that
would whisk it away to be catalogued.

Underneath all of that metalwork and copper wiring was the
masonry of a Wall Prefecture. Aaron was surprised to see how good it
all looked, given what it had seen for the last two years. Not a single
crack, smooth like an eggshell, except the stone was easily two feet
thick. The engineers were stripping this place bare.

"When I move out, I try to leave the landlord with some light
fixtures at least," Fiona snarked.

Talania was not amused. "You've never lived anywhere you
weren't squatting in."

"One half of ownership is possession."

Aaron didn't leave them time to continue that fight. A firm grip
on the door handle, and a thousand microprocessors checked his
biometrics—from the scarred palm print to the unique murmur of his
heart. Satisfied, the door locks clicked, and Aaron pushed the door
open with a hush.

Bray was already lodging his objections before the door seal had
even broken. Using his outside voice too. "It's *gulaw* stupidity is what
it is, Goldilocks."

Nora, a ball of condensed human scar tissue that had gained
sentience and a drinking habit, was squared off with him, arms folded
across her chest. Several old injuries were etched on her forearms,
creeping out from under her Capital jumpsuit sleeves. The longer
she served, the more disheveled that uniform got. "What are we going
to do instead, Gunny? Leave him in the trunk of a cruiser? Punt him
into the plains for the Jergad to play with?"

"The Jergad are coming too," Aaron added.

That made both Nora and Bray hiccup, both turning to the open
door. Bray got to his protest first. "You're going to cram two-tons of
leathery space demon into the cargo haul of an industrial freighter?"

"Not one. I'm bringing all of 'em," Aaron said. "There's only about a hundred of them left, and I'm not leaving them for the Empire to wipe out. Why do you think we needed a freighter, Bray?"

The blood drained out of Nora's face. "Do we know how they'll do in space flight?"

Having precisely no context, Fiona chirped, "You look like you left half your skin on a different planet and you're worried about how *they'll* do?"

Nora wasn't going to dignify that with a response. "Aaron, it's going to be cramped. If you can't control them—"

"I can."

"*If you can't*...they panic inside a tin can going half the speed of light—which is not even an unreasonable response for a subterranean pack animal—"

Aaron couldn't believe he heard that. "You're really going with 'pack animal?'" A sentient hive mind species with clear signs of intelligent thought and she was going to reduce them to a herd of cattle?

Nora stuck to her guns. "Jergad aren't exactly rocket scientists. They're *burrowers*, Aaron. They might rip open a bulkhead, take the whole ship out, and we die in a cold, dark vacuum."

Bray was in agreement. "And our little revolution doesn't make it off the porch."

Fiona leaned over to Talania, whispering, "What's a Jergad?"

"Two-ton leathery space demon just about sums it up," Talania quipped.

"Fair 'nuff."

Aaron waved a hand in the air, swirling up all of the sound and squashing the dissent in a clenched fist. "I'm not doing this without 'em. Full stop. How's our guest?"

Bray sighed, turning to the battery of cameras behind him, showing the young Naval captain pacing about his cell. "He's...petulant."

"How do you insist that you're the most important person in the world while also knowing absolutely nothing about anything?" Nora asked, rhetorical.

"Be sixteen?" Fiona offered.

Bray glared but Aaron had to bite his lip to hold back the laugh.

By all accounts, Wolcott looked well enough. He marched from one end of the room to the other, keeping time. Hair was oiled and matted. His uniform had been torn and scuffed, but nothing that couldn't be accounted to a—largely effective—crash landing from forty-one miles in the sky straight down. His natural hard shoulders and rounded face said good breeding from a rich family, likely Lunar Guild folk.

"He knows something's up," Aaron explained. "He can hear us working outside, but he's trying to avoid thinking about a potential rescue."

It didn't take a mind wizard to go from there. Talania leaned over to study the camera feed, smug. "It's not working. He can't help himself."

She was right. His pace was picking up, wringing his hands. He bit his lip—"There!" Aaron pointed at the screen, as Wolcott did a one-two-three hop on his toes, almost giddy.

Fiona shook her head in disbelief. "You've got him all kinds of spun up."

Sounds of industry, a two-week captivity. The timeline was right. Maybe, maybe, the Imperials had arrived and were preparing a second attack. Liberty soon at hand, the boy thinks. Soon, home to Sol and off this dreary brown dustball.

"Let's go get the luggage," Aaron agreed.

It was a short walk over to the cell, where Aaron pushed open the door. And he was ready for Wolcott to rush him. The punch came for Aaron's cheek, and Aaron didn't even have to break stride. He felt the decision to punch, the chambering of the shoulder and the release as it came.

Aaron snagged the boy's wrist and yanked it back to introduce it to his shoulder blades.

Ever the fighter, Wolcott mule-kicked blindly. Aaron simply lifted his foot out of the way and stamped down onto Wolcott's standing leg, bringing Wolcott down hard onto that knee. The bone-on-stone sound reverberated around the room, but Wolcott didn't make more than a grunt.

Aaron leaned in close. "I swear to God, nothing you do is going to surprise me. So just save your strength."

To his credit, the boy didn't try anything else, but tension remained in his muscles, coiled but steady. Aaron never let go of the boy's wrist. "If you play your cards right, today will be the last you see of this cell."

"My name is Ulrich Wolcott, Captain, Imperial Navy. You are committing a Capital offense!"

"Yeah," Aaron drawled, "that's not a real evocative threat to somebody in my position."

Sensing the tension relax, Aaron released the boy's wrist. Wolcott retreated, whirling away from Aaron into a dark corner. Sunlight pierced through a plexiglass window, thick beams of radiance illuminating the dust and almost obscuring his face. But he said nothing, just favoring his wrist.

"I don't need your secrets. I don't need your connections," Aaron said, soft and calm. "I'm going to take you home, and I'm going to do it personally."

A trap. It had to be a trap. Perhaps some mind game or a sadistic ploy. Wolcott's eyes darted around like they were going to pop out of his head. "For what?"

Good opportunity to be honest. Deckard was worried about Wolcott, worried enough to hurt Eden.

"For...nothing," Aaron said. "We're going to go visit Deckard Tiberiet. And—"

The boy got to the conclusion all on his own, spitting, "And he won't shoot you on sight if I'm aboard your ship."

"That's right." Aaron nodded. "I want to talk to him."

Wolcott stood as tall as he could while still leaning on the wall, afraid to leave it, like it provided him any security at all. The cold stone felt soothing on his palm. "Well, you can forget it, *skel*. I'm not your shield. He won't negotiate for my return."

Aaron pursed his lips, and called out, "Fiona? Eyes on the screen."

More darting eyes as Wolcott searched the room for a surprise that might be related to whatever Aaron had just said. Panic hit his heart and his lungs were only ever half-full. And yet, he still tried that brave face. "My name is Ulrich Wolcott, Captain, Imperial Navy—"

"I-I know," Aaron said, backing him off the speech with a waved hand, and squatting down. Be small, nonthreatening.

"You heard me the first time?" They both said at the same time, overlapped like a harmonious chorus. Wolcott damn near swallowed his tongue. Aaron'd had the same cadence, same intonation as he had. Like the same voice from a different mouth.

"What the Hell are you...trying to..." Every time he'd start, Aaron was right there with him. "How?" Wolcott asked in sync with Aaron.

Aaron couldn't help but smirk. "Weird, right?"

But Wolcott wanted to test this. "Rosewater. Venutian Black-tar Farmland. A shot of whiskey makes the heart an imaginary part, in need of a cold restart."

And that's when Aaron's eyes flickered blue, like a hot flame was somewhere in the back of his skull, projecting out an alien warmth. "I know what you're thinking. That you can...withstand me, outlast me. But I'm not trying to break you, Ulrich Wolcott. I know that you want to go home—to the fresh smell of buttered pastries and your sister practicing her cello in the next room, to the scent of fresh laundry and heavy rainfall. You miss that most of all. There's a...texture to the sound, when rain hits pavement."

Aaron almost choked up at that memory, that piece of himself. He could still hear the difference, when the water hit a puddle rather than the road.

Wolcott's face slipped into abject terror of the monster in his presence. He had never felt such intrusion and yet, hadn't felt any at all. How had this abomination reached into his mind and plucked out such secrets without so much as knocking on the door? No wonder there'd been no interrogation—if Aaron wanted something, he'd simply go take it.

Aaron knew the expression very well. He had himself stood in the presence of an alien deity, the Jergad core consciousness, and it had touched him the same way. It had learned about him by visiting memories, distinct and painful.

And it had not asked for permission. It had no concept of privacy.

Aaron could see Wolcott's mother getting sick. How his father threw himself into his work. How Wolcott took to leadership, just eight years old, took care of his sisters while his father recovered. How proud they all were when he was accepted to the Academie Bellator—

How scared he was on the deck of the *Pompeii* as it fell, how he did nothing, said nothing as the crew looked to him. He couldn't help them. Command was a sacred trust, between crew and captain.

And he had failed them.

Aaron took a breath, letting the memories fly through him. Wolcott's face twisted in confusion, trying to sort out what Aaron was doing.

A wet sniff, and Aaron stood up. "I'm taking you home, Captain. Sometimes, you're just lucky."

CHAPTER
SIX
FIONA

AARON HAD BROWN EYES, flecks of amber in the core, like sweetened coffee. Pretty enough in sunlight, but plain and simple. But then, in an instant, the entire socket glowed an iridescent blue, like they'd frozen solid, polished glassy ice.

She'd seen her share of the universe, from gunslingers to sooth-sayers—but nothing like this.

Okay, so he had her attention. And now, she couldn't sleep. Well, given that she had seen an otherwise normal person's eyes pulse with blue fire, like something had replaced the human with some new cosmic devilry...staring at the ceiling in wonderment wasn't alto-gether an inappropriate response.

The dormitory that Talania had arranged for her was an upgrade from Fiona's last two stops. This roof was intact, for one. A far cry from the banquet halls and copper inlays of her home. But then, that building had some rather...foundational adjustments, free of charge from the Navy's best and brightest. In order to rebuild her asteroid home, she'd have to find the asteroid it once sat on. Half of it had probably fallen into the Boolean star. The other half, scattered across the system.

Empires, she scoffed to herself. Built upon sin, but most espe-cially, out of pride. And an Empire shamed was a vengeful creature.

Fiona laid on the too-stiff bed, staring up at the smooth recessed ceiling of her room, that small pocket of absence looking back at her. In reality, it was designed to make the compartment 'feel' bigger, but in practice? It felt like something was missing.

Who had lived here before her? This place had been furnished by someone with minimalist taste, not unappreciated. But little specks of a person were everywhere. They struggled with their storage cabinets, one of them wiggling on its hinge. And the charge sockets were scuffed and scraped by unsteady hands.

Whoever they were, they were dead now.

This wasn't a room to sleep in. This was a room worker bees went to await the next sunrise and the next droning shift at the proverbial grindstone.

So, Fiona went for a late-night walk through this up-jumped metropolis. Through three grinding rusty doors and a banging, clunking lift all the way down to the ground floor, Fiona walked half-awake, drinking in the uneasy silence. She had to have passed a dozen doors of other homes and not one cheery voice, no music or screams of frustration, no passionate moans or crying children. It was like walking through the halls of an aging manor, once full of activity. Now, only memories and hauntings.

The streets weren't much better. She stepped out into the night and the rubber walkways bounced under her feet, like she could break into an easy sprint at the drop of a hat. She was in the center of town, the beating heart of humanity on this dustball. But still limping from siege, the city had clammed up, taciturn and wary, naught but glimmers of neon light reflecting off the leaning towers overhead. Except for where craters in the steel had been carved out, exposing the ugly material within.

Piles of debris had been cleared and sorted into great piles in the square, with impromptu walkways cut by the most common foot traf-fic. It was the natural sorting of what had been so carefully constructed. People always found their way, even if it was past the mass graves of their dead neighbors.

She could smell it in the air, the solvent used to chemically break down the bodies, masked with a hint of pine. It made her stomach turn, but she supposed it was better than the true scent of death.

That was more saccharine, like syrup gone foul.

This little pocket of civilization had thought itself so high and mighty, humanity's arrogant fist rising from the desolate savannah, supreme over the wild. They had fled the Core Worlds to escape exactly this kind of life, of steel and stone, only to plagiarize that metal origin. Like they had composed, out of a more idyllic way of life, something exactly like the old.

Imperial was all they knew.

But, despite the despair and the damage and the defeat, Fiona could make out the distinct brassy sound of music on the air. Thin, barely piercing the languid atmosphere, like it was its own act of rebellion. Somewhere, someone was having one last ride before certain annihilation.

Her kind of people.

She followed that sound. It wasn't far, just a turn around the block, and amongst the cold night and silver steel, she could see the warm glow of a pub's front door. Like a candle in the dark.

A drunken fool pushed his way out of the door, which groaned at his touch like a well-paid lover. Inside somewhere, a stereo system blasted some metallic pop music, and there was a hint of acoustic manipulation—subconscious wavelengths buried in the song, manipulating the psyche, suggesting good times and physical entertainments.

Even at this distance, Fiona shivered, imagining a pair of hands running up her arms and across her shoulders to her neck, all while a second set of fingers teased her thighs...

She shook her head. Flagrant open acoustic manipulation, free flowing alcohol, and a populace on the edge of apocalypse? Yes. This, now *this* felt like home.

Fiona entered that corner pub and let the music wash over her. Cement slab floor with a wood-stamp on it, and cast-iron tables scattered about in a choreographed chaos. But they'd dressed up the place with lights, paint, trying to brighten the decidedly industrial mood. The music was coming from a crackling old speaker, and a holographic display was playing something: sports or an indecent display, it wasn't obvious. Maybe someone was channel surfing.

With each step forward into the bar, she felt eyes track onto her. These were grungy colonists on the Reaches with simple clothes of brown and tan, some uniforms and workman's gear. Those that weren't laborers and scientists still clung to their Capital jumpsuits, hand stitched modifications and mending.

And here she was, with a red waistcoat of fine silks.

She marked them as she entered, several disparate groups. Some were heads down enjoying their meal and drink, sinking into the melodies and the flavors after a long day. Some Capitals reacted like they knew her, tilting glasses and softly nodding in her direction.

At one favored table by the corner, Fiona spied the brusque ball of blonde scar tissue: the Capital bruiser, Nora. She sat next to Keira's pet snake, Solomon, and that stiff grizzled fossil, Bray.

The Capitals Three sat with curled backs and hunched shoulders, drinks clutched close in shared silence. Despite their very common uniforms, there was a healthy berth around the trio, like no one dared stray too close to their gravity well.

Fiona strode up to the bar, settling one hip on the stool with her other leg staked hard to the ground. The bartender approached, polishing a glass in that eternal Sisyphean task that every bartender was trapped in. "Whiskey," she said.

He rolled his eyes. "What kind?"

"The alcoholic kind."

The bartender shook his head, reaching back for one of his liquor hoses. He snagged the most generic whiskey-flavored whiskey of the bunch.

Before her social lubricant could appear, however, some brave soul sidled up next to her. And his voice leaked grease. "You must be the famous Captain Harlowe. I don't believe we've met."

She felt gross just listening to him, his easy tone polished to unsettlingly smooth. Fiona didn't look over at this aspiring charmer. Eye contact was power. Refuse it and she could deny access. "I've met everybody I need to." She slid her credit forward for the bartender.

But a second card appeared, under slender manicured fingers. "A lady doesn't pay for her own drinks."

"Good thing I ain't so fancy then."

He turned around, leaning on the bar on propped elbows, like he might be able to peek around into her view. She looked askance, but she couldn't avoid a glimpse of his tussled brown hair. "Good thing this isn't a social call, either. I require your services, Captain."

Work intrudes.

She sighed, looking over at him. His face was chiseled from a block of stone, his eyes sharp and attuned. He looked vat-born, chemically designed to appeal to the largest swath of people possible. And that kind of focus-tested face always made her cringe. "I'm otherwise engaged."

"Whatever they're paying," the golem said, "I can assure you, I will more than compensate you for the inconvenience."

She heard chairs squeak, as several people got up all at once.

Really? She hadn't even gotten a drink yet, and the overture was already starting? These powder kegs must've been primed and ready to blow well before she got there.

Fiona squinted, studying her suitor for a moment. "Looking for passage?"

He nodded. "Me and my friends need to make our way to the nearest Imperial station. Can you help us?"

Ah. Loyalists. They wanted out of the blast zone before their precious Empire confused them with the hated Enemy. Again.

The bartender slid over a glass of cheap ambrosia. She palmed it with one hand, tapping a generous payment into her card, enough to make the bartender's eyes bulge.

End of the world. Money was meant to be spent.

As she lifted the glass to her lips, she slid this Imperial lackey's card back to him. "Captain Harlowe might have helped you," she said. "Unfortunately, he's dead."

His brow furrowed, confused and unhappy with this development. "And who might you be, friend, with Captain Harlowe's legally registered vessel?"

She took a sip of the liquor, savoring the burn at the back of her throat, the notes of vanilla and cardamom buried underneath it all. Making him wait for her answer, letting that tension build. "My name is Fiona McCorty," she said, "Master of the Boolean Edge, and Imperial Most Wanted. I built a kingdom out of Piracy and Crime. I sank an Imperial fleet carrier that had the temerity to invade my space. And I am no friend of yours."

He seemed...pleased by that confession. He smiled, thin lips gripping tight to his jaw, like his face didn't quite fit his skull, too small. The way he projected his voice, he was no longer speaking to her but to the entire pub. "A fugitive from justice. And a *pirate*...come to the aid of terrorists. They are not going to help you. They are not going to protect you!"

"Oh, *shut up*, Whitby!" Nora finally barked from her table.

'Whitby' turned away from Fiona, playing to the crowd like someone had a bouquet of roses chambered in the cheap seats. "Our home used to be a jewel, an example to the rest of the outer Reaches. And now, after almost a year of 'independent' leadership, of forgiveness and reconciliation, what have we bought?"

"I'll buy you a new voicebox," Bray muttered.

"Government by threats and intimidation!" Whitby said, aiming a finger back at Bray. "But I tell you now, we are not yet gone from the Pilgrim's light. We can yet be redeemed!"

For a man feigning faith and political weight, he was depending quite highly on the muscles of the five goons marching over to the bar.

She'd met enough sleazy politicians to recognize a nascent mafioso when she saw one.

And they were going to detain this 'fugitive' as an example of his moral leadership.

"You know, it's hard to see the Pilgrim's light through all the smoke you're blowing up my ass," Fiona quipped.

He didn't respond. Whitby just jerked his head. And the grunts were all too happy, a spring in their step as they cracked their fat knuckles.

All she had wanted was a whiskey and some good music. Now she was going to have to break some fingers. Oh, well. They didn't know her very well in this neck of the woods.

They'd remember her after this.

The first one laid a hand on her augmented wrist, and she let them pull it back behind her. Idiot. You can't wristlock someone with an artificial wrist.

She rolled with the motion, twisting and cartwheeling around the augmented elbow joint with the freedom and flexibility only technology can buy. He stared gormlessly at her, befuddled by this acrobatic development. So, she kept the spin going, cartwheeling a second time to hook her foot around the back of his neck at the top of the rotation. She brought him cracking into the ground, jaw first, the rest of his body ragdolled behind him.

His friend didn't wait, trying to grab Fiona while she was occupied, pin the little acrobat. He swung his arms wide, trying to wrap up the woman and leave her nowhere to escape.

Big moves, wide moves, were slow moves. She bent over backward, tapping her fingers on the steel floor for balance. And his flailing attempt found only air.

She tucked her knee as she tumbled, snapping it out into the underside of his jaw. He popped into the air like a string had yanked on his spine. She rolled to her feet and squared up, all before he hit the ground.

Nora didn't wait another moment. She swiped her highball glass and hurled it across the pub, popping the next attacker right in the temple. The glass didn't break, but his skull made a very satisfying thunk.

By the way his eyes crossed and everything went limp, he suffered some minor brain damage. Fiona just pushed him to the floor, before he hurt himself further.

"*Zu gloriam!*" Whitby shouted, a call to collective arms against the Capital usurpers.

And those words activated the taciturn Gunnery Sergeant Thomas Bray, like the politician had shouted some kind of slur. Bray flipped over his table, showering the wall with liquor and glass. And he barreled straight at Whitby, a runaway train, a roar leaking from behind his clenched teeth.

The sweatiest bear of a man Fiona had ever seen—who probably did nothing but turn very large wrenches for a living—intercepted the old soldier, trying to drive Bray off track.

But Bray was a Navy Regular with decades in the saddle. He knew how to turn his enemy's strengths into their weakness. He picked up his feet, letting the laborer carry him off—because Bray quickly wrapped up the man's beefy legs and brought the considerable weight slamming into the pub's floor.

Fiona grabbed her whiskey glass, giving a gracious tilt to the bartender before pounding it back. She could hear the scuffle intensifying behind her, but she had a moment to enjoy the complexity hiding in the cheap drink—despite the burn, the distiller had added warming spice on the tail end, a lingering cinnamon.

It was always invigorating blending sensations: blood and fun.

The music picked up its pace, like it adjusted to the different tone the night had taken on. It felt like sparks running the length of her forearm and down to her pinky finger, but the tinny echoes of bodies hitting the cement floor was a sweet afternote. Couple that with the cheap whiskey stinging her tongue, and it was a fine evening after all.

"You seem awfully calm," Fiona observed, the bartender just going about his business.

He shrugged. "I have my routine. They have theirs."

A hand grabbed at her leg, the same unlucky bastard that tried to wrist lock her. She slipped her foot from his grasp and drove her heel across his face, knocking him out cold. Didn't spill a drop.

Nora was pelting Whitby's goons with bottles and other found weapons. Bray squeezed his arms around the big one's neck, like a fifty-foot python around fatted cattle.

And then there was Solomon, squaring off with his own loyalist opponent. Soulless eyes pierced right through flesh and bone, assessing, breathing, anticipating.

Fiona heard the slick of steel against leather. A raised eyebrow, Fiona looked over to see the flash of an Imperial quick knife in the Loyalist's rough hands.

A lethal weapon in an otherwise friendly bar fight? What was this wannabe bruiser doing?

Solomon didn't mind. Solomon's eyes went dead, like he'd been unplugged and the lights had gone out. And with a twitch of his wrist, a slender blade dropped from up his sleeve, a slick curved number with a gutting hook on the end of it.

Still stained with blood.

The simple sight of the blade was enough. The bruiser dropped his knife to the floor and kicked it over, hands shoved high in surrender. No need for any of that business.

Solomon's eyes fluttered, disappointed.

Some drunk came sailing in at Fiona, interrupting her view. It wasn't terribly clear if he had a dog in the fight or was just drunk enough to enjoy a late-night dust-up. He threw a wild and ill-advised haymaker at her head.

Fiona grabbed him by his swinging wrist and spun him around hard enough to bring him to his knees. Then she clapped his head against the bar, politely stunning him just enough to reset his inner ear and knocking that fool notion right out of him. The man stumbled, got to his feet and went off to sit against the wall.

Nora looked over at Fiona, all heavy breathing and a little cut over her eyebrow. "You have time to *sit down*?"

"Bring me something worth doing," Fiona remarked, "I'll do it."

Whitby, little slug, had seen how quickly the tide was turning. He was scarpering right to the pub's door. But it swung open before he could get there.

And everyone stopped. Solomon pocketed his knife with a groan. Nora put the bottles down. And Bray let his goon loose.

Aaron Havenes didn't need his glowing blue eyes to command the attention of the room. Legatus, all five foot something of him, strode in to the pub. He was a few inches shorter than Whitby, but the way the coward hunched over, genuflecting in the presence of real power? Fiona'd never have known Aaron wasn't eight feet tall.

Aaron hadn't said a damn thing—but the world warped around him in compliance.

He looked right through the tattered suit, measuring every dust-up and scrape, every foul word and cruel intent, shriveling the man into a schoolboy with nothing but a stare.

Whitby had no secrets here.

"I'm never quite done with you, am I, Whitby?" Aaron asked. "First the mountain. Now this? How did you expect this to go? An escape from Vanguard? Failing that, you start a bar fight late at night in the Commerce District. That transforms into some groundswell of support for your cause from some silent majority just waiting for your transformative leadership? Appeals to faith and patriotism restore you to your rightful place in the Statesmen, banishing tyranny and villainy. And we can forget how our Imperial Master & Commander threatened to burn out our homes for the unforgivable crime of...that we didn't sing his name loud enough? Or have you forgotten how this all started, how it was *Imperial hands* that drew *our* blood?"

Whitby jibbered something akin to a response. "I-I have the right to free expression of my—"

"No. *You* don't." Aaron's brown eyes didn't waver. "Do your feet still hurt from the last nature hike? Or do you want a jail cell this time?"

Whitby swallowed his bile and his pride, whispering, "Jail, please."

Aaron looked around the room, ready for any other pretenders, but no one said a thing. Frankly, Solomon looked like he was going to sheepishly click his heels together.

Aaron raised an eyebrow at Bray. "Doing a little community outreach?"

Bray dusted off his knees and straightened his jacket. "Just getting a sense of public opinion."

Aaron jerked a thumb at Whitby. "Get him to Security in one piece. And don't threaten him this time?"

"This time?" Fiona remarked.

Nora huffed, suppressing a laugh. "See you all next week?"

Bray grumbled, grabbing Whitby by the wrist. He snapped a scolding finger at Nora to follow along. A single withering look from Solomon was enough to route any loyalist thug still standing, and they all fell in line right behind the Gunny, ready for their night in the drunk tank.

And just like that, the night's trouble shuffled out of the bar.

Aaron looked over at Fiona, big brown eyes and speculation. He looked like he was trying to pick her apart with his mind, take her down brick by brick, but just couldn't figure out where to start.

She mocked a two-finger salute at him. And his strength vanished, his eyes fluttering as he turned to the door.

Fiona slid her glass to the bartender, propping her foot up on the unconscious goon at her feet. "Can I get another one of those? That was remarkable."

CHAPTER
SEVEN
FIONA

THE GROUND CREW had done an admirable job of patching up her ship, though it was quite obvious where harvested ruddy metal covered critical damage. It had made the aged freighter look like it was draped in an old quilt, pockmarked with patches from a hundred different wrecks.

Disgusting. But she'd fly.

A few hundred colonists were at the perimeter, held at bay by a line of armed Capitals. The protestors had brought their civil rights with them, shouting epithets at anyone that crossed the picket line they had drawn in their heads. And they brought art to illustrate their displeasure.

The Governor must've kept a tight grip on the Capitals, Fiona mused, as the body politic openly spat insults in front of a cadre of armed guards. Back home, Fiona would have had the enforcers drag the offender out of the line and elucidate for his fellows what a lack of forward thinking it was to insult anybody with a gun.

Of course, the large firearms draped across their chest rigs might be just for show. And what a tragedy in leadership that would be.

"Excuse me! *Excuse me*, Madam!" A voice called out from the line. Fiona could recognize when polite verbiage was used to issue demands, and this voice had that familiar bite to it. "Ma'am, do you *really* believe there's a reactor leak aboard this ship?"

Fiona threw a glance over her shoulder, at nobody in particular. "You keep bothering me, I'll make one using your teeth."

Shocks, gasps, the audacity! The absolute gall! It rippled through the crowd as they all told each other what had just transpired in a game of offended telephone. Nobody even gave a damn what she said, only that she had answered a perfectly justified question with a threat. How dare!

Fiona sauntered up the gangway, jacket folded over her arm, as she watched the engineers scurry around. It was like someone had disturbed some colony of insects and they were furiously at work, scuttling about in separate dance numbers.

"This bucket," a snide little voice said, "has three bulk Jupiter Assim impulse engines, twenty-two cargo bearing hardpoints, living quarters for twelve, a medical suite, and a fully-stocked bar."

Floating down the gangway in a maglev chair was a muscular young woman. No older than seventeen, still slight of frame but all sinew and toned edges. From underneath a mop of surly red hair that was bright enough to signal passing starships, a glowing red eye implant squinted and tracked Fiona's every edge.

She was exaggerating the movement, letting the implant wander independently of its squishy neighbor. This overactive adrenal gland of a person was trying to cause Fiona discomfort.

But Fiona had an augment of her own. She pointedly rolled out the elbow joint, twirling her metal arm behind her to scratch her back in a way no human should be able to. "Are you waiting for me to add something to that assessment?"

"Nope," the chair-bound rubber band said. "Just if the *Esteban* had been stocked like this, I'd still be there."

Ah ha. The Naval Defector—last one standing anyway. "You're the Jockey?"

"Aisling Danahy. What's left of her."

Fiona cocked her head, examining the floating chair. "They just let you run away with hospital equipment?"

"I don't fly with my feet, pie rat."

Pie rat. Pirate. Wordplay. Wordplay she'd heard before over open comms in a scrappy edge of space she used to call her backyard. This little jockey had probably been a part of the very same Imperial fleet that had busted up Fiona's nascent fiefdom.

Fiona squinted at her. "Well, you can put up your feet, plug," she said, "because I do all my own flying."

Aisling puckered at the remark. She craned her neck to examine the pocked underbelly of the ship over their heads. "Maybe that's why she looks like someone ran her through a thicket of picket mines."

Fiona gave an approving nod. Touché. "Grab yourself a drink on me. From the top shelf."

Aisling flipped her an approving finger. "Don't think I won't get it."

Fiona chuckled at that image, all of the tools that would be needed. And she had no doubt she'd find broken glass in the galley before they'd made the first Jump.

Fiona marched up the ramp through the cargo hold. "Bosun? Pre-flight."

The AI assembled its head out of pixelated blocks, floating along-side her as she walked. Every so often it would skip as she moved out of range of one projector and into the next. "Of course, ma'am. Do we have a charted course?"

"I'll get you one," Fiona dismissed. "For now, just run the check-list. And let me know if anybody starts pressing buttons."

A clang and a bang, some power tools up ahead. Fiona rolled her eyes, stalking up the corridor to the living quarters. Two engineers were busy reinforcing a door with pocket welders, while Nora and Bray looked away from the sparks and burning light.

"Look, I know it's in bad shape," Fiona said, "but I don't think we need to condemn the whole room like it's haunted."

"One of us will be posted within sight of this door at all times," Bray repeated for her benefit. "He'll be fed at regular intervals and provided full quarter."

Fiona raised her eyebrows, looking back and forth between the two soldiers. "There's going to be one, two...six deadly killers on this ship, plus a very tall politician, an old geezer"—she pointed at Bray—"a plughead jockey, and a cargo hold full of alien horrors. Sergeant, if he wants to start slinging, I think we can take him."

"M-hmm," Nora vocalized behind tight lips, quiet confirmation of a long-held opinion.

They weren't worried about Wolcott. They were worried about a certain pirate lord noted for her history in kidnap and ransom deciding to collect on a high value target.

That extra security was to keep her out, not keep him in.

"Bosun?" Fiona asked. "Open hatch C-19."

A grind, a crunch, and the door ripped open the weak welding joints and sheared off the metal burs. Nora and Bray gawked at the interior of the cabin.

A very confused Wolcott stared back at them from his bed, the old grimy screen in the wall scrolling some fanciful something he'd been reading. The wide-eyed surprise he was giving them looked like a twelve-year-old boy caught leafing through the forbidden and salacious parts of the Extranet, hand in the proverbial cookie jar.

And Bray slowly reached over, tapping the keypad at the doorframe, closing the door again and wiping the prisoner from view. The Sergeant then threw two menacing looks at the engineers, both of which were suddenly very interested in their shoes.

"I'll leave you to it," Fiona said, sliding between them all and onward. There wasn't any shouting, no creative slurs or violent promises. But the snap of welding filled the air with renewed zeal.

Fiona stepped over the doorframe into the galley. It wasn't a large room—just a narrow hall with seating against one side and the industrial replicator sunk into the opposing wall. Get lunch, turn around to sit and eat, back to work. It was an industrial freighter, designed for capitalism and efficiency, not human life. Of course, she'd installed some shelving, housing some of her favorite liquors, two rows of elegant glassware made by genuine artists. A little exposed copper fringe, and it almost felt like home.

But by the way Graccus hunched over his meal, shoving an oat paste into his face in the most undignified manner, Fiona would have thought this was a diner on the fringe of Ilum's Sunset line. A place where the drunk and recently drunk commiserated over their comfort foods and avoided the hot gaze of the sun.

The Imperial didn't look up. Rather, he stiffened at her approach. He was so unremarkable, with his simple brown hair with an off-center part and glassy gray eyes, he might blend in with the furniture. He pouted, his smile like some kind of rodent with its cheeks full of a winter's supply. "Eat when you can."

She'd heard the refrain before. "'Don't know when the opportunity will come again.' Don't mind me. Tank up." She slid past his seat and on up toward the Jump Deck.

She'd made it four steps when she felt the rush of wind. She turned, and there he was, staring at her from inside dagger range again. He liked that move.

And his smile that had been warm and playful a moment ago was now plastic and hollow. "I want to make something abundantly clear."

"Now's as good a time as any."

"You jeopardize this mission," Graccus said, "you jeopardize *him*...and I will yank your spine out and use it as a hanger to dry my laundry."

"You got an awful lot of loyalty for a crew you joined like a month ago."

"I had more loyalty when I was seven than you've ever had in your entire life, pirate."

"You're not the only one who took an upgrade, Oskie," she said, flexing her metal arm.

"Yours are more commercial grade, sweetheart."

"You guys called *me*, remember?" Fiona remarked. "And if you do kill me for whatever reason, the Bosun will flood every compartment with helium gas. So not only will you slowly asphyxiate in the cold and the dark..." She leaned in close, close enough to feel the electric snap of the current running under his skin. "...but it'll be funny too."

Graccus huffed and sidled back over to his bland porridge. She quietly hoped he'd melt into it, returning to the beige dishwater from whence he came. Fiona reached up, plucking a bottle of something blue, and resumed her death march up the length of the ship.

Who might be waiting for her in the next room, and what particular objections did they have?

From the galley, it was a short hop up to the Jump Deck. The cold and blank cube would've been a quiet retreat from all of the hustle, but she found the inhumanly tall Governor draped over the crunchy command chair like she had tripped into it. Talania bounced her foot in the air to some unseen rhythm, her eyes tracing the empty space overhead. Like she could see all the stars twirling somewhere up there.

"You're in my spot," Fiona stated, thwacking the foot with an open palm.

Talania craned her neck to see who had invaded her private moment. "Good morning, Ms. McCorty. How did you sleep?"

"Like I'd been tranqed," Fiona said, "but whiskey will have that effect."

The Governor laid her head clean back over the top of the chair to check, and Fiona winced. "That cannot be comfortable."

"When you're my height," Talania said, "you're never comfortable."

And yet, she was still sitting there. "Get up."

"No."

Fiona sighed. She knew where this was going. "You're like the fifth person in the last ten minutes to explain to me 'my place' in your little situation. And I gotta say, I'm going to shoot the sixth."

"Depending on who's left, I may want to take bets on that fight."

Fiona did a headcount in her head. "Well, I haven't seen Aaron or Solomon yet this morning. Get out of my chair."

"I refer you to my previous answer."

"Bosun," Fiona ordered, "give the captain a wake-up shot."

Talania had a whole speech prepared, but she cut short with a yelp, practically levitating out of the command chair. She looked back at it, a mixture of offended and surprised. And the few hairs not pulled tight into her ponytail were standing on end, reaching out for the silksteel above her.

"You see?" Fiona crooned with a devilish grin. "Now would that have happened if you just did what I told you to do the first time?"

Talania straightened up, looming over Fiona. "You're a bad person."

"You're just gettin' that now?" Fiona asked as she settled into the chair. She could still feel the residual electric charge in the headrest.

Talania laid a hand right next to her ear and started in. "I was elected by this Colony with sixty-two percent of the vote. That's unheard of."

"High score."

"The Governor gets their power as a mandate from those people."

"Was I one of those people?"

"You know where you get your power?" Talania asked. And Fiona was ready to break the woman's jaw. "From people being scared of you. You take it from them. And I have power because they gave it to me."

"Mine's cheaper," Fiona said, waving a hand toward the door.

Talania studied her for a moment. "When was the last time you spent a single day without looking over your shoulder?"

Last spring, she'd paid a squad of Yellowjackets to escort her, paid them well. Two years before that, she'd dropped off the grid and assumed an alias to vacation in the Reaches. For a full month after she'd had her arm done, she wasn't afraid of anything. But really, truly, *didn't* look over her shoulder? The last time?

Her name was Keira Ladd and she'd kept Fiona safe. Fiona hadn't been there to do the same.

"Get off my Jump Deck, Talania Dedria."

Disappointment in the air, Talania retreated down the causeway and Fiona sealed the hatch behind her. The Bosun wouldn't let anyone in while she drank in solitude.

———

It didn't work. She had solitude, sure, but the sound of grinding steel rang through the whole ship like a drum. Rivets being shot, rust ground away. It was like living inside an anvil. She could go back to the dormitory Talania had arranged for her, but she didn't want to give the slender titan the satisfaction.

Instead, Fiona took to wandering the ship, in deep dark places where the engineers weren't clanging away on the hull.

That meant the cargo bays.

This freighter didn't have interior bays. Instead, it relied on docking collars and struts to grab prepackaged containers and ferry them from place to place. It made for great open track, running for nearly a quarter mile. Back and forth, she could be alone.

But one time she reached the end and found a hatch open. The colonists had hauled up a container and hooked it up. Inside, nothing but corrugated steel. It reeked of salt and rice, some basic foodstuffs. Authentic. Beat the stuff that came out of a computer program and a carbon printer, but harder to come by.

What was going in here?

She sighed and turned—and her heart damn near leapt out of her throat to seek safer ground.

Standing before her, ten feet tall with rough mottled hide, stood a beast straight out of nightmares. Its thick carapace scattered with old injuries and divots, while a single bone talon extended out from each wrist, articulating and snapping at the air. A crystal blue eye with no discernable pupil stared back at her from the dark, the other sunken

63

socket marred in scar tissue. A bifurcated jaw and crushing flat teeth issued hot heavy breaths, dripping a viscous slime onto the deck.

This was a ton and a half of leather and terror.

And behind this beast, a wall of matching eyes, like horrors in the forest, behind the draped blanket of night.

The scarred face drew forward, chittering eagerly from deep within its chest. A rivulet of something thick oozing from its maw.

"There you are!" She heard Aaron's voice call out.

Her hand moved on its own, waving him back, urging him not to get closer. Her other hand unhooked the retention strap on her pistol.

But Aaron moved right past her, sauntering right up to the big beast and dropping his hand hard on the crusty exoskeleton. She could swear a cloud of dust fluffed off its hide, softening the hollow thud of the affectionate hit.

Aaron cooed, "What're you doing all the way back here, Scar?"

"The..." Fiona took a moment to cram her heart back down her throat. "The locals, I assume?"

The lead clicked its teeth together, prompting Aaron to issue a sharp grunt. "Hey! Be nice."

"I don't think your friends like me very much," Fiona said.

His eyes slid off of her. "What's not to like?"

"I meant the human kind."

"They'll come around. They *still* don't like Graccus all that much."

She watched those shoulders as they rose and fell. Strong and lean muscles, but thin—he'd been abused, denied food. It had stunted his growth. Was that why he was so short? Grew up poor, not enough food?

The big scarred alien hunkered low, a growl deep in its throat just at the edge of hearing. Fiona knew a threat display when she saw one, and she immediately took two steps back, giving ground. She quietly wondered if she could outrun them, get to some small passage they wouldn't fit in. But then she recalled—they were burrowers. There's likely no place aboard that'd be safe from them.

But playing that creative moment in her head made Fiona catch on a word choice. "*They'll* come around?" Fiona asked.

They. Not us. They.

"Yeah," Aaron said, blowing right past her observation. "They've been through a lot. That's all."

Huh. He might be that dense, but her instincts said he was avoiding the topic.

"I...don't have any news on...on Callum," he agonized over his word choice. "With the ExtraNet access cut and our transmission privileges restricted, we can't get a whole lot of traffic."

Fiona forced the air out of her lungs in a dramatic huff. Then she had to remember to draw some air in. It tasted like rotten eggs. How had these things snuck up on her?

She looked over at Aaron. "There's a quicker way."

He raised an eyebrow, and it looked like Scarface McNightmare did too. "I'm listening."

"...There's a refueling depot on the other side of the Jump Point: Akagi Station."

"How'd you get past it?" he asked.

She shrugged. "Not every Jump Point is...well regulated."

"So why would we go this 'well regulated' way?" Aaron's hand slid off of Scar's hide and marched over to her. "One guarded by Imperial soldiers—"

"Many of whom," Fiona pointed out, "would've been commandeered by your friend Deckard as he came on through to kick your ass. The base should still be on a skeleton crew. Especially with Deckard running around Imperial space unaccounted for—they have other priorities. Failing to reinforce old garrisons *is* something of a theme of theirs."

Scar didn't like her interrupting Aaron, and he chirped in her direction, a warning grumbling in its throat. But Aaron waved him down. "Setting aside why *attacking* an Imperial outpost with six triggers and a tugboat is a stupid idea...say we get to the station in one piece? What then?"

"Akagi isn't the station," Fiona explained. "It's the AI onboard. It records every passage through its space, incoming and outgoing. It'll know where Deckard went. Where Callum went."

Aaron hung his head. "And so, what, I leave Vanguard defenseless?"

"You really need every bit of it spelled out, don'tcha?" Fiona said. "Superhuman leader of a historic rebellion and he can't do basic math."

"If we go out to attack the depot, we'll..." He stopped.

And Fiona smiled. "Here it comes."

And it hit him like a firework going off behind his brown eyes. "Without the depot...there'd be no one to record who came or went. Rescue ships could get in, refugees could get out. Nobody would have a record of who went where."

"And he crosses the finish line." Fiona booped his nose, causing his entire brain to reset. "Day late and a little short, but he got there."

Aaron tried his best to keep his temper, taking a controlled breath. "I'm...not *that* short."

Scar grunted behind him, a clear disagreement. And Fiona had to choke back her laughter.

"Akagi's a valuable little tool," Aaron noted. "Won't they have some kind of tracker on it?"

"Absolutely. Which is why you carry him off in a Faraday cage, blocking any outgoing signal. In fact..." She paused, considering. "...we might be able to throw that panicked cry for help onto a half dozen other ships fleeing the scene of the crime."

"And drop Imperial attack dogs onto innocent people," Aaron pointed out.

"If that's your biggest moral hangup, fighting a war is going to be real rough on your sleep schedule." She shrugged off the perfectly legitimate point. "Well, if your wee beasties are going to lurk in the dark the whole trip. I'm going to string up more lights."

"I'll share the good word," Aaron said. He gave Scar a dirty look, clicking his tongue. And like a herd of demons, the other beasts followed him astern to their holding pen. The rolling thunder of their weight and the click of their talons on the deck, Fiona had no idea how she hadn't heard them approach.

If they wanted to be silent, they could. And if they wanted her gone, she'd be gone.

"Fiona?" She looked back up at him. He stood in some happy spot in the lighting, where she could only make out his silhouette. But his brown eyes caught the light just right as it cast down across his face, reflecting their brilliance. "It's a good plan."

"I *have* been doing this for a while," Fiona said.

He nodded, receding into the dark with his alien horrors. And Fiona's heart started beating again.

CHAPTER
EIGHT
DECKARD

HE COULD FEEL their eyes tracking him around the ship, lingering observations, like trying to guess when the volcano would finally erupt and take them all down in a hot flash. He was used to the gravity, to the distance admiralty brought, but not this wariness. Some leaders cultivated it, carefully and with forethought, built up the fear. They wanted each young officer to walk like the ground might fall out from under them at any moment. He'd served with more than a few of that stripe.

Not Deckard. This was alien, foreign, hostile. It was isolating. And it made him walk faster.

Apparently, Trevor Lindell wasn't so afflicted. To the contrary, the deck officer wasn't giving him an inch of space. The plucky regulation savant went the other direction entirely, becoming more familiar and direct. Maybe because the regs didn't apply to former admirals openly derided by the Ministry.

Lindell was waiting for Deckard outside the lift. He came into view just as Deckard cranked the manual release, the steel doors curling back to reveal his slender frame. His perfectly shaped beard, stretching down to his chest, appeared almost before he did. Lindell was brushing a hand along his crew cut, like he was trying to push the hair down through his skull to join his beard, but he was really pressing down nerves.

When he noticed the sliding doors revealing Deckard's stocky frame, Lindell immediately tilted forward, changing tone in an instant. "Can I just say, sir, that this is a *very* bad idea."

Deckard rolled his eyes, stepping out of the lift. "Has there been some development to modify your earlier disapproval?"

Lindell fell in right beside him, matching his pace as they stalked toward the Jump Deck. "Only my commanding officer's apparent dismissal of my alarms, sir."

"My, that must be frustrating. I'll have a talk with him, shall I?"

"Sir—"

Deckard waved him off for the moment, raising a hand to catch the attention of a passing face. "Doctor Findley!"

Doctor Cotchwell Findley was a casual man, wearing a fitted cotton shirt and rugged pants. A serious square face and a permanent scowl cursed his visage and his personality to boot.

He tried to act like he hadn't heard the admiral call out, so Deckard called his name again. "Findley?"

"What?" Gruff responses like that weren't altogether out of character.

But Lindell didn't care for the disrespect. "That's Admiral Tiberiet, Doctor."

Findley gave a little wave of his hands in mock fear at the title. "What can I do for you?"

"How's Mayfield?" Deckard asked.

Findley shrugged, more out of disinterest than out of ignorance. "She sprained her knee. Try not to order any hundred-yard dashes."

"I'll keep it in mind."

Findley mocked out a salute with two fingers and resumed dragging himself off to find the source of all foul temper in the local cluster.

Deckard shook off the grouchy tingle that was left in the doctor's wake. But Lindell must've gotten some stuck in his impressive facial hair. The Warrant Officer hopped ahead, turning to walk backwards, like that would somehow command more attention. "Sir, Cassandra Meilos is not a military officer. She's not Ministry. She's not—"

"Neither is Findley, so they're not bound by Regulation," Deckard cut him off. "She'll meet with me where a hundred others wouldn't."

Lindell stopped in his tracks, wrestling with his words before arriving at the only ones that he could. "She's a *slave* merchant."

"Slavery is illegal."

"Except as punishment for a crime," Lindell said, "and she accepts payment for her roster. How is that not slavery?"

Deckard looked back at Lindell, taking in the young man's raised eyebrows and narrow face. Five years in the service had left nary a mark on him, not even a broken nose. But the navigator's augments could be picked out along his scalp and his sleeves, always rolled up. He couldn't cover the adaptors lining his forearm. He looked like he was fresh from the box, mint, the plastic smell still hanging about him.

"She trades in human bodies. There's no other way to put it," Lindell implored. "Why would you trust her?"

Deckard huffed. "Worried about a certain *Capital*?" he asked.

Lindell's head bobbed back and forth as he weighed his words. "And worried about those in his orbit."

Himself. But also, the crew, his friends. And Deckard too. Big picture.

"She's not trustworthy," Deckard assured him. "She's a snake who's made a fortune marrying industry with criminal justice. She hasn't met a person alive she hasn't attached a numerical value to. So long as we provide her returns that exceed anything else...she'll cooperate."

"Yes, sir," Lindell capitulated, straightening up again.

Deckard beckoned him to follow. "*Be* nervous, Officer. That's a good thing. That means you're not stupid."

They approached the large archway to the Jump Deck. It had seen some tender love and care since the battle over Vanguard, but there were still some computer panels left exposed, maintenance work incomplete. The various half-moon consoles of each battle station were scattered haphazardly about the floor, an officer or two at each one. Gunnery Officer Saubert stood at his, rakish grin and glint in his eye.

Deckard glared at him. *Wipe that look off your face, you'll spoil the moment.* And Saubert tightened his lips, trying to put pressure back on his weakening gasket. Deckard swore he was actually squeaking.

The Sergeant-at-Arms, Elena Mayfield, stood at her post right next to Deckard's command chair. Her leg was still braced but you'd never know it from her solid posture; a dislocated knee hadn't kept her off her feet for long. Her chin popped up at the sight of Deckard and a cheeky grin appeared. "Ten-HUT!"

"As you were," Deckard conferred before anyone could finish standing. "Mayfield, you're looking positively spry."

"Doc Findley does good work," Mayfield said, giving her injured leg a little swing in the air. Whatever soft tissue harm had been done, it would soon be on the mend.

"Yes, he does, when he chooses to do so," Deckard grumbled. Lindell peeled off to head for his station, but Deckard grabbed him by the shoulder. "Mayfield, what day is today?"

The Sergeant's smirk grew worse, as the game was now afoot. "It's Wednesday, sir."

"Not that," Deckard remarked, playful. "I meant what day of the year."

Lindell was now firmly convinced he was asleep. His eyes had gone wide, but his shoulder slackened. Whatever weirdness was happening was going to happen with or without his consent, so it was time to brace for the storm.

"It's the thirtieth of Neptune," Saubert said, implying weight.

"One hundred and ninety-two years since the Pilgrim walked the

Path," Deckard said. "And the anniversary of Warrant Officer Trevor Lindell joining the crew of the *Tartarus*."

The Jump Deck erupted into pleasant applause. And Lindell sunk into his shoes, amused and embarrassed. Of course, they'd remember, what with the High Holy Day syncing up with his deployment orders in such serendipity. "And what a year it's been, sir," he muttered under his breath.

"Stick around, it gets better," Mayfield whispered to him.

"Who's driving this taxi cab, anyway," Deckard considered, playing up the showman, "when I'm not around?"

"The Commandant," some idiot offered, to some heckles and laughter. Another supplied a "Citizen Tiberiet!" cheer.

Deckard pointed a finger, marking the mouthy brat that took that particular liberty, but he continued with his prepared remarks. "Our Navy is not flown by algorithms and mathematics. No amount of programming can substitute. The Pathfinders were *aided* by machines, but they themselves were flesh and blood, challenging the void. These skies...they are patrolled by sailors and Regulars. And in the face of devastation, one man among you stood up to power and did what he thought was right, even knowing that it might cost him his career. He did this without so much as a second thought."

Lindell tensed. Was this some elaborate public execution? Maybe it was his nerves bleeding from one topic into this one, because Deckard thought he was being quite obvious where this was leading.

With his free hand, Deckard pinched and unclipped a medal from his collar. The cold metal fell into his palm like a spent cartridge. A small tapered bar with twin red stripes coiled around its center.

"For his bravery under fire and service to his fellows, it is my honor to present Warrant Officer Trevor Lindell with the Copper Battle Service."

Lindell's eyes bounced around with a thousand questions. And Deckard's smile softened. "It's not official, us being disgraced and dishonored. But...you deserve it."

Mayfield took the medal from Deckard's hand, affixing it to Lindell's jacket with a crisp, "Congratulations."

"Thank you, Sergeant," Lindell said, breathless.

"Alright, back to your duties," Deckard ordered. "Commandant? Begin Jump Preparation." Lindell went for his console, but Deckard pulled him close. "When I'm on that station, these people are going to need leadership. Can I trust you, Lindell?"

Somewhere between ecstatic laughter, tearful joy, and a reality disconnect, Lindell scoffed. "I think you have a terrible judge of character, sir."

Deckard looked into the man's eyes, back toward the Academy graduate and plucky cadet that looked starry-eyed into the heavens with a prayer to follow in the footsteps of the Pilgrim. And here he now stood, being offered command of one of the greatest battle machines made by human hands. "You should think more highly of yourself, Officer."

———

The *Tartarus* emerged in the Kuiper belt a mere hour's impulse from the prison moon. They kept to the field as much as possible, trying to avoid detection by satellites around Jupiter. It took some careful positioning, but they managed to glide in toward Pluto's solitary moon:

Charon.

Deckard took a detachment of Regulars led by Mayfield to a shuttle, and from there to the surface installation. It was a terse quiet. Every soldier aboard knew what this meeting might turn into, and they held their weapons close, the occasional leather squeak as gloved fingers tightened. Would they be greeted by Imperial loyalists, zealots who would gun them down to the last?

Sitting across from Deckard, bound to her chair with magnetic restraints, was Eden Neria. Many a prisoner in a similar situation might spit, thrash, scream in anguish. But not her: this rebel Capital, this calm insurgent, just stared at him with patrician intent, eyes twitching to and fro as she studied his face, committing it to memory. Her guarded stoicism was unsettling.

Quiet from a prisoner, broken, hollowed, and empty? That was expected. But she was so alert, so calculating. This silence was not out of deference or even self-preservation. This was a mind at work.

Deckard looked away. If she didn't want to bargain for her freedom, then there was no reason for him to explain himself.

Then why did he want to? So that she'd understand, maybe even sympathize with him? She never would. He came to her world as a conqueror and it was his men that had marched in the streets. Oh, woe is him, because he felt so awkward about it now?

Minister Caldwell would never approve of him, and neither would this diminutive woman.

Charon had no atmosphere, and a surface temperature that would shock, if there were any visible light to even read biometrics. It was so far removed from Sol that the great yellow star might as well have been just another speck in the night sky. Exit from the mines would lead you to true desolation and oppressive darkness. No need for heavy security—where were you going to go?

Escape from Charon just meant death.

Mayfield hit a button near her seat. "Charon Control, this is SSV-42 Niner, on approach for prisoner transfer."

"Copy 42-Niner. You are cleared to approach."

On that desolate lonely rock, the Mining Guild had burrowed, seeking out the valuable minerals over a hundred years ago. They'd long since moved on, but the subterranean refinery remained—and in swept the Ministry of Justice. Machines did heavy lifting, but they needed people to maintain the equipment at mining sites all across the Empire.

And the Ministry of Justice had some bodies to donate to the cause. Thus, the Capital labor program had been born, an innovation that sparked dozens of explorations into the Reaches of Imperial space. A cheap, renewable labor force for dangerous conditions.

Here on Charon, those prisoners were conditioned and trained, before being shipped out. And Deckard might just be volunteering himself for it at this very moment.

"Bless our burdens," Deckard intoned, "for they weigh on our shoulders."

"Huah," somebody muttered.

And the shuttle clanked to the ground. Nobody moved. Not a muscle.

Until Deckard stood up, stooping as he made his way to the back of the shuttle. He grabbed the lever, feeling the shocking heat sting his palm, the heat of the Charon mines. And he turned the handle.

The shuttle hatch creaked open, and hot air rushed in, nearly knocking his cap off his head. And with it came the rank stench of sweat, along with the almost aromatic bouquet that Deckard had come to know as death. Orange light spilled inside, like painting the bulkheads with sickly sap.

Outside, semi-circled around the shuttle, were four private security guards. They wore hardened armor, bulky and heavy—made to take kinetic hits rather than absorb energy. And their weapons, while a generation behind the Navy, were still fully functional automatic Gauss rifles.

The military surplus had to end up somewhere.

Beyond them were featureless industrial hallways, steel beams and grungy bulkheads. That orange glow leaked from around every corner, like a gateway to Hell lingered out of sight. Grinding machines and hydraulic hisses filled the air, and every single surface had oil caked on thick. But Deckard didn't miss the two ports in the wall, where automated turrets lay sleeping.

Spotless at the center of the pad, was Cassandra, affable and smiling, a flawless art piece amongst industrial equipment. Her jacket was slung over her shoulders, the heavy fabric hanging behind her, gold braids draped off of one side. A tightly tailored tunic and slacks made of fine white silk did little to hide her left leg, which was narrowed and tapered below the knee—an ivory augment claw gripping the stone ground like a ship's anchor.

Flanking her were two large dogs, dark as night with eyes to match their fur. The athletic creatures stood as tall as her hip and stock still. Their noses twitched, taking in the smells rolling off that shuttle.

Deckard was certain that with a single motion of her head, those two beasts would lunge for his throat.

Cassandra extended both hands, no expression. And her predatory eyes did not match her accommodating tone. "Deckard Tiberiet, you old autumn wolf. Blessed be your steps."

He dragged himself out of the shuttle, taking her hands in his own and planting a kiss on her right hand. "For the road is long, Miss Meilos. Thank you for your hospitality." He tried not to stare as the dogs tensed up.

"Welcome to Fort Augustine proper." Mayfield and the Regulars disembarked, and Cassandra shook her head. "Deckard, you hardly needed to bring a *boarding party*. We're all friends here."

Deckard faked a smile, twitching at the corners of his mouth. "Maybe they were just eager to see this jewel of the Empire, Cassandra." Mayfield audibly scoffed from behind. "But I didn't bring them for me."

Cassandra's eyes widened. Thirsty. "Have you brought me a gift, Deckard?"

He pursed his lips. He didn't quite know how to introduce her, so he didn't. A glance back toward the shuttle, and Mayfield pulled Eden out into view.

Cassandra's shoulders squirmed under her jacket, a pleasant shiver. "A trophy?"

"One of Aaron Havenes' close lieutenants," Deckard said.

"I'm acquainted," Cassandra whispered. "317-YT."

The designation drew a disdainful scoff from Eden, the first noise she'd made in the entire trip.

Cassandra inspected her prize from head to toe, assessing every inch. There was something more than hunger behind her eyes. There was...anticipation, like a vampiric thirst eager for the first sip.

And Deckard immediately regretted stepping onto this revolting station to meet this malignant woman.

"Come." Cassandra drew a hand back, ushering Deckard's party into Charon's glowing interior. "Let's get you to your accommodations."

Lindell was right: this had been a mistake.

CHAPTER
NINE

EDEN

IT STILL SMELLED THE SAME, that blend of copper and wet and salt and a touch of something electric. Five years away from Charon and she might as well have left yesterday. It made her hair stand on end and her skin tingle and her ears burn.

In all that time, everything might have felt the same, but everything was new. The corridors had been remapped and reinforced as the diggers cut new channels into the glorified asteroid. All the cold spots she had memorized for a moment's refreshment from the humidity were gone, covered up by the thermal generators. The fusion reactors made Charon hospitable to organic life, but there wasn't exactly an emphasis on comfort.

And with all of that change, there remained one truth: when Eden awoke in her cell, the door was open and there were no guards. She rolled onto her back, feeling the uneven stone jab and prod her in a sadistic manner.

Some prisons were pockets inside civilization, kept insulated and under tight fists. But this? This was deep in Imperial territory on a moon hostile to the very idea of life. Aaron and the others, they weren't going to come get her, not here.

Whatever happened next, she was on her own.

Eden sighed, rubbing at the lacerations on her wrists. The steel cuffs weren't sharp, but they had pinched and torn at her skin after weeks in captivity. There didn't appear to be any damage to the muscles, and she had full rotation in each joint. She painstakingly rolled out each finger to ensure everything was in good shape.

And then she pressed herself to standing, squaring up on the door like it was a gladiator in the Coliseum.

She'd survived Charon as a medical resident, just sixteen years old, cold and afraid. She'd wanted to do right; she'd thought she had done right. And then suddenly, she was in prison, stripped of everything, even her name.

Now, she'd seen true horrors, colonists butchered by alien claws mere feet from her; entire cities burning in the morning light; she'd survived Marcus Riley; she'd survived the siege of Vanguard.

She was still a doctor, still a soldier, still Eden.

This? This was going back in time to a place she had once feared, only to discover that it...annoyed her.

Outside of her cell, there were a dozen or so identical empty doorways, hewn from the stone by hand. Security doors had been socketed into the rock. But those were mostly for safety from other prisoners than for imprisonment.

At each shift change, the appropriate doors would swing open and release freshly rested teams to tend to the great drilling machines below. End of the day, prisoners would retire to their rooms, and the doors would slap shut behind them, releasing the next crew. Capitals would find safety and community among their own teams; any Capital caught outside when they should be asleep likely found themselves fair game, no protection.

That rumble under the floor was almost friendly. Somewhere below, in the heart of Charon, several HML Model 68 autonomous mining drones gnawed on the guts of a planet, seeking precious minerals long since extracted. Here, the Capitals learned how to maintain those great dragons, work in teams to keep them singing.

What would Jensen say right now, hearing that idle hum through the stone? Or Quinn, the little squirrel? Or Carmona?

Her heart fluttered for a moment, a smile brought to her face by memories of theirs.

No. They weren't here to help. But they can shuffle the rooms around all they want—this place was exactly the same.

She sauntered down the hallways, lackadaisical, drifting from one side of the hallway to the other. Extending one hand, she dragged her fingers along Charon's stone walls. They were hot to the touch, and wet, like the rock was sweating. The stone was harsh and rough to her fingertips, scraping like sandpaper. Bits of it came off in her fingers, knocking free. She could feel the vibrations of the drilling rigs vibrating up from below, rolling thunder.

She paused, her breath catching in her throat.

No. The Jergad were not coming. That was a drilling rig. She was on Charon and they were far away, Aaron was far away. Talania was...

Eden blinked away the thought and resumed walking down the corridor.

All she had to do was follow the noise, clanking, squeaking, grinding metal. She passed a handful of Capitals in the corridor, heads down and power-walking to whatever task they had for the day. They didn't even look up as she passed.

And yes...not a single guard.

But soon she came upon a large cavern, possibly a natural formation. Catwalks had been built up high, encircling the space like arena seating. They were meant to provide maintenance to the large three-story tall crucibles, glowing full of molten metal. On the ground floor, almost half a mile wide, an assortment of tools and gear for attending both the refinery here and the drilling rigs below. Several elevators were sunk into the wall on the far side of the cavern, ferrying workers down for their shift. There'd be half a dozen dig sites at different depths, connected only by those elevators and the conveyors for the raw ore.

"You're late," a voice called out.

Eden rolled her eyes. The tone of voice attached a moral judgement, something hilarious given the place they were at and the company they kept.

She turned to see a stout figure, head roughly but closely shorn with a rough homemade blade. Patches of brown felt peeked out on their tanned dome. And they were trying to appear...broad, flexing their shoulders outwards, despite a slender frame.

Eden bit her lip. "You're the Foreman, yeah?"

"And you're late." They were pitching their voice down, trying to be domineering, but the natural original high pitch just made them sound like a tuba. "317-YT?"

"Eden Neria," she said, extending a hand.

As expected, they didn't take it. "Not down here, it isn't."

"Well, you can shout numbers at me all day long. I'm not answering to 'em."

They sneered. "You will."

"Do I look like fresh meat to you?" Eden asked them.

That confused them, but the Foreman wasn't above a little amusement. "You look like they all do."

"Mhmm." Eden nodded. "Guards are stationed on orbital platforms and only come down for corporate visits. Otherwise, they just control us by raising the temperature a few degrees an hour until we all give up. Most of the time, we're left to run the house ourselves. Cheaper that way. Set our own schedules, so long as we hit our quotas. But *really* step out of line, and there's always the Hot Boxes. Sweat it out in pitch darkness. Is the mess hall still down that way? They moved everything else."

The Foreman blinked away their confusion. "Where you come from?"

"I was pulling rock in this dank dark hole back when you had a name," Eden said. "What is your name, by the way? I promise, I won't go shouting it."

It was dumbfounded silence for a long moment. The Foreman

looked around to see if anybody had decided to watch that drama. Sheepish, they kicked a toe into the dirt. "I don't remember."

"That's the fun part," Eden comforted them. "Sometimes down here, you get to pick a new one."

"You're not scared at all, are you?" they asked.

Eden shook her head. "I'm just passin' through."

"Passing through," they said with a scoff. "Nobody escapes Charon. How did you get away?"

Eden's eyes glazed over as the last four years went by in a blink. "I didn't."

Screams. She pricked up her ears. Not rage, not fear. But pain, shattering pain. And for a free-associating instant, she could smell the gunpowder and the alcohol, that lemon and pine scent they used to try and hide the smell of cleaning solvent, that metallic tang. Vanguard's hospital had been caked in blood. And a single baleful scream had brought her straight back into that triage center.

But the Foreman hadn't heard that piercing howl, not over the industrial work filling the cavern. "Well, if you're thinking of trying anything on my shift—"

"Shut up."

That got them all haughty. "Hey! I'm the Foreman. This is my block. You're going to—"

The scream again, and they both turned to the elevator. A muscular woman was carrying a body, heaving the security gate open with her foot.

Someone above in the catwalks bellowed: "Blooood-y steak!"

Eden didn't need to be close to see the man's injuries; she'd seen them plenty of times. A gear rat—a small crafty type that could worm up into the rig—had gotten a limb caught in something hydraulic. And it hadn't cared two wits for this fleshy bag of water and meat. They were carrying him because he didn't have his left leg anymore.

And he was dripping red from the ribbons, leaving a thick trail. Crushing, tearing, gnashing. Not a clean cut. Meant the arteries were smashed, not severed. They wouldn't constrict shut. They would've left half of his blood inside the mechanism that ate him, and he would gush out the rest with each passing second.

Eden tracked on the goons above them on the catwalks watching the show, more than a few laughing and pointing. She quietly reminded herself that this *was* a prison; some people in here weren't so nice.

The Foreman pushed past her, jogging over to the wounded Capital. "Wha' happened?!"

"I don't know!" the brawny woman carrying him babbled. "We had a stoppage on—I called on stoppage on Four. Bit was grinding on something."

The injured man clung to his savior like a man drowning with some driftwood.

"You sent him in to clean?" the Foreman asked Brawny.

"I called a stoppage!" she snarled. "He's far up its ass, doing his thing. Next thing I know, the beast is roaring, and he becomes *red paste!*"

It was a story all too familiar, from Charon and from Vanguard. Heavy machinery didn't give a damn. It pulled bone and sinew just as easily as rock and stone.

The man blubbered in her arms. "You gotta—go back. Gotta—my leg!"

Eden stalked over, easily slipping between the two Capitals. She yanked on the patient's knee, drawing it out straight and eliciting yet another scream. Blood gushed out over her hands, hot and warm. Strips of flesh, like torn reeds, mashed into the fabric of his jumpsuit. There was no way to fix this, not down here.

But maybe—

Predictably, a hand launched down to seize Eden in a grip that could crack a bone.

"Who—*fra tow xi*—are you?" The brawny Capital demanded with all of her chest. Her shoulder sleeve said some incomprehensible string of numbers and letters Eden wasn't going to commit to memory anyway, but she had some beautiful tattoos on the ball of her shoulder, a stark white-on-black feather symbol. Looked religious, might be just impressive.

"I'm trying to help," Eden said.

Maybe it was her tone of voice or her demeanor, but Tattoo let her go, instantly code-shifting to a mother cradling a child, that powerful voice cracking just a bit. "Can you?"

Eden didn't wait to answer. She quickly scanned the tools at her disposal. Something flexible, something strong. Chains? No, that would do more harm than good. Of course, they didn't leave anything she could use! Unless...

"Where's the mess hall? You all stocked up?"

"What?"

"Do you have a *still*? A distillery?!" All she got was blank stares, so Eden turned to the room. "Does anybody here have a contraband still?!"

The Foreman raised a meaty paw. "Ain't nobody got nothin' they're not supposed to. Now let's keep our voices down."

Eden whirled back to the brawny woman. "Tattoo, what's your name? Quick. Chop-chop."

The brawny woman's brain hiccupped, halfway between rage and confused. "Isolde."

"Isolde," Eden repeated. That was the end of her politeness. "Take him to the Mess Hall right now. Pour two full cups of pure alcohol on a table, get it as clean as you can. Then wash your hands in hot water." She pointed at two other workers nearby. "You both, help her! Now!"

Having totally lost control of the situation, the Foreman grabbed a pipe and rang it against the nearest steel support they could find, sending a metal gong into the air. "Nobody...do any of that."

"Oh, for the love of..." Eden grumbled. Were we really going to be doing the sacred hierarchy dance *right now*?

The Foreman pointed their blunt instrument at her. It was low enough she could look right down the end of it like a telescope. They didn't mean it as a threat, but it was kind of hard not to take it as one. Their voice went low and hushed, like they could keep this as their little secret from the Powers Above. "There ain't nothin' we can do for him," the Foreman advised. "We jus' have to go back to work now."

"I don't have time for a chin check, jackass. This man is more than just leaking. So, you either bash my skull in—or you help."

The wounded Capital got another lungful of air and let loose with a scream that could break glass. And that was the step too far.

The Foreman tossed their pipe back into the rack of tools. "What do you need?"

Isolde used that moment to take off with the patient, jogging away. Eden reached into the rack, pulling out a long screw, using it to pin her hair back behind her ear. And then she grabbed a shovel. "You do any metalwork?"

"It's a refinery," the Foreman chirped. "Yes, I've done metalwork."

She tossed them the shovel. "Mold the sides over, use your knee as a form if you have to. Then get it white hot and meet us in the Mess."

"Use my knee—*white* hot?" the Foreman had made the unhappy guess of where this was going.

"It'll be red by the time you get to us and any colder won't do the job. Now go." Eden turned to jog out back into the hallways. She didn't have to guess which turn to take. There was a neat blood trail on the steel grating. The orange light did make it rather hard to make out, but it shined against the matte of the metal.

The halls might have changed but the mess was exactly as she remembered: long, low tables in a long, low room. A kitchen was tucked behind a counter on the far side, with silksteel grungy tools. The stone floor had been polished by hundreds of feet over hundreds of days. It was almost soft.

One shift was busy having their meal when Isolde started snapping out her own orders. They had cleared a table and two grunts were holding his arms down. For as big as she was, Isolde was surprisingly agile, vaulting the counter to the kitchen and shoving her hands under hot water.

Eden marched over to the patient. Two Capitals tried to block her path, producing some ever-classic prison shivs made of shards of rock and a silksteel spoon.

"Do I *look* dangerous to you?" Eden asked.

The two meatheads looked at each other, hoping to rub together their brain cells to form a collective intelligence.

But hey, the shivs looked sharp. Eden snagged one from their hands and pushed through.

Before anyone could grab her, she lunged in close to the patient's head, right by his ear. "I don't know who you are, and we can swap stories later. But right now, I need your undivided attention. Your leg is gone, and it's not coming back. I do not have anesthetic, I do not have a surgical suite, I do not have an AutoDoc. If we're doing this, we're going to do this medieval. There's every chance it'll hurt like Hell, you'll get a post-operative infection, and you'll still die. Nod if you understand?"

The Patient bobbed his head up and down, gritting his teeth.

"Good," Eden said. "We have two choices. We go crazy and try to fix this. Or..."

She never got to say the other thing. The Patient opened his pale blue eyes, stared right back into her soul, all the way back to her first year of residency and said four words. "Fix my fuckin' leg."

Eden nodded. "Clean the table. I need to scrub up. Get something in his mouth before he bites his tongue off."

Isolde was back from over the counter with a tin bucket that positively reeked of bathtub whiskey—somebody had managed to ferment their porridge. It would have to do. Eden guided them through it as they lifted the Patient off the table and did a backyard sanitization. And then, they washed out the wound with alcohol.

The blood draining from his leg refused to mix with their home-made antiseptic, painting small red rivers across the surface of the table.

Eden took the shiv, testing the edge. Delicate, but sharp.

"This is going to hurt," she cautioned.

"Everything hurts," he panted through the balled-up shirt in his mouth. "Jus' do your thing."

If the Patient felt her cutting away the long strands of his skin and muscle, he didn't complain any more than he already was. She had to get the wound site clean and clear, or the next bit wouldn't take. They'd create a hundred little pockets for bacteria to grow.

And even still, this might not work.

Covered in blood up to her forearms. Scraps of flesh piling up on the floor. Bone shards plucked from the bloody bog. She even got a Capital onlooker to be on sweat duty, dabbing her brow with a rag and cleaning up the Patient's face. A crowd of onlookers had gathered, an audience to the macabre, a mixture of horror, glee, interest, and fear.

It always took longer than she felt it did. And the Patient was slipping in and out of consciousness.

And that's when the Foreman arrived with a glowing shovel, like Satan's hockey stick. The head was molded into a neat cup. He jogged over like he was holding aloft a torch.

She hated this part in school and that's when they had used a laser form. This wasn't her first time cauterizing a wound in strange conditions—but it was going to be the largest.

"Well, if blood loss hasn't killed him," Eden muttered, "this might. Hold him down."

Isolde laid over the top of the Patient, using her impressive size. Eden grabbed the shovel from the Foreman—and pressed it into the leg.

It always smelled a bit like beef in a cast iron pan. Same sizzle too. Of course, dinner didn't usually scream.

The Patient went limp. The room went quiet. And Eden lifted the shovel away. But the blood had stopped.

There was a great deal more care that needed to happen. She'd effectively created a burn site that now needed its own care. He might still bleed internally, pool and abscess. He might have an infection. He might die of shock.

But all was quiet now.

Which is why everyone could hear the clack of a charging handle and the whine of the capacitor winding up. Guards stood in the Mess Hall doorway, their weapons nestled into their hips, ready to spray the entire room with indiscriminate death.

And standing at their center was the Lady of the House. Cassandra's eyes sorted through the crowd and each Capital stepped out of the way in turn, as though she could leaf through their number with just a flick of her chin.

Her perfect brow didn't flinch when she saw the graphic horror on the table.

And nobody said a word when they led Eden away.

———

Eden had been in darkness before, deep in the mountains over Vanguard and in alien tunnels underneath the savannah. But the way the sound of her breath bounced back at her, she knew this darkness wasn't just complete, but close to her skin, pressing in. It was like a coffin, inches from her face and her shoulders and her legs. It reeked of salt and metal, but Eden knew it wasn't the container—it was the blood still caked onto her hands.

Every exhale, and she felt her own hot breath blasting back against her face. And the walls around her, the rough metal cage, sizzled against her skin if she tried to lean or relax.

The Hot Boxes.

Was she buried under one of the crucibles, liquid metal inches away? Or was she against whatever Hellfire device kept Charon's innards hospitable?

Wherever she was, she was not beyond the reach of Cassandra's voice. "I thought that Deckard had brought me a gift, but now I see, he has brought me...trouble."

Piped in through a small tube overhead, echoing in her little chamber, those drips of venom felt like they were crawling from under her skin.

Don't speak. Don't beg, don't fight, don't rage, don't cry. She wanted Eden to respond. Give her nothing.

Silence didn't dissuade the Lady of the House. "It was fine work. I might congratulate you. The man will live. Were it not for your quick action, he would have bled out right there on my foundry floor. Your time in the field has tempered you."

Eden tried to mask the sharp intake of breath, the slight pleasure that this little trip wasn't in vain. She'd successfully purchased the man's life.

"You're in my halls for less than a day. And you organized half of the day's detail into a trauma ward." If Eden hadn't known any better, that sounded like a compliment. She knew it wasn't.

Cassandra sighed. "Every person that took instruction from you has been disciplined in accordance. They take their orders from the Foreman, who takes their orders from someone with a name. From the moment you entered my facility, you became mine, Capital."

Eden knew this speech well enough. She was alive because the Empire allowed it. Her crimes were great and her punishment final. There was no redemption for those convicted of Capital offenses. There would be no mercy.

She swore she could hear the bitch smile, some tone in her voice, a girlish laugh somewhere in the back of her throat. "You've got some fire in you. That's good. Keep that close. But burn too bright, and someone will snuff you out."

Someone like her? Or another prisoner she paid to do it? No, don't answer her.

"Your life is now bereft of the protections you once enjoyed. That is a truth as solid as the ground under your feet. You have to survive now. And you cannot survive by making such a racket. You understand? Don't make noise. But do not aim to be quiet either. Too quiet, and the fiends in these halls will smell it. Find the delicate balance. Be neither predator nor prey. Not a danger...not a weakness."

Well, that was a very long play, Eden thought. Don't drive out the light, but leave enough to stay alive?

Of course. She wasn't in the business of punishment or isolation. She was, in point of fact, in *business*.

"You're a terrorist now, darling." Cassandra's voice was drips of wicking moisture through the vent. "The powers at play here, they'll want you dead. I don't. But I can't keep your secret if you go making that much noise. Someone is going to notice you, and they will come to this moon with a whole new litany of charges. And you won't escape treason alive, child. But I cannot protect you if you don't help me. Come out of your hole with chin high and belting out orders, someone will silence you. Instead, come out resilient, come out strong...but above all, come out quiet."

For the longest moment, Cassandra didn't have any follow up to that. And Eden wasn't going to fill that air.

But then Cassandra laughed, pleased, behind tight lips. "Very good. You'll be out soon enough. And we'll speak again, before then."

She heard the boots retreating, and Eden was alone in the dark again. Cassandra had taken Eden's silence and turned it, made it a tool, an asset. She'd made punishment a benefit and her word the only balm. Her advice made sense, and her words felt cool, refreshing.

Narcissistic bitch.

Eden was alive because they allowed it? That was a song she already knew. No amount of resistance, no amount of thrashing was going to dissuade Cassandra from this playbook.

The Lady of the House was patient. Nobody was going to 'find out' about 'their secret.' That wasn't a thing.

Was it?

Eden could quietly resist or thrash till her arms fell off. Cassandra would just bleed her with one hand and tend to her wounds with the other, for however long it took. Until Eden accepted the program.

Eden had to find a way off Charon, or Cassandra Meilos was going to break her.

CHAPTER
TEN
AARON

SOFT VIOLET GRASS under his head. Glittering stars in the sky. There was an overwhelming calm, a peace in his chest like being wrapped in a heavy, soft blanket. And the lights that flickered in the sky were dancing to and fro.

And he felt...glad.

The only home he'd ever known was a three story walk up in a city that was perpetually shrouded under smog and night. So why did this feel so much like a heart lifted, free of its troubles, like every muscle in his body wanted to relax? Why was this place, full of rolling lilac grain and gentle hillsides and green sunsets...why did this feel like home?

Some flexing steel in the hull of Fiona's freighter startled him awake. The bang echoed down the hull, rippling like a skipping stone. Whatever hydraulic system that suffered ran all the way down the fuselage. He didn't expect the freighter to be quiet during flight, but two solid weeks of travel, and this old boat rattled like a toolbox.

The Jergad were huddled in the center of their container, pressing together into a single leathery shell. And yet, when Aaron had laid against them, they were soft and welcoming. Maybe that blanket he'd been dreaming about?

Scar moaned underneath him, and Aaron rolled over to see the big guy staring up at him, a single weary eye. Aaron sighed, patting the beast with one hand. "I'm okay, big guy...just a nightmare."

"You too?"

Aaron looked up to see Sergeant Bray framed in the door, some steaming cup in his hand.

"What time is it?"

"Late enough," Bray grunted.

Aaron smirked. "Then what are you doin' up, old man?"

"Reading a history book and griping about the youth. Isn't that what I'm s'posed to do?"

Aaron chuckled, letting his head fall back onto Scar's big warm flank. He rose and fell with the creature's breathing, and it was like being rocked to sleep.

But Bray clearly wanted to talk. "You uh...not able to sleep in your bunk?"

Bray thought it odd that Aaron was electing to spend time with the Jergad. He thought the beasts smelled funny, and he hadn't really gotten over years of fighting them. He still had images of battle etched into his—

"Don't do that," Bray said.

"Do what?" Aaron felt the Jergad tighten underneath him.

Bray leaned on the doorframe. "Don't go rootin' through my head like it's going to make you feel better. It won't help me. And it won't help you."

Aaron shrugged. "I'm not..."

"You're not what?" Bray asked.

Bray was combative by nature, sure, but he hadn't come here looking for a fight. That was just how he showed his love.

"See, that right there," Bray said. "You get this look in your eye and you go somewhere else and then you know what I'm going to say."

Bray came into this room because he couldn't sleep. He had

wandered the ship for the better part of twenty minutes looking for anybody else awake. Why was he awake?

"You can't sleep?" Bray asked him, projecting his own issues.

Aaron sighed, sitting up and choosing to stare at a bulkhead instead of into his friend's mind. Everything Bray thought was so loud.

So instead, he just said, "Not for very long anyway."

"Well, Nora's out like a drunk," Bray said. "Talania snores, would not have called that bet. I'm not sure Solomon sleeps."

"Nah, he just turns off his brain and waits," Aaron quipped. If he couldn't feel Solomon zonked out a hundred feet astern, he'd believe that man undead.

"Aisling played music until she passed out."

Bray was right. Aaron could hear it echoing up through the grating. Some techno piece, with a slight hit of something underneath, some alpha wave to stimulate calm. It wasn't exactly the safest way to knock out. Go too deep into that, and she might not wake up. "She's medicating."

"Rolling acoustic?" Bray raised an eyebrow. "Great, the jockey's an addict."

Not an addict, Aaron thought. But she was hypnotizing herself away from dealing with her troubles. Suppose it was better than the opposite, playing music to fly high as a kite or pump herself full of adrenaline. Acoustic mods were a good party trick, not a long-term solution to mental health.

But for those precious moments, with the music ebbing and flowing...she forgot the touch of Keeper's skin on her own.

Aaron grimaced. "She's got her treatments. And you've got a cup of—what exactly?"

Bray slurped at his coffee. "You know damn well what it is."

"And you're coming at *me* about sleep?"

"Don't start. I earned this." The old warhorse wanted the extra zip, the extra step. Without it, he felt sluggish, like every part of him had to press through jelly, like there was a fog in his mind, like there was some cable holding him back that he had to pull with every step. Everything was heavier. And if he was slow, even a little...people died.

But Aaron just said, "Well...Thanks for checkin' on me."

Bray raised his glass. "Sleep in your bed, Legatus. It's worked for ten thousand years and we ain't modified the design all that much. It works."

The door slid shut. And Aaron laid back, staring at the ceiling for hours until the lights came on.

———

"Event horizon in three minutes," Fiona announced into the intercom. "Closing thermal vents and routing aux power to the Jump Drive. This ship is pretty old, so we might pop out the other side with some new breezy windows. But it's a good day to die, and I like a light show. So, grab a seat, hang on, and let's ride the rail. Bless whatever your burdens, for the road is long, yadda yadda." She clicked the overhead switch, her sign-off as dry as stale bread.

Aaron stepped over the open hatch into the gray, featureless box, taking in the bare necessities that made up the Jump Deck. "Not exactly a luxury liner."

"Yeah, your higher-class ships tend to have security lined up for troublemakers."

"Am I a troublemaker?"

"No," Fiona admitted, "but you make one rule for everybody, or they'll all just think you're special. Get off the Deck."

"Do I really have to sit down for this?" Aaron asked.

"You're also *supposed* to not eat four hours before a Jump. But who the Hell does that?"

Aaron examined the bulkhead, trying to find whatever pinprick she must be looking through to see the outside. There wasn't a single glowing panel without some indecipherable code flowing across it, no image to speak of. How did she know how close they were?

Fiona must've noticed his gawking because she raised a hand—and with a flick of her wrist, the whole cabin came to life with brilliant reds and hot orange and deep violet-black. The walls and floor faded away and the cold steel was replaced with the sparkling void, and the roiling brown and red nebula around them.

"Where are we?" he asked.

She took in that vista herself. "Main Street, wise guy. Two weeks out from Vanguard, you've got this little gas cloud with a pretty happy gravity well holding it in place. Ten thousand years, who knows, maybe a new star gets born in here."

"You ever wonder why the Jump Points are so conveniently located?" Aaron asked.

"What?"

"They're all near habitable planets or resource pockets. No dead ends. That's not weird to you?"

"Sure," she said, "if they were random, we'd be a piss poor Galactic Empire. Stuck in Sol, waving our very shiny stick at the Cosmos."

Heh. The reason didn't matter to her. The effect did.

She looked up at him, the colors of the nebula reflecting in her hair and along her steel arm. It made the green in her eyes absolutely explode with color. But the dark that swirled around her made his stomach turn itself inside out.

Aaron reached up for the intercom switch, tabbing it open. "Last chance to check and test your weapons. Depot's right on the other side. Take care of who's next to you, they'll take care of you."

He felt each person onboard take a steeling breath, and the Jergad collectively chittered, a bone rattle somewhere in the aft of the ship. Fiona's eyes widened at that sound. "Yup. Yup, I'll hear *that* in my nightmares for at least a year. Bosun? Can you give us some peppy music please?"

"Of course, ma'am," the Bosun's voice echoed from every surface, like the invisible floor and walls thrummed with its words. And as soon as that tremor ceased, a pleasant string orchestra began to play.

And Fiona closed her eyes, fingers on her right hand dancing along with the tune.

Aaron chuckled. No acoustic manipulation. The lady just liked her music.

Somewhere out there beyond the limits of the human eye was a gravity well that would crush all matter down to a single point of space.

"You don't really buy that sale, do you?" Fiona asked, tilting her head with each movement of the orchestra. "Take care of who's next to you?"

"Not to be too mean about it," Aaron said, "but I don't expect a pirate to understand."

"Naw, it's a fair hit." Fiona rolled out her neck, and Aaron could hear the slight crack as she did. "Pirate or soldier, people are people. And I've found in half a decade of piracy that what people *believe* to be valuable, has value."

"And you can sell it?" he asked her.

She smiled, devilish. "You can steal it."

Aaron had Jumped a handful of times, but it had been years since the blocky bulk transport had ferried him and Jensen out to the colonial Reaches to toil away in Vanguard's copper mines. He had forgotten how it pulled at the skin, like a million pins underneath his skin were pushing for escape. His eyes scratched and itched and his lips fused together.

And the Bosun ran the calculation faster than his brain could process what was happening.

Space rippled around him, flexing and bending, before settling again. He stumbled, the gravity generator skipping as it came back online. And that beautiful nebula vanished, winking out of existence.

"Bosun?" Fiona asked.

The pixelated head assembled itself like a glowing blue sand sculpture. "All systems nominal, ma'am. Point oh two three placement drift. Multiple Naval signatures detected in the vicinity."

"Jump complete," Fiona said into the intercom. "Opening

97

thermal vents. Thumb those safeties, raiders. We're flying in somebody else's skies now."

Aaron craned his neck, scanning the projected dome around them, but all he could see painted on the walls was space and more space.

Then, like a candle in the dark, he saw them all. Five thousand people, give or take, and more than a little plant and animal life, floating on a brick in the middle of nowhere. He was transfixed, the throbbing rainbow glow against the black.

Fiona studied him for a moment, a slight curl to her lip. She raised a hand, pinching her fingers in the air to zoom the image in.

There it was: Akagi Station. Six long arms reaching out from a core, spinning around like the arms of a dancer. Hundreds of small ships swirled around it, shuttles and fighters on patrol. It was like a storm of glitter or a swarm of bees hugging close to a rotten tree husk. Chromatic twinkling lights.

"See that fat bastard off to the right?" Fiona asked, pointing. "That'll be his weekly fuel run. Keeping the station stocked. Looks like a dozen or so freighters are in today. Good crowd to hide in."

What happens to them in all this, all those innocent ships? Will the Navy just kill them all, Aaron wondered, to be sure that they'd contained the pirate threat?

Aaron squinted, raising his own hands to pinch and zoom the image, but nothing happened. Fiona raised an eyebrow. "What is it?"

"Just..." Aaron pointed. "Zoom in there."

She obliged—and they both swallowed hard. The lean shard of a ship loomed over the station, a mother over its nest. And it dwarfed every other ship in view.

"That's an *Alighieri*-class Fleet Carrier," Aaron said with a hushed tone. "Over four hundred crew, a squadron of Bearcats, and enough kinetic batteries to blow that whole station to dust. They'll flood that place with armed and angry Regulars in under a minute."

"Yeah," Fiona said, with a touch of cursing in her voice. "I've met the type."

Aaron shook his head. "We need to abort. We push that station, we'll never get off it."

"What's the matter, baby boy?" Fiona asked, that perfect curl in her lip. "Afraid to make a little noise?"

Don't make noise. Don't be quiet. Don't burn bright, but do not hide in the dark. The words were etched under his eyelids, had guided his every step for three long years. He'd survived this long by being unremarkable, but not being weak, neither predator nor prey.

No...he could stand to make some noise.

PART TWO
ORPHEUS

CHAPTER
ELEVEN
FIONA

WALKING around refueling depots always felt claustrophobic, and Akagi Station was no different. Most of the hulking steel structure was for fuel and supplies, with barely enough room left open for a crew to stretch their legs. Ceilings were low, and the walls were tight, like a big steel compression box.

It reminded her of a prison cell—a really *long* prison cell.

But any place that people gathered, there was trade. And where there was trade, there were merchants.

When the hatch opened and hot air flushed through into the freighter, her nose filled with the stench of fry oil, salt, and sweets. The cacophony of friendly chatter filled the air like some kind of percussive texture.

She drank it in. It sounded like...like home. The air crackled with a soft pleasure, accompanied by sharp barks from the stall owners hawking their wares to the dismissive captains passing by.

Now, unregulated commerce brought crime: mugging, theft, black markets. So, the Navy wasn't far behind, installing a few token guards and big walk-in scanners. They'd cross-reference the biometrics of any arrivals against Extranet databases.

Any wanted person—like a certain beautiful pirate who had

declared herself Master of the Edge, one who had single-handedly sank a fleet carrier into the side of a star—would alert every vessel within three Jumps. They'd descend on the station to secure her arrest.

And Aaron Havenes...well, he might raise a few alarms of his own.

Legatus, the Capital Rebel, Capital Commander—he stepped off of her freighter with proper ease and authority, gliding over the airlock hatch like he was walking on water. Drifting upon the invisible currents with his eyes closed, he felt his way over to the security checkpoint.

It was a brightly lit spot, no shadows, nooks, or crannies: a decent kill box. The Navy had set themselves up for victory.

On the other side of the scanners, the market was having a modest day. Ship captains trading in small goods and tools, mechanics telling them how they have to fix this or that. A little over a dozen innocent bystanders, all tolled.

But they were all going to clear out of the way in just a moment.

Three Regulars: ceramic plates and some focused laser sidearms. Probably officers too useless to be given real postings on active Naval patrols. They were bored and chubby, gnawing on sweetbreads from a shared container. This is what inevitably happened when left to self-report their own physical fitness while being in deep space rotation with access to fried food.

In fairness, it's not as though there was a lot going on.

The Regulars were only paying half attention as Aaron marched up to the scanner. One grunt with a very bushy soul patch shoved the last chunk of greasy bread into his yawning maw and mashed it into his cheek with two fingers. He hopped off his seat and flipped up the holographic screen on his Entiglass. He quickly briefed himself on the ship, captain, and manifest that came up, beckoning Aaron into the scanner with two fingers.

Aaron obliged and the arches started to whirl around him, collecting all kinds of data to compare against the official record.

Fiona braced herself for what came next.

"Captain Harlowe," Soul Patch mumbled past the food stashed under his tongue. "Welcome to Akagi Station. Please present your manifest for inspection. We are at Threat Condition Two, so you must surrender any firearms or weapons for the duration of your stay. This is a reminder that all transport of biological cargo must be declared, and decontam procedures observed before you—"

He never got to the end of the sentence. Because the scanner froze in place and released a red warning light, along with a klaxon so loud she felt it vibrate her augment socket. Soul Patch's jaw slackened a little bit, crumbs dribbling down his front, as he looked up from his screen.

Aaron raised his head and cracked open his eyes—casting an evanescent blue so bright Fiona could see it glowing across Soul Patch's own fat cattle face. The alarm seemed to change its pitch, raising in importance.

And in that split second, half of the Imperial Navy received word, the most terrible secret: the Capital terrorist Aaron Havenes was no longer trapped on Vanguard.

Good hunting.

The market crowd paused, eyes up to watch the unfolding drama. They didn't see that alarm go off every day. What was all this now?

Soul Patch's chin quivered. But whatever Soul Patch was thinking, Aaron could read ten steps ahead. He just shook his head and said one word: "Don't."

It was at this moment that Soul Patch remembered he was armed. He fumbled for his sidearm—and Aaron lunged. He punched a hand out, seizing Soul Patch's limp wrist and locking the weapon in its holster. His other hand came up, striking Soul Patch's nose with an elbow.

Before the Regular could stumble back, Aaron reached an arm up and wrapped his neck in a bind, bringing the man's head down into his arm pit. Wherever Aaron turned, Soul Patch followed blindly, flailing his stubby arms and legs.

But Soul Patch had friends.

And Aaron felt them coming even with his back turned. Aaron spun off the mark, and the first two shots went past Aaron's shoulder. The red lances pierced where he had been and found only air, carbon scoring the opposite wall.

Which is when Aaron drew his own pistol from his waistband, slipping it right past Soul Patch's helpless head. The poor Naval thug got to listen intently to the thwump of the magnets—the round snapped directly to his friend's ceramic chest plate. The thick armor shattered, throwing him to the ground.

If the people weren't screaming and running before, they sure did when they heard kinetic gunfire. The sound of a bullet hitting ceramic was louder than anything else in the terminal. It sounded like a brick had hit a wall.

The entire market screamed as a collective, and they fled like they actually possessed functioning self-preservation instincts.

Guard number three, well, he tried to be a hero. He stepped up to cover his downed friend, firing erratically all over the terminal. Suppressing fire like that was liable to hit Soul Patch as much as Aaron.

But Aaron was a slippery little snake, whirling both himself and Soul Patch out of the way of incoming hot death. Both of the Regular's fat legs came off the ground, leaving his neck as the only load-bearing point, draped across Aaron's forearm. Aaron squeezed just a touch, and Soul Patch's panicked flailing slackened and slumped, hugging him off to sleep.

The last remaining Regular still standing shook in his boots, like he was ready for takeoff. All that gunfire, all that hustle, and now he hesitated.

Aaron gently propped Soul Patch up against the wall. He gave a single tap to the man's flabby cheek, almost adoring the sleeping grunt, before turning.

This heroic moron just watched Aaron advance for a second, unsure if he was dreaming this or not. Maybe a spot of cheese or gravy had gotten the better of him, granting him this waking night-mare. Fiona couldn't help but giggle at the man's dawning realization: this vexing hallucination was quite real.

The little man renewed his subscription on courage and squeezed the trigger. But Aaron seemed to slip aside with every blast, casually leaning away as hot beams of energy slipped inches away from him.

Over the shoulder, beside his head, twist out of the way—every time. Aaron was never standing in the way of the shot, despite confidently marching straight ahead.

Six shots in, and the coward suddenly dropped his gun with a clatter, shoving his hands in the air. "You know what, I'm not stupid. Let's all chill out now, okay?!"

Aaron cocked his head, giving the guy a curt nod, as if to say, *I'm good, if you'll be good.*

Fiona drank in the smell of ionized air and the singed carbon. It made the skin on her neck tingle. "*Damn* fine show, Capital." She sauntered through the scanner, issuing a whole new battery of klaxons and lights.

"More like 'show off,'" chirped Nora, leading the rest of the Capitals off the ship, along with a bound Wolcott at gunpoint.

Bray pointed at the downed guard. "Get him some medical."

Fiona leaned over to check on the writhing man. "Movin'. No blood. He's fine."

"Was I talking to you, pie rat?" Bray glowered, before snapping his fingers at the surrendering Regular. Quivering, the grunt glanced at Fiona, as if to seek permission. She rolled her eyes and nodded, letting him go to his friend.

The market had largely cleared out, the last footfalls of retreating patrons fleeing into the station. After all, nobody past the checkpoint was armed to defend themselves. What remained was a ghost town, shanties of sheet metal, echoes of shouting deeper within. The klaxon echoed up the halls, a heartbeat of danger.

And that's when the Imperial screamed like his voice was trying to leave his body. Not because of his friend; Fiona knew for a fact that a ten-millimeter Horus center-mass wouldn't penetrate the standard-issue ceramic armor. No, this was a scream of abject childhood terror.

Because Scar, and the rest of the Jergad brigade, began to clamber out of the airlock. Curious at first, picking at the surroundings, tentative and uneasy. They...didn't really fit through the door, all skull fans and glowing eyes and leathery carapace. But they were determined, warping the metal bulkhead with each testing push.

The coward abandoned his friend and beat feet into the station, scrambling away like he was carrying an unwelcome deposit in his trousers.

Funny as it was to watch, she didn't entirely blame him. Scar looked like some fantasy beast that tormented a pre-literate medieval village. This thing was a nightmare horror made manifest. Running away was a perfectly logical choice.

Still, a Naval survivor loose on Akagi could properly inform and prepare the rest of the station's defenders. Fiona slipped her carbine off her boot and took aim at the coward's retreat.

But Aaron laid a hand on the barrel, bringing it down with a disapproving look. "In his back?"

"Fine," Fiona said, holstering the weapon, "but whatever surprises are up ahead are now *your* fault."

"Yeah, Aaron. Since the rest of us lowly humans can actually *get* ambushed..." Nora said with a shrug.

Fiona threw her a glance. The little ball of scar tissue was actually agreeing with pirate scum? Nora avoided her eyes, trying to not give Fiona the credence.

"I thought you liked surprises," Aaron said, tossing the stolen pistol over to Nora.

She went to catch the gun—but couldn't quite snag it, and it clattered to the ground. Nora put her hands on her hips, staring daggers. "Don't. Throw. Guns. *Aaron.*"

"That carrier will have told half the universe about my ship," Fiona said, "so once we pluck that AI, we'll need a new ride. Slip away like we're just scared law-abiding folk."

"Nora, Solomon," Aaron gathered them up with a wave of a hand, "get us a good big ship that can take the Jergad in the hold. Graccus, you're with me and Fiona. We're going heisting."

Graccus bounced on his toes and shook out his wrists, loosening up for what was to come.

Bray jostled Wolcott by his restraints, tweaking the boy's shoulder. "I'm the babysitter, I take it?"

"You *could* give him to me," Solomon offered, eyes glittering with something other than greed. And that made Wolcott's face go pale.

Talania stepped up, towering over everyone else. She clutched a rounded case in her hands, soft corners and thick cables coiled on top with care. It was the Bosun, gingerly removed from his housing in the ship and awaiting his next adventure.

Talania looked around, expectant. "And what should I do?"

Fiona stalked over to her, laying a possessive hand on the Bosun. "You drop him, and I drop you. Copacetic?"

Aaron threw a look at Scar and the rest of the demonic horde waiting patiently for orders. There were entire databases that contained less information than what passed between those blue eyes in half a second. And the affirmative chuff that came out of Scar still made her skin crawl.

The Jergad reached out with their claws, tearing into a bulkhead. Entrance carved, they disappeared one by one into the bowels of the station. A hundred alien demons...behind any bulkhead, under any floor of Akagi.

Those biological tanks compressed into tight spaces far better than should be possible.

Nora gave a playful salute to Aaron. "We'll see you soon, shortstack."

No reason to worry about directions or a rendezvous point. Aaron would be able to find them wherever they went.

Fiona marched over to a wall console, grabbing its edges with her augmented fingers and ripping it free. Drawing some loose cord from her wrist, she plugged in—

Test matrix, rerouting. Hostile breach in sector Five-Niner-One. Rerouting. Please remain calm and proceed to evacuation docks in an orderly fashion. Attention: KC-801B Model freighter, tagged and marked—

Electric impulses up her arm, pulling her to the source. Deep, down into the Station's heart...

"I see you," Fiona muttered. She drew the cable back, letting it wind back up into her wrist. "We're close. You boys ready?"

Graccus had to tap her shoulder, jerking his head back to where Aaron had stopped, staring up at the lean-tos and market stalls. He was transfixed with nothing but sheet metal and etched designs. Maybe he thought the grease stains held the secret to his future?

No, that was wistful memory. This looked familiar to him somehow.

"Oi." Fiona drew his attention. "We're on something of a schedule."

He looked so sad, eyebrows raised, somewhere far away. But he nodded, his only answer a breathy, "Yeah."

For half a second, he had gone somewhere else, disoriented to wake up and find himself where he actually was. He walked over to them, but his eyes lingered on that corrugated steel.

Fiona led the way, marching up the corridor. She tucked her carbine into her shoulder, but let her augment drag along the wall. Feeling for vibrations.

Beyond the checkpoint security, there was no real resistance. She followed the electrical currents in the walls, drawing answers back as fast as it sent pulses outward.

The great immutable source of Akagi Station.

They came upon an archway—it might as well have been a temple gate, but Fiona knew that it was constructed to mask the enormity of the routed cables. She supposed nobody wanted to stare at the ugly conduits day after day. It'd be like living inside a circuit board. And, of course, drunk crewmen or anarchistic captains might tamper or sabotage the lines.

There was an awful lot of traffic that wasn't leaving the next room, isolated just short of these beating arteries. It would bounce from the AI Core, hit several subsystems, then report back. What could all that traffic be? A security door, maybe, with a rapidly altering helix lock? Some other security response?

It was a lot of noise...

But Aaron didn't see all that, or care why she had stopped. So, he just stepped right out into open space, completely blind to what was on the other side.

Overconfident, so used to his superpowers.

Fiona reached out for him, vainly trying to pull him back to safety. But Graccus was faster. Her fingers passed through where Aaron had once been like he was made of gas. Graccus threw Aaron to the ground, sliding and squeaking to the far side of the archway—

And bullets came screaming out, scraping and sparking off the metal, like they were angry to have been denied their prize.

"What was that?!" Aaron shouted, favoring his shoulder. Graccus had hit him hard enough; he'd probably bruised him nice and purple.

Graccus stacked up behind Fiona, back flat to the wall. "Combat Mechs! A lot of 'em."

Of course. Aaron couldn't see what wasn't alive. That was a simple piece of modern tech that turned Aaron back into any old mediocre grunt. The metal quadrupeds inside would be walking turrets, piloted by the station AI as it defended itself. They couldn't be bled, they couldn't be frightened, they couldn't be negotiated with.

Lovely.

"Can you get through?" Aaron asked Graccus.

The Imp shook his head. "I'm fast. But you can't dodge a wall."

Good thing they brought her then. Fiona palmed a small sphere out of her pocket. "What model are they?"

"What?"

"Are they thermal or infrared?" she demanded.

Graccus sucked on his lip, thinking. Then his body flickered as he blinked at lightspeed out to take a look—accompanied by a fresh blast of bullets snapping through the archway. "Full suite. They can probably figure your family medical history from across a city block."

She couldn't blind them, then. She was going to have to stun them.

"Your implants? Are they shielded?" she asked.

Graccus nodded, following her line of thinking. He backed up a ways, almost like he was getting a running start. But he was just getting clear of the blast radius. "Depends. How much EMF will ya throw off?"

Fiona gripped the sphere tight, counter-twisting its top and bottom till a small seam appeared. It expanded in her hand with a whine. "You're going to have one second. Maybe less."

"You going to cause some havoc?" Aaron asked.

"No," she said. "Your shadow's about to."

Graccus cracked his neck. Fiona raised her augmented hand in the air, like a starting flag at the race track.

And he gave her the nod.

Fiona threw the ball, bouncing it against the doorframe of the arch and into the room. She heard it skitter to a stop. And for a moment, ugly silence.

She hated that silence. It always made her think the damn thing was a dud.

There was no bang, no light, no ceremony. Nothing in the visual spectrum for her eyes to see. But her augment went numb, dropping from over her head down limp to her side.

Graccus knew his signal. And he vanished, his passing a tornado of squealing rubber on metal flooring. Her hair buffeted around her, whipped by the passing storm.

And inside that room, it sounded like a garbage scow had overturned its load. Gunshots rang out, metal strained, and she could swear she heard a strained electronic scream. Clanks, bangs, flashing red laser fire.

And then nothing.

She peeked her head around the corner, tentative, ready to

receive an iron rebuttal. But what she saw was nothing short of horrifying.

Five combat mechs alright, fanned out to cover the murder funnel that was the doorway. And in that one second of down time, the drones had been overwhelmed. There were streaks and divots in the metal floor where Graccus had moved, each change of direction carving examples of physics into the steel.

The Oskie had moved hard and without mercy. Hell, one drone had been simply decapitated by the sheer force of the impact. It was like looking at a scrap yard.

And Graccus stood over their wrecks, metal bits dangling from his fingertips like mechanical viscera, glowing yellow lines from head to toe. He held a mech's severed gun-arm in one hand, the ammo belt still trailing out of the side, a robotic intestine. The sweat on his skin sizzled and snapped, as he heaved each consecutive breath.

And Fiona had decided to hunt one of these freaks? How was she going to bring him down? Harsh language?

Graccus tossed the arm down on the pile and propped his hands on his hips. He windmilled a hand in the air. "I had less than half a second, lady!" He gasped. "But...y'know, everything worked out okay, so..."

"Okay?" Fiona admitted, her mouth still hanging from the display. "It's a *gulaw* recycling center in here."

Graccus propped his hands on his knees, bending over and sucking air. "Anybody got a...ration bar or something? Goddamn..."

Aaron stepped out from cover, with a sidelong look at Fiona. "We'll get you food and a cold shower back on the ship."

"You better," Graccus gasped, fishing out a water line from his pack. He bit on the straw and sucked hard on cool, refreshing H2O. "My forehead could cook an egg right now."

Fiona walked up to Graccus, crossing her arms. "You did all this with your bare hands?"

"Yeah," he grunted. "They may be made of metal, but physics is still a bitch."

Her eyes narrowed. "How do your hands live through punching an armor plate?"

Graccus straightened up, the patchwork of yellow still glowing under his skin like toxic bloodwork. It occurred to her right then that the yellow was coolant. She looked him in the eye, and she saw the same yellow reflecting back at her.

He weighed his answer, looking down at his bloody knuckles. "They don't. They've just been dead for a very long time."

"Can you get this open?" Aaron asked, grunting through exertion. He was digging his fingers into the wall, trying to force a hinge.

Fiona reached over, yanking the laser pistol from Graccus' hip. He was too tired to stop her right now, anyway. "Get back."

Aaron jumped away, just as Fiona slagged the hinges on the panel with two quick shots. It dropped with a hollow bang.

"Don't work harder, Aaron. Work smarter." Fiona tossed the pistol back to Graccus, who flickered for a second as he deftly caught it without concern. The pistol might as well have teleported into its holster again.

Aaron shook his head and reached into the panel. He was so short and slender, he was halfway into the wall in about five seconds, with his adorable feet kicking in the air for some kind of leverage. He was basically a little kid jammed into a vent, ass in the air.

A pretty good ass too. Good musculature, well proportioned.

Graccus clicked his tongue, disappointed and disapproving.

She side-eyed the aging operative. "You disagree?"

He shrugged. "Honestly? Once you've turned a man inside out, nothing looks like anything anymore."

She had no idea how serious he was being. Maybe it was the fact he'd just dismantled a firing squad of top-tier combat mechs with his bare hands and a sidearm. He was literally *phosphorescent* at that moment. She quickly imagined him doing that to people...and she realized why he might be more disconnected.

A gasp, a pop, and a snap. And she could feel the whole of Akagi Station stutter. Success.

Aaron eased himself out of the wall, holding a small box in his hands, rounded corners. A foot across, give or take. But she'd swapped the Bosun around enough times to recognize a Sixth-Generation AI Core when she saw one.

This might be an aging device by Imperial standards, but it was a sophisticated batch of hard-drives and neural networks. For all intents and purposes, he was holding a living organism.

This side up, don't drop.

"Nicely done, shortstack,'" Fiona teased.

Nora's charming nickname for the hero didn't land like she'd hoped and Aaron's face instantly soured. "Don't call me that."

"Fair enough. Let's move to the escaping part of today's agenda."

CHAPTER
TWELVE
AARON

THE BOX he had pulled from the wall, all steel and wires and silicon pathways, didn't feel all that alive to him. It had felt warm to the touch, smooth under his fingers. But it was a series of electrical pathways, dark and devoid of anything alive. And now even colder, tucked inside a nondescript case with a mesh cage.

But, come to think of it, Fiona was equally dark to his Sight. And she was every bit the living, breathing, cussing human. Darkness didn't mean absence. So what did he really know about anything?

He could've used his Sight, followed Talania and the Capitals to the dock on the far side of the station. But as it turned out, he could just follow the sounds of shouting and gunfire. Graccus was still shaking off his last exertion, sweating and gasping for air. He leaned against the nearest wall anytime they paused for longer than a few seconds.

A grating flipped open and a woman peeked her head out, greasy hair and mousy eyes. Her clothes were little more than a bag she'd thrown over her head—duct rat, impoverished children of the ventilation system. She looked left and right, freezing when she saw the trio approaching.

Aaron waved her back into her hole, back to safety. But she

just stared, frightened and transfixed. Fiona rolled her eyes and grabbed the grating, flipping it closed on the woman's forehead with a bang.

"I swear," Fiona muttered, "nobody wants to save themselves anymore."

Aaron peeked into the grating as they passed, checking to ensure the woman was okay. Grumpy, and rubbing the crown of her head, but okay. Three small children were in there with her, wide cartoon eyes peering back up at him.

No time to stop and apologize or make nice. They had a ride to catch.

They came to a pressure door and Fiona pulled out the conduit from her wrist.

"Can you get it open?" Aaron asked.

She nodded. "The only thing that was running interference, honey, is in your hot little hands."

Aaron closed his eyes, reaching out. Beyond the door was a proper clusterfuck.

It was so loud and painful and bright. Aisling was working on an airlock hatch—graciously left alone, as there were louder and more pointed threats than her.

Solomon and Nora, on the other hand, were overextended and pinched, left to crouch behind some crates with nowhere left to go. Bray was further back, popping what shots he could, while Talania kept her gun pressed into Wolcott's side.

Wolcott weighed his options and trying to measure the Governor: would she actually shoot him if he tried anything? What would he even try, with his hands bound?

The other end of this pipeline full of bullets was a platoon of Naval Regulars, fresh from the carrier, some still piling off their landing craft. And not all of them riflemen.

A hulking figure—a soldier in what amounted to a simple exosuit—stomped through the hatch. Normal soldiers wielded guns with stocks and propellants and focusing lens. This behemoth of a figure held a wand, with a round knob at the end. And he had no need to shoulder it, because this weapon had no recoil.

The Regulars ceased fire and ducked—luring Nora out from cover just enough. A lick of lightning arced off of the soldier's wand, snapping across the space. It didn't hit with accuracy or precision, but grabbed on to any metallic surface nearby, scoring the bulkheads and crates.

Rubber soled boots were fine, but if a soldier had themselves pressed against their cover—like the Capitals were—they were given the shock of a lifetime. Nora, Bray, Solomon all leapt away from their cover.

But poor Aisling shrieked, the electric current leaping right up her augment.

The Regulars stood up, ready to finish the exposed Capitals. Aaron was going to watch his friends—

This was not Bray's first anything, and the Tesla-wielding grunt did not stun him in the slightest. As he slipped from cover, he raised his gun high, aiming for the pressurized coolant overhead. Two magnetic thumps, and a dense white gas filled the corridor, blocking them from sight. Not even thermal goggles would penetrate that.

But the lightning was bright enough. Solomon and Nora took aim, racing each other to the headshot. They squeezed the triggers almost simultaneously—and the Tesla trooper's head exploded.

"I got him!" Nora claimed, competitive. And Solomon gave her a derisive nod and thumbs up. *Sure, you did.*

The Regulars used the window to advance up. And Aaron's eyes narrowed.

Time to even the odds.

It took just a thought, a suggestion. But Scar and the others leapt at the idea. Oh, this was familiar to them.

Aaron felt the rumble under his feet as they passed by, hidden in spaces between the decks. He heard the duct woman and her children scream surprise, short and sharp. But the Jergad left them alone, moving on.

Fiona got the door open—just in time for everyone to see with their own eyes. The Imperial Regulars were pressing their advantage bought by the Tesla unit, slicing wide to get flanking angles. A few moved forward as their allies leveled suppression fire, keeping Nora and Solomon pinned.

The Capitals would be dead in seconds.

But four claws, more than two feet long each, cut up through the floor underneath. And in one motion, they wrenched downward, and the very ground fell out from under the Regulars' feet. Almost as soon as the first few unlucky bastards fell out of sight, the Jergad surged upward into the remaining Regulars.

The aliens always knew how to bring biological scythes to a gunfight—and win.

Fiona threw a glance back at Aaron. She knew full well where that horrifying order had come from.

"Great!" Nora shouted. "Where were we keeping *that* this whole time?"

"A hundred left in the entire species," Aaron said as he stomped past her, "I'm not sacrificing a few just to keep your heart rate down. Huah?"

"Hoo-ah," Nora heckled at his back, nasally.

Aaron paused, glancing down the hallway. Amongst the severed limbs and burbling bloody death, a quivering man hunched against the wall. It was the guard from the checkpoint, the one who fled. He stared down at the Jergad working their bloody magic in the hole below. Too afraid to flee, too shocked to look away.

He had warned the Imperials, told them what horrors had gotten off that ship. They hadn't listened. And now...

Aaron could feel his pain, and do nothing to help him.

Solomon leaned over his crate, propping his head up on his sinewy arms like a bipod, as he watched the Jergad work their brutal magic. In stark contrast to the guard's existential horror, he looked like he was enjoying a particularly beautiful sunset.

Bray dropped to one knee by Aisling. "Copacetic?"

"Yeah!" Aisling shouted back at him with bleary eyes, knocking her ear with the heel of her palm. "You guys hear those bells ringing?"

Aaron stomped over to Wolcott, locking eyes with the young officer. "How 'bout you?"

"What do you care?" Wolcott snapped. He was too busy processing the meatpacking plant down the hallway. He knew who had ordered it, and he knew that Aaron could stop it. It was pure horror and disgust. He looked at Aaron like he had seen the face of Evil.

Talania jostled the kid by the wrists. "One day, a person is going to inquire about your wellbeing, and you're going to accept that it's because they're actually interested in the answer."

"I think I've got it!" Aisling bellowed over the tinnitus in her ears. The airlock hatch clanked as the block released.

Fiona tucked her own cable back up into her augment and glanced at the monitor over Aisling's head. The ship docked was knobbly and old, decent cargo capacity. A smuggler's favorite. Should do just fine.

But Fiona disagreed. "Not that one."

"Oh," Nora moaned, "we're getting picky now?"

A KC-28 Perseus model freighter. Aaron wasn't familiar with it, but Fiona shook her head. "I said 'no.' Let's grab *that* one."

Two berths down, over by the screaming pile of stew meat that had once been an infantry platoon, the board showed a bulbous transport craft. A gas hauler by the look of it, the kind of ship that drove out into the dark to rescue ships that had run dry, or haul back liquid O2 for the depot.

A text crudely painted to the hull: *Asphodel*.

Innocent, large, and more importantly, still docked to the station. But there was something...blurry, something not quite...Aaron couldn't nail it down. There was a lifeform on that ship, and it wasn't human. Lingering, like a fog.

"What's up, shortstack?" Nora asked. "You going to veto that one too?"

"We're not shopping," Fiona said. "This is the one."

"Yeah," Aaron muttered. "This'll do fine."

"Let's go," Bray grunted, grabbing Wolcott by the collar, "before they get impatient and blow the station in half."

———

It was a beast of a ship, meant to push quite a bit of mass with all of the fuel it could hold. It wasn't altogether that different from Fiona's ship, with a central spine and containers strapped to its exterior—perhaps that had been her interest in it. Familiarity?

Fiona's augment had the airlock open in half a second. Nora and Aisling pushed themselves up to the Jump Deck, while the others filed onboard. Talania whisked the Bosun away to some safe location, while Bray stomped off with Wolcott in search of a different type of storage.

Aaron waited by the hatch, ensuring every last blood-stained Jergad got onboard. Solomon made sure none of the Imperials they'd left behind were alive to suffer.

Solomon followed the last alien onboard, and Aaron shut the hatch. He jammed his finger into the intercom. "Nora! Full house! Let's go."

The message was passed up and Aisling's voice rang out over the speakers. "Emergency detachment, full burn on my mark. Hang on to something."

The ship shuddered under Aaron's feet and he reached overhead to grab one of the many brace bars lining the hallway. The Jergad hunkered low and Solomon did the same. When the gas hauler pulsed its engines, Aaron felt it in his ribs, as the ship pressed off of Akagi station and away into the night. The sound vibrated up through the hull, a grumpy, lumbering beast.

And Aaron felt the living fog, that quiet life...shift.

Lovely.

"We've got a problem," Aaron said. "Stowaway."

Solomon smiled, cycling in a fresh magazine on his rifle. "Where?"

"Aft of the ship, near the reactor," Aaron warned. "Careful. It's not human."

Solomon drew an electric, excited breath. Aaron meant that as a warning, and Solomon looked like he'd taken an adrenaline shot directly into his carotid. The slender murder-ball was halfway down the corridor before Aaron could say another word.

"...o-kay," Aaron murmured, turning back to the front of the ship.

A Jergad moaned in a kind of dissonant song. Talania side-stepped it on her way back to Aaron. "What's with them?"

"They're subterranean burrowers," he explained. "They can feel there's nothing underneath them. It's kinda wiggin' 'em out."

"Problem?" she asked, pointed.

"Maybe. But it's not like we have other options right now."

"Maybe we could sing them a lullaby?"

Aaron blinked at that suggestion. "We're in the middle of a daring escape from an Imperial outpost in a stolen ship. You want to start *singing*?"

"Would it really be the craziest thing we've done today?" Talania said, dangling from the overhead handlebars like she was on a jungle gym.

Aisling's voice echoed from the loudspeaker. "We've got ourselves a General Imperial Edict: That carrier is ordering all fleeing vessels to cut power or be destroyed."

Aaron bumped the radio on the wall with his fist. "I think this goes without saying, but do not stop."

"Well," Aisling responded, "we can't outrun them in this barque."

"Bosun?"

The Bosun's head materialized next to Aaron. "Network infiltration of military interceptors would be futile, but I have limited access to forty three percent of fleeing civilian vessels."

"Time to sow some panic," Aaron ordered.

The Bosun didn't have a very expressive face, but Aaron could swear, it smiled with just its eyes. "Thirty eight different vessels have begun broadcasting the Akagi's distress signature."

Aaron keyed the radio. "Aisling, run for the hills."

"You all might want to hang on to something."

Talania was positively buzzing, her heart pumping like mad, her eyes wild. She was sweating. But she asked him, "You okay, Aaron?"

He could ask her the same question, but he knew the answer. Sure, she'd been in a warzone before. She'd been psychologically tortured. She'd seen battlefields packed with bodies, wet and shredded like linen fabric.

But it was an entirely different feeling, without compare, hearing a bullet crack past her own head. She wanted to pretend she was fine for everyone else, and she was very good at it.

She was just one more pressure point away from cracking. Before today, the war was somebody else's affair, something ephemeral and ideological. Today? She dipped her feet into it.

So, he just nodded. "Yeah, I'm fine."

"Oh, hero?" Echoed up the sing-song voice of Solomon. "You should come take a look at this."

Both Talania and Aaron winced at that chilling melody, sharing a pained look. "God," Aaron grunted, "I knew he was going to do it. But it didn't help. At all."

Aaron and Talania jogged aft, feet pounding on the metal grating. As they moved further, the shape of the hull bowed inward, swelling as they approached a row of mounted gas tanks. Each one could probably hold thousands of gallons of gas or liquid, whatever pressurized nonsense. He didn't envy whoever was small enough to get inside to clean it. A ship like this likely couldn't afford a drone to do it.

Solomon sat cross-legged on the causeway, looking down and to the side. A set of worker's tools sat beside him, a welding kit dropped to the deck. It was quiet and dark, but a slagged pit of metal laid cold at its head.

Somebody had dropped it hot and not had time to turn it off before they fled. Or were taken.

"What is it?" Talania asked.

"I think someone else was here first," Solomon said, a slender hand pointing down—to a two-foot diameter hole torn in the tank below. Tanks like this could burst if over pressurized, peeling open... but this looked more like a fist had slammed out, taking a sizable amount of material with it.

Aaron scoffed at the welding kit. "Somebody thought they were just going to *weld* this back together?"

The ship lurched—as Aisling made a maneuver—and the kit tumbled off the walkway and into the open hole. It fell a long ways, seconds counting off, before it gonged off the outside shell.

Solomon waggled his eyebrows at that. "Well, bloodhound? Whatchu pickin' up?"

Talania looked at Aaron, expectant. So, Aaron closed his eyes.

Blurry, unclear. One creature? Or many? So frightened, alone, weak. It couldn't breathe. Gasping.

And moving forward. Seeking. Hunting.

Aaron jogged back to the airlock, trailing Solomon and Talania behind him. He hammered his fist on the radio link. "Everybody seal your compartments and prime your weapons. We've got something in here with us, and I don't know what. Don't shoot it unless you have to."

"Don't shoot it?" Talania asked. "That's ominous."

"It's scared," Aaron said, "that's all. I can work with scared. But if we piss it off..."

The ship rattled underneath them. Aisling's voice: "To the shock of nobody rational, the Imperial carrier is freaking out about the very many Akagi signatures—but that's not stopping them from shooting at us."

Talania sucked on her lip. "Alright, gamblers: who kills us first? Weird thing? Or the consequences of our actions? Even money. Any takers? Who dies first?"

Solomon pointed right at her nose. She sneered at him, right back down his crooked finger.

Gunshots, from ahead. No screams. Then silence.

Aaron took off at a sprint, racing down the hallway and throwing open doors as he came to them. Up a small incline and around the bend, he came upon Bray. He had Wolcott pressed against the wall with one hand, gun extended towards an open door with the other. He had been busy securing the prisoner—and found something.

"What happened?" Aaron demanded.

Wolcott had the gibbering answer. "Black—dark—tentacle thing."

Bray's wild eyes didn't dare stray from that open door. "It sunk right through the *gulaw* floor, Aaron."

Aaron flattened himself against the wall as the ship rocked under his feet, like a boat in angry water. He craned his neck to look, not eager to get close to the doorframe where this ghostly sight had last appeared.

It was an empty room, barely larger than a closet. Every amenity hinged out of a wall or surface, maximizing the space. And the floor grating, painted with some rust-resistant spongy material, looked positively sticky, like it had been left to air-dry and never quite lost its moisture.

Three punchouts in the opposite wall, where Bray had placed compressed iron slugs.

"Safe to assume shooting it didn't do a damn thing?" Aaron asked.

Bray sniffed the air, not answering. Too disturbed by what he'd just seen. A ghost.

That's when Wolcott yelped.

Everyone spun to see the young Naval officer yanked up to the ceiling, slamming hard into the grating overhead. Some inky blackness beyond him, like a cloud of buzzing static. A tendril was coiled around Wolcott's throat and the boy's face was already blue.

"Grab him!" Talania shouted, wrapping her arms around Wolcott's legs.

But the creature lurched ahead, pulling Wolcott along the roof, like he was being garroted by a pulley system. His feet swung with the movement, kicking Talania to the ground and nearly swiping a foot across Aaron's jaw.

Solomon and Bray raised their weapons—

"Wait!" Aaron shouted, putting his hands out.

They didn't. Peppering shots into the ceiling above Wolcott, sending sparks spurting down on him. The magnetic thumps of their weapons sent metal slugs into the rafters, shaving off of the grating and peppering Wolcott with shards.

Wolcott yelped as his leg suddenly spat blood.

The creature pulled away, bending Wolcott's neck against the grating as it tried to pull him through. His head was bent over its tendril, wheezing and choking.

Aaron ran over, underneath the creature. And the walls around him reflected back the blue in his eyes.

Fear. Scared. It couldn't breathe.

And here were these pools of air, life-giving oxygen throbbing through their veins. It had swum in its oceans without a care until the steel casing and the pounding dark. It had burst free of its prison, only to lose what oxygen it had. Asphyxiating in this oppressive containment, it drank what it could.

It couldn't breathe, and they had been so full.

Wolcott's breathing had gone soft. Slack. His eyes fluttering...

"Let him go," Aaron whispered. "I can help you."

It was so scared. Scared of dying. It's family? Far away. Where was it? How could this pool of oxygen help it survive?

And yet, the vampiric cloud eased its grip. Wolcott slumped to the floor, coughing and hacking. Talania rushed over, grabbing under the arms and pulling him away.

Aaron looked up through the grating, two inches of cross-hatched steel separating him from the fog. Thousands of minds, maybe a million. A swarm?

Bray and Solomon inched forward, weapons trained on this inky black.

"Our favorite Imperial marksmen have given up lobbing darts our way," Aisling reported over the loudspeaker. "So, could one of you take a moment and explain what the *Hell* is going on back there?!"

"Is there any O2 still in the pods?" Aaron asked the crew behind him.

"No idea," Bray said. "We just got here."

"Find out for me. Right now, please."

———

The ship's log had called it the *Asphodel*, but it didn't appear to have that name in any official documentation. It had been scooping oxygen from a gas giant's upper atmosphere, filtering and pressurizing it for delivery to Akagi Station.

The ship was found drifting, the crew never found. Official records claimed it was a ghost ship. Now Aaron knew why.

They had, quite by accident, lifted something from the planet—or to be more precise, about a half a million microscopic things. And in their confusion and panic, that half a million particles had killed the crew trying to survive. They didn't know that the little bags of oxygen were other living things, that breathing from them would extinguish them. They were just as confused as Aaron.

This story worked in their favor now. Whatever the Naval jockeys reported back to their carrier group, all they had was a cursed ship that didn't respond to hails.

Aaron opened the oxygen filtration on one of the pressurized cargo pods. To ensure the load in the tank was pure, the filter would separate the chemical compounds. Anything heavier than O2 would be trapped in the filter, while smaller molecules would pass through with ease. The Akagi Station's refinery would take it from there.

The foggy dark creature hovered nearby, watching Aaron work with urgent perplexity. They had no concept of plans or subterfuge.

They had no worry that he was misleading them—honesty was not a word they knew. But they were distressed, gasping, cramped.

And alone. So very alone.

He understood well enough. The trauma of being ripped from your home, lifted into a world you could not have believed nor understood. Being driven by fear, how that fear fueled rage. How that rage could harm.

...He still remembered the dark and the heat and the salty taste of the air...

Aaron took a breath. He didn't need to speak. Words were just vibrations, battering waves in an already thin ocean. They wouldn't understand. But they would know his intent.

Go inside. You'll be safe until we can get you home.

It could smell the richness, the fulfillment down the pipe. Tendrils of black dropped down from the ceiling, balling up into an odd shape. Like a human head, featureless and smooth. The roiling fluid matching his shape.

And then, it melted, a rushing wind diving into the pipe and gone. Aaron closed the filter and took a breath, savoring the air in his lungs.

CHAPTER
THIRTEEN
FIONA

THE *ASPHODEL* WAS A SUITABLE SHIP—A little
worse for wear and aching joints, but enough engine power to
maneuver itself out of a pinch. No armor to speak of, and its deflector
shield wasn't rated for high speed projectiles. Even a meteorite going
at the right speed would ruin the day, but the relativity of finding that
was low enough risk for whatever insurance company had backed
this purchase.

The Capitals had secured their Imperial prisoner into a nice little
cabin. But with the depot raid behind them and a close encounter of
the xeno kind, they'd eased up their security. Too exhausted to be
stringent anymore, she supposed.

Now? There was just a lock on the door, and no posted guard.
Everyone taking rest.

And with the Bosun properly installed, a lock couldn't stop her.

The door slid open at Fiona's command. Wolcott sat on his bunk,
knees tucked to his chest. A medical kit was unfolded in front of him,
as he painted a bandage on his shin. Looked like a skipped bullet or
shrapnel had punched through the meat.

It wasn't his first leg wound either—his knees were scarred up fairly well, gnarled patches where a little boy had fallen dozens of times—and a cadet who had broken his legs in truly ugly fashion.

He looked up at her approach and his jaw tightened.

"You know who I am?" she asked.

"I know you're not one of them."

She stepped inside and the door slapped shut behind her, prison bars. "You were the Commanding Officer of the *Pompeii* when it went down."

His lower lip twitched. "My name is Ulrich Wolcott, Captain, Imperial Navy. You are committing a Capital Offense."

She mouthed the words along with him, like an imitation of prayer. "Illuminating," she mocked. "My name is Fiona McCorty, Master of the Boolean Edge. My very existence is a Capital Offense. So, you're going to have to dig deeper than that."

He eyed the medical kit, searching for a tool that might help him. A scalpel, some sutures, anything sharp. But the Capitals had been forward-thinking enough to leave him only with a bottle of bandages and alcohol. Best he could do is tie her up and get her drunk.

"Of course," Fiona said, "I could always let that ghost back out of its cage. Now that he's had a taste, I imagine he'll want to finish the meal."

Wolcott swallowed hard. "They didn't kill it?"

"Lord knows, I would have. But Aaron's sentimental like that. Y'know, they say he's more alien than human? More so by the day."

The brat blinked, resisting the urge to react more than that. But his voice still shook: "What do you want, pie rat?"

"First and foremost, I'd like you to adjust your tone. You could be dead in the next five seconds and nobody would even find your body."

"Kill me," Wolcott said with a puff to his chest, "and the rest of them will come crashing down on you."

"Now *there's* a man starting to recognize his value." She circled over to the opposite wall, leaning against it with arms folded across her chest. "You were in command of the ground offensive on Vanguard?"

"My name is Ulrich Wolcott—"

"I'm not asking you for the command codes to the *Rio de Bravos*. Were you in command of the ground offensive on Vanguard? Yes or no." He didn't answer, so she pressed him. "This is hardly a disputable fact, kid. Concentration camps? Strategic strikes at *hospitals*? You know, from what I heard, Imperials were melting that city like it was a bad memory."

"We had orders—"

"Orders to cut up people into giblets?" Fiona asked. "Must've been *some* order. You take lunch orders too, or just the genocidal ones?"

Make him angry. Make him defend himself, his honor. He'll start blustering, start justifying himself. He'll say something useful while trying to prove he's still a good person.

"I am a patriot," Wolcott started right out of the jingoistic playbook. "I do what I do for the betterment of the Empire."

"For the betterment of some, sure. But not everybody. Some people...well, they're just holding us back, aren't they?"

His brow furrowed and his lip curled. "Some people want to do us harm."

"You know, I'm a firm believer in a little schoolyard violence. A black eye can reset the brain. When you know what a fight costs, then...you know what you can buy with it. I wonder if your masters have ever had to fight for a single thing in their lives. Why? When they got you all spooled up and ready to do it for them."

Wolcott snarled, all childish spite. "What do you want?"

Fiona's eyes darkened and her voice dropped low. "Help me, and I can help you get your leg patched up."

He eyed the wound. It hurt, sure. And he was no medic. But what Faustian bargain was he about to make?

"You've got the bleeding stopped," Fiona said, "but you positively soaked yourself in alcohol. The bandage will dilute and break apart.

What follows is the secondary infection, days later, when you expose a now-open wound to bacteria and fungus. You get fever, fatigue..." She raised her augmented arm, exhibit A. "And you end up like me."

"You get shot fighting a ghost?"

"I got sliced up fighting another inmate over a bowl of soup. It was my soup. He disagreed. He doesn't do much anymore."

Wolcott shivered, involuntary, a chill up his leg and back. "*Zu gloriam*, bitch."

"'To glory.' Were you in command of the ground offensive?" No answer. "Let's do some free association then. I'll tell you about one man, and you'll tell me something else about him."

He snorted, derisive. But not dismissing her, his eyes lingering. Which meant he was open to the idea...

"You ready?" She pulled a picture out of her Entiglas, turning it to show him. It was a large man, with a scar down his cheek and onto his throat. Haircut tight across his scalp. And a predator's raptor gaze. "Orbital Strike Command: Captain Callum Remus."

She waited. And Wolcott took a breath, bracing himself for the torture to come. "My name is Ulrich Wolcott..."

Disappointment. "Suit yourself." She pushed off the wall and sauntered to the door. It opened for her without a word, and it slammed shut behind her, just in time for her to hear his body bounce off the steel frame.

He'd tell her what she wanted to know. Eventually.

———

On any given ship, there were only enough outlets for a single AI unit. Used to be in the old days, the core would take up an entire room with all of the processors needed to formulate a convincing artificial personality.

Nowadays, the hardware and the core were completely modular. She could take the Bosun with her and hook it up to any starship she liked and it would seamlessly integrate with the hardware.

But to hook up one AI to another, bypassing wireless securities and override the read/write privileges of a hostile entity? Now that took some computer science.

The Bosun talked her through it as best as the digital guy could. It was difficult to focus as the neural network of an entire other being issued handshakes with its own. It had to be like having a conversation while someone screeches in your ear.

The Capital crew huddled around the Jump Deck as Fiona tried to slip narrow conduits into fiddly open ports on the stolen Akagi core. The Deck was more elaborate than most she'd ever seen. Three identical blank consoles were arranged left, right, and center—probably more interesting when they were bright and active. When operated, they'd glow with information and data. Now? Just featureless flat slates.

A steep stairwell carried up to a causeway that half-moon encircled above them, providing two more consoles for crewmembers and the captain's chair.

This ship would likely be coordinating fuel drops as well as deep space rescue operations. Lots to do, requiring lots of seating.

The Bosun's voice hummed from the ship's speakers. "Now connect-con-connect the extension cable with—*kzzt*—outface panel?"

"Was that a question or a direction?" Fiona asked. No answer. "Bosun?"

"Processing."

Bray rubbed the bridge of his nose. "This is going great."

Nora shoved off of the wall and started for the door. "Well, I could use a drink. Tal? You want anything?"

"I'm fine," the uptight politician said with a grind to her jaw. She was neither fine nor comfortable, and Fiona figured that a finger of whiskey would likely do her some comfort. But whatever lines she had drawn for herself, she was not going to cross.

Nora didn't read that much into it and turned to leave. Aisling waved a hand in the air. "I'll take a bit of whatever's open."

"You'll take what I give you, ya drunk!" Nora shouted back at her.

Aaron and Talania shared a look. He shook his head, and she squinted at him. Mutual sneers and then more shaking of heads. It was like watching two siblings have an entire fight they'd reference two years from now despite the fact nobody said anything.

It was an argument she'd seen a thousand times.

I'm fine! You're not fine. You don't trust me? I only trust Mom. You really shouldn't, you know how she is. Shut up. You too.

Solomon had his quick knife out, spinning it sidelong on his darkened console. The blade seemed to sing as it helicoptered across the surface, and Solomon was considering with each concentric spin if something should be dropped in front of it. Imagining what that would look like, the patterns the spray would create on the Jump Deck's smooth and featureless furniture.

Bray windmilled his hand at Fiona, urging her on, but his eyes were on Aaron too. He saw the tension in the air and wanted to draw some other focal point for the energy.

Fiona tongued her cheek and jammed the conduit into whatever outfacing port she assumed the Bosun had intended.

And the Deck came alive for half a second, every single console projecting a kaleidoscope of colors and images. Charts and graphs and a myriad of symbols painted on the walls. The speakers crackled and groaned. Three dimensional images leaping up from the desks and sinking back down into them. It was like being inside a rainbow's death cycle.

The entire time, Solomon didn't even flinch. Never stopped spinning that knife.

Then, abruptly, the room fell dark again.

Nobody said anything, eyes wide as they looked to and fro.

"Um...guys?" Nora's voice echoed up the hall. "*Fra tow zhu li, si'van?!*"

"We didn't see anything up here. Why, what did you see?"

Aisling chuckled to herself, but her eye implant was still darting around, looking for the next surprise.

"Fiona...did we just upload a virus designed to incapacitate bad guys just like us?" Aaron asked, entirely too self-aware.

"No!" Fiona chuckled, quietly praying that wasn't the case. "Bosun?"

Instead of the pleasant and polite voice of her AI co-pilot, the consoles glittered to life again with a cacophony of static and colors. Symbols seemed to hurl out of the desktops like out of a cannon, too fast to comprehend.

Fiona ripped the conduit out of the Akagi core, tossing it to the floor.

"Bosun, full status report," Talania demanded. Fiona would've snapped at her, but mostly because the suit had beaten her to the question, almost verbatim.

And it was increasingly distressing how quiet the Bosun had become.

Fiona raised her voice. "Bosun, answer the nice lady."

A static burp, almost like a cough, from the speakers. Then the Bosun's charming voice: "Apologies, Mis-Mistress. I am encountering quite a bit of resistance access—*kzzt*—this core's memory databanks. Direct interface is proving...troublesome."

"Elaborate?" Talania asked.

But Solomon stopped playing with his knife. "It's screaming."

"An adequate approximation," the Bosun agreed. "While AIs do not have human pain, we do have systems designed to alert us to physical threats to our person."

"Sounds an awful lot like pain to me," Aaron said, hushed and low. His eyes fiercely locked on the glorified hard drive at Fiona's feet.

"Can I cut those systems?" Fiona's question drew at least three alarmed stares from around the deck. She didn't have time for their ethical dilemmas. "Bosun?"

But Talania cut off any answer the computer could give. "Hey, hang on here. That's not a calculator in your hands. That's a living intelligence. Aware of itself, aware that it's in *danger*."

Fiona shrugged. "And it knows something we want to know. What's your point?"

"Pie rat." Was Bray's only rebuttal to that.

"I'm sorry, blue 'n white, did you want to just drive around out here calling Red Rover, Red Rover? Or did you want to find your friend?"

"Aaron!" Talania looked to him for help. But he was too busy eyeballing the Akagi core, searching for something lost in the steel hide.

Fiona was done waiting. "Bosun, can I cut through the noise?"

"Not directly," the Bosun said. A green light grew out of the ceiling reaching down to highlight a panel on the side of the Akagi. "But there are a number of computer cores that could be removed without disrupting primary function. That reduction in processing capacity would allow me to bypass its systems and shut down—"

That prompted Bray to draw his sidearm. "You're not going to lobotomize a livin' thing, pie rat. End of discussion."

"Woah!" Aisling raised up her hands. "We skipped some levels here."

"It's a computer," Fiona said, as she gingerly peeled the access panel free. Four visible shards of silicon, glittering like gold in sunlight. "I can put the cores back in just as easily as take them out."

"Somebody took your arm off. You feel just the same as you did before?" Talania sniped.

"Let's all cool down a notch," Aisling tried to cut in.

But her voice was buried by Fiona's rebuttal. "It's an *Imperial* computer system. And it has what we need."

"So, the *paint job* is what justifies dismemberment?" Talania said. "Why don't we just filet Wolcott while we're at it?"

"Your friend is twisting under the hands of an angry Imperial taskmaster. If Wolcott knew where she was, what would you do?"

Talania didn't blink, a darkness in her eyes that Fiona had not expected. "I'd peel him apart with a rusty screwdriver."

But Bray'd had enough. "Step away from the core, pie rat. Last warning."

It had been a rough year for her. Fiona had seen plenty of gun barrels. The rifling, striations back into dark infinity, had a kind of comfort to them. A repeating pattern. And between a career in criminal piracy, her fall from rather lavish heights, and months on the run, she'd seen it so much, it had rather lost its dramatic impact. "Bray, shoot me or shut the fuck up."

"Maybe I should," Bray growled.

"One more word outta you, and I'll *make* you shoot me."

Graccus melted out from the wall behind her. How long had he been back there, watching her? "One word from him, and you'll be dead before you hit the floor," hissed the human representation of grayscale.

"*Gulaw pasob ka*, you bleedin' hearts," Fiona cursed.

And the room exploded into barking chaos. Bray and his threats, while Aisling tried to talk him down. Talania shouted her ethics and Solomon muttered dark prayers. Graccus was still against the wall, a coiled spring, ready to stop the violence with one well-placed strike.

And amongst it all, Aaron just stared at the Akagi, like he wasn't even in the room with them anymore. He looked like someone had flicked his switch and sent him into sleep mode, pensively waiting for something to happen.

Enough of this. Fiona stood up, presenting her forehead for Bray's gun. Her boot hit the grating with a declarative bang, a cannon shot in that enclosed space.

Aaron lurched forward. He slipped Talania's outstretched hand like she'd greased up her fingers. And he lunged for the Akagi, ripping a shard free.

That's when the gun went off, missing Fiona to track on to the new motion...drilling a half inch hole in the wall right beside Aaron's head.

Total silence.

Nobody breathed for a few agonizing seconds. Aaron didn't look up at the punctured steel or at the old gunhand. He just stared at the silicon shard in his hand.

Fiona could swear to her dead mother that she could make out the tracer lines of yellow lingering in the air where Graccus had streaked forward. Bray's pistol still smoked from the barrel, while Graccus's fingers squeezed Bray's wrist. Flickers of yellow coolant under the Oskie's knuckles, tracing the veins in his flesh.

One wrong move, and Graccus would pull so hard that Bray would lose his hand like it just didn't belong to him anymore. If Bray was in pain, he didn't show it. His face was twisted into a kind of horror, staring at the puncture in the wall and at Aaron. Unable to apologize, unable to defend. Frightened by himself, by the sound, by what Aaron might do in response.

Nora stood in the hatchway, a thermos of booze in one hand. "Alright...what did I miss?"

Talania exhaled shakily, her ears still ringing from the gunshot. Weak, she said, "Bosun? Will that do?"

"Adequately," the AI responded. "With the computing power of the *Asphodel,* I should now be more than a match for Akagi's counter-measures."

Talania turned away from the sight. "Then do it already."

Fiona side-eyed Aaron, gauging his intent. No expression. No alarm in his eyes or tension in his jaw. Stone faced, he just nodded.

And with that approval, she reached down to the core and plugged the cable back into place.

The whole deck flickered one last time, symbols and colors, before whining on down to a single point. And a happy chime rang out.

Bray loosed his grip on the pistol, letting it dangle off his one finger in the trigger guard. Graccus let go of the Sergeant's wrist and secured the firearm for safekeeping. His yellowed eyes tracked on every movement of Bray's face, before finally giving one good step back—olive branch.

Only thing broken was a bulkhead. No need for further violence.

They were really going to let Bray get away with running loose like that?!

"What've you got for us, Bosun?" Fiona asked, her acidic distaste leaking out of her voice.

A detailed amber projection of an Eisenclad dreadnought appeared in the center of the room between them all. The city-sized ship resembled a metropolis that had been ripped from the ground, with tall spires reaching upward, and an armored belly with visible gun emplacements. This was a ship designed to orbit a planet and decimate it, while leaving its crucial systems hidden on the dark side.

"The *Tartarus* passed Akagi station one month ago," the Bosun said. "It had no declared flight plan, and evaded Imperial patrols. Most forces in the area only tracked the vessel's movements—any open confrontation with a ship of that class would surely result in their destruction."

"So where did it go?" Graccus asked.

The projection shrunk away as the relative view zoomed out, revealing a single red dot in the Milky Way galaxy. The dot traced its way back...

Towards Sol.

"Earth?" Talania asked. "That can't be right."

"He's got a dreadnought, not a death wish," Aisling said, with an incredulous shake to her head. "Earth Defense would melt him before he broke the Belt."

"He's not going to Earth..." Fiona concluded with a sigh. "He's got a Capital prisoner onboard and an Imperial knife at his neck. There's only one place he can go."

Aaron tensed up, starting in his heels. He got half an inch taller at just the mention of that name. "Charon."

Home of the Capitals.

She remembered it well enough. Hot stone under her bare feet, dry and humid and burning and cold. Steel doors sunk into rough stone, with glaring lights. Never a guard in sight, but she was never free. It was a place that felt like a hand gripping her shoulder, so hard her collar ached.

She remembered it like she was still trapped in its labyrinthine tunnels.

And the pristine stillness of the bitch that owned every cavern, every twisted body within it. She never smiled. Always frowning. Speaking in poetic riddles. Patient, narcissistic, methodical. Fiona felt the tingle on her skin just thinking about it.

Fiona looked up at Aaron, his eyes fluttering and his throat clamped up.

"There's nothing on Charon but dust and ice," Aisling said. "Why would he go there?"

Fiona never took her eyes off Aaron as his strength wicked away like candle wax. "To make a deal."

"What's Charon?" Bray asked, rubbing at the wrist Graccus had nearly removed. Talania shrugged and Aisling looked about. None of them knew a thing about it.

But the Capitals all turned away. Nora, Solomon...they had words, none that could be spoken out loud. How to even begin?

But Graccus—oh, that fount of unsettling, that skinshifter, that dead-eyed freak—he had the answer. "Fort Augustine—it's a prison in the Oort cloud just barely inside Sol's SOI. On Charon, moon of Pluto. We dump undesirables out there, and it turns out..." Graccus looked at the recoiling Capitals. "Well, turns out *them*."

Aisling muttered something, a prayer under her breath. Fiona had to stop herself from scoffing. They knew about Capital labor, but they never asked where it came from? Of course not—that would require self-reflection.

"You didn't think we came out of the box like this, did ya, Gunny?" Nora asked him, wiping her lips of some blue liquor.

"Hardened criminals go in, and a labor force comes out. Conditioned, obedient. And that far out from the warmth of the Sun?

Nothing survives out there—perfect prison." Graccus was not complimenting the design. "Nothing escapes, not even bacteria."

Fiona looked up at the Imperial spy. "Oh, really? How do you think I met Keira?"

Solomon sneered. "Chasing butterflies?"

"You're not the only person she ever connected with, snake."

His upper lip twitched and his pupils dilated, likely painting elaborate watercolor reliefs of Fiona's bloody demise.

"She helped you escape," Talania said, connecting the dots. "That's how you know Keira. You're a Capital."

Everyone turned, like she held cosmic gravity, pulling them in closer to her. For just that moment, she was the center of their universe.

Everyone but Aaron. He hadn't moved since the gunshot. He still stared at that silicon chip. But that wasn't what had shaken him. The fingers on his left hand were quivering against his side. An old injury?

Didn't matter. He wanted privacy, or he'd say something.

"Master of the Boolean Edge," Graccus said, like he was introducing her to court, "and a Capital extraordinaire."

Fiona huffed. "You're only a Capital if you let them make you one."

The Imperial stepped forward, less a commanding presence and more the dutiful student with total focus to the matter at hand. "You've escaped Fort Augustine before? I need you to tell me everything you know about that planet."

She nodded. Cards on the table time. "Charon isn't a planet; it's barely more than an asteroid. Loaded down with mining gear and prison cells. The guards and the warden, they live on a small orbiting platform. They're rarely down on the moon for anything."

"And if the prisoners revolt?" Graccus asked.

"Simple," Fiona said. "You turn up the heat. Charon is too far from the Sun to be habitable, so they have pretty strict environmental controls. Somebody does something untoward, they just raise the temperature. Bitch about the heat? Raise the temperature again. And for special offenders, they put you in an isolation cell right next to the thermal output."

"The Hot Boxes..." Nora muttered to herself.

"How do we get in, and more importantly, how do we get out?" Bray asked.

Fiona's head bobbled. "The same way I did. Charon has—"

All she had to do was say the name of that place one too many times. A burst of movement, as Aaron dropped the silicon shard. He was halfway to the hatch before it clattered against the deck, chipping a corner on impact.

Nora reached out a hand to him, and he almost checked her into the wall. Nobody said a thing as Aaron retreated into the bowels of the *Asphodel*.

Graccus glared at Bray. "Next time you shoot at him? I'm planting whatever's left of your gun inside your chest cavity."

"The only way Bray hits Aaron, is if Aaron wants him to," Fiona remarked. "That's not what's under his skin."

———

She found him mid-ship. The halls out there were built for heavy lifting gear, so the Jergad had packed it in close, huddling together like they were one quivering shell. She'd heard the beasties make plenty of nauseating sounds, but this pathetic whimpering en masse? She had to admit, pulled at the heartstrings.

And there Aaron was, crumpled beside Scar, his back pressed hard against the demon tank. It nuzzled against his hand, and he didn't respond. His breathing shallow and sharp, irregular, pushing air and unable to get enough to replace it. His head was tucked between his bent legs, squeezing on his ears with his knees.

She knew what he was doing. The pressure, it felt good. Still a little human after all.

As Fiona approached, Scar perked up—snorting a dramatic chuff in her direction. She didn't need a translator to understand 'stay away from my human.'

She raised a hand, trying to coax the big guy back into calm. And she stooped low. "Hey, Aaron. It's okay. Alright?"

He didn't move. But she could see him wringing out his stress, his left hand gripping his right wrist so tight the skin was starting to go pale.

"Listen to my voice," she said as she inched closer. "You're on the *Asphodel*. Your friends are here."

Scar barked at her, a solid bass-filled thump. And Fiona stopped in her tracks. That was close enough.

But it looked down at Aaron, quivering, shaking. And it looked back up at her, one piercing blue eye.

Imploring her. Do something.

"It's okay, Aaron. You're having a panic attack." Aaron trembled, a shiver rolling through him at the sound of her voice. "Put your hand down, on the floor. Touch the ground."

Slowly, his hand crept off of his knee, pushing past whatever tension held it taut to his side. It looked like he was stuck in some resistant web, or that his hand was bound to his hip and he had to find the strength to wrench it free. Scar cooed encouragement.

A graze of the fingertips at first, feeling out the uneven texture of the corrugated steel. Then he pressed his knuckles into it, dragging over the surface.

Tactile. Bring him back to the now. Bring him out of that hole.

"That's right. You feel that?" she whispered. "Touch it. Really feel it. Feel the vibrations in the hull. That's the engines, the heat exchanger. Feel the rust. The cold."

Tears spilled down his face, active rivers cutting through layers of caked-on dust. He pressed his palm to the deck, pressing down now, tension rolling in waves through the ball of his shoulder. She saw the shake and Scar must have felt it, as it chuffed in support.

"You're with friends," Fiona whispered. "It's okay now."

She inched forward, checking in with the two-tons of bladed

leather dog with each step. Scar let her advance, bit by bit. She reached out her hand, gingerly at first, as if expecting Scar to lift a blade in defense of his human. But Scar just watched.

Her fingers crept along the floor, until finally one finger touched the back of Aaron's hand. He didn't recoil, but he twitched away, an involuntary spasm. Like she'd shocked him. And he grimaced between his knees, whimpering.

"Breathe," she said. "Just feel it. In and out. Breathe."

She held out her hand, near enough to his. And she waited.

Finally, like he could sense her presence, his hand drifted back over to hers. His fingers brushed over the back of her hand, finding the burn scars on her knuckles. Then they slid up to her wrist, and she let him explore. There wasn't anything to find, but her wrist always felt so warm where the manacles had shocked her again and again. Doctors said the nerves had fried out, cooked.

He slipped his fingers down, wrapping them into her hand, squeezing so softly. Probably as tightly as he could.

"That's it," she said. "It's okay. We're right here."

A full deep, cooling breath. And Aaron lifted his head up. His teary eyes took in the room, a moment of mania. He didn't know where he was.

But now, he felt Scar at his back and the warmth of her hand, and the cold steel floor, that ozone charge that filled recycled air. And he sighed with relief, a thousand pounds sloughing off of his shoulders.

"...You're a Capital?" he asked.

She didn't say the words out loud. A Capital was a criminal, bound to chains. But had she been to Charon, languished in its pits and its heat? Had she too been abused and forgotten, like he had? Like they all had?

Her voice cracked as she spoke. "Yeah..."

"You never said."

She had never thought that she was, not really. Not like the others. They had not taken her name from her, failed to extinguish her spirit, break her will. She had believed herself stronger than that.

Aaron looked up at Fiona, sniffing back his waterworks. "I can't go back there," he muttered. "I can't. I can't."

Fiona was taken aback at that. He had been so adamant about saving his friend. He had made it very clear that nothing Fiona did was going to impede that mission. But the barest hint of Charon...and he shattered.

Fiona struggled with the words. "What about the others?"

"They don't need me." The words came to him like a reflex.

"I can think of at least one person locked in Hell who does."

"The only reason she's back there is *because* of me."

"Aaron..." Fiona bit her lip. "You're very pretty, but you can be very stupid."

Scar grunted, almost like some deranged cattle mooing its objection. But Aaron chuckled at the blunt delivery.

"Your friend got where she is by her own choice. I promise you that. But I'll tell you one thing, nobody gets out of that prison by their choice alone. She can't. I didn't. And you will carry that place with *you*...forever. Unless you let me help you."

"Help me? With what?"

She squeezed his hand and her eyes darkened. "Burn the whole thing down. For Keira, for Eden. For everybody else that didn't get out. You and me. What do you say?"

He didn't say anything. But he squeezed her hand.

CHAPTER
FOURTEEN
EDEN

SHE DIDN'T KNOW when it happened, but they finally decided to move her out of her special suite with a half-moon balcony overlooking Hell. Every source of light burned her eyes, the glow of the fixtures piercing through even as she squeezed her lids shut, like hot coals were crackling inside her head. She vaguely remembered someone touching her, grabbing her about the wrists and ankles, checking her over. Then dismissively shoving her on to the grubby floor of her cell block.

Last thing she remembered with any clarity was the scalding wall of the Hot Box. She was pressing her shoulder against the hot metal, trying to use the pain to wake up, keep sharp. But when she blinked, there was suddenly the scalding lights of her little Capital dorm, sedimentary walls crumbling under her fingertips, and an unfeeling metal door. Even this dim, warm light felt like thumbs pressing on her eyes, pushing them backward against her brain.

She must've passed out, her body finally giving up and relenting. Her shoulder ached, her neck frozen by the cramp. And her knees shook underneath her, refusing to take her weight.

Water, food. She needed food first. Then she could set about with escaping this hole.

146

She stumbled into the hall and followed the sounds of people. She passed the main foundry floor, looking in. The Foreman was directing folk, assigning tasks, exactly how they'd been when she first found them.

Days ago, weeks? Assuming it hadn't moved again, the mess hall was just a few short corridors away.

Her chest ached and she paused to catch her breath on the wall for just a second—for all she knew, she lingered there for an hour. The stone bit into her palm, jagged rock like tiny glass shards.

How many hands had scored themselves on these walls?

She finally turned the right corner and the hallways opened up. There were a couple dozen Capitals seated at steel tables, slurping on protein slurry and jabbering on about the rocks they'd moved that day. Metric tons of this and that.

And every single one of them silenced when they saw her.

She blinked a few times, trying to confirm if she was hallucinating or not. Nobody said a thing, not even a whistle or a cracked knuckle. Either she looked like garbage, or she'd done something truly terrifying. Satisfied that she wasn't in a stress-induced fugue state, she ambled over to a stack of trays.

First tray, then bowl, then food in the bowl. Take it step by step.

And nobody spoke for the longest time.

During meal times, this line would be shoulder-to-shoulder with sweaty and aggravated workers trying their best to be cheery as they stared down vats of gray protein stew. Eden's dour and dry face didn't even fake a smile as she reached for a ladle of protein.

But someone's hand got there first, gloved and thin. "We thought you were dead."

She didn't have the energy to look up. "Were I so lucky." Her head hung heavy on her shoulders, and she looked back at the rest of the hall. Everyone averted their gaze, hiding in their meals.

"Care to swap stories?" the voice asked from behind the counter. "Or should I just keep it to a 'thank you' and go about my day?"

Eden blinked the sweat out of her eyes and squinted at the

shape across from her. Apron, tall—but that wasn't saying much. Everyone was tall to her. This man ambled irregular, some kind of walking aid. He had a below-knee amputation—that was still fresh and bandaged.

Her Patient.

He leaned on a steel rod tucked under his arm, a makeshift crutch. That had to be killing his shoulder, but what else was he going to do?

"How long was I in there?" she asked.

He pursed his lips. "I look that good, do I?"

"You look...better."

He shrugged, playful smile across his narrow jaw. "Eh, well. Eyes on the bright side 'n all that. You, on the other hand, look like the wrong side of a sick cow."

"Dry and full of shit?" she asked.

"I was going to go with 'chafing,'" he said. He pointed to the number stitched on his chest. "I'm QT-412 by the way. I answer to just about anything but QT."

"Cutie. I imagine that got pretty old pretty fast?"

"In prison? No, why do you ask?"

Eden coughed, but she didn't have enough energy to smirk. "What's your real name?"

He squinted. "See, it's that kind of talk that got you Boxed in the first place."

"I got Boxed for saving your life, so maybe less with the backtalk?"

"You'll learn that I am an endless fountain of backtalk." He spooned a healthy puddle of slop onto her tray, dropping in two solid cubes. "Stir those in, let them break up, and you will thank me."

She knew a beef bouillon cube when she saw one, so she didn't ask any more questions. A hit of flavor and salt in her stew was worth gold in this hellhole.

"Well, you gotta give me something, or I'm just going to stick with Cutie."

He shrugged. "You can call me Four-Twelve, for all I care about it."

"Really?"

He gave a crooked smile. "A name is just a collection of grunts and whistles that we all decide means something. So long as you call me something I'm comfortable with, what does it matter?"

A fair point. Eden stared at her sludge. "So, a gear rat relegated to the kitchen?" she asked.

He looked up and away, trying to hide the quiver in his lip behind a fast mouth and a cheery tone. "Not much of a gear rat with one leg. But I *can* hop between pots. Gotta say, the last prison planet I was on, we didn't have run of our own kitchen."

The contrast turned Eden's brain askew. This place had taken his leg from him, and he was still grateful to be here and not somewhere else.

Eden dropped the beef cubes into her stew and stirred them up. "You've a mind for machines?"

"Computers, mostly," he said. "I used to do a little government work back in the day."

"That 'government work' get you Capitalized?"

And he wasn't going to divulge what it was. He mocked up wide eyes and a matching dopey grin. "Somebody should tell the Magistrate. There's been a huge misunderstanding!" That was the truth of it, but he'd clearly stopped saying it in earnest a long time ago. Now it was a catchphrase played for laughs to hide his pain.

She studied him for a long moment, the way his fingers danced independent of one another but with absolute precision.

Well, government work was unlikely for a musician, so it had to be something more science or engineering. "You in for theft?"

"I guess you could say that," he grunted. "Use of expendable company resources could be spun that way."

He made something, but out of consumable resources that were expensive enough for a life sentence. Government employee good with his hands and a half decent chef. "You a chemist?

He froze, eyes wide. "How did you do that?"

"You're not my first mystery case."

So, good with his fingers, educated, and experienced with electricity. Duly noted. She'd met just the people she needed to.

With a grateful nod, Eden slipped off to the nearest table. She paused for a second, looking down at the polished dull shine of the surface that Twelve had been draped across, screaming and bleeding. Now, it lacked any evidence of his passing.

She sat down, and half a dozen folk stood up with their half-finished food, slinking away. Nobody wanted anything to do with her. Nobody wanted to be perceived as her friend.

That was fine with her. Where she was going, they'd only slow her down. She only needed a handful...

———

She was small, and with delicate hands. A natural job for her in the mines would've been replacing Twelve as the crew's 'gear rat'—climbing up inside damaged rigs to make repairs, whether the big mechanical beasts had stopped moving or not. But the grateful Foreman managed to swing a new position for her.

Turned out that work resumed faster when the crew had adequate and prompt medical care. Who knew?

Maintaining a crew had the same effect as maintaining any machine—it didn't need to be completely replaced so often if you regularly took care of it. She patched up scrapes and the occasional broken bone. Mostly shaft fractures. The crew took blunt trauma and falls on the daily, and they lacked other safety equipment.

And the cherry on top? Nobody wanted to screw with the crew's one source of medicine. She was stern, small, and bulletproof.

As the weeks went by, she had plenty of time to think. Working a shift, going back into her cell and watching the door lock itself for the night, only to wake up to work the next shift.

Klaxons would sound and every prisoner would stop their work and return to their cells to wait until whatever business had concluded. Sometimes prisoners would be brought out for inspection; sometimes nothing at all.

Business. That was the root of it. They were a product, and there was business. And security was trying to do more than just secure the prisoners during this vulnerable time, but also mask their goings on.

That meant only one thing: during the klaxon was when Eden would escape.

Eden rode the lift down into the pits, a single twinkling yellow light over her head. A large circular gear ran exposed over her head, turning and turning whatever crank system supported the steel box. The warmth of the foundry slipped away with each rotation, and her skin crawled with the sudden chill.

Then a spill of light filled the elevator, dozens of work lights and silhouettes of moving bodies. Two small buildings—HML Model 68 drilling rigs—stood tall in opposing corners of the cavern, their geologic meals temporarily on hold. Eden couldn't resist a grin as she remembered chewing through the colony's border wall with one of those titans.

No. That was Vanguard. You're here now, in a dark hole. Focus.

A big hand attached to a bigger person waved her over to the foot of one of the rigs: it was the Tattoo woman—Isolde. She was clutching at her thigh, but the smile on her face dialed back the worry.

Eden slung her tool bag and stomped on over. "What did you do to yourself?"

"Nothing," Isolde said, rolling out the knee. "Boys needed a water break and we hadn't called you down yet today, so..."

Eden cast a look back at the elevator.

"Settle. Nobody watchin' us in the Pits," Isolde said.

Right. Eden shook her head at that naive notion. For all her muscle, Isolde must be new enough to still believe the autonomy pill that Cassandra pushed. There weren't any guards running them around a prison yard, sure—but they were not alone. They were being watched, graded, observed. They must be.

They would never let convicted prisoners *own* anything.

Eden crouched down, inspecting Isolde's calf. "Can I ask a multi-million kind of question?"

Isolde slurped from her waterskin, chucking it to someone nearby. "You got that kind of money and they locked you up?"

"Where's the water come from?"

Blinking, as the brute had to hard reboot her brain. "What?"

"Come on, you've been here a few months now. You're not ice miners. Yet your boys are having a little impromptu water break. Where's the water comin' from? Is somebody stepping outside to refine some of the ice?"

"Hell should I know?" Isolde asked, brusque and defensive.

"Charon's over forty percent ice," Eden said. "I used to lick the walls for hydration. But the water we're drinking tastes wrong. It's not Charon water. So, they have to be bringing it in: for us, for the guards, for Cassandra. How are they doing it?"

"Why?" Isolde was too intrigued to play dumb, but too cautious to connect the dots on her own. She didn't want to get lured into her own trip into a Hot Box.

"Because no one escapes Charon," Eden reminded her. "No one's coming for us. Once they get us out here on this rock, they don't need to guard us. Now what they do have to guard...is how *they* get here."

Now the gears were turning in the big girl's head. "Not a local source. That means a ship."

"Food, water, personnel, luxuries for the Lady of the House. They all have to be brought in. And they will guard that boat with everything they've got—because it's the only way off this rock."

"Which is exactly why this is suicide," Isolde pointed out.

"For anybody choosing the front door, sure," Eden said. "So, we gotta make a big of point of rushing the door...and then go somewhere else instead."

Isolde's eyes darted around her skull, like she was looking for the missing puzzle piece Eden had dropped on the ground. "Finish the thought, girl!"

"They drop off water," Eden said. "They also have to take off waste."

"A sewer escape?"

"It'll only work if we have a diversion." Eden pressed down on Isolde's ankle, eliciting a sharp but happy pop.

"Ow!" Isolde said, but her voice quickly slipped into relief. She didn't even know she'd been carrying a kink in the joint.

Eden dusted off her hands. "While we make our far more discrete escape, we make it look like they've got the situation handled."

"They'll be locked down once the alarm goes," Isolde pointed out. "No ship will be allowed to break mooring."

"You're assuming they're not worried about a breach. They can't wreck the reactor. With the expertise in the population, we'll just fix it. If they're worried, we'll take a fully functioning ship, they'll make an emergency launch to strand us and leave whoever's expendable," Eden said. "But we'll already be onboard. By the time they manage a headcount, we're long gone."

A glimmer of something resembling hope in Isolde's eye. "You really think that'll work?"

"Now..." Eden grabbed Isolde's ankle, turning it out wide in a stretch. "Shipments like that have to be on some kind of schedule. They can't help themselves. How often do you have lockdowns? Everyone tucked in their cells at the same time?"

Isolde forced a laugh. "You more comfortable in the Hot Box, are you?"

"Where I come from," Eden said, "we work as a team. No more of this every Capital to themselves crap. You want to survive, see the sun again? Get onboard."

It was an alluring concept, and Isolde's eyes sharpened at the notion. "What do you need?"

"The Foreman knows the schedule. They'll get us the shot we need," Eden said, "and Twelve will get us onboard."

"That's as big as the club gets?"

Eden nodded. "Any bigger and somebody will talk. It's already bigger than I'd like."

Isolde sat forward. "And what's my job?"

"You've got a reputation for violence. At some point in this process...we'll need that."

No smiles, not on her lips anyway. But there was a spark to her eye, like some kindling had finally caught. "You know, I'm pretty sure after we mine the rock, somebody puts the rocks back again so we just mine forever."

"Oh, definitely," Eden said. "Fifty years of mining Charon, we'd have burrowed the thing out by now if they didn't."

———

Later that night, her cell door opened. The Foreman stood in the doorway, with a bag in one hand. They tossed it onto the floor with a heavy, metallic thud. Eden eyed it, waiting for the guards to appear with batons and gleeful sneers.

But nothing. The Foreman had kept their word.

So, Eden descended on the bag, flipping open the leather cover to take inventory.

"Are you sure this will work?" the Foreman asked, their eyes wild.

Eden braced herself against the wall, sucking in the last breath of fresh air she was liable to get for a while. "Aw, hell, Foreman. I'm not *certain* the sun is still out there. Do you trust me?"

They thought about it for a while. "Against my better judgement, but yes. I do."

"That's usually how trust feels." Eden pulled a slender hooked tool from the bag. That had to be what Twelve had requested.

"Because if this doesn't work," the Foreman said, "it won't just be you sitting in a Box, okay?"

"Foreman, if it *does* work, and they ever catch up to us, they'll kill us." Eden closed the bag, remembering the mud and blood of her Capital trials, when Riley had overseen the recruitment of a prison militia. She remembered the crumbling city, under Riley's thumb and under Deckard's boot.

The mulched bloody mess of a nurse who had dared to aid the enemy.

And Callum's hateful sneer as Eden dangled from his Warcom's clenched fist. Her life wasn't a life to them.

She looked up at the Foreman. "But if we call if off...they'll just kill us *later*. We have to try."

"I know," the Foreman said, halfhearted. "Still scared."

"Good," Eden said. "That means your brain's working."

The Foreman nodded. "I'll tell them uh...I'll tell them we're on."

Eden handed the bag back to the Foreman. "You given a name any more thought?"

They paused, their mind trawling through a hundred vague memories and trying to grasp just one of them. And finally, she saw them light up as they sank their talons into it, eyes watering and the barest hint of a smile. "Khalid."

"Khalid?"

The Foreman nodded. "I don't know...w....why. It feels like it means something to me, but I don't remember what anymore."

"Well, now I'll help you find out...Khalid."

They drank in that moment, and it was like they grew twice as tall, back straightening and chest puffing up, the stout person refilled with something. Full of pride and expectation, newly possessed. "I'll see you in the morning...Eden."

FIFTEEN

FIONA

IT WAS AWFULLY quiet for first thing in the morning. Only a handful of the Capitals had emerged from their various cabins. She hadn't exactly set up a duty roster or assigned tasks to be done, but she didn't much care for sloth. And this was going to be funny.

The bunks on the *Asphodel* were situated high and low along ladders, set on either side of the main corridor that ran the length of the ship. Not unlike other ships of its class. It also meant that most everyone asleep was within the same forty square feet.

Fiona keyed the PA system with a whistle to the Bosun—and the Bosun himself repeated that high-pitched two-tone throughout the entire ship.

And then, Fiona's voice echoed from every corner. "Good morning to all manner of scum and villainy. In case you hadn't noticed, it's day time and I'm deactivating the Replicator in fifteen minutes. So, if you want to be fed anytime in the next six hours, come and get it now."

A hostile grunt and a huff of hot air. Fiona looked over her shoulder to see Scar lurking in the hatch a few meters back. Bleary eyes and a slumped posture.

"What do you want, an apology?" she asked.

Scar's eye narrowed, coughing some guttural throat noise at her. And she just sneered right back at it. Soon enough, Scar broke eye contact and shuffled off to some dark corner of the ship to resume its slumber.

The first one out of their bunk, gangly and awkwardly slipping down their ladder, was Talania. She already had a thermos in hand, ready for a morning coffee. "You're turning off the Replicator?"

"Yes, ma'am," Fiona confirmed.

"Why?"

Fiona shrugged. "You're up, aren't you?"

Talania grumbled and sidled past her towards the mess hall. Graccus came jogging up the causeway, rolling out his shoulders in morning calisthenics. "See if you got up when I did, you wouldn't be so out of it."

"Fuck you."

"I deserved that."

Fiona crossed her arms. "Oskies need to work out?"

Graccus didn't even stop running, his feet pounding on the grating. "And if you ran every morning, you could punch through a brick wall too."

"And eat your vegetables, right? See in the dark?" Fiona turned to follow Talania into the mess hall. Some morning drink and a nice Eggs Benedict sounded lovely.

With a pep in her step, she bounced into the room—stopping, balancing on one foot when she saw Aisling...standing up to pull a dish from a cupboard. "Hold the—"

"I told you. Top shelf isn't safe from me."

"So, we're only like eighty percent chairbound?"

"Hey *asshole*, my spine is compacted, not liquid." Aisling settled back down in the chair with a pained gasp, tucking a clean plate to her lap. "This should not be a miracle to you."

Fiona nodded. "Fair enough. Hey, were you rolling acoustic last night?"

Aisling's eyes narrowed. "If I was?"

Fiona gave her a thumbs up. "Play it louder next time. I was just shy of catching a high myself, and it was real frustrating."

That got a face scrunch and a moment of thought, as Aisling gauged if Fiona was yanking her chain. But then—"Can do, lady. Hey, Sol."

Solomon didn't say a word. He just shoulder checked Fiona as he entered the room. And Fiona was halfway to pulling a knife out of pure reflex. Solomon heard the sound, leering at her.

Fiona's eyes narrowed, drawing her coat back to show off the sheathe on her waist. Classic stand-off.

Talania noisily poured her coffee into her thermos, on the edge of her proverbial seat.

And when Aisling clapped her hands, both Fiona and Solomon grabbed for their knives—but Fiona stood up bolt straight when she saw Solomon pulled out a spoon. A dingy, scuffed, and scratched...spoon.

"I'm sorry, *what?*"

Solomon looked at it, quizzical, trying to sort out the nature of her problem. "It's a good spoon."

"We're doing quickdraws and you pull a *spoon?*"

"Yeah," he said with a shrug. "It works."

"You killed a lot of people with your soup spoon?" Fiona asked, incredulous.

"Yes," Talania and Aisling both confirmed in unison.

Well, that was an unsettling notion. Solomon dropped the spoon into a bowl with a clatter and never broke eye contact as he went for the Replicator.

Aisling shivered with a giggle, like she was shaking off a layer of ice. "I'm making clam chowder. Who wants some?"

———

She hadn't expected their laughter to be quite so enthusiastic. Even Graccus was wiping tears from his eyes, coughing off the last gleeful moments. Bray pounded his hammer of fist on the table, splashing everyone's soup. Fiona soaked up their adulation.

But Aisling wanted details, leaning forward with an inquisitive, gawking look. "So, wait a minute. You stopped *time*?"

"Time is relative," Fiona explained. "You and me, sitting here? Time is constant, but to an electron? He had the same communication implant I do. We could chat at the speed of light and all he can do—" she cracked up, losing her composure. She raised her fist in the air, illustrating. "So, here's what he sees: a clenched fist hanging in space, inching toward him *so very slowly*...with every intent of breaking his jaw. And he...can't move out of the way."

"Do you have any idea how psychologically damaging that must have been?" Talania asked, slack-jawed.

"Yes."

Graccus was sobbing, gasping. Implant humor, space-time relativity: this spoke to the Oskie's personal experience. Bray, on the other hand, Bray was just a little bit cruel enough to find violence funny.

Nora had her lips puckered, arms folded across her chest, already composing her superior story.

Talania leaned away on the back two legs of her chair, casting herself out into space. "He was going to get hit no matter what. So, you just hung him out...to torture him?"

"Eh," Fiona grunted, "he deserved it."

"You stopped time...to torture your ex?"

Fiona jumped at that with an objecting finger. "Not my ex. And I'm pretty sure he's in love with a computer anyway."

Aisling draped herself over the table. "What *is* your life?"

"Right?"

The laughter simmered for a second, before breaking out anew at the visual of a young man forced to stare at imminent deserved pain. It was refreshing, invigorating.

She was smiling. When was the last time she smiled like this? It was like...

Like being home.

"I can beat it," Nora barked.

Graccus and Bray coughed their obvious disapproval. And Talania raised a perfect eyebrow. "You can beat 'stopped time for my ex?'"

"Not my ex."

"Oh, loosen your corset, lady. Your brain is starving for air."

Nora leaned forward, propping herself on her elbows like the tent poles of a circus and framing her face with her hands. "Okay, so picture—if you are able—downtown San Francisco, 2238. It's a cold summer—"

"'Worst winter was a summer in San Francisco,'" Bray and Graccus quoted in unison, like they were connected at the brainstem.

"Shut up." Nora slid her way back on track. "Cold summer. So, everybody's dressed for sun and getting blasted with an ice storm. They end up packed into my bar. Turns out two guys, real machismo ideals, right? They decide it's not that cold outside and decide to go for a stroll. Try to impress some of the lady folk." She spun one hand to indicate she was one of the aforementioned lady folk. "Well, this guy gropes me, whispers that he'll be right back, and then *died* of hypothermia!"

Pause for effect. But the rousing applause and bombastic approval did not arrive.

Nora's eyes flitted about the room, taking in the variety of responses. "What, was that not a good story?"

"No!" the choir said in mutual horror, drowning out Solomon's giggled, "Yes."

"A man died," Fiona said. "Have some respect."

"You respect every man you killed?"

"I respect the fact that they're dead."

Boots hit the doorway, and everyone looked up. Aaron hung in the arch for a second, assessing the room. And then, he wilted. He averted his eyes and made his way over to the kitchenette, pulling together a tray of food.

Nobody said a word, choking down the merriment of just seconds earlier. It was like they were trying to be sensitive to a hungover partner, keeping quiet and still. But when Fiona caught Bray's eye, or Graccus', they studied the tops of their shoes instead.

What the hell?

Aaron fixed his tray of food, measuring out a cup of soup and grabbing a pear. He gave one last look back at the table—and jerked back a bit, reeling on his feet like he'd been slapped. But his raised eyebrows and watery eyes on the verge of tears, said he was sorry.

And he retreated back out the hatch, to some dark secluded corner.

After a sufficient polite distance, Fiona put on her best regal Imperial airs. "Okay, I am a guest. New face, new story. But I'm not...what's the word I'm looking for...oblivious?"

"It's complicated," Talania deflected.

"No, honey. When the United States annexed the Moon...*that* was complicated. This right here? I've been in enough cults to know."

Aisling raised a hand, with a very dry point of order. "How many is enough?"

"Two. You guys have discovered your patron saint ain't all he's cut out to be."

Talania'd had enough. "You don't know what you're talking about."

"I don't?"

Nora already had a stick up her ass from before, so this was a perfect opportunity to rip it out and beat Fiona with it. "He turned out to be *exactly* who we thought he could be, and more. That's why. Even when he was human, he never really sat around with the rest of us. Always brooding, always removed. And now he's a psychic superman who prefers the company of aliens. You weren't here all the times we—"

"*When* he was human?"

And that cut Nora's monologue dead, as they all soaked in that observation.

Fiona cast her eyes around the room. Graccus met her stare out of sheer habit, but no rebuttal. Bray averted his gaze. Nora was too busy squeezing her fists to engage, and Talania was sucking on her teeth, absorbing the truth of it all.

They didn't see him as one of their own. Not anymore, if at all.

"Sleep on that bullshit," Fiona said, getting up from the table. "Because he'd take a bullet for any one of you."

If they had anything else to say, Fiona didn't wait to hear it. She stomped away from the little insulated coven of 'humanity.' They weren't all that much fun anyway.

———

In fairness, he didn't look all that human, snacking on his breakfast staring at a bulkhead with all the same warmth one might share a meal with a delirious grandparent. Made all the more sinister by Scar looming behind him. The Jergad cooed and clucked, like it was trying to coax something out of the dark.

It suddenly clicked for Fiona what they were doing, where they were. The oxygen vampire cloud—they were sitting outside the tank system, like an aquarium visit.

"You given it a name yet?" Fiona asked.

Aaron shrugged. "That'd be like giving a school of fish one name."

"You really are a nutcase, aren't you?" His eyes fluttered, and his armor cracked, and she immediately felt like garbage. She'd hit a man when he's strong, or armed, or pissing her off—but that right there, that was just being a bully.

The distaste fell off Aaron's face quickly enough, shoveling the next bit of soup and bread into his mouth.

"For what it's worth," Fiona started, "I like crazy."

"You'd almost have to," he said, reaching back to scratch Scar under the chin, "living like you did. Kidnapping, ransom, murder."

Was he really going the judgement route? "Solomon's killed more people than I have and for worse reasons. Bray and Talania are career government, one of them at the end of a gun. Graccus is a state-sponsored assassin. You've got worse company than me."

"I understand them. They don't like somebody rooting around in their unmentionables. And I can't help it. So, they think of something to say to me, maybe tell me to knock it off. And I already know what it is, so they don't say it, and I know that too—and we circle around for a few minutes, before everybody gives up. It has to be really frustrating. I know it is, because it frustrates them, and I can't *not*...See that."

"But I'm a great big mystery?" she asked.

He laid two fingers on the bulkhead in front of him, like he was exploring the steel. "I can't See you."

She didn't quite pick up what he meant for a second, but the lingering silence gave her time to work it out. See her. *See her.*

He didn't mean with his squishy eyeballs. His super Sight didn't work on her. Her alone. Of everyone here, only her. He saw life, and he couldn't see her...

There was only one truly unique part of her history that could explain that.

"What *do* you See?"

Aaron's hand flattened against the bulkhead, pressing himself up to standing. He turned, closing the distance between the two, drawing within a knife's reach.

And she let him.

"I See..." He shook his head. "Nothing. It's like...it's nothing. No motive. No feeling. No plan. I can't see your ulterior motives, old secrets, or the next thing you're going to say. It's like..."

He was so close. Did she really have to say it?

She still remembered Keira reaching down, pulling her back...

"Who are you, really?" he asked her.

"Damn," she cursed. "He's figured out how to penetrate my elaborate defenses."

"Fiona—"

"The word of power. Who am I, *'really'*. Well, now I'm stuck."

Aaron pointed at the bulkhead he'd been meditating to. "Thousands of individual life forms. I know they're frightened. Alone. They're confused and lost and hurting. They want help, but they don't know what to ask for or how to ask for it. I...I want to help them, but—but I don't know what they need. I know more about that Ghost than I know about you."

"You named it."

"Don't patronize me!" He stomped a few feet back up the hallway before whirling back around. "Everybody else? I know their every thought, every emotion, all the time. Aisling is mourning while trying not to mourn; Talania's practically sparking off of every surface, she's so worried."

"And you can't See me?"

His voice went meek and hollow, a whisper in a cave. "Not a thing."

"Because I died."

Aaron froze up. He cranked his head around, brow scrunched up. He wasn't sure he heard that correctly.

Fiona nodded. "It was on Charon. They told me I was dead for...twenty minutes. We were desperate. Didn't have a way out, so I...I looked down. Into the tunnels. Charon's got hundreds of these little pockets in the stone, goes down maybe a few hundred meters. Practically to the other side of the damn rock. And I...suffocated. There's no air outside the mine's radius. It got thinner and thinner and I...blacked out."

His eyes narrowed, suspicious. "What did you find down there?"

She shook her head. "Nothing I remember. I died, remember?"

"...And Keira brought you back?"

"She hauled my ass out of the tunnels, performed CPR on a corpse—like a lunatic. Three people grabbed her, trying to haul her off of me. And I just...woke up." Fiona counted off her fingers. "I had three broken ribs from her chest compressions."

"That's how you know you're doin' it right."

Fiona chuckled at that, tonguing her cheek as she considered her next reveal. "I shouldn't be alive. That's why you can't See me. I left some part of me in those tunnels that I'll never get back."

"You think you'd live a bit more careful," Aaron commented, "having been dead once."

She shook her head. "I'm already dead. What more can they do to me?"

Aaron's eyes went distant. "A lot more."

Scar chittered from behind her, words of comfort for his friend. And Aaron gave Scar a thankful nod.

Fiona bit her lip. "So...you can't See me? Means you just...have to talk to me like a normal person then, huh?"

Normal. The notion hit him, washed over him, electrified him. "Yeah."

"You want to know something about me?" she offered.

"Something more?"

She drew herself up to his side, almost towering over him in her heeled boots. She looked down into his eyes, taking his full and undivided attention. His lips parted like he was going to say something, but he just let out a ragged exhale instead.

How far did she want to take this? His shoulders tight under his shirt, and his eyes sharp, and he smelled like autumn leaves.

"I killed my first when I was fourteen years old," she said.

What would he do with that? That she'd killed a man in prison, in Charon. That her childhood had been nothing but sweat and torment and bloodshed? What would he do with that peek into her history?

He huffed, a wry curve to his lip. "Me too."

———

The door slid open with a hush and Wolcott didn't even look up from his tablet. The soft yellow glow on his face washed out his soft features. Even his voice had gone dry and annoyed with their game. "My name is Ulrich Wolcott—"

Fiona strode into the makeshift cell, letting the door clack shut behind her. "Captain, Imperial Navy. What are you reading?"

With a sigh, he confessed, "The Jezero Daily Mirror."

She blinked. "You're reading a Martian gossip magazine?"

"From five years ago. And it's a local archived copy. Your stupid AI won't grant me Extranet access."

"Yeah," Fiona drawled, "remind me to give the Bosun a cookie for doing his job." He returned to his reading with a sigh. Fiona tongued her cheek, considering how to open this particular can of worms. "I'm not a good person, Wolcott, I don't think that's a hard sell."

"You sank an Imperial Fleet Carrier and every soul aboard," Wolcott growled.

"I had good reasons," Fiona snapped, before quietly adding, "And a...few selfish ones."

Wolcott rolled his wrist, turning the article to the next page. He wasn't going to give her any ground to stand on there.

"You don't need to trust me," Fiona said. "And good judgement would say, you should never trust me. But you *should* trust these people."

His eyes lifted off the page, focusing through the translucent scrawl of celebrity pabulum to lock on her face. "These people?"

"I'm here to kill somebody. They're here to *save* somebody. And if you took your head out of your ass for two seconds, you'd see that."

"I'm in prison."

Her eyes darkened. "You've got your own bunk, a functioning jaw, access to reading material, and three square meals. You don't know what prison *is*, boy."

"I'm not giving you anything. On Callum Remus, or anyone else!"

She threw up her hands. "Don't! Or do! It doesn't matter! Or it does. I don't know. I don't *care* anymore. But these people are not the blood-soaked villains you think they are. I know, because *I'm* the blood-soaked villain you think I am."

Wolcott pinched the holographic reading back into his bracer, the amber light winking out of existence. He sat up, a sardonic kind of pep in his voice, "My name is—"

"Shut. Up." Her voice might very well have stolen the warmth from his blood. "I will kill Callum Remus, with or without your help. But if you don't help me, you should help *them*. Your entire career is drenched in more blood than I can even imagine, and you've barely got facial hair. You think I've got crimes to atone for? Those people out there are risking their lives...to save just one person. They are bigger than either of us. How old are you?"

Wolcott thought hard before he answered, no doubt consulting the regulations they burned into the back of his skull to see if someone would rap his knuckles in some future debrief. "Sixteen."

"Sixteen?" she said, breathless. "Old enough to burn a planet. Too young to know any better. Bosun?"

The disembodied voice thrummed. "Yes, ma'am?"

"Cut archive access to Wolcott's Cabin. And cut the lights too."

The room was plunged into darkness, and Fiona left Wolcott with nothing but his thoughts.

CHAPTER
SIXTEEN
EDEN

THESE WERE days always fraught with a kind of terror. No matter how many times Eden had awaited a mission—checked her gear and assessed the terrain—she had always held her breath, like if she had exhaled at the wrong moment, she might change the way the day fell.

The klaxon came as expected, sending every prisoner to their cells. Before any formal business could be conducted by Cassandra, the guards would perform a sweep and ensure that every soul was contained, exactly as they should be. Anything amiss, and the delivery would be delayed.

She had to lure them in close before she snapped the trap around their unsuspecting feet. Get the supply ship in close, get it moored and stuck. If she was too soon, the ship would break off before her team could get there. Too late, and the ship would repel any invasion. It had to be just right.

And so, obedient and small, she returned to her room. Khalid, Twelve, and Isolde returned to theirs; hundreds of prisoners marching off to be confined to their stone cubes.

The guards inspected the locked doors for a good seal, they checked electronics for any funny business. They checked the mess hall and the Pits and the enormous drilling rigs for any prisoner thinking they might stowaway.

Only after the guards were satisfied...

The visits had a time limit, averaging out to just forty-two minutes. So, in the gloom of her cell, Eden counted. There was no way to be precise, no way to be sure. So they had to guess, try to hit them right in the middle of the transaction.

The fortieth second on the twentieth minute—and Eden stood up. She marched up to her door and rolled her fingernails on the steel. Cold tickety-tack. Not loud enough to sound an alarm, but loud enough for the cell next door to hear.

She waited. And the tickety-tack of more fingernails answering, passing the one-note message on down the line.

Twelve would know what to do from there.

Wild things, humans were, Eden mused. Leave them blind and deaf in the most hostile environment imaginable, and they'd still find a way to communicate.

The cell doors were fail-safed to lock closed. So cutting a line would not suffice. They would actually have to signal the all-clear, as though no ship were docked. Twelve theorized that this was hard-wired into the airlocks themselves, hidden somewhere in the stone. Even if a guard was paid off to throw the lever, the doors wouldn't open with a ship still docked to the complex.

So they had to trick the station into thinking the ship had already left—or never arrived. They searched and searched, trying to find the mysterious airlock that Eden remembered coming in. No luck. It was hidden beyond hidden. Maybe it had been buried and moved like everything else in this labyrinth?

But every prisoner knew where the cell blocks were. And for that failsafe to work, some hardwire connection had to go out. It was simply a matter of determining which line in the floor was the lock.

And, well, Twelve was a smart man. She trusted he'd figure out the right line.

Twelve went to work, Isolde limbered up her gigantic arms, as

Khalid greased the right pair of hands. And Eden waited for the first prison riot in Charon history.

The resounding chorus of doors slamming open all at once almost made her cry, like a percussive symphony of squeaking metal fingers against slate. There was a collective hitch in the air, as everyone in every cell took a similar breath.

Before the plunge.

A battle-cry, no language she knew. Someone screamed. Something primordial, something emotional, and full of hot hatred. A dozen angry and rested bodies came hurtling past her door, running toward some unseen threat.

And that's when she heard the first gunshot.

Time to go to work.

She darted out of her room, creeping along the wall as fast as she dared. She could hear the crackling of electricity, the snaps of gunfire. The guards were doing their best against the surprise attack.

One wrong turn and Eden would end up in a firing line. Listen to the fighting, find the heart of it. Steer clear.

Ahead of her, grunts of exertion, distress, whimpering. Something hard baton-ing into soft flesh. Eden pressed herself against the wall, seeking the nearest shadow and inching along.

The fighting up ahead intensified, carnal snarling. That didn't sound like guards or gunfire.

Well, the Capitals weren't all imprisoned for their charity work. Some of these folks were not kind, and Eden had just removed the one semblance of civilization from their world.

No time to debate the ethics of her decision right now. Somebody needed her help.

Eden peeked around the corner, and her body immediately relaxed. Isolde stood over three crumpled Capital men, each of them sporting bloodied faces. One of them curled around an arm, his wrist already swelling where she had done something...uncharitable.

"Hey! Tattoo!" Eden called out to her. "You're already mashing faces?"

Isolde jerked her head in acknowledgment, stepping on the body of one challenger on her way over. "So what? I can't go to prison twice."

"How the Hell do you think *I* got here? Come on."

Isolde scooped up a wrench, feeling the weight in her hands and rolling it over. Did she want the teeth forward, or use the backside like a hammer?

Eden led the way through the tunnels, moving from corner to corner, chancing her way past any open or bright areas. The shouting was getting worse, even as the shooting calmed down.

The tunnel shook under them, like the planet was rolling, and it nearly took Eden's feet out from under her. She crumpled into the wall, hard enough to pop her head against the rock.

But she never found the ground. Isolde picked her up like Eden was luggage, and this tattooed behemoth was late for a train.

"What was that?" she asked, mid sprint, far faster than Eden was comfortable going.

The ground rumbled under them again, rolling thunder, and for a split second, her mind tricked her. Blue eyes. Growling in her ears, somewhere in the dark.

No. Remember where you are.

"They got to a driller," Eden guessed. "Trying to cut their way out."

"And go where?" Isolde huffed.

She could hear the klaxon sounding again, a furious parent repeating with increasing urgency, paired with the percussive beat of firearms and the snap of electric batons. It was positively medieval.

Hell, they couldn't even utilize their favorite method of simply cooking the prison. No, now they had to go back to 20th century methods—bruising the meat.

But while the prisoners made a push wherever the guards resisted, Eden led Isolde away from it all. They darted past the main foundry floor and into the kitchen, where Khalid and Twelve waited.

"Took the scenic route?" Khalid barked. "We almost left without ya."

"You wouldn't get far," Isolde stated, more fact than threat.

Twelve grunted from under the sink. "Yeah...we wouldn't get anywhere."

"What? Why?" Khalid asked.

Eden shook her head, hopping over the counter. He was looking in entirely the wrong place.

But Isolde loomed over them. "There a problem?"

Twelve leaned back to reveal the graywater pipe that was just six inches across, rancid, moldy smells stinging the nostrils as fluids rushed into several different drains the size of pinheads. "How are we supposed to fit through that?"

"We don't," Eden said.

This made Khalid start to panic like she'd lit a fuse. "You started a prison riot and *didn't have a way out?*!"

"Devious," Twelve said, "the plan that is no plan at all."

Eden marched right to the back of the kitchen, where boxes were stacked to the ceiling. And she started pulling them aside.

"We have to get back to our cells!" Khalid urged. "They'll punish everyone, but they won't single us out if we don't resist."

"Speak for yourself," Isolde said, cracking her neck.

"You're always in trouble," Khalid said. "Me? I've never gotten so much as a parking ticket!"

"You're in prison, buddy."

Khalid's jaw worked, chewing on the words that all wanted to climb out at once in some useable format. But they ultimately shut their trap. Whatever defense they had against that wasn't making an appearance.

Twelve hobbled over to Eden, leaning on a nearby counter in a mockery of casual. "What are you doing?"

And she pulled aside the last box, revealing a square hatch, a little under two feet across. "I told ya," Eden said, "they have to get this stuff in somehow."

"You lied to us," Isolde said with a squint. "You said we were going out with waste and trash."

"I lied," Eden said, "but I got you here, and now if anybody talked, guards will be waiting for us—in the wrong place."

Twelve bit his lip, nodding. "Like I said. Devious."

Khalid caught on, and despite the fear in their voice, they were intrigued. "There won't be gravity controls in that compartment. No heat, no air."

"You don't have to explain hypoxia to a doctor." Eden waved for Isolde's help. The tattooed behemoth marched over with her wrench in one hand. With a single hard motion, she popped the hinge on the hatch and chucked the steel plate aside.

Twelve shrugged. "I could hop around a prison, or down a rabbit hole. Why do I hate both of these options?"

Eden glanced down the hole. The small space was more than enough for her shoulders but would be a tight squeeze for Isolde and Khalid. It was a yawning dark, no light to lure her forward. A crisp air blew across her face, like the cold breath of an icy dragon, some great wyrm from folklore.

The klaxon sounded again, and the gunfire sharpened. Somewhere, there was a firing line cutting into angry prisoners as they approached an airlock.

This little escape attempt was just about out of time.

What would Aaron do? Or Nora? Aaron would take the plunge, do it for the others, lead by example. Nora would leap without thinking and somehow come out alive, despite missing half of her face.

Talania. She would say something brilliant. She would take some dramatic sip from a flask, wipe her thin lip on her elegant sleeve and say more in ten words than Eden could in a hundred.

Eden looked at the three prisoners behind her, and her voice caught in her throat. They were looking for a reason to follow her. They wanted to, they really did. But they had programming, months

—if not years—of it. They were struggling to stand their ground, let alone follow her further.

What would Talania say?

Eden cleared her throat. "In there, out here; either way, we don't know what to expect. At least in there, we'll find it on our own terms. We'll find what we deserve."

Twelve swelled up, puffing out his chest. Isolde nodded silently. Khalid...Khalid was sweating, jaw twitching. Afraid.

And so, Eden climbed into the hole, into the dark. She had no idea if they followed her. There was no way to look back and check. It was like she had wrapped her head in a blanket. The metal warped and groaned after every movement, a cold wind rushing past her ears and stinging her cheeks.

Keep crawling, she thought. Keep crawling and you'll get there. Because if she didn't, there'd be nothing at all. Or perhaps the vacuum of space, ready to pull her and her friends out into oblivion to consider their folly while their blood boiled in their lungs.

Her stomach turned at the thought. No, her inner ear was turning, and she couldn't get purchase on the shaft!

She'd moved out of the gravity generator. The cold wind was still pressing her backward, nudging her across the threshold of the field again. She shook her head and pressed both hands into the walls. The metal burned her fingertips, so cold they bit and held on to her.

And she pushed off, throwing herself ahead. It wasn't a perfect launch; Charon had its own natural gravity—minimal as it was—and it was impossible to aim at anything in the pitch black. So, she skipped off the walls, dragging her shoulders on the cheap pot metal.

But then she bonked her head on something, something hard. And she came to a stop.

She palmed around her. No, no. There was no way forward, down, to the side. The tunnel just ended.

But that didn't make sense! Where was the wind coming from? Had they missed a turn? In a cargo tunnel meant to spit crates planetside with little regard? No, there had to be some kind of exit. There had to be!

Her forehead hurt, right above her right eyebrow. And she could feel pressure on her eyes and jaw. It pulsed with a certain beat, like music.

What was the song? It reminded her of a song. A simple popular—

Low oxygen environment. Of course. She was asphyxiating, and delirious. Gas pushing through the tunnel didn't mean it was oxygenated.

Find the escaping gas. Where was it coming from? Because it wasn't coming from a vacuum. It had to be coming from somewhere, and that somewhere had people, and those people needed oxygen.

Go take it from them.

A seam in the wall, blasting freezing air against her fingertips. A hatch.

She couldn't turn around in the confined space, so she braced against the walls. And jerked her forehead up like a battering ram. Once, twice.

It wasn't helping the headache. It had taken on a harsher rhythm, and underlying accompaniment from the throbbing in her temples.

She had to get this open.

Talania. That raven hair, those green eyes, that harsh jaw and strong shoulders. The power in her voice. The feel of her silk shirt sleeves.

She's somewhere behind this door.

Eden gave it one big hit—and the rivets popped. Her stomach turned. And blinding light.

She tumbled out onto a pile of boxes and something wet slapped the back of her neck. She was being held down, pinned. No, that was gravity. She had gravity again.

Get air. You need air.

She pushed down and the wet sucked into her fingers, pulled on her hair and her feet. A beige slime, knee deep. Plexiglass walls. A crane hung overhead with an empty crate poised.

Ah, the crane would package up the slime and send it down the chute for the prison. In here, no oxygen, nothing to contaminate it.

Food. This was a vat of food stuffs.

They were on the ship! They'd done it. Eden lifted her head—

And Cassandra was staring back at her from beyond the glass, a wedge of guards standing behind her. They made no move, no rush to aid or kill. They were just here to watch, to be sure.

How? How did they know that she'd be here?

Her vision blurred. Was it Cassandra beyond the slimy glass? Maybe it was a ship captain and crew? Maybe this headache was getting the best of her.

Maybe she could bargain with them? She didn't mean any harm. She was a doctor.

No emotion, no reaction from Cassandra. She didn't even blink. She just watched, like a student in the operating room, as Eden struggled and thrashed and slumped down into the muck.

Break. The. Glass.

Can't. Arms won't move. She couldn't even get her feet out of this bog. Her eyelids drifted and her fingers twitched. That song kept pounding in her head.

That song.

The voice of a planet. *Blue eyes in the dark.*

And Isolde surged over her head, swinging that wrench. It gonged against the plexiglass. Again and again. Expressionless gargoyle, Cassandra just watched as Isolde swung away.

Eden looked back to see Khalid and Twelve draped out of the tunnel. Twelve was already unconscious, drowning in the soup. Khalid quietly wept, clutching their friend to their chest.

One final war cry, Isolde put her foot against the wall, smearing protein paste on the glass.

Nothing. She heaved off of it, lifting herself up just enough—to snag the crane overhead. And her weight ripped it right out of its socket.

Wind rushed in, holy blessed wonderful wind. Full of air. Eden took a deep breath.

And Cassandra frowned.

CHAPTER
SEVENTEEN
DECKARD

"HOW OFTEN DOES THIS HAPPEN?" he asked, swirling the whiskey around the bottom of the glass.

Cassandra lifted up the decanter, refreshing his glass with more. "Regularly. But not often. A given percentage of new arrivals think they alone can break the mold." She settled into her chair, letting one hand dangle off the armrest to scratch at a dog's crooked ear.

The Lady of the House had quite the extravagant set-up here. Her desk was hewn directly from the stone, a work of sculpted brutalist art. Meanwhile, laminate flooring had been laid to cover the rest of Charon's bare rock, hiding the planet behind faux wood walls —or was that real birchwood? Interpretive art pieces hung on the walls, splashes of color and shapes that shifted as he leaned. He imagined they had a more cohesive image from Cassandra's seat. Her high back throne of a chair was all exaggerated curves and sweeping angles.

And her two dogs sat by her side, ears perked and eyes sharp on Deckard—he recognized a bodyguard when he saw one. At their feet were scraps of their last meal, bone shards and dried meat not yet fully consumed. Among them was a brown and mottled bone that looked an awful lot like a human tibia.

Where could they have gotten that, he wondered morbidly.

"How many make it onto a ship?" Deckard asked, pointed.

Her eye twitched. If it had been slower, he'd have thought she was winking at him, coy and reserved. But this was the crack in a shield, a computer glitching, before an icy smile. "It's been done."

One of the dogs growled at something. Deckard glanced at it, and the dog sneered back up at him. It might have been disturbed by a passerby in the hall, or by a smell on the air, but Deckard had just volunteered to be the focus of its ire.

Cassandra reached down, tapping one long finger on its shoulder and the dog silenced like she'd cast a spell on it. "For a man drinking my expensive whiskey, you're awfully tense, Admiral."

"I suppose I'm eager to hear Philippe's response to our predicament."

Cassandra took a sip of scotch, savoring the flavor. Not answering.

Deckard's eyes narrowed. "It's been two weeks, Cassandra. Has there been no response at all?"

She considered the intricate orchid carved into the bottom of her glass. "Not a peep. But that's not altogether unusual for Philippe."

Deckard stared into his own glass, looking for that patriotic flower behind the amber liquor. The flower looked twisted through the liquid, like a talon or claw. "He was sighted coming through Akagi. He'll be coming straight here."

Cassandra remained motionless, but she couldn't stop her eyes from snapping up. That black shard of her mask shimmered in the light. "And when he does, you'll be rewarded for your service. But not before, Admiral."

This was beginning to sound more and more like bounty hunting, or mercenary work. He smirked. Deckard would be some kind of freelancer, next level power with a dreadnought at his call. This here, this wasn't the behavior befitting a Naval officer, but quite expected from someone paid for their violence.

"Something amusing you?" Cassandra asked.

He shook his head. "Less amusing and more...acidic."

"You expected a quick response," Cassandra surmised. "That old friends would come racing down the hill to your aid when you called?"

"I expected..." Deckard stopped himself. What did he really expect? Did he really think he'd be able to dig his way out of this hole with nothing but good intentions?

Cassandra set her glass down. "Let me offer something free of charge. Stop living by *their* expectations of you."

"Excuse me?"

"Heresy, right?" Cassandra said with a mocking smile. "But it's true. Philippe, Caldwell, the Dunsweir—they maintain control with a single human emotion: disappointment. You can give it all you have, leave it all on the field. Blood, sweat, and tears, and they'll be disappointed you didn't take it one more step. And let's say you do? Next time, you...haul yourself that one extra step. And they move the goalposts, disappointed...that you didn't make it two extra steps."

She stood up, circling around the stonework desk to sit on the corner, looming over him. "Set your own expectations...and then meet them. And you'll never be disappointed again."

A chime at the door. And her nostrils flared and her blood seemed to pump fresh through her. "I promise you...I did not time that."

"Who's at the door, Cassandra?"

She circled back behind her desk to key the necessary lock. "An object lesson."

He tried not to react to that vaguely threatening sentiment, but he must've done something, because the dogs were both staring at him again. Beady black eyes, ears pricked up, tension in their legs. One foot draped possessively over its bone.

A dull hum. Deckard always wanted to pick at his ears when he heard maglev nearby—it didn't really sound like anything, but sounded like the absence of sound, somehow. Like there was something he could almost make out, but something was stuck in his ear.

But the blood drained from his face when he saw what—who—was hovering at his side. Arms and legs pinned back, hog-tied, hands and feet encased in steel blocks, her face bruised and battered to go with the crimson stain on her eye she must've sustained from hypoxia.

He thought that Eden looked bad dangling in his brig, but this? This wasn't something done to a human. This was done to chattel.

Eden still mustered up the ability to spit a wad of blood on to the floor. One dog snapped its head down, lapping it up with one quick lick, and then back to its post.

Cassandra laid a hand on the dog's shoulder, and it stiffened like she'd shocked it. She locked eyes with Deckard, taking his measure on the situation.

Deckard cursed silently. He was as much under suspicion now as the Capital was. Who was he kidding? Until Cassandra said otherwise, he was no better than Eden.

"Who told you about the supply ship?" Cassandra asked, never breaking eye contact with the admiral.

"Nobody told me anything," Eden said. "I'm just not an idiot."

Cassandra wasn't dissuaded. "Who told you...about the supply ship?"

"We can do this all day." Suddenly, Eden tensed, grunting, gritting her teeth.

Deckard's brow furrowed. He could see the tendons in the girl's neck strain. There was no sound, but he could smell the singing skin at the contacts.

Cassandra was electrocuting her.

Eden sagged and he could hear her shoulder pop out of its socket. She didn't care. It wasn't any more pain than anything else she'd endured.

"Who told you...about...the supply ship?"

Stop this. He had to put a stop to this. "Oh, fuckin' Hell—"

"Language, Deckard," Cassandra scolded him like they were over a common dinner table.

"You're cooking this girl in her skin," Deckard snapped. "What good is this going to do?"

"Oh, I didn't expect it would yield anything. But you must always play the hand to its end." Cassandra drew an image up from her bracer, throwing the amber video feed up onto a wall. "Do you see this?"

Eden waffled, struggled to raise her head. But Deckard rose from his chair and set his glass down on the desk.

On the screen, three figures were splayed out on the foundry floor, similarly hog-tied. They were convulsing non-stop, pools of sweat drenching their clothes, blood leaking from ears and mouths.

A muscular tattooed woman, a one-legged waif of a man, and a stout portly figure.

"What am I looking at?" Deckard demanded.

"Did one of *them* tell you about the ship?" Cassandra asked. Though the question was aimed at Eden, her eyes pierced through Deckard.

No. She wasn't asking Eden.

She was directing every bit of this at him.

"I didn't tell her anything, Cassandra," he said.

"Don't play her game—" Eden tried to interject, but she seized practically the moment she opened her mouth.

"I didn't tell them anything!" Deckard bellowed.

"Don't assume I'm expecting something, Deckard. I'm simply asking—who told you about the supply ship?"

What did she want? Why did she care so much about the supply ship?! Unless...

Unless this tactic has been done before. By Capital sympathizers. Traitors. Someone with the leverage and ability to get Capitals off the station.

Someone like a rogue Imperial admiral.

Deckard stuck his chin out. "Kill her, kill me, you won't find whatever you're looking for."

A softness in her eyes and a steel in her stance. "Deckard...darling...you're alive because I allow it. Do not test the limits of my patience."

Grunts at the door, something crumpling to the ground.

Cassandra rolled her eyes—

—as the door opened, revealing Sergeant Mayfield. She had a guard's hand limply draped over the door handle, freeing the lock. Her other hand held her service weapon. "Admiral?"

"I'm fine." Deckard looked down at the dogs. They hadn't moved, coils of tight energy staring down Mayfield's entrance. A drip of saliva off of one snout.

Cassandra clicked her tongue and shook her head. "Imagine what Phillipe will say now. After you've assaulted my men."

Mayfield dumped the guard on the floor and strode into the room. "Admiral, I need you to come with me now."

It didn't take great genius at this point. "Philippe doesn't know a damn thing about this, does he? You didn't send a single message, and he has no idea I'm here."

"And what a feat that would be," she said, small and proud, "keeping secrets from the Spymaster."

Hell. It had been a long-shot anyway.

Deckard nodded. "We're leaving." He looked down at Eden, and he saw...forgiveness in her eyes. He had hoped he'd find cruelty, even anger. Instead, it was like she was urging him on.

Get out.

Too late. Prison guards formed up on the door, weapons drawn. Mayfield took a breath, gauging how hard it would be to take them both. She was about to get shot, certainly, and on a bum leg already? How well could she handle?

"Deckard," Cassandra cajoled, "it's a simple enough question. Who told you about the supply ship?"

"And you've received my very simple answer," Deckard said. "I've no connection to whatever insanity you have cooking here. Let me leave with my men now, or the *Tartarus* will scrape Charon from human history with the push of a button."

It was like Cassandra didn't even register the threat. "So, you know nothing about this?"

Cassandra let her eyes fall, drifting down toward Eden. She studied every bruise, every welt, every burn and committed them to her reptilian memory in less than a second.

And closed the book. "Sulphur? Mercury?"

The dogs stood up at their names, ears pricked for the command to follow. Mayfield's eyes slid from the dogs to the guards, trying to gauge the threat.

But Deckard knew that his throat would be torn out and available for his study before Mayfield could do anything. And poor Eden—if she wasn't among the dead herself—would be forced to watch the two hounds feast.

Cassandra's lip curled, like she was chambering a round and savoring the pleasant ping. But before she could spit the words...

A happy chime from her desk, pleasantly clashing with the gravity of the moment. It was musical, like spun candy for the ears.

And Cassandra held her tongue.

Deckard raised an eyebrow as it chimed again. "You going to get that?"

Cassandra lowered a hand to her desk, pinching the unseen call button. "Yes?"

A voice like jazz. "Howdy-ho there, boy scouts. It is Neptune the 23rd in the Pilgrim's Wake. I have a special delivery for one Admiral Tiberiet."

Cassandra's eyes narrowed, quickly interpreting the data flowing across her desktop like leaves down a river. "I'm going to freely suppose that you are not the captain of the *Asphodel*?"

"Not on any documentation, no ma'am. But I am *a* Captain. Graccus Ontarim, Orbital Strike Command, Ident number C26354. And I have two prisoners for transfer to Fort Augustine Reformation & Reclamation."

"You've come an awfully long way for two prisoners, Captain," Cassandra noted. "Who are they?"

"Aaron Havenes," Graccus paused to let that land.

Deckard let out a sigh of relief. It had worked—Aaron had left his little safe haven to pursue his friend and got himself captured. Deckard Tiberiet had, through mission of action, taken Legatus.

But Eden whimpered, something under her breath. Exhaustion. Grief. Failure. Some cursing of the fools.

But then the second name hit the room. "And Fiona McCorty."

Cassandra's eyes went wide, her nostrils flared, and Deckard could swear, a droplet of sweat tumbled down her forehead. The guards at the door dared not move, but they leaned away, like they were resisting the pull of an incredible abyssal force.

Cassandra's words dripped, molten metal from the crucible. "Welcome, Graccus Ontarim. Blessed be your steps."

CHAPTER
EIGHTEEN
AARON

THERE WERE one thousand and forty-six living, beating hearts on Charon: A hundred and two guards, eight Imperial officers accompanying Admiral Deckard Tiberiet, two hungry snarling dogs...and Eden.

She had not been idle. Aaron could feel his friend, see her light. In agony, but also...steel. Resolve. The only cracks? Aaron's name. She hadn't believed. She hadn't thought it possible.

She hadn't thought it possible they could be so stupid. This wasn't heroism. This was suicide.

Because there was cold fire on that desolate rock, brighter than every other light, washing them out, blinding radiance, scorching Aaron's mind.

It was *her*, the Lady of the House: Cassandra Meilos. He could see right into her sadistic mind, like staring into the heart of a young star, hot and angry, but the waters on the surface were so still, masking the turbulence beneath. She was an unholy torch in the dark, all consuming, all encompassing. Nothing compared. Nothing could drown her. She was inevitable as the sea, waves beating against a shore until they washed away all resistance.

She *was* patience.

And the arrival of Aaron Havenes had awoken the storm. Cassandra Meilos breathed in as if for the first time, and that light...he could see it even when he turned his back.

Graccus knelt down to check the fittings on Aaron's restraints. He didn't want to cut off circulation. "Tighter," Aaron said, correcting the Imperial's instincts. "We don't want them suspicious."

"Suppose I could beat you about the head a bit," Graccus offered, "if you think it would help."

It just might. It might get Aaron's eye off of that pulsating glow, a light that dimmed every other by sheer proximity. Was she really that much more alive than everybody else, more powerful? It cemented everything he'd ever thought of her, that she was somehow...

More.

Fiona pulled at her wrists, fighting at the magnetic lock that pinned her and Aaron to the wall. "I could do with tighter too. But I should say, my safe word is—"

"Nobody cares."

Her eyes sparkled, but she refused to smile, letting her amusement creep out in her voice. "How'd you know?"

Graccus shook his head, walking over to the stairs and practically hurling himself up to the Captain's seat on the balcony above.

Fiona looked over at Aaron, her gemstone eyes assessing him, softening. Her lips parted, composing her thought. "Don't worry, big guy. I've been in this pit before. I know the way out of it."

"And you're the only one who does?" he asked, his voice cracking a bit.

"Only one available. But I'm better than the rest anyway."

Graccus settled in the captain's seat, reaching up for the intercom. "You all better be in your places, because we are cruising for contact."

Nora's voice barked the rebuke. "It's a smuggler ship, Graccus. You do your job and they won't find us."

"Well, then we're off to a great start," Graccus muttered under his breath, more nervous than he wanted to let on. Aaron could feel his skin crawling.

Funny. He always thought Oskies were conditioned and disciplined, modified to the point of barely human. But here Graccus was, nervous like anybody else. Super speed and super strength must not do much for anxiety, when you were doing super things.

Good. Then he wasn't alone.

This plan wasn't made to be done silently. It just had to be quiet for long enough. Nora and the others were secreted in the end cap of one oxygen silo. Any guard that inspected the space would just find an empty compartment, unless he climbed inside and inspected a hinge on the far end of a sixty-foot-long tube. Or be smart enough to know the actual silo was forty feet longer than that.

The same was true of three other containers. A hundred Jergad drones laid in wait, along with a handful of psychopathic Capital renegades.

When the trap was sprung, they'd retake the ship—but they wouldn't have the firepower to take Charon. Instead, they'd simply have to hold long enough for Aaron, Eden, and Fiona to get back onboard through the food and waste conduit.

Simple enough. If anything went wrong, the Jergad would dig them out.

Callum Remus was unlikely to cross their path. Aaron had him pinpointed on the *Tartarus* in orbit, out of reach. He'd have to wait.

He trusted the plan, the team. Even Fiona.

Yeah. He trusted her. So why did Aaron's chest hurt?

Fiona raised an eyebrow at him. "Don't go all weak in the knees on me now."

He shook his head. "If I go down, I'm taking you with me."

Her eyes narrowed, a child taking that dare and doubling down with some rebuttal in her mind. Instead, she glanced up at the empty air over their heads. "Bosun? Transfer command protocols to Graccus Ontarim. Confirmation code: BooleanNFW01. Fly safe."

The pleasant voice came from a speaker behind Aaron's head. "Very well, ma'am. Fair skies to you as well. It has been an honor."

"You change his settings, Imp, and I'mma peel your skin off," Fiona called up to Graccus. "I mean it."

"I'm going to program him to share patriotic trivia every few days," Graccus said. "You're never going to know where I put it or how to turn it off."

"Please sir," Bosun said, "I believe she is quite serious." Fiona smirked.

"Six generations of the Pilgrim's descendants," Graccus shouted. "Six whole generations, Fiona. The Dunsweir are the literal chosen people, and they lead us small folk out into the stars. We owe them our allegiance. And this election year, vote your faith."

"Peel your skin. Right off your face."

She was playful, snarking and joking. But it didn't take special sight for Aaron to figure out how frightened Fiona was. Jokes, forced smiles, but sharp breathing and swallowing hard on the lump in her throat.

She was back where she swore she'd never return, and she was doing so in chains. She had more than likely made promises to herself how she would never do this exact thing.

And here she was: chained, dethroned, dominated. If she had ever returned to Charon, she would see it destroyed. She broke that promise today.

Graccus keyed an open radio channel. "*Tartarus* Control, this is SSV-19225 Bravo. Requesting clearance to approach Fort Augustine Reformation for prisoner transfer."

"Clearance granted, 25-Bravo. Set transponder to 1300. Reduce speed to 453.7 and turn to present for lateral docking arm."

Graccus cracked his knuckles on his chair. "Copy all, transponder 1300, reduce speed 453.7, turn to present, 25-Bravo."

"Sector clear, 25-Bravo. Welcome to Fort Augustine."

Aaron tried to remind himself to breathe. "One wrong move and they blow us to pieces."

"Come on," Fiona purred. "They'd have to catch us first."

———

He thought he was prepared. He could feel her approach, every gleeful step. He could feel the sweat sticking to her palms and the itch at the back of her skull.

But when the doors opened and the hot air rushed in, stinking of grime and oil, when Graccus put his foot into Aaron's knee, forcing him to genuflect before her...he felt so small.

There she was exactly as he remembered, porcelain and still, bated breath and regal clothes. The last time he had seen her, he was sixteen years old. And now, Cassandra Meilos stood over him, like a benevolent deity, looking down from her pedestal with a mixture of compassion and derision. Look at this small creature, look at its pathetic attempts to change its fate.

And he was a child all over again.

He saw every movement behind the proverbial curtain, had access to her every secret. But it wasn't enough. Because her secrets did not gall her, and her weaknesses did not threaten her.

He knew how her father had run a respectable import/export company on Mars; how every pet she had as a child went missing eventually; how she had graduated top of her class; how she broke every barrier in her company and the occasional finger; how she bought out her own family business and sent her father to the poor house.

He knew what she would do before she did it. And it was horrifying, because with every insight, he knew he would still lose.

She said two words. "Welcome back." And they were almost friendly.

Fiona reared up and hocked a wad of spit into Cassandra's face. She didn't even blink, but the dogs both growled and tensed, ready to launch themselves for Fiona's throat. Aaron could see the synapses firing, the reflexive gear. This was a trained response, to give one warning before unleashing unfettered violence.

Aaron scowled at Fiona, shaking his head. Now was not the time.

Cassandra lifted one gloved hand, swiping the fluid from her cheek. That black shard on her mask drew Aaron's eye, like a jawbone made from condensed void. "ZR-097. You remain repulsive."

"That's only because you know me," Fiona demurred. "Most people find me despicable."

Cassandra shook her head, slow and sad. "What happened to you, little one?"

"What happened to your face?" Fiona spat back. "Dramatic."

Cassandra's eyes worked over every inch of Fiona, assessing and sneering. She snapped her fingers. "Remove her augmentations. And prepare her for orientation."

Two guards moved forward, seizing Fiona by her restraints. The maglev system kicked in with a hum and they easily lifted her off the ground, dangling her like a pig from a spit. She thrashed and grunted, putting on a good show.

And the only assurance she gave was a playful wink before she disappeared behind Cassandra's silhouette.

He didn't say a thing. Which only seemed to please the Lady of the House. Cassandra's eyes narrowed. "You remember your training well, 626. A fire kept close is hard to extinguish. A fire too bright...draws the monsters." She threw a meaningful glance over her shoulder, at the retreating guards and the echoing shouts from Fiona.

Cassandra knew how to adjust her tactics based on the prey. They exhibit aggression, apply pressure. Exhibit weakness, and supply strength. She had always feigned secret kindness for Aaron, providing infrequent drips of constitution. She had ensured he'd survive his time on Charon...and ensured she was the reason he had, creating dependency. Creating subservience.

He knew her game now, saw the moving pieces. He could resist her. This time.

But it was like Cassandra saw that decision, and her lips pulled tight in disapproval. "Process him."

Hands grabbed him and lifted him up. They did everything they could to disorient him, jostling him and banging him against the cave walls. One of them had gambling debts to the other, and their tension was pressing on him. His father disapproved of his career, but he personally wouldn't characterize this as a 'career.'

"You miss your father, don't you?" Aaron asked.

And the guard unhooked his baton.

———

Aaron awoke in his cell. It was exactly how he remembered. The ground was damp and abrasive against his fingers, scraping his cheek. His hands were bound, the chains reaching back and into the wall to some mechanism that kept the lines tense, tight. The tips of the fingers on his left had gone numb.

Hardly new. Why change something if it works?

The ship was still docked, Nora and the crew undisturbed in their hiding spot. High above, a whole separate floor, Graccus sat with Cassandra. No doubt discussing his curious tale. How an Orbital Strike Commando had opposed Deckard, only to deliver his prize, unscathed and unspoiled.

The prisoners were all bound in their cells, mixtures of begrudging and...relaxed. Like their minds and hearts had cut power, simply waiting for activation. They waited for the door to open, when the life they were allowed could resume.

And Eden. She was in a different block, but not far. So close.

What would he say to her? What would *she* say to him? There was a number of fleeting thoughts at the edges of her consciousness, but nothing concrete.

Asleep? Maybe even drugged.

But now he'd lost Fiona too. He'd have to find her the old-fashioned way before they could leave.

Two guards on patrol, the gambler and the prodigal son. No, not patrol. They were carrying a load. And they talked and jeered and—

Fiona. They had Fiona. He couldn't see her, but they were thinking of her. She was...in pieces.

Aaron's chains tightened, hard, yanking his wrists and ankles. He stumbled, tipping forward only to be yanked backward. He could hear the whine of an angry, soiled gear as it pulled. He curled forward, trying to protect the back of his head. It didn't work—he struck the wall with enough force, it whipped his skull into the rock. A flash of white—

Blue eyes in the dark. A rolling field of purple grass. Dark skies.

His eyes fluttered, unable to focus, unable to think. A rush of hot, dry air. A door creaking, like a distant haunted voice whispering for him to close his eyes, hushing his moaning pains with gothic gasps.

He flexed his arms, kicking his toes against the ground. Suspended, only just.

And the door shut. They left something behind. They left her. But just out of sight, a slit of sickly yellow light cutting just over her head. He could just about make out the bedraggled mop of her red hair.

He opened his eyes, but it was just too dark to see.

"Hey..." her voice croaked.

They kept him pinned. They wanted him to see this, but not be able to do anything.

A sticky salty smell clung to his nose and throat, all of a sudden, too much.

Blood.

"How bad is it?" he asked, blind.

A laugh, or maybe a cough. And she stepped into the light.

Her augment arm was gone, cut crudely from its socket, leaving an empty plug and shorn wiring dangling from the joint. A bandage wrapped about her skull and across one eye, damp and brown with dried blood. Her clothes had been torn away, leaving her in an ill-fitted Capital jumpsuit. Bruises were already showing around her

193

nose and jaw, yellow splotches staining her skin. And her lip quivered with something more than pain.

Fear.

"Well, now—we've gone and done it, honey," she said. "No turning back now."

CHAPTER
NINETEEN
DECKARD

IT'S NOT AS THOUGH he was in her good graces before, but now she'd shut her door on him. He stood outside in the hallway like some kind of disruptive student. His jaw hung slack, and his arms wrapped tight across his front, lest he break a hand on the doorframe. "Can you believe this?"

Mayfield shrugged. "She was about to feed us to two slobbering hellhounds. To be honest, sir, I'll take rude in place of lunch."

"And can you believe *that*?" he hissed, trying to keep his voice down. "Threatening an Imperial Admiral at gunpoint?"

"I don't have to. I was there. Sir."

He sucked in a breath and pushed it out, trying to evacuate all of the stress and anger. And failing. "Do I detect a hint of insubordination?"

"Only when it's called for, sir."

Deckard looked over at the Regular. Where he was pacing and grinding and growling, she was stalwart, stoic, almost like a sculpture. She followed him with her eyes, but never broke her parade rest, did not pivot or lean. It was like she was compressing all of her rebellion into as few syllables as possible, lest she rip the orchid insignia off her sleeve.

"Use it more often," Deckard cautioned. "A day or two in a brig is better than killing somebody."

"I respectfully disagree."

"There you go again. Do you even know how to curse?"

There was the barest hint of a smirk. "Not in uniform, I don't."

Deckard tried to pace his breathing again, but the realities of the situation always came rushing back. "We're not getting off this station without shooting our way out."

"No, sir," she said in agreement.

"The main docking collar will be too well protected, even for your team."

She nodded. "We got to see how well that worked in real time. They're still scraping Capital out of the ceiling."

The Capitals had rioted. They'd unified. They'd pushed the collar like a mindless horde. And a pair of GA-57 Repeater cannons had pulled them apart like cotton fibers. It had looked all too much like the streets of Vanguard.

And every other street on every other rebellious world. Deckard had gotten quite sick of the sight of sinew and bone.

"But that can't be the only way out of here," he mused.

"If I was building a prison—"

Deckard cut her off. "But you're not. She is. Get yourself into her..." He paused, fishing for the word. "Chitinous shell."

Mayfield raised a bushy blonde eyebrow. "Her *what*, sir?"

Deckard painted the picture with his hands. "Three hours ago, the stage is set, but this time Cassandra is on the station. There's a riot. Blood, screaming. She's losing control."

Mayfield jerked a thumb at the closed door. "You think that crustacean can even conceive of losing control?"

"She's a narcissist, Mayfield. Set expectations, meet them, disappointment? 'Losing control' is a concept that lives in a corner office of her head every single day since she was five years old. She'll have fallback plans for the fallback plans, and the ability to pin failure on something..." Deckard took another calming breath. "On *someone* else."

And that's when the blood drained from Mayfield's face. "A powder keg of a prison. Here comes a Duster rebel with a history of inspiring rhetoric. And us, right in the middle of it."

Deckard nodded. "She's been waiting for this day for a long time. The day she takes her chips down and plants the blame for every inefficiency, every disappointment. And I walked us right into it. She's going to scuttle Charon, deprive the Empire of a labor force...and she gets to blame us."

Mayfield's eyes sharpened. "How do we stop her?"

Deckard's heart sank. She had such passion in her yet. Youth, not yet beaten into the mold. "Sergeant...we're the ones who've been stopped. Outplayed. I needed the good will of a creature that hasn't shown good will to its own mother. I took the shot. I missed. We're Capitals now. For good."

"That can't be the only play," Mayfield urged.

Deckard had bent his knee to the Blue and White Orchid, served the Dunsweir with pride, for thirty years. But if they ordered it, would he lay his head on the chopping block? For the Pilgrim? For the Empire?

No.

It was like she saw the decision click behind his eyes. And she stiffened. "Is it, sir?"

Those words didn't have time to really sink in, because her firm question was drowned out by a far more aggressive one. "Where is he?!"

Deckard felt the breeze before he saw the man. Callum whistled past right up to the office door, stopping at the barricade. He still had that lingering gold glow about him, as his implants cooled off from a surge.

Based on how he tilted forward at the closed door, jutting his chin out and puffing his chest, he wasn't asking Deckard or Mayfield. They just happened to be present to hear the question. He might as well have been asking the stone under his feet. Had it been possible under conventional physics, Deckard had no doubt that Callum would've blown right through that door, cutting out a silhouette in the steel that forensics could've identified him with.

Now, the porous and soft rock? He might've actually been able to do that, jump right through it with a shower of debris.

"Where is who, Captain?" Deckard dared to ask.

Callum turned so fast, it was like his head flickered with yellow streaks traced in the air. His charred scar had started to bleed again, blood oozing from the cracked carbon black. He spoke harsh but slow, like he was trying to speak for an imbecile. "Graccus Ontarim."

Deckard tongued his cheek. He wasn't going to hold a man that angry up to regulations and rank. Not that Deckard held rank or was beholden to regulations anymore. Instead, he gingerly extended a finger towards the door that Callum had almost slammed through. "He's with the Lady of the House."

Callum's eyes bored a hole clean through Deckard's head into the rock wall beyond, as he pictured what must be happening behind that door. His nostrils flared and his shoulders swelled with homicidal intent. But his words were gentle, like he was trying to avoid spooking a herd of animals. "Would you mind?"

"You have no idea how much I'd *prefer* if you did."

Callum nodded, like he was confirming one last time. But then he turned and dug his fingers into the door, finding purchase in the seam—

Except that they opened on their own, and a slender man stared back at them. He appeared...average. Average build, average height, unremarkable frame and clothes. His hair draped around his ears and across his forehead like it might obscure his features. And every aspect of his admittedly handsome face seemed fit to blend in with every other handsome man that had ever lived. He was unremarkable, by design and selection.

"Oh, hi." The smarmy pearly white grin, his voice like a silky brass instrument. He looked back into the room, toward the rigid Cassandra and her dogs. "We were just finishing up."

Flashes were for lightning, cameras, and explosive materials. Some gunpowder still burned like a flash.

This wasn't a flash. The two men were suddenly a blur of yellow streaks and muted flesh, the squeal of rubber soles scraping on the floor, leaving tread marks on the ground. Sparks flew off the door-frame where—something—hit it. But a short breath later, both men had come to a standstill six feet into the room, gasping for breath and taking stock of one another.

Callum held a scrap of Graccus's clothes in his clenched fist.

Deckard watched as the door tried to close, the warped frame now locking one side of the door inside the wall. The gears whined in a childish tantrum, vainly pushing on the obstruction. The other half of the door reached out at full extension, moaning that it couldn't find its pair, before sliding back and lurching forward again, praying that this time would be the one where it found its brother and a proper seal.

The admiral stuck his hand out, pushing the unhappy door back into the wall and striding into the room. "I take it there is history on display?"

"Whatever he's told you," Callum growled like a starved lion eying its first meal in months, "is a saccharine lie."

Graccus cocked his head. "Well, that's not very nice. When have I ever lied to you?"

"That's all you ever *did*!" Cassandra's office wasn't a large space, but Callum made it echo like it was an amphitheater. Somehow, his words hung in the air, clung to them, like hateful cobwebs.

The Lady of the House threw a wide-eyed look Deckard's way, a friend with an inside joke. Like she hadn't tried to kill him just a short while ago. "And that's why I'm opposed to monogamy."

"Admiral." Callum didn't turn, growling at his opponent like he had his jaw locked onto a limb. "Destroy that ship, kill this man. And kill Aaron Havenes right now."

Cassandra's eyes drew target lock. "626 is *my* prisoner," she said, cool and calm. She wasn't declaring ownership; she was alerting the room to the imminent demise of anyone who claimed ownership of what was hers.

"How do you know my officer?" Deckard demanded of Graccus.

Before Graccus could answer, Callum cut in. "Holkstad Academy, ten years ago. Then Jupiter. Ilum. *Concordia!*"

"That's not true," Graccus said, "I've never been to Ilum. The rest of it was pretty spot on though."

"He's a rogue agent. Wanted by the Ministry and Holkstad, both. A traitor and a mongrel rat."

Graccus cocked his head, disbelief and awe. "Espionage never was your forte. I infiltrated the ranks of enemy combatants, captured my target—plus one—and did it without a drop of blood or all the..." He waved a hand at Deckard. "Sanctimony. No offense."

Deckard squinted at the operative. This Oskie was fast on his mouth. Too fast. Almost...prepared?

"How many Imperial Regulars died in your 'bloodless' pursuit?" Callum snarled.

"Philippe doesn't clear his operations through Naval Command. And neither do I. Get out of my way while I'm doing a job."

"You tried to kill me on Vanguard!"

"Emphasis on 'tried' or we wouldn't be having this conversation!"

Deckard stepped between the two apex predators. "Enough!"

They both tensed, as the line of sight was broken, but each waited for the other to make the first move. And neither did.

Deckard glared at Callum, trying to catch the man's eye. "Stand down, Captain."

Callum took a step back, as ordered, but notably blocked the doorway.

Deckard turned toward Cassandra, and—based on how Graccus stepped into her orbit—her new pet assassin. "Cassandra? What do you make of this?"

Play to her ego, bend to her will. Try to drive her sails with artificial wind.

But she didn't take the bait. "My opinion is my own, Deckard."

"Aren't you a Capital now? 'Deckard?'" Graccus mused.

He could feel Callum practically sizzle off of the little gray man's voice. Not because Deckard had been challenged, but simply because Graccus had spoken.

Callum didn't disagree. Interesting.

He threw a glance at Mayfield. She was a Naval Regular, and certainly not a rank-and-file bit of heavy muscle. Excellent or not, she would be pulled apart like cotton candy in this room. Without Callum's backing, Deckard didn't have the room.

So, he had to take it another way. Defy their expectations.

"And as a Capital—" Deckard's throat clenched on the word. "...my life is not my own. What would the Lady of the House have of me?"

That wasn't subservience. That was a dare.

And she took it like one. There was no expression on that reptilian face. He couldn't beat her at a game where she had drawn up the rules. Her voice was so homely, so pleasant. "Have dinner with us, Deckard."

"I for one, am starving," Graccus urged, doubling down on her bet. He either found this whole debacle highly entertaining—or simply knew how to choose the winning team.

Mayfield stepped forward. "Unfortunately, the admiral has official duties that require his attention."

Deckard didn't even have time to curse her impulsiveness. Cassandra leapt on the mistake, playing the gracious host. "Let's not do this again," she crowed. "It's time for new beginnings."

"You intend to keep the prisoners alive?" Callum coughed, incredulous. "After all the damage they've done collectively between them?"

Cassandra's eyes remained fixed on Deckard, like she was waiting for him to blink. "Havoc, my good man, can be a powerful ally."

She knew they'd try to escape. She knew they'd raise havoc. She knew how to make it Deckard's fault. And she had the firepower to pull this insane gambit off. And she'd pick some other rock to set up shop and go right on torturing whoever the State deemed was acceptable for her to torture.

Damn it.

Deckard growled. "This 'havoc' seems to follow me wherever I go..."

"Mhm. Entropy," she mused, with more than a little whimsy.

And that was the step too far for him. "I didn't realize entropy included hostage taking and sabotage."

"Admiral, my word. I simply asked you to dinner." Cassandra played up the wounded bystander.

She was no fool, not forgetful or forgiving. She was playing to a fresh audience, making him out to be the villain. That big show of challenging him before, asking him about the supply ship—that had simply been to drive up his ire. And now, by acting like that stand-off hadn't even happened in front of new faces, it made him out to be the aggressor.

After all, Graccus and Callum had not been present for the 'interrogation' of the escaped convicts. And the Oskies would likely go unharmed in whatever scuffle was to follow.

They'd make ideal witnesses for his trial post mortem.

And she was daring him to make his case. Go on, do it. Accuse the diplomatic businesswoman of impropriety, with all of her connections and all of her reputation. What did he have?

After all...he was just a Capital.

Deckard straightened up, but his heart sank as he swallowed his pride. "Your invitation...how very kind of you, Cassandra. Of course, I would like nothing better."

Her nostrils flared, and she smiled. "That's a good boy."

CHAPTER
TWENTY
FIONA

IT FELT like being in the dark, but...locked in it. Clothed in it, draped around her shoulders and tight around her throat and squeezing her face.

She couldn't feel her hand. She had memories of feeling it. But not anymore. Those dangling wires off her socket, exposed to the hot air, had a nice little safety feature built-in to deactivate the feed when not in a circuit, lest she live in excruciating exposed agony.

All she could think of was Keira reaching down to her in the dark...grasping her hand...

That hand had been taken, along with every trick and secret it held. The nape of her neck was damp with what she hoped was sweat, but quietly knew to be blood; they had taken her radio implant and done so without care or patience. Who gives a damn if a Capital gets a post-op infection in her *gulaw* brain?

Good thing she was here to rescue a doctor.

Everything ached, even parts of her they hadn't hacked on. But that was the most familiar feeling, almost like seeing an old friend across the street and thinking for a moment that she knew that face.

In five years away, they hadn't even changed the door locks. Still the same old ring systems: just a closed loop of electrical current, failed into the closed position. Child's play.

In truth, it didn't especially matter. Fort Augustine *was* the lock, the cell, the yard—an island prison with stormy seas. Who gave a hot damn if the gears were rusty and the guards were fat? Where was anyone going to go?

She popped the lock on Aaron's cell one-handed in about five minutes. She needed his help pulling the electrical out where she could see, but that was about it. He had good little hands, dexterous and careful. Suppose a gear rat like him didn't get to keep all ten fingers if they were clumsy.

They waited for a few hours to let the shifts change over, before she cracked the door and let them out into the hallway. "So, where's your friend?" she whispered, pressing her back against the stone wall.

Aaron stood next to her, almost oafish. "She's uh...a-a hundred feet forward. Six feet down."

"Six feet?" Fiona mused. "Girl got herself in a Hot Box. Tsk, tsk."

He was dripping in sweat. Hands shaking. Tremors.

She slipped her hand into his, giving it a squeeze. "Is it everything you remember?"

He nodded. "I'd forgotten the smell."

Hot searing air. There'd been some recent trouble, a fair bit of it. The Lady of the House must've dialed up the temperature as punishment. And fresh blood cooking on the rocks always made the stomach do cartwheels.

She squeezed his hand, and he squeezed back. But he crouched down next to her, his voice lowering to a hush. "We can uh...we can make our way to the foundry floor. Access the uh...Boxes from there."

She appraised him, slack-jawed. He was an impossible thing. Nothing threatened him, not really. Nothing concerned him. He could walk from one end of this Hellhole to the other and back without ever fearing a shiv, a guard, or the Lady herself. He'd be a ghost in the cruel machine, coming and going as he pleased.

And he was still frightened, like nothing was true. What he could hear, see, touch—none of it could be believed anymore.

He was just a boy again, in prison, frightened. Alone.

"You're sure that's where she is?" Fiona asked.

He nodded, and a droplet of sweat fell off of his sharp jaw. He rolled his shoulders, trying to work out some growing kink in his lean muscles.

"And are there any guards?"

He shook his head, trying to clear the fog in his brain. "A few. Most are picking apart the ship. A couple of roving duos hunting for stragglers."

This strange, strange man, she thought in amazement. He'd be a remarkable criminal, marking out patrols and sussing out the truth in a hostage. She might never know if he was going to betray her...but he would know everyone who was.

She'd never be safer anywhere than standing right next to him.

"How's your little friend holding up?" Fiona asked.

He squinted, reaching out to access that more acute information. "She's gone numb in the fingers of her left hand and she—" He paused, wincing. "She has a splitting headache. And there's three others."

She rolled her eyes. "Do we care? We're escaping prison, not liberating it."

He wasn't offended by the question, too wrapped up in his study. "They...know her. They were a part of something. Oh no..."

Fiona waited for him to follow up on that suspenseful notion, but he never did.

So, she punched him, driving the hard metal socket of her elbow directly into a good nerve on his shoulder. He grimaced, rolling out his now tingling arm as he eyeballed her. "Ow."

"You don't just say 'oh no' and not follow that up with the thing!" she hissed.

"You hit hard."

"I will find something to *stab* you with if you don't start talkin'."

205

His tone was suddenly familial and regular, just like the day she met him. A blow to the arm and she brought him right back to himself.

Shit, if she'd known it had been that easy. But then again, he'd probably not like her all that much if she hit that reset button too often.

He cocked his head. "Eden tried your escape plan, to the letter. That's why they're Boxed. Cassandra was waiting for them."

Of course. The Warden would've been well briefed on *how* Fiona and the others had escaped. But instead of patch the weakness, she laid a trap over it, a spider's web.

Devious. She figured that someone on the outside was offering aid and comfort, and she could catch that traitor. Or, that Fiona and her group might come back to rescue more of their kin.

By rights, Fiona should've started thinking of a new plan right there in the hallway. She should've considered their options, readied herself for the chaos to come.

But instead, only one thought rang around between her pirate ears. "She was here two weeks and figured out somethin' that took Keira and I a whole *year*."

"I told you," Aaron said with a shrug, "she's good."

"You told me she was a *doctor*, not an escape artist."

"Hang out with me more. You get good at all kinds of stuff. Let's go," he said with that damned perfect smile, and Fiona felt her scalp tingle. It was hard not to follow someone with that much reckless energy.

Aaron led the way forward, weaving his way through Charon's tunnels like the dim light meant nothing to him. He turned corners with unearned confidence, like he was prepared to kill whatever was on the other side simply by walking through it.

Suddenly, he waved her down, pressing her against the wall with one hand. She crouched down, turning her face into the wall to hide the whites of her eyes, so she didn't see what happened next.

Aaron lunged away from her and she heard a soft crunch. A

man's voice gargled and gasped, trying to scream or shout. But nothing.

Fiona opened her eyes. One guard was flopping on the ground, clutching at his throat and eyes bulging—a blow to his throat had collapsed his larynx. She slid over, laying her knee over his hands and pressing her body weight through to his neck until he stopped moving.

She looked up to see Aaron tangled in the second guard, hand over his mouth but unable to secure the chokehold. And the guard was stretching out to his waist, reaching for his weapon...

Fiona swiped the baton off of her guard's prone body, giving him a bash across the jaw for good measure—and hearing a satisfying crack of bone. Satisfied he was handled, she rushed Aaron's guard and slammed the baton into the meat of his leg, stunning the muscle. The man's support crumpled, and he slipped down, letting Aaron's forearm come up under his chin, securing the hold.

But this guard, he was fiery. He leapt up to try and kick at Fiona. Aaron must've felt—or Seen—it coming, because he quickly yanked backward, pulling the man down on top of him. The guard flailed and kicked and fought, but the battle was lost now. Aaron just held until he slipped into unconsciousness.

Aaron pushed the guard off of him and took a deep, gasping breath. So, Fiona walked over and popped the guard across the temple with the baton.

"Oy," Aaron objected through his exhaustion. "He was out."

She shrugged. "Jus' making sure."

He shook his head, no energy to fight her on it.

"Take their uniforms?" Fiona suggested.

"And be the miraculous one-armed bleeding guard and her jar-opening companion?"

She raised an eyebrow. "You're giving me back chatter while lying on the ground?"

"Oh, would you get over yourself?"

She lent him a hand, pulling him up to standing. "We leave 'em out, they're going to get found."

"They'll get found," Aaron assured. "But we'll be long gone when they do."

She believed him. He'd know where everybody else was, how they were feeling today, and how committed to their pay scale.

It was a brief walk ahead to the Foundry floor. It was something of an open secret that the Hot Boxes were buried into the refinery's decking. In point of fact, they were an inspired innovation to existing engineering. The source of the heat had to be at the Foundry in order to melt the crucibles full of mineral ore. But if a Capital were to be buried right near that heat exchange, why that would be truly miserable!

And it was.

Aaron paused as they entered the vaulted space: the catwalks overhead, the vats of molten metal left unattended.

But it was the lift on the far side of the room that simply commanded his attention. It was a basic factory lift, ferrying workers to the drill site below. It was empty and quiet now, with nothing to do. And he was...transfixed.

"You alright, sunshine?" Fiona asked him.

He blinked away whatever illusion had captivated him. "Jus'...memories."

"Well, reminisce when we're long gone. Where is she?"

Aaron's eyes darted to a specific floor panel. Really, the entire floor was just a series of riveted steel sheets, none unlike any of the rest. But that kept the working surface level.

So they could mask what was underneath...

Fiona grabbed a prybar. But Aaron shook his head. His eyes? Glowing blue. "No time for that. I'm bringing in some heavy machinery."

She nodded, tossing the bar aside. "Okay, I understand euphemism. But...what heavy machinery did you have in mind?"

Shouts. Screams. Gunfire. Lots of gunfire. And Aaron was just standing in the center of the room.

Fiona bent over the prybar again. "Uh...Aaron? I think we're about to have problems."

He didn't move. He just stared with those blue eyes into some distant place, like he was meditating.

And the ground trembled under her feet.

"The heavy machinery?" Fiona asked, pointing down.

He nodded. "Rolling thunder."

And right on queue—the dramatic bitch—came a Jergad, blasting clean through a rocky wall, drenched in blood and viscera. A fleshy bag that must've been a guard at some point rocketed out from it, slamming into a support beam and spilling all over the floor.

The bloody Jergad whipped its head over to Aaron. Mottled flesh with divots in its skull fan, and a single scarred eye.

The gunfire picked up its intensity, as did the shouting. It was growing more coordinated. The jailbreak offensive was in full swing. Bray, Nora, and Solomon were in full form, and a hundred Jergad beasts were now roving the *Asphodel* cleaning house.

Fiona was never happier to see that nightmare creature.

Aaron greeted the Jergad with warmth, saying something urgent under his breath. And Scar was more than happy to oblige. It took two big steps over, pausing to give Fiona a little nod, chittering concern.

Ah. She was missing parts, bleeding, in distress. Scar was worried about her? How cute.

But Aaron waved at her. "You need to...get out of the way."

"I knew it was something," Fiona said, hopping off to one side. Scar huffed affirmation and lowered its claws against the steel.

It popped the rivets like they were made of glass, ripping the entire floor panel up and tossing it aside. Fiona watched a chunk of steel the size of a desk sail across the room like a razor edge disc and she couldn't help but picture what would happen if the Jergad had meant to throw that as a weapon.

Peeking out of the ruddy stone looked like a hatch. Nobody had a chance to reach for it, because Scar quite simply popped the tin. A blast of air, hotter even still, almost like the space had been under pressure.

The first thing Fiona noticed was the god-awful smell of burning hair, followed by sickly sweet sweat, ammonia. But she didn't see anything.

Scar reached down into the dark can, gingerly, like he was dipping his claw into shadowy waters. And a hand reached back, clasping around the bone.

Eden.

Scar lifted her up out of the bin and set her on the ground, whereupon she immediately fell into the creature's flank, wrapping her arms around the big boy. "I never thought I'd see you again." Scar chirruped and groaned back comfort. And Eden laughed like she understood anything it said.

And that's when she noticed Aaron. And her disposition immediately darkened.

He raised a hand. "I know what you're going to say."

Eden might have been weak, croaking through a dried voice, and forced to lean on the big bladed space alien, but she was not going to be stopped. "You're an idiot, you know that? You're a first-class idiot."

Fiona smiled. "But sometimes its therapeutic to say it, I guess."

"Who else is here?!" Edendemanded.

"Everybody," Aaron said, looking at his shoes.

"*Fra tow ni laska*, Aaron! You're going to get everybody *killed*!"

Fiona looked at Scar with tight lips, rubbing the back of her neck. She knew this story. She'd lived it on occasion.

They'd been a thing. They were no longer a thing. They still felt responsibility to one another, even though they're not supposed to. Fiery exchange ensues.

"They talked me into it," was Aaron's piss poor defense.

Eden pushed herself off of Scar, wobbly on her feet. "Then they're stupid too! You're supposed to keep them safe."

Aaron's head snapped up, looking to the sky, like a dog that had heard the dinner bell. "We have to go. Right now."

"Thank you!" Fiona said, readying her prybar.

"And who the hell is this?!" Eden shouted.

"Hi," Fiona said, extending her stump like she still had a hand, "Fiona McCorty: new girl, pie rat, and all-around bad influence. Good enough?"

Scar ripped up another panel, revealing another two Hot Boxes.

"We have time for this?" Fiona asked.

Aaron nodded. "Graccus bought us all the time we're going to get."

"Graccus is here too?!" Eden balked.

"In my defense," Aaron said, "Graccus is probably the *best* person to do this kind of thing."

Eden had to shrug, no real rebuttal for that.

Aaron suddenly tensed from end to end. He snapped his fingers at Scar. "Hurry up, big guy!"

"Hurry up with what now?" Fiona didn't much care for being kept in the dark. And Aaron, for all of his politeness, had read every demand Eden had the moment she had it.

"She's not leaving without the three folks in the Boxes. And we need to leave. *Now.*"

Eden clapped her hands together, like she was going to do any of the labor that Scar was halfway done with. "Let's get 'em out."

Aaron glanced sidelong at Fiona. And he didn't say it. He didn't have to.

Fiona felt her hair catch fire. Her skin crawl. Her throat clench. And she felt a hunger. "It's Callum Remus, isn't it?"

"...Yes."

Keira's body on that stretcher.

Cut to pieces. Cause of death: asphyxiation.

She'd been cut in half, and before she could die of shock or blood loss, she'd drowned as her lungs collapsed.

She'd reached down and plucked Fiona out of the darkest holes.

She'd been a comrade. She'd been a friend. Fiona hadn't been there to return the favor.

And the man responsible. Was coming. Here. Now.

She was going to kill him.

Fiona stalked to the exit. And suddenly, Aaron was in her way, hands outstretched.

"Fiona, you can't—"

"Get out of my way, pretty boy, before I rearrange your features."

"He's *Orbital*," Aaron said, like she cared. "He's not someone you just walk up to."

New girl had been out of her cage for seventy seconds, and now she had an opinion too. "He's right. You try to dance with an Oskie, and he's going to paint the room with you."

"He killed Keira." That wasn't a statement of fact. It wasn't a promise, or a threat. She could hear the sheet being pulled back, crinkling and crunching, revealing what had happened to her friend.

"And he will kill you too. We can help you," Aaron said, "*I* can help you. But not right now."

"When?"

"*Not now*! First, we get out of here—"

They leave now, and this little band of heroes would forget they ever needed the pie rat. They'd drop their allegiances, their promises, their civility. They'd shoot her in the back the moment she blinked.

And Aaron would feel it coming and do nothing. Just like he was doing nothing now.

She thought about Keira on that table, and Fiona swore she could see her old friend gasp awake—

Aaron laid a hand on her shoulder. "Fiona, we'll do this—"

She slipped the prybar under his wrist, leveraging his hand off of her and striking him across the face in one motion. He tumbled out of her way, shielding himself from further attack. Scar roared its protest, but nobody followed her out of the Foundry.

And nobody was going to get in her way.

PART THREE
ACHERON

CHAPTER
TWENTY-ONE
AARON

HE WASN'T ENTIRELY sure the contents of his head were still in his skull. He remembered how fixed artillery pieces had blasted on his ears and chest, like they were using his ribcage as a drum. This was a crushing throbbing pain on just one side and crept along his scalp like spiderwebbing cracks in a sheet of glass.

Eden stumbled over to him, almost falling on top of him. She couldn't help herself, her doctor fingers searching along his hairline, looking for any seeping wound or swelling.

He blinked, bleary eyes trying to refocus. A dulcet tone of a bell filled his ears, his vision blurry, like he was trying to look through the surface of a lake disturbed by a stone's throw—

Soft violet grass under his fingers. Twinkling stars.

Eden stood over him, those almond eyes and her ragged oily hair, burns on her neck and wrists. Singes on her suit's left shoulder, where it had laid against a heating element. And here she was, tending to *him*.

"Where'd she go?" Aaron grumbled.

"You're in no condition," Eden barked. A barrage of distant gunfire caught her attention, and she looked up. "Where's our ride?"

Aaron pressed his hands onto the ground, heaving himself up.

His stomach protested, immediately flipping over in his gut. "Fiona?!"

He glanced to the doorway, deeper into Charon's labyrinth. Maybe she was somewhere in the room? Behind the Crucibles, or down that lift—

Jensen smiled at him from behind the gate, face covered in blood. "Hey, shortstack."

Eden took his hand. "Aaron, we have to get out of here."

Scar was helping the last of the three others out of their Boxes, and all of them were transfixed by the mighty alien. A wiry little man with one leg assessed the demonic visage with remarkable comfort, as if to say, 'Sure, why not?'

Aaron shook his head, but he couldn't lose the sound of—

Cards riffling between skilled fingers. The last card stained with blood.

A tattooed behemoth of a woman stalked over to Aaron, as if she hadn't spent the last however long stewing in hundred-degree heat. "Who're you?"

Aaron looked at her—and his mind was flooded with so many memories.

Isolde: her sister was dead, at least she believed so; she enjoyed popsicles and working with her hands. "Sorry about your sister."

Her nostrils flared and he could see the muscles in her back flex and flare out like wings. "Answer my question, little man, before I fold you in half."

"Don't even try it," Eden and Aaron said in unison. And Isolde's eyes went wide, leering back at them both. It took Eden half a moment longer to notice what had happened. Aaron raised an eyebrow at her, smug.

"That's new," Eden murmured.

His eyes focused, sharpened, darkened. Along with his voice. "Where is Fiona?"

"You can't See her?"

He shook his head, eyes drifting off. "Never have."

No time to process that. Eden snapped her fingers at Isolde. "Grab Twelve and get Khalid on their feet. We gotta move."

Isolde nodded, and in two loping steps, she was already heaving the one-legged man into her arms. The third, logically, was Khalid, who had yet to take their eyes off of Scar. "Is it going to eat us?"

"Once upon a time," Eden said.

Aaron looked back toward the *Asphodel*. Bray and Nora had managed to secure the gangway, posted up on opposing sides. Solomon had actually crept forward on to the station, trying to offer the occasional bit of crucial flanking pressure while remaining hidden in shadows. Who knows how long that risky position would hold up before the guards caught on and cut him to pieces?

Aisling was scrambling with the ship's systems, likely working with Bosun to keep hacking efforts from shutting down the engines. Talania was following directions, constantly looking back up at Aisling for the next wire to rip out of the wall with all of the dexterity of a zoo animal. It was certainly *one* way to fight a hostile AI—block up the roads, stall the approach. It would buy seconds, but that might be the deciding half of a heartbeat they needed to escape.

The Jergad, well...the Jergad were burrowing. They had surged out of the *Asphodel* and dove immediately into that sweet familiar ground. It was their planet now. They dug better than the machines ever could. They were making tunnels and filling them in again, popping out only to wreak havoc before vanishing into the stone again. Step wrong, and a claw would snag the boot, yanking down into supposedly solid stone.

The planet itself had spawned a hellish vitriolic response to its human invaders, invoking two hundred years of emotional pain and anguish back on to those that had inflicted it. Nowhere was safe anymore.

But the Jergad were taking losses. This place wasn't Vanguard. It was cold, the stone hard. They were slower, sluggish. Gunfire flicked out the Jergad one by one. Their lights were growing so distant.

They couldn't hold the dock for long.

Where was Fiona? Where was she?!

He had to find Graccus. The gray man was riding in with Deckard and Callum. He had to get to Graccus before Fiona did, stop her from attempting something insane.

Fiona would know where the shuttle dock was. No one else alive knew this station's secrets like her. She'd find the dock and ready an ambush for anybody that stepped off.

But Callum would almost certainly hear her proud heart beating, would feel her breath shifting the air. And he would stop both before she could so much as clench her fist.

She hadn't fought Oskies. She had no idea what she was stepping into—

Riley's blade buried into Jensen's chest. Pulsing yellow coolant under the Oskie's skin. And he set his bloodshot eyes on Aaron, hungry and angry.

Aaron squeezed Eden's shoulder. "I'm not leaving without her. Scar? Get them home."

"So you can go after the cripple all by yourself? Not happening."

"You're not going to have any better odds. You're half dead as it is."

"I didn't go to Hell *twice* for you to go off all by yourself!" Eden spat.

Enough. Aaron snapped. "And I did not come all the way out here to lose you now! Get back to the ship. I will meet you there. I promise. Now go!" He shoved her at Scar, and took off into Charon's torturous halls.

His feet beat against the uneven stonework, packed down smooth by thousands of feet over a hundred years. How many lives had ended in these halls? How often had these halls been changed, just to flummox the inmates and shatter their will?

He remembered the sullen faces. He remembered the stench of sweat and bile and blood. The acrid air, the boiling metal, the grind of gears.

Jensen. When the monsters had come for Aaron, Jensen had

stood by him. He'd always stood by him. That stupid smile. Maybe because Aaron was so short, just a child? He couldn't stomach letting the prison and its worst elements tear up a child?

Aaron rounded a corner—

Jensen leaned on a wall, big meaty arms crossed his chest. He looked up as Aaron approached. Riley's quick knife was still plunged to the hilt through his ribs, three other wounds dripping hot blood to the floor. But that big smile on his face could not be dimmed. "You have to let go, boss."

Aaron shook his head, blowing right past the hallucination. But the voice didn't quit, like it was following him step for step.

"You saved me too, y'know. This place...it's only powerful if you're alone. And she"— Cassandra's face flashed across his mind—*"she was always an expert at pulling folk out of the crowd. Making them alone. Trapping 'em there."*

He could feel where Callum was landing. He could feel him getting closer. Wherever he was, Aaron would certainly find Fiona. He pressed harder. No guards between him and the landing. They were busy with the surprise invasion.

Aaron had a clear shot straight there.

Jensen's voice was clarion between his ears. "You didn't kill me, shortstack. You helped me live the way I wanted to. I wouldn't have it any other way."

The shuttle docked with a bang. Wind, as the door hushed open. Aaron turned the corner—

—in time to see Fiona's body crack against the stone wall like a piece of rotten fruit. She clung to the stonework for a moment, like she had fused into it. Now a piece of Charon, like she belonged to it. But after a breathless moment, she slipped to the ground, limp and lifeless.

Callum lowered his fist. He'd swatted her aside like an insect, and with about as much concern. And his eyes settled now on Aaron standing on the far end of the hall.

Aaron looked at Fiona. Was she alive? Was she alive?! But all he saw was the same darkness, that empty nothing.

Callum took a step forward, letting Deckard Tiberiet out of the shuttle. "Hello, Aaron."

Aaron swallowed. Nothing to say.

And neither did Deckard. His throat clenched, trying to formulate something. Thousands of lives lost, a world laid siege, and the bastard didn't have a thing to say.

Because he was torn. He didn't command respect or authority. With his vaunted privileges stricken from him one by one, he had become so small, and was well aware of the transition. His power was granted to him and was just as easily taken.

He couldn't look down at Aaron anymore.

Callum cocked his head, his stare leaning back towards Deckard. What was Aaron so fixated on? An ally perhaps? A traitor?

Aaron looked up at Graccus. The gray man was on the tips of his toes, tilting, ready. But to do what? Give the order.

Aaron wouldn't have time to speak it. Callum would be on him before he finished the first syllable. A glance would be as obvious as swinging a flag in the air. The twenty yards would be closed so fast it would be like Callum was simply extending a hand for Aaron's throat.

So, Aaron closed his eyes. And reached out with his mind. And he started counting.

One.

The ground rolled under his feet. He felt the angle of the rock shift, tilting him backwards—and he leapt into a run like he was coming out of sprinter blocks.

Callum almost took off after him—but Graccus drew his attention. Not to attack. The double agent dove for Fiona, tumbling across her body and pulling her over his shoulders in a fireman's carry.

Two.

Graccus was fast, but Callum was just as fast. Pound for pound stronger, too.

Which is why he wasn't expecting Deckard to pull a gun. Deckard got it halfway out of his holster, but the slide of metal on leather betrayed him. Callum broke his arm like a chicken bone.

The admiral was trying to help, earn his way back into grace. But that was grace given, not taken. And Callum had decided the fate of Deckard Tiberiet.

Deckard didn't even get to scream as Callum hurled him to the ground by his broken arm, and Aaron heard the pop of something else all the way down the hall.

Three.

Graccus slipped by Callum, roughly tossing Fiona into a corner of the shuttle. And with naught but a wistful glance, he closed the door.

Four.

Callum hit the hatch with both fists, as if he could grab hold of the shuttle with his glistening golden arms and hold forty tons of spaceship in place. But Graccus was gone, along with Fiona.

And so Callum turned to the problem he could solve, eyes dark—

—*Riley's hungry eyes looked just like that, amidst the toxic fumes and dripping blood.*

Five...is when the Jergad warrior drone slipped from the ground, leading with its enormous claws. It growled and roared, a vibrato from somewhere deep and tortured.

Callum caught the Jergad's claws in his own two hands, squaring off with the beast four times his size. And he growled right back. It snapped and snarled, reaching vainly for his face with its bifurcated jaws.

Callum snapped his own teeth, miming a bite back at the creature—before ripping one arm clean from the shoulder, and slamming the scythe blade down into the Jergad's skull. The sheer force of the strike toppled the giant alien onto its side. Callum put a boot into the Jergad's head, wrenching the arm free.

Aaron's mind flashed, burned, grinding! He stumbled but caught himself with a palm off the ground.

The Jergad whimpered—and Callum brought the blade back down, finishing the creature with a squelch.

Aaron didn't dare look back, but Callum's voice called out to him. "There's nowhere for you to run, 626. This doesn't have to be an ordeal."

Bare feet against the rock, Aaron fled. The lights whirled over-head, whipping by.

He felt the Jergad all over the station turn to his aid.

No. They had to get to the *Asphodel*. Get away. He'll kill you.

They weren't going to leave him.

Aaron wasn't planning on getting left. But they couldn't stop Callum, not even if they brought all of their combined strength. They had to run.

He could see Scar at the docking collar, head pricked up and eyes tracking through a million pounds of rock. It watched Aaron, wistful and mourning. It crowed out a baleful roar Aaron heard echoing through halls.

Aaron wasn't going to make it. And Scar knew. And it was so, so sorry.

It stayed in the threshold, taking one last look, even as Bray tried to shove the beast back aboard the *Asphodel*. The old sergeant looked over his shoulder, searching for whatever the Jergad could see amongst the encroaching dangers. Bray didn't see anything worth waiting for, but nothing Aaron could pick out—

That meant mechanized threats mobilizing to engage, spitting hellfire and absorbing all the responding gunplay.

He could see Eden, flailing all four limbs, clawing and scraping, practically hurling herself back into the fray. Ready to dive back on to Charon, even as thirty caliber slugs skipped around her. She'd been through wilderness, through war; she would not leave Aaron alone in Hell.

Nora had an arm slung about Eden's waist, hauling her back onto the safety of the *Asphodel*. Eden's new friend Isolde tried to shout sense into the young doctor. Khalid and Twelve strapped themselves in, readying for the roller coaster to come.

Solomon scrambled back across the hatch, and with gritted teeth, he hit the button—

And Eden screamed as the hatch closed, shutting her off from view.

The mountaintop. The Jergad closing in. Jensen screaming Aaron's name as the Howler doors closed.

Aaron's ears filled with ear piercing screeches, a hundred alien voices calling out despair. He dropped to the ground, sliding and tumbling along the uneven dirt.

Pain. Screaming. Threats. Anger. So much anger. He couldn't shut them out. Their songs, so loud. Discordant and full of empty rage, as the *Asphodel* broke dock and slipped away into the void.

The Jergad were screaming his name, the banshee cry of mourning.

And underneath all the din, the rising of a thrumming bass, the encroaching icy waters—

Callum.

He was working through the tunnels the Jergad had carved. Circling under the surface, out of sight. The darkness was no enemy to someone of his skill, with his tools.

And his voice seemed to drip out of the very bedrock. "Capitals are all the same: you take and take and take..."

Aaron pushed himself up to a seat, watching Callum's glow dart through the arteries of the planet like an infection. Oskies were not invulnerable, and Callum was relishing this moment like he was.

Aaron had a track record of killing his kind, and he could do it again. He could. He had to.

If Aaron could overwhelm him, taunt him into a mistake...

A hand extended down to him, blood trickling off the rough fingertips. Jensen. He wordlessly urged Aaron to take his hand. Take his help.

"You're dead," Aaron muttered. "You're not real."

Jensen's smile faltered, but his eyes softened. "You've never fought alone. And you don't have to."

How? How would that even work? Was this...

Was this what it was like for the Queen, to be the shared consciousness? Was this what it meant to take on that role? To lose the self and become the many?

And could it save him?

Aaron took Jensen's hand—*and he felt Jensen pull him to his feet.*

"You're not alone, boss," Jensen said. *"Never again."* And his *bright and happy eyes came alight with blue fire.*

Duck. Why? Just do it.

He could feel it coming like pinpricks along his skin, a shiver from his toes to his scalp.

Callum's hand reached through the stone like he was pushing through a cloud, chips of rock sailing through the air, bits of flechette. The Jergad claw bone in his hand chiseled through with surprising ease, and with the strength of an Oskie behind it, it might as well have been attached to its owner still.

Aaron bent low, whirling away—and Callum found only air.

Glowing yellow streams pumped along his arms. But Aaron could see those yellow streaks reaching out ahead of him, forward trailing, like bright yellow tendrils reaching out into the air. It was almost like seeing tracers from moving lights.

Callum was fast—but Aaron wasn't seeing him, reacting to the blazing speed of an augmented super soldier, no. He could see where the Oskie was *going* to be before he'd made the move, before he'd actually decided to do it. Aaron could see his own response—and the Oskie's response to that, how he countered, and how Aaron adjusted his move, until finally...

Callum struck, the Jergad claw aiming straight for Aaron's throat, ready to slash every vital thread and separate Aaron's head from his shoulders.

But Callum missed.

Aaron spun away, ducking the tracer—and the blade sailed along that path just as predicted.

The look of confusion that drew up on Callum's face was saccharine sweet. How was this possible, the Oskie thought to himself. Aaron wasn't faster than him, stronger than him, smarter than him. These were quantifiable metrics, measured, optimized, and tested. Callum was, in every available way, superior to this Duster Capital laborer.

Callum tensed up, and Aaron could see the calculations taking place, as he considered. Perhaps this Capital had some back-alley augmentations? Maybe Graccus had shared the secrets of Holkstad and this little prophet had subjected himself to the risky procedures?

The battle-hardened veteran adjusted his strategy, but Aaron could feel his growing frustration. This wasn't supposed to be a fight. This was supposed to be a triumph!

Aaron saw the yellow lights grow and reach out, mapping along the trajectory of Callum's path before the Oskie had even flinched. It was like watching a glow sharpen into a line, as all the possibilities narrowed to the one. As Aaron considered his move, he saw the tendrils shift and react, winding vines of light, as Callum's own path changed to match. Like streaks of yellow lightning slowly looking for ground.

The last moment, the last second. And Callum struck—and again, Aaron was out of reach. Every swipe the Oskie took, Aaron simply bowed out of the way, keeping out of reach from the ghost-like sketches of where the Oskie would go.

Callum kept striking. He changed stances, shifting it up. He bounded off of walls with elbow strikes, and slid along the floor, trying to bind up Aaron's legs. He tried to grapple, he tried to strike hard, he tried to strike quick.

But nothing seemed to work!

Aaron was not too fast. He was just inside Callum's head, seeing the move before it happened. Speed was an advantage, moving before an opponent could respond, and allowing physics to work its cruel magic.

But what good was speed if the opponent knew the play even before the person calling it?

And the veteran's chest began to ache. His breath wheezed. Sweat beaded on his forehead, starting to steam. He was overworked, his implants beginning to cook him in his own skin. The alien bone was charred black at the Oskie's fingertips.

And he was slowing down. Slowing down just enough.

Jensen whispered in Aaron's ear. "Kick his ass."

Aaron could see the next path, see Callum's exhausted body straining to reach him. He wouldn't need to do anything but...

Callum slashed with the bone claw—and Aaron threw a counter, catching Callum at his wrist. The Oskie's hand went numb, sending the claw sailing off into the dark halls.

Panic. Callum's eyes went wide. And Aaron's eyes darkened.

Fiona's body hit the wall, crumpled. Wet, limp.

Aaron advanced on Callum.

The veteran threw a snap kick for Aaron's head. Reaching, overextending, backing up and off balance. And Aaron punished him. He bent low, letting the strike sail harmlessly overhead. And Aaron lashed out at Callum's anchoring leg.

The Oskie fell, catching himself before cracking his head on the ground. And fear pumped through him in one burst. This lesser, this fleshy human rebel, a Capital...had struck him.

"You tortured Eden Neria," Aaron said.

Eden dangled from her wrists, crying out to drown out the crack-ling arcs burning her flesh.

Aaron stomped over to the Jergad claw. "You killed Keira Ladd."

Keira gasped for breath, half of her body lying still three feet away—

He kicked the bone up to his hand, feeling the charred leathery flesh still warm from the Oskie's skin. He stared at Callum, his lower lip quivering. "You killed...Fiona McCorty."

Fiona cocked her head, and her smile flashed in the dark—

Aaron clenched his fist around the claw. Nothing more to say. Pure focus on this moment.

He saw the tracers. He saw where Callum was going. He could be there, ready, with the killing blow.

And he raised the claw—

A flash in the dark, blinding him, filling every corner of his Sight. And a growl.

What?

He never saw it coming, as the dog's teeth locked onto the Jergad claw. Aaron stumbled, staggered by the sixty-pound weight suddenly snarling on the other end of his weapon.

The bone cracked between its clenched teeth, and it snarled as it pulled.

Pure anger and fear behind its eyes, drilled and refined. Loyalty built, constructed with care and abuse. It didn't hate him, didn't hunger. It just feared its owner more than any danger in the dark.

Aaron's eyes glowed blue, highlights playing off of the dog's rich brown fur. This wasn't what it was made for, meant for. It didn't *want* this anymore. She called it Mercury, but that was not its name...

He saw the small puppy, floppy ears and big wet eyes, being handed off to—

The second dog hit him like a hammer, rough claws sticking into his shoulders. Sharp teeth bit into his wrist, crushing down into the bone. Wet slobber mixed with blood, smearing warmth.

But just as suddenly the dog let go without so much as a word—because Callum's fingers wrapped around Aaron's throat, hot like a brand iron. Lifting him up. And the fingers dug in, getting a solid grip on the cords and arteries within.

Jensen. Eden. Keira. Everyone. Anyone. All of their faces slipping away into the fog. Vanishing.

"Very good," came the applauding words from the dark. "Very good."

The dogs sat down next to one another, like soldiers at attention.

Waiting for their next command. And on the tip of their every thought was a branding iron, driving them to stillness.

Aaron clenched his eyes shut, trying to block out their pain.

It didn't hide the alternating click of a heel and clank of a metal leg as Cassandra Meilos approached. For all of the blood spilled, he knew there was not a hair out of place, her porcelain face like a molded mask.

"He dies," was all Callum said.

Cassandra's voice was politic, light, and menacing. "You believe you know suffering, Mr. Remus. If you kill him even one second before I give the order...I will redefine the word for you."

And Callum believed her. He didn't put Aaron down, but his fingers slackened their grasp on his important bits.

She did not plan for this specifically. But she planned for chaos. She planned for disruption. She planned for Aaron and the rebels to try something.

Now, Aaron knew Deckard's fate was sealed and, he was captured and...and...

And that melodious voice dripped venom into his ear. "626...you disappoint me."

CHAPTER
TWENTY-TWO
FIONA

"WE HAVE TO GO BACK!" She kept saying that. The grungy little woman was never happier than saying those four words at escalating volumes. Eden had been saying it since Fiona's shuttle doors opened, and she had said little else.

Graccus, understandably, wasn't saying much. He could've stayed, saved Aaron, been trapped there too. Killed Callum.

Instead, he'd plucked Fiona off the floor and ran away like a coward. He didn't meet anyone's eyes and offered no explanation. Suppose he didn't owe anyone anything. And no one could successfully compel him, anyhow.

Fiona's back cracked like someone had shoved popcorn between her shoulder blades and her head pulsed like a reactor had sprung a leak. No time to check that out. There was a dreadnought in high orbit and they were deep in Imperial space, tagged leaving a pile of spent brass and dead bodies. They might as well have done it on camera for the world to see.

No Deckard meant their Wolcott shield was meaningless. They'd be blown to bits before they even got half way to the Jump. The Navy might even drag this out like a good ol' fox chase. Have some fun with it.

"We have to go back!" Eden repeated her favorite words.

Nora had her about the shoulders, screaming just as loud back into her face. "We can't go back! He's gone!"

"No, he's not!"

Bray paged the Jump Deck, soft and hesitant, like the toggle was the final nail in the coffin. "Aisling, get us out of here."

To where? Fiona huffed. The Imperials could take their time, blow away the *Asphodel* at their leisure. The Capitals could run and they would just die tired.

Graccus leaned in close to her. "You should really sit down." She didn't want to hear it. But he wasn't letting up. "You've gone tachycardic, and you have acute swelling in the brain. You should be happy you didn't leave any gray matter back there."

"You can *see* my concussion?" Fiona asked.

"I saw you go headfirst into a stone wall. I don't need augments, just common sense. Sit down before you fall down." He tried to reach for her shoulder, soothe her, but she threw off his hands.

Every touch felt like acid anyway.

Eden thrashed at Nora, trying to break free. "We have to—"

Nora practically slammed Eden into the bulkhead. "He is *gone!*"

Maybe it was the blunt force trauma, or the fact that Nora's outburst eclipsed her frantic energy, but Eden finally simmered. And so did everybody else. Nobody said a thing for a long moment. They just stewed in that knowledge.

Aaron was trapped. Beyond their reach. Probably dead.

Dead...he better hope they kill him.

Scar nestled up against the closed airlock, curling up and folding together into a cozy little faux rock. It mewled and cooed, vocalizing...grief. Like it was laying its head against a grave stone.

What were they...without Aaron, Fiona thought.

What was she? Just another pirate, another Capital with delusions of grandeur? Arrogant? Short-sighted?

Boots pounded on grating, and Talania's sylvan frame stooped through a hatchway, freezing there like she didn't expect what she found.

She didn't take in the whole sight. Just Eden.

Eden looked up from Nora and their eyes locked. And Talania's face fell, ashamed. Her jaw worked, searching for something to say, but all she could muster was a weak "...Hi."

The corner of Eden's mouth curled up. Angry that these people came for her, but the simple one syllable was enough to cut through the fog. She was just so grateful to see that face, that face she'd told herself she'd never see again.

At least they'd all die happy.

Fiona turned and stalked down the hallway, rolling out her shoulder. She heard somebody berate her for leaving, like she was disrupting some kind of solemn ceremony.

To hell with that. Hell with them all.

There was only one way they weren't going to all die right here, right now. "Bosun?" Fiona groaned.

His voice was far too cheery. Her head throbbed and his voice was hitting the right pitch to make it all worse. "Welcome back, ma'am."

"Assume navigational control. Set course for the *Tartarus*, half speed."

"Are you quite sure that is wise, ma'am?"

"Just do it!"

The ship lurched as it pulsed retro thrusters, twisting for a course corrective burn. Their little freighter was about to go straight for the dreadnought, like a wounded fish swimming straight for the shark. They'd be an easy target. If the *Tartarus* wanted them dead, they'd have no ability to resist.

But she still had one move left.

Fiona paused at a wall locker, keying in the security code. The doors swung open to reveal the remnants of the pilfered armory the Capitals had looted for their assault. Empty racks and open shelving.

But there was still a single pistol left: an M&J Series 92 magnetic slug thrower, chambered with flechettes. That would do.

The intercom crackled next to the locker: "Fiona, what did you do?" Aisling asked, frantic. Fiona could hear fingers tinkling against holographic controls and getting a chiming error each time.

She offered the jockey no answers. Fiona just closed the locker door and walked the twenty-seven brief steps to Captain Wolcott's bunk masquerading as an improvised cell. Fiona opened the door—and immediately rolled her eyes.

The Naval brat was wrist deep in a wall panel, yanking on some conduit of indeterminate value. He looked up with gawking eyes, frozen in place, like he'd just been found in a state of undress.

But that expression snapped to one of concern as he saw her state: her torn clothes, her missing augments, blood and bruises all over her. The way he stared at only one of her eyes, made her think she must've done something foul to it. It *was* the side of her head that had connected with a rock wall. Who knows what her eye looked like?

"Oh my God," Wolcott gasped in sympathetic horror.

"And I was only there for four hours," Fiona said with ice.

Hand in the proverbial cookie jar, he quickly tried to jam the conduit back into place. Nothing he could do about the exposed panel. But whatever hijinks the boy had been trying to engage in, Fiona didn't care.

She just drew his undivided attention by racking a round into her pistol. "Leave it. Come with me. Let's go."

Wolcott felt he was in a position to demand answers. "Where are you taking me?"

"We'll find out together," Fiona mused, her head swimming. "One way or another, this is your last day in prison."

Aisling's voice echoed throughout the ship. "Fiona's locked me out of the controls, and we're now on a Hohman transfer right for the *Tartarus*."

Wolcott huffed, almost a chuckle. He couldn't believe his luck but was immediately disheartened by Fiona's complete lack of surprise.

And his eyes went wide. She wouldn't dare.

"I told you. You should've helped them." She raised the pistol. "Start walking."

He didn't. Instead, he shouted. "She's got a gun!"

Fiona whipped the pistol around, blasting a three-inch-wide hole in the door controls. Safety mechanisms kicked in and the door slammed shut—not a second too soon, as Graccus's fist dented the steel from the outside.

"Bosun, flood the ship."

"Verification, ma'am?"

More banging on the door. It curled and bent under the assault but refused to buckle. He'd be inside in a matter of minutes.

Fiona gave the order. "Boolean-QR-Delta-C, Osyen Belt. Flood the ship."

Every room but the one she was standing in was about to get very light-headed, as the oxygen was slowly replaced with nitrogen gas. A proper nitrogen mixture was always important to human survival, but too much of it would cause narcosis, painlessly neutralizing... killing the entire crew. They'd feel drunk, a stupor, and would just go to sleep. Dioxide poisoning made the body panic; the brain recognized too much CO_2 in the blood, in the lungs.

But this? This would just slip them all away. Painless, quiet.

"Fiona!" Graccus shouted. "Fiona, open this *gulaw* door or I will peel your remaining arm off and beat you to death with it!"

She brought her gun back around to Wolcott, letting him study the live firearm in all its exquisite detail. "You saw what this did to that console? Two and half pounds of pressure, it'll do that to you. And I'll be starting with your hands and feet."

The boy was surprisingly fast with his mouth now. "I don't know anything about Callum Remus."

"Very wrong answer."

"I warned you," he was babbling now, scrambling for the collection of sounds that would help him. "I told you about OSC, I told you how dangerous—"

She squeezed a shot into the bulkhead, the metal peeling and scraping up like a blossoming flower. Thankfully, flechette wasn't mean enough to go clean through the hull. Instead, it skipped around the room, showering them with sparks.

Wolcott dropped into a crouch, shielding his head. "What are you doing?!"

More pounding on the door, but a different voice. "Fiona! Open this door! *Fra tow gyo-sha!*" Nora's threats were less explicit, but the intent was there in every hard consonant.

"She blew out the console," Graccus explained. "Get into the subfloor!"

Clever boy. But they'd all be dead before they could get in.

Fiona snarled at Wolcott. "We're past Callum. We're *way* past Callum. You had a moment to help, and you didn't. Now we're going to see the consequences of that choice."

Wolcott started his stupid Naval mantra, like it might grant him strength and serenity. "My service is to the People—"

"The People?!" Fiona barked at him. "That's *hilarious*. When your leaders get to choose who gets the *right* to be called a person—you're not serving the People when you get to choose who the People even *are*!"

He cast his eyes to the floor, his brain locking on that, like she'd poured concrete into his ear.

She heard them tearing at the floor outside. Graccus was trying to force his way past rivets and hardened steel. The others were tossing and clearing whatever he could pull free.

He was fast. He wouldn't be fast enough.

Fiona cocked her head and curled her lip. "Bosun? Give our little friend here Extranet access."

Wolcott's brow furrowed. A chirp and a happy little bell accompanied with the pleasant reverb of the Bosun. "Granted, ma'am."

Fiona trained the pistol on Wolcott's leg. "Call them."

Wolcott blinked, the words choking him up. "C-Call who?"

"Call for help."

She swore she could hear his spine crackle as he slumped down. His eyes watered and his mind broken. But through all that, his voice was still able to squeak out two words, spitting them. "Pie rat."

"You know how I became the 'pie rat' Master?" she asked. "How I consolidated an entire sector under my hand? I killed whoever got in my way."

"I die," the boy croaked, "so do you. You'll never pull that trigger."

She could blow his foot off right there. It might even be a kindness, seeing the poor bandaging done to his wounds from his encounter with the oxygen ghost. One year ago, she'd have smeared his brains against the back wall and called it an art exhibit. She'd killed men for less.

But today, all she could think of was Aaron's disapproving eyes, flickers of blue against the brown, full of pain and understanding. Empathy.

"You're killing all of them just to save yourself," Wolcott sneered through the tears starting to well in his eyes, finding his courage. "I won't help you. So do what you do, pie rat. You can't help it."

She should kill him right now, just for that. No, rip his throat out, so that he never speaks again. Make him live with that offense forever scarred into him, a walking memorandum to the world never to cross Fiona McCorty or the Boolean Edge.

She remembered Aaron's eyes in that corridor, eating his meals alone. How he understood her. And how he wouldn't understand this.

"Fiona, I know what you're doing."

Her eyes flitted back to the doorframe. Over the sounds of crunching metal and exertion, there was that new voice: the girl from the prison, Eden.

She wasn't angry or judgmental. That was pity staining her words.

While the rest of the crew tried to claw their way in, Eden had settled down beside the door, sitting with her back against the cold steel like she was sitting against a grave marker.

Talking to the dead.

"I was a medical resident in the Lower Wards of Detroit. Before all of this. You're flooding the ship with an inert gas. Drowning us."

Yeah. She was. And there was nothing Eden or anybody else could do about it.

"It won't work. Oh, you'll get us. We'll be dead in a few minutes. But the Jergad? They're...unpredictable without Aaron. They don't understand space travel. They'll panic, they'll try to escape—right through the hull of this ship. They'll kill themselves and take you with them."

Fiona hissed a breath past her clenched teeth to mask her internal screaming. Eden was right. The Jergad were more than capable of tearing the *Asphodel* apart from the inside, peel it open like a can of meat. She couldn't subdue the bladed space demons with gas or guns.

"I'll always be a doctor," Eden said. "Three years in prison and labor camps will never take that away from me. I was a soldier on the frontlines for almost a year. I wish I could leave that behind, but I can't. Not while my friends are in danger. But I don't have to be a *Capital* anymore. And neither do you. They made you a Capital...so you became a pirate, a killer: just to survive. You can choose to be whatever you want to be. It doesn't have to be *this*. You did this because of what they chose. But it's still your choice. And you can choose...anything else. What you've done before is what you know: it feels safe, comfortable. But you don't *have* to be that."

What other choice did she have? She started a Civil War for vanity; she sank a Fleet Carrier just to say that she did; she came all this way just to kill one person, and she'd kill any number for another shot at that one man.

She was never getting out of Imperial space alive. They'd sacrifice a thousand good and loyal men like Wolcott for a shot at her, for what her insolence represented.

"Maybe I'm...biased, but I never felt killing...ever made the world a better place. But saving someone? That..." Eden was slowing down, breathless and listing. "That *always*...was worth something."

Saving someone? The Capitals called Fiona to ask her help in saving someone. They offered to help her kill someone.

Who could she save beyond herself?

Aaron?

Fiona lowered the gun and Wolcott started breathing again. "Bosun? Terminate protocol. Captain's override."

"Very good, ma'am."

The door didn't open properly anymore, and the subfloors weren't as deep as they had hoped. They had to cut the door open, showering the room with sparks. When Fiona saw their faces, she half-expected them to execute her, cuff her, or feed her to the Jergad.

And the stern look on Graccus' face told her it had been discussed.

But Eden took the lead, stepping right past him. She had an ugly limp—the hot boxes and the torture had probably done a number on her back and leg. But she made her way over with confidence, extending an open hand with a firm request—give her the gun.

Fiona looked down at the firearm. Magnetic capacitor charged, it could loose thirty rounds as fast as she could pull the trigger. Her augmented arm could place those accurately in eight seconds. This hand? It had a tremor. Not a lot, just enough to remind her of years of nerve damage.

She huffed, considering that notion. Her first thought with a weapon in her hand was how effective she could be with it, weighing and measuring odds...guilting herself for every lost inch.

She'd been running for so long...she'd forgotten how to walk.

She spun the pistol around, handing it grip-first to Eden. Eden reached out gingerly, like she was cautious not to spook the feral animal. But Fiona gave no resistance when Eden's slender fingers slipped around the weapon.

And Bray exhaled something akin to relief, whirling away from the room and out of sight. A very grumpy Nora took his place, sliding in to lean against the doorframe.

"You can't lay siege to a prison twice in one day," Fiona pointed out. "They'll know you're coming."

"And they'll kill Deckard and Aaron before we even hit the airlock," Graccus said.

"They'll what?"

Eden's eyes sharpened, looking past Fiona.

To Wolcott. The young man was perked up, like a wild animal that spied a predator on the horizon.

Graccus took a breath, trying to phrase this delicately. "Admiral Deckard Tiberiet has been stripped of his command and branded Capital, for disobeying orders—and trying to save you, kid. He's on that station right now, probably going through processing."

"They'll kill him!" The words burst out of Wolcott like a pressure leak. "He's an Imperial officer. Those prisoners will eat him alive."

"That's usually the idea," Nora said from the doorway. "They don't brand you a Capital because they care about your wellbeing."

"We need a new way on to Charon," Graccus declared.

Fiona grimaced. "And we need it in the next ninety seconds before the *Tartarus* decides to hit us with a cannon bigger than our ship."

"Your pupils are dilated," Graccus observed, concerned. "You should sit down."

Fiona rolled her eyes. "Weren't you going to kill me like two minutes ago?"

"Don't suppose we can ask the *Tartarus* real nicely?" Talania offered. "It's *their* admiral down there."

Nora thought it was ridiculous but didn't have a better idea. "Depends on how nice. What're you offering?"

"That's our way in." Everyone turned at that. They all looked back towards Wolcott. The Naval officer was rubbing his hands together, like he had a ball of clay between them. An idea taking shape. "We ask...real nice."

"*Our* way in?" Eden asked.

Wolcott straightened. "Get me on the *Tartarus*. And I'll get you on that station." He raised a finger, pointing at the roof. And he looked to Fiona with his questions, before instinctively breaking eye contact to look at just about anyone else. "What's its name? Bosun?"

Fiona nodded just as the computer's pleasant voice chimed in. "Did you have a query, Master Wolcott?"

"Yeah, uh..." The little boy scout squared his shoulders and deepened his voice. "Hail *Tartarus* Actual with priority message. Signed Captain Ulrich Wolcott, Imperial Navy. Requesting clearance to dock."

CHAPTER
TWENTY-THREE
AARON

HE COULDN'T FEEL it anymore, the violet grasses against the back of his neck, tickling his ears. He couldn't see the starlight or the distant mountains or the comforting warmth of the air against his skin. Instead...

He saw fire. Blinding white hot fire, drowning out every other light. He always knew Charon had pain, residue from a hundred years of Capital correctional work. But now? Something new, something that hadn't been here just an hour before. It was like a curtain had been drawn back, and beyond that shroud was a life so bright it drowned all of the others.

Eden. Scar. He couldn't feel them. Couldn't find them. It was so very bright. Overwhelming. Isolating.

Fiona? Was she dead? Her darkness always stood out amongst the twinkling lights. But now, he couldn't even find that. There was a light so close and so radiant, it washed out every corner of his sight. Blinded him to all else.

Cassandra.

She stood outside of his cell now, lingering. Like she could taste his discomfort on the air.

He pulled on his chains, and the links tensed, the mild hum of a machine in the wall reacting to his force and pulling all four limbs taut. The more he fought, the more it pulled, keeping him strung out but never unsupported. A firm hand holding him upright.

"They changed you..." Cassandra spoke through the steel, her precise voice lingering on each syllable. "Didn't they? Those creatures? They gave you...something."

Aaron couldn't look at her. It was just too much. Why hadn't he seen it before? Why had she seemed so...so normal?

A solid piece of steel. No scuffs, no rivets, no joints to break. And the blazing phoenix beyond it.

"When you left this place, you were little more than a boy. And you come back to me now...so much more. What did they do to you, out there on that rock?" He heard the muted chirp of her Entiglas opening a file. "HR-2056. 'Vanguard.' No alien ruins. No artifacts. No recorded visit from the Pilgrim. Just a rock. Just valuable material and the worthless drones tasked to retrieve it for an ungrateful sovereign."

"You were somethin' once," Aaron hissed at the flat face of the door. "But I've tangled with monsters a helluva lot scarier than you."

"Scare you? My boy, I never meant to frighten you. Not now, not ever." She sounded almost maternal, wounded that he'd ever insinuate her hostile intent. "You would've been killed by this place in a matter of weeks. And as memory serves, you almost were. A beast of a man...chased you through these halls. And you survived as you always have: you went where he could not follow. Me? I never threatened you. On the contrary, I urged you onward."

The owner of the labyrinth does not get to claim innocence from the deeds of its inhabitants. Distance from the act made it no less cruel.

She certainly thought so. She contained monsters, enriched them. Sculpted and formed them, like wild stallions into faithful companions. But always cautious of the true nature of an animal: wild and dangerous. She saw herself not as a warden—but something akin to a farmer.

"You can read my mind," she said, her voice pitchy with that discovery. "That's what it is, isn't it? You have some...insight into my soul? Tell me...what do you see?"

She laid her hand against the door, pressing her hot palm against the icy steel. Asking, almost pleading him. Like it would be some form of release.

He blinked, flustered. Her light waxed and waned, fluxing like there was something in control of it, like the phases of a moon. She kept that flame, tended it.

She could fake it.

"I see..." Aaron stumbled on his words, trying to lock down the shifting illusions and pluck out the truth. "I see a woman in a mask."

A light, affable chuckle. "I'll tell you what I see. I see a boy who thinks himself a legend. I see a prodigal son come back to his roots. He thinks to confront his demons, to exert himself...to triumph over shadow. And he has found the valley is deeper than he remembers."

A prison was a prison, chains were chains. And she was a warden like any other. At least, he tried to tell himself that. He squeezed his eyes shut and looked for the blue eyes in the dark, and for the faintest moment, he thought he found them. But Cassandra's light drowned them, the light of an entire star in the room next to him.

Aaron tugged on his restraints again, testing how hard they'd pull back. And he found them somehow squeezing on his wrists and ankles, almost as much as they pulled him backward. "Y'know, this little community theater is starting to piss me off."

"They tried to crack you, didn't they, 626?" she asked, "They wanted your secrets, even if it meant opening you up like a treasure box. Forcing the lock with drugs and knives. The brutes. Men in uniforms and lab coats, they tried to peel you apart like you were some kind of science project. A utility that could be refined, monetized, and saddled. They only ever saw in you...what they could take."

Riley—so fixated on war and glory, that he saw peace as a threat to his authority. Deckard—so proper and upstanding, he saw war as a clean and just affair. Aaron was just another roadblock to them both.

Not to her.

She didn't see a tool, a weapon, a threat, or an inferior.

He was not so distant and unknowable to her. She'd seen thousands of criminals and malcontents. And she'd always had a talent for what made a man tick. She had become quite the musician.

"Empathy. Insight. It doesn't need technology or magic or your very alien senses," she purred. "You just...need to listen to people. And they'll tell you everything."

Her light, her life...effervescent, all-consuming. Dwarfing every other. She felt herself so superior to every other form of life.

"I'm nothing like you," Aaron said, rejecting her assertion.

He could feel her smile behind the door. Swelling with conviction. "You're the *only one* like me...Aaron."

She used his name. Not his number. Not some cold designation. He *deserved* a name. He was more than this rabble, this disposable resource. He was unique. He was special.

She treasured him.

———

The prison had yet to resume mining operations. Too much to clean up.

Aaron found Deckard on the Foundry floor. Bodies draped in Capital jumpsuits were piled six feet high on either end. Grinders had been brought in—or brought out of storage, and the living were tasked with loading their dead compatriots into the gnashing metal teeth.

Somewhere on the other side of it all, compressed and simple biological material was being processed. Red and gooey bricks emerged on conveyor belts, dehydrated and rancid. A second team of Capitals loaded the bricks into the Foundry ovens, their hands stained with the blackened red clay.

All of this could be automated. This was so the Capitals would be reminded of what happens, let it pass on to newcomers like folklore. Resist, and you will become fuel for the great fires, serving the Empire one final time.

The hair in Aaron's nose burnt at the smell. The guards had tried being hands-off, they had tried passive punishments. Now, they were escalating their cruelty.

Deckard lifted bricks off that assembly line. His broken arm lay swaddled against his side—he'd torn a leg off his jumpsuit to make a sling—no way to set bone or treat the pain. His good hand was caked in human blood, crusting under his fingernails, smears and spackling of it across his forehead.

Aaron approached him, looking around at the other Capitals on the line. Nobody said a word. Nobody even looked up.

"...I'm sorry, Deckard."

"Piss off." That was the pain talking, but more than a little anger.

Aaron blinked at that response. Of course. The prison was full of people abused by the Imperial system, and he was a former Imperial admiral. One whisper of Deckard's past, and Deckard would be dismembered before the night bell.

"I'm not here to threaten you," Aaron assured him.

"Well, you're not getting a pat on the head."

"All I ever wanted to do was talk to you, Deckard."

Deckard hissed, "And I should've *glassed* your planet when I had the chance."

Because if he had, if he had opened with the cleansing fire of a righteous man, he'd be left with nothing but a sour conscience, as he and his men ruefully returned to the Empire for their next crimson assignment.

Instead, he was here. He'd lost his titles, his reputation...everything.

Not everything. Wolcott still lived. Out there. It was worth it.

Aaron looked down at the conveyor belt, considering the juicy blocks as they paraded down the line. "How many died in Eden's riot?"

"To give you an accurate answer, they'd have to give a damn. I know I don't."

"Yes, you do. You can't help yourself. It's the same reason you *didn't* glass Vanguard. You've never been able to hide behind the numbers—"

"Get out of my head, freak."

Aaron pressed. "That's why your son doesn't talk to you anymore. He's off catching criminals and saving lives, while you were taking them. Does he know you're a Capital now?"

Deckard never stopped lifting the bricks. "My son is a decorated Cleric of the Academie Pacem, and you have now attacked *two* Imperial installations that were nowhere near your precious little planet."

"Chasing a friend you stole. You had to know I'd come after her."

Deckard snarled. "I counted on Capitals...doing what Capitals do. It's in your nature."

He didn't believe that. He couldn't anymore. Because he was now a Capital, and he was no monster. He didn't think so. He prayed that he wasn't. And the cognitive dissonance was tearing him apart. Everything he'd ever been taught over a fifty-year lifetime, everything he'd taught his son, taught Wolcott: every Capital was lost to the Pilgrim's light, cursed, damned, monstrous. They had to be isolated for everyone's well-being.

Was it true? Was he lost as well?

Aaron looked aside, at the growing number of eyes watching them. Hoping for a fight, something to break up their monotony. But they all went back to work off of Aaron's cold stare.

"I suppose I'm alive right now because you allow it?" Aaron asked.

"I know that ten thousand colonists on Vanguard are dead because I allowed it to happen," Deckard admitted without missing a beat, a mixture of shame and rage.

Wolcott was a young boy, scared and armed. He had pulled the trigger, but someone else had given him a gun. Deckard took responsibility. But that wasn't his fault, not really.

Aaron's lips parted as he saw the name on Deckard's lips, the face in his mind, and the hate swelling in the admiral's chest. "Who is Alvin Caldwell?"

It was like he'd set Deckard ablaze. "Alvin Caldwell—didn't take a sixteen-year-old boy hostage."

"He was old enough for you to bring him into a war," Aaron shot back. "You can't have it both ways. He's either old enough to fight, or not old enough to know what he's doing. But then again, that's the whole point of the war college only accepting children, isn't it? They don't know better!"

Some broad-shouldered ogre with half of his teeth and an artificial eye barked at them. "Shut it, the both of ya's and get back to—!"

Aaron glared at the man twice his size. He did nothing else, simply stared, hyper focused, unblinking. He could've told the man off, could've spouted off about the ogre's father, could've recounted all of the curses his wife had slung at him, but no.

Instead, Aaron just channeled his inner Solomon. Like he was imagining the various sounds the man would make when kicked into the grinder behind him.

And the ogre...sheepishly went back to his own work.

Aaron turned back to Deckard, trying to lower his own temperature. "Pardon the pun, but where's your right hand? I don't see her on the work line."

Deckard paused, glancing at his broken arm and taking a moment to process what Aaron really meant. "Mayfield...was ordered back to the *Tartarus*, to resume her post."

Every single member of that crew would take Deckard's place in a heartbeat, but Deckard wouldn't have it. His disobedience was his and his alone. The rest of them followed orders, his orders.

It was his responsibility.

"Aren't you rather old to still be serving?" Aaron asked.

Deckard flinched, but kept working. It was a phrase he'd heard often. And he had his response chambered. "I'll serve until they kill me or there's nothing left to serve."

The flag was his very identity, and now the flag was ripped from his shoulder. That blue and white orchid, that which was all good and true in this universe, had deemed him unworthy of its grace. And he accepted its judgement.

But it wasn't the treasured ideal doing the judging. It was Alvin Caldwell and those like him. And that thought crept through Deckard's mind like a growing fog.

"I had been of service. I was uh...I was a court clerk," Aaron offered. "Eastern Seaboard, Sixth Criminal Adjudication. First job they had at the Economic Center."

Deckard scanned him up and down, with a raised eyebrow. "You weren't there for terribly long, apparently."

"No," Aaron chuckled. "No, I uh...you could say I didn't last."

"You know, your file has more gaping holes in it than the Chicago crater?"

"I didn't." Aaron stooped down to pluck the next brick off the conveyor, stealing Deckard's task. "But I kinda figured, what with me being guilty of murder."

Deckard squared up on him, ready to punch Aaron, take the brick back, and resume whatever service his treasured Empire deemed fit for its former admiral.

He had so much more to live for than a flag. He just couldn't see it yet.

"Who did you kill?" Deckard asked through clenched teeth.

He could still feel the rain on his skin, and for a blink of an eye, he could see the market stalls juxtaposed against Charon's rock walls. "A drunk Holkstad cadet. Had his augments, but..."

Deckard raised an eyebrow. "Fourteen years old, and you killed an Oskie?"

"Not on purpose. He came at me and I just reacted..."

"You killed an Oskie on *accident*?" Deckard huffed, turning back to the belt for new passing bricks. "Aaron Havenes, you may be in prison, but you did the world a favor. Any Oskie, cadet or veteran, that can be killed by a child doesn't deserve his boots."

What a perverted way to look at life. "He had gray eyes," Aaron whispered. "And I don't even know his name."

Deckard nodded, solemnly. The Oskie had been drilled, conditioned. Aaron was just a kid when he had taken a life, no training to prepare him for the moment after. "Do you care?"

Not especially, Aaron thought. It wasn't going to help him sleep any better.

"How is your son these days?" Aaron asked.

"None of your concern."

"You miss him?" Aaron extended the brick for the admiral to take.

Deckard didn't take it. "You're a sick son of a bitch."

"Maybe," Aaron shrugged. "But I'm not the one who put you in here."

"Oy, Foreman!" someone called out.

The elevator door hurled open and three workers stumbled out, holding a fourth in their arms. Aaron squinted at them. Surely, they weren't down below mining? The rigs were silent and the floor was still.

No...some of the prisoners must've fled into Charon's depths, hoping to find some secret escape or to simply hide from the chaos. Like Fiona had tried, years ago.

They would've died alone in the dark. Now these Capitals were tasked with clearing out the dead...

But they found something.

The ogre lumbered over to them to examine their burden, but immediately lurched away in horror. "*Gulaw zu s'ivan! Hok zu y'trit*"

Aaron jogged over, and the ogre didn't stop him. The three workers looked to Aaron for some kind of guidance or aid, panic welling up in their eyes.

They carried one of their own, recently dead, but his flesh was emaciated, eyes sunken and skin gray. A permanent visage of fright and pain was locked onto his shriveled features, a final scream before whatever killed him petrified it for all time.

Like he'd been smothered or exposed to a vacuum. The deep tunnels were low on oxygen, but this...this was something else.

Deckard approached, covering his nose and mouth with the sleeve of his jumpsuit. "What happened to him?"

The prisoners started to babble all at once. "We was going down below, crawling through them tunnels, ya? Looking for bodies that tried to escape and-and—We'd found three *skull* already! And then— something—grabbed Hamish, and-and-and—"

"Slow down," Deckard urged them. "Take a breath."

Funny choice of words. Aaron squinted, looking down deep into the planet's heart, searching...

Was this what Fiona had found, what had killed her years ago? No...no he recognized this. This came on the *Asphodel*, slipped away in the fighting...

To hunt.

"When we found him..." the Capital trailed off into a whimper, unable to articulate the image.

But Deckard stared at Aaron, his eyes burning a hole in the side of Aaron's skull. "What did this, Aaron?"

He couldn't see it down there. Perhaps it had scattered, spread out into too fine a mist. There wasn't anything strong enough to stand out to him. "For now? Nobody goes anywhere alone."

THE *ASPHODEL* WAS NOT a small ship, but it was still small enough for the *Tartarus*'s docking bays to swallow it like a mid-afternoon snack. Dreadnoughts were fleets unto themselves, capable of serving in all manner of ways. The hangar bay they were stowed in contained almost two dozen mid-size fighters, with deck crews attending to their daily maintenance.

But everyone was hanging up their work to gawk at the *Asphodel* today. The Capitals emerged from the ship with Wolcott at their head, walking down the gangway towards a firing line of waiting Naval Regulars.

Talania leaned over to Eden, talking out of the side of her mouth, "I guess I'll be seeing you on the Sojourn."

"We'll get through this," Eden soothed her. "Just be cool."

Talania was not soothed. "Anybody got anything they'd like to confess?"

"Not me," said Aisling, "I'm clean as a whistle." Solomon grunted some laughs under his breath. And Aisling glowered over at him. "Honey, you're one to talk."

"Heaven's going to be a shit show," Nora grumbled.

Fiona chimed in from the back. "You bring the liquor, I'll bring the boys. We'll be up all night."

Graccus perked up at that. "I'm game. What are we playing?"

An alarm klaxon and everybody stopped walking just short of the base of the gangway. The Regulars did not budge, and nobody said anything for a long moment. Eden reached over and squeezed Talania's hand. "Whatever happens, stay with me."

And Talania squeezed back. "Don't go running off this time."

A clean-faced corporal with a voice like asphalt shouted over the sights of his rifle. "Surrender your weapons and prepare for processing."

Before Wolcott could take the lead as planned, Bray stated his single calm rebuttal behind barely contained laughter. "No."

"Excuse me?"

"I don't like to repeat myself," Bray said, as Eden's jaw dropped. Well, this was going sideways with alarming speed.

"Drop. Your. Weapons!"

And that's when Eden heard a tone of voice that sent her back in time, back to muddy trial courses and a dingy barracks. Bray barked so loud, the young Corporal's soul nearly left his body. "Son, if I was going to shoot you, I'd have done it already. The ten of us are not taking a dreadnought by ourselves. You can cool your safety-hatch. But I shouldn't wonder with your intellect, that you can't do some basic arithmetic: count us, count you. Who wins? Dear God, boy, you are an insult to mammals everywhere! Now you are free to march at my six with a gun in my back like you're happy to see me, but you're taking this here rifle from me only after I break both of your arms and give your mother the best night of her life. Am I understood?"

Eden could feel Graccus practically shaking at her back, desperate to not bust up laughing, as the poor Corporal and his platoon were caught between natural instinct and their orders. They looked back and forth to each other, trying to gather a consensus.

Wolcott glanced at Bray, who surrendered the floor with a bow of his head, like he'd just properly prepared the troops for their visiting commanding officer. The young captain cleared his throat. "Corporal Griggs. Captain Ulrich Wolcott, requesting permission to come aboard."

The corporal took a moment to realize that was aimed at him. "Uh...permission granted, sir. Welcome back?"

Was that a question? Bray had taken this poor boy's brain out, mashed it, and shoved it back in.

"I need to see the commander right away," Wolcott said. "Who has the Con?"

Griggs finally lowered his weapon down to a ready position—still shouldered, but at least they weren't staring at a couple dozen hot barrels. "That'll be Warrant Officer Lindell."

"Take me there."

The Regulars were more than happy to escort the group. But convincing the squad of hot-headed Navy grunts to *not* sweep the *Asphodel* for threats was another matter entirely. There was, after all, close to a hundred confused and angry space demons near the ship's true center, huddling together for warmth and comfort. And if they felt in danger...

Reactor leak. That was the story. And judging on the ship's raggedy exterior, the soldiers elected to take some diagnostic readings.

And they found, what do you know, active radiation. That...was meant to be a bluff.

Fiona leaned over to Eden. "We've been flying around in a glowbox and nobody said nothin'?"

"You've been flying around," Eden corrected. "I just got here."

"It's not a *big* leak," Khalid offered up, inserting themselves in the conversation and looming over both women. They had the smile of a dog who had helped and was now looking for a treat.

Fiona studied them for a moment. "Who are you again?"

"Khalid," they offered. "You saved me and my friends from—from Charon?"

"Yeah, okay. Prison social disaster? If I can check your dental records while talking to you, you are standing *way* too close."

Message received, and Khalid took one big and meek step back.

"Will our *friends* be okay in there?" Eden asked.

Khalid shrugged. "I have no idea. What are they?"

With a reactor leak, no one was to go aboard the little freighter. It wasn't a threat—they had the ship under lock and key. If they wanted to destroy the ship, they need only press a button and vent it into space.

Eden had walked inside of—an admittedly upside down—Imperial ship before. But being in one as grand as the *Tartarus* was a whole other matter. It was like moving from a tunnel into the open sky. Everything was so much more open. And a horribly sterile gray, all exposed rivets and bolts and cheap steel.

There were exquisite steel boxes sliding along tracks to ferry folk and material quickly to their destinations, but with the size of the party and the security detail that walked with them, there was hardly room for them all. So they marched the length of the ship, like a final mile before execution.

But Wolcott walked the ship's corridors with conviction, authority, and purpose. Made sense. This was his ground.

The corridor came to a stop at a broad set of sliding doors, with a powerful woman blocking the way. Her right leg was locked up in a brace—some kind of knee injury, perhaps from the battle or the fall from orbit. She had her hands folded across her front, a sour look to her face. "Welcome back to the *Tartarus*, Captain."

"Sergeant Mayfield," Wolcott said. "I'd like to speak to *Tartarus* Actual, if I may."

"We're at Condition Two," Mayfield said. "Nobody's going on the Jump Deck, and...visitors are confined to quarters."

"Visitors. That euphemism is doing a lotta heavy lifting," Nora quipped.

Wolcott coughed, trying to cover Nora's rude comment. "I'm a serving Imperial officer."

Mayfield raised an eyebrow. "One in need of debrief and not cleared for active duty."

"If I may?" Talania raised a hand. "Hi. Talania Dedria. Governor of a planet you tried to wipe off the map. What's Condition Two?"

"Enhanced threat position," Graccus succinctly explained.

Talania waited for more than those three words and got nothing. "...You're real helpful."

"They've imprisoned the Admiral," Wolcott urged. "And I can't help but see you standing idle."

"You'd prefer we bombard a sovereign Imperial station?" Mayfield quipped. "We're engaged in communication and are negotiating."

Bray stepped forward, prompting Griggs to prod him with his rifle. "There's nothing to—Corporal, touch me with that again and I will remove your teeth with the heel of my boot. There's nothing to negotiate, Sergeant. You have a dreadnought, they don't."

Mayfield was not in the mood, and while Bray could project his voice for the back row, Sergeant Mayfield had no difficulty matching his volume. "Wearing brown doesn't mean you still have rank, and if you raise your voice to me again, I'll put two in your forehead and get a commendation."

This was getting out of control. They were getting heated. But with a gun at her back in the heart of the Imperial war machine, what was Eden going to do?

Wolcott puffed out his chest. "Deckard Tiberiet—"

"Defied direct orders, and regulations are clear on this matter."

Bray had some guff for that. "When the orders are shit, shit on the orders."

"The orders are Gospel!"

"'And you'll be asked to write your own verse,' is the end of that quote," Wolcott barked back.

Nora's jaw dropped and her eyes bugged out. "That's a super crazy line of thinkin' with a lot of wiggle room in it. Am I the only one with that read?"

"Don't get me started," Graccus muttered, with an exhausted look in his eye.

Mayfield looked to the platoon leader. "Corporal Griggs? Escort Captain Wolcott and his entourage off the Deck."

"Belay that order, Corporal," Wolcott snapped.

The panic that shot through the Corporal's eyes, as he received two contradictory orders from superiors. Eden didn't envy the man. It was moments like this that training came into conflict with the internal moral compass. In less than a second, he'd have to make a potentially painful value judgement.

But Mayfield saved him by taking one powerful step forward, her metal brace clanking on the deck like a steel boot. And her voice went low and menacing. "Captain Wolcott. Stand down."

Captain Ulrich Wolcott was a lot of things. Among his many qualities, he was young, hot-headed, and self-assured. So, he simply dared Mayfield to shoot him.

He took a step. She drew her sidearm, the hiss of metal against polymer—

And the door opened, like curtains parted at the theater. Out stepped a stiff young man, like he'd been starched into his uniform, tall and broad, with a playful curl to his thin lip. His enormous beard draped down to the top of his chest, perfectly shaped and coiffed.

And Wolcott exhaled. "Officer Lindell."

Lindell snapped off a salute to the much younger Wolcott, and Eden was able to see the wrist-mounted augment still dangling a cable out of his sleeve. "Officer on deck!"

Mayfield holstered her weapon and saluted Wolcott out of reflex, but the sting in her eyes was obvious to a blind man.

Wolcott smiled, vibrating with warmth and barely contained glee. He shook Lindell's hand with far too much force, like he was trying to break it off and keep it. "Trevor. Damn good to see you!"

"Likewise, Wolcott," Lindell said. He glanced at the assemblage of riff-raff and chaos behind the Captain. "How'd you get them to surrender?"

Wolcott bit his lip. "I didn't."

"Here comes the fun bit." Aisling whispered with dread.

Lindell glanced down at Wolcott, suddenly rigid. "Sergeant? Detain these traitors and escort them to the brig."

Graccus cracked his neck. "This is going to be funny."

Lindell was not the most observant, because he didn't take the threat from the Oskie with the gravity it deserved. "Enemies of the Empire *will* be detained pending summary execution for their crimes."

Wolcott tried to redirect the moment. "They have Deckard down there. These people have critical intelligence that can be used in his recovery."

Lindell barely got the words past his clenched throat. "I will not jeopardize the safety of this ship or its crew. The Admiral gave me responsibility—"

Aisling grunted. "This is a waste of time." And she started to shove herself back down the hallway, like she could just get back on the *Asphodel* and leave.

Which nobody cared for, least of all Lindell. "Stop that woman, right there."

Aisling didn't even slow down. "What're you going to do? Shoot me in the back? You've already done that, and it didn't take."

"Capitals don't have civil protections." It was said like a warning and was fact of law, sure—but one that he said like a slur.

Wolcott wanted to object. Talania wanted to interject with her own lengthy education. All sorts of 'Hey Now' and 'Now wait just a minute' issued from the crowd.

But Solomon simply drew his quick knife. Griggs and his Regulars all snapped their weapons up, a chorus of charging capacitors and gritting teeth.

And Aisling's voice drowned them all out. She spun her chair around, a single force filling the hallway with her voice, bellowing back at them like the heart of a maelstrom. "His name was Conrad Eskell, you piece of shit. Your triggers gunned him out of the sky as he was carrying wounded off a battlefield. You shot down a *goddamn medevac*! You—and everyone on this ship—are nothing. Just bullies and cowards. Might makes right, and you had all the power. You killed because you could get away with it. And now that you're about to face consequences for the first time in your miserable lives...you don't know what to do!"

Lindell stood, stone-faced, like his brain was stuck loading its response to that diatribe. Solomon's eyes slid from left to right, plotting which shooter he'd take first. Graccus sunk into his stance, ready to burst into movement.

And Wolcott tried to take over the moment. He squared off with Lindell like a child with his hat in his hand. Begging. "Trevor, I let someone I respected tell me what to do back on Vanguard, and I didn't think for myself. I didn't care. I didn't...I have to believe that I can still do the right thing."

Lindell's response was canned. "Our Service is to the People—"

"Our Service is to *each other!*" Wolcott shouted, tears spilling down one cheek. And he pushed towards Lindell with one step. "To each other!"

Gunshot.

The magnetic thump was magnified by the interior halls. Eden convinced herself she'd heard the blood spatter against the bulkhead. Because almost in the same sound, that wet slop against dry metal, Mayfield cried out.

Two finger bones had erupted from the back of her hand. Graccus had moved to her side in the blink of an eye, twisting the pistol in her grip. Her fingers were caught up in the trigger guard, and the bones in her hand shattered like kindling.

Griggs and his Regulars took one clean step back and tracked their weapons. Fingers itchy with sympathetic violence. But Lindell bellowed over the deck, somehow cutting them off before a massacre. "Cease fire! Cease fire!"

Eden saw Mayfield's pistol smoking, one shot discharged. Griggs and his men demanded at gunpoint that Graccus release her. Bray and Nora waved their weapons, trying to create space. Mayfield cried out with empty lungs, still dangling by her wounded hand.

Lindell shouted for order. Talania shouted for calm. Aisling stared from the back, horror painted on her face.

And Eden wiped the blood spatter from her cheek. Wolcott turned, clutching his gut. There was no exit wound but he could...feel something horribly wrong. Like a bee sting loading him with horrible toxins, leeching away his strength.

Ten-millimeter Horus, pre-fragmented anti-personnel load for soft body targets. The round would've hit him and immediately shredded like flower petals in a strong breeze, ripping through his tissues.

Blood was already dripping down his back, where the bullet had entered. She could hear the wheeze in his breath.

She knew what to do.

Eden dropped a knee behind Wolcott, easing the wounded man to the ground. With her other hand, she waved for room. "Wolcott! Wolcott—Ulrich, look at me! Keep those eyes open."

He couldn't speak. Couldn't get enough air. The shot was in his gut, but something must've gone higher than she thought, ripped into his lungs. Maybe a piece of shrap had skipped off a rib—or a bone shard blown off from impact?

She folded his hands over his gut. "Do not close your eyes, do you hear me—"

Someone yanked her away, throwing her to the ground. Her cheek collided with the riveted steel of the floor and her head rang. She thrashed and screamed, struggled. "No! NO!"

He was her patient. She had to help him. But someone had a knee in the small of her back.

She could vaguely hear the orders. "Commandant! Alert Meditech! Trauma code blue. GSW, Senior Officer. Prep the surgical suite. And get these Capitals off the deck!"

Wolcott's eyes met hers, fluttering and unfocused. But he knew it was her, just out of reach. He was confused, mouth chewing on his words, unable to get anything out. He was trying to ask a question.

But nothing came to him.

CHAPTER
TWENTY-FIVE

EDEN

NO ONE HAD SAID anything since. Eden knew her old cell
well enough: featureless white room, blistering light from every
surface, and a dull noise that seemed to cut through all else. It made
her breathing stutter, like the brain's internal clock was thrown off.
There was no entry or exit, like they'd been placed in some pocket
dimension away from all aid.

It was unsettling by design.

Graccus paced like a caged tiger, dragging his fingers along the
outside edge. Constantly reminding himself of how big the space was,
lest he think he was trapped in some endless nothing. Solomon sat on
the floor, humming some guttural tune to himself.

Aisling lay crumpled in the corner. They'd taken her chair. The
others had offered to help her, but she'd refused them. She pulled
herself into the most isolated spot she could find and said some quiet
prayers.

Nora laid her head against Bray, and he held a rough hand about
the ball of her shoulder, squeezing it every so often. She was his little
girl, and he would hold the monsters at bay. Her eyes danced in her
skull, playing through her memories.

And how it all ended like this. The both of them expected to go out like soldiers, not caged.

Eden knew well enough that people never got to choose how.

Twelve and Isolde tried to comfort the inconsolable Khalid, weeping about what it would be like returning to Charon. They had tasted the open sky, and now they'd have to go back.

At least she'd given them that, that one last taste before it all came crashing down.

Lindell came to the cell two hours into their confinement. The wall opened up and in he stepped, covered in blood up to his elbow, eyes frantic. The bricks built up behind him again, locking him inside.

"You're a doctor?" he asked, hollow.

Everyone looked at her. Some urging her not to answer. Some knowingly nodding.

She stood up, drawing herself to her modest full height. "How is he?"

"You're a doctor?"

"Is he going to make it?"

"Doc Findley won't operate."

Eden's brow furrowed. "Why not?"

"Are you a doctor or not?! Yes or no."

Why wouldn't they operate? This ship's Meditech wing would have all of the finest facilities available, and ready to treat mass casualties, both of its own crew and to support ground operations. They had all of the ability....

Of course. They had none of the will.

She answered his question with a sharp nod.

Lindell took a heavy breath, regretting every decision that brought him to this moment. "Open the cell."

Somewhere out of sight, a maglock disengaged with a clunk and a chunk of white brick receded into the floor. It was like it let darkness into the room, relieving everyone. She looked back at Nora, at the others. They looked at her, expectant. This was her choice to make.

Imperials weren't tricksters. All the power made them blunt instruments, not deceitful. They only came here because they needed her.

Wolcott needed her.

Bray gave her a jerk of the head. "Go, kid. Do what you do."

Eden took a hard breath, rocking herself onto her toes, like she was trying to balance on the edge of a cliff...before taking her first step out of the cell. "Where is he?"

Lindell led the way—and Eden did not miss the two armed guards that were at her ten and two o'clock, lockstep. "We've got a full surgical suite, primed and hot."

Primed meant it hadn't been doing anything for two long hours too many. "Who's the attending? Doc 'Findley', you said?"

Lindell nodded. "Ship's Chief Thoracic, leads a team of specialists."

Then why didn't any of the others operate, she wondered. But she knew there was only one reason a doctor wouldn't operate on a patient and block others from doing so.

He wanted the patient to die.

Lindell led her to one of the sliding lifts. The door hushed open and closed behind them. "Commandant? Meditech. Priority Transit."

The authoritative baritone of the Commandant's voice hit her ears like she was sitting inside a drum. "Confirmed. Meditech."

The floor lurched underneath her, nearly taking her off balance. The three Imperials didn't seem bothered in the slightest, practiced and prepared for it.

Lindell leaned down to her. "Let me make this abundantly clear. I could be court martialed for doing this."

Eden shook her head. "That's like one of several things you're going to be court martialed for. Are you going to let 'em?"

He couldn't decide if he liked that or not, but he pawed at his beard. It was a very full beard, and well-kept. It smelled like sawdust and sweat, filling the small chamber.

And when the door opened, her nose was hit with iron, disinfectant, and plastic. The lift had brought them right into the suite. Inside a plastic dome, was maybe the fanciest AutoDoc Eden had ever seen, with two different surgical arms and a holographic diagnostic display —and Wolcott laid up on its bed. His blood was dripping off the side like a sanguine summer rain, some incidental spatter on the inside of the dome, put there by whoever carried him in.

And she heard Doc Findley's sandpaper bullshit before she saw him. "Oy, that's just fine. Brought some muscle with ya this time?"

Eden stepped out of the lift. A large door blocked the surgical suite from the rest of Meditech, but it was open to accommodate the lift's passage. Rows of medical beds far as the eye could see and they were mostly filled with aching and pained Imperial soldiers. A cursory triage saw lots of recovering patients, some ill in zero pressure tents, but nothing critical.

Findley, she assumed, was the plainclothes surly jackass stomping over. He had a square set jaw and a bald head polished to a shine, his small eyes hiding back behind a stylish set of glasses. She noticed the scrawl of text flowing over the lenses, likely patient records. His right hand was clearly a prosthetic, a deeper color than his face, and the tectonic lines along the wrist told her he had most of his daily tools tucked inside, deployed with the flick of his wrist. She wouldn't be surprised if they were being sanitized inside there too.

"What's his vitals?" Eden demanded.

Findley's eyes flicked over her, once, twice, then back to Lindell. "Who is this? You brought a kid?"

Eden's eyes narrowed. "Medical Resident in Detroit Lower Wards, battlefield medic, and half your age. Nice to meet you."

"You're no longer treating Captain Wolcott," Lindell said, conceding the point of a two-hour argument that Eden had missed. "I brought another doctor."

Findley's whole face seemed to recoil, lips curling and eyes widening. "AutoDoc won't take anybody's orders but mine. Even the

Commandant can't overrule it. So, if you've got needle and thread, little lady, you can have at it."

"You're going to unlock the AutoDoc," Lindell ordered, "and then go back to whatever pissing contest you like."

Findley crossed his arms. "And if I don't, Warrant Officer? What are you going to do? Tell your daddy about it? Or is he very far away right now, kickin' rocks?"

Eden glanced to the side and froze.

Mayfield. She was sitting upright in a bed, her hand immobilized in a rig with pins holding the bones in place. Neat and fine stitching on the back of her hand.

Wolcott's assassin had seen medical care before he had.

Lindell was about ready to draw some more blood in the medical suite. "Doctor Findley. I order you to open the AutoDoc."

"*Doctor* is right," Findley sneered. "I'm a civilian, roughneck. I don't take orders. And I might be the last loyal Imperial citizen in this whole bucket."

"Oh, enough of this." Eden turned toward the AutoDoc. A bed was a bed. She didn't need a computer.

"You can't help him!" Findley was somewhere between telling her it was futile and vainly ordering her not to.

Some doctor he was. Eden rattled off her diagnosis. "GSW to the thorax. No damage to arterial, or he'd be dead already. Possible perforated bowel and I heard wheezing before, so he may have fluid in his lungs. But the first thing he's going to need is a blood transfusion *right now*."

"Well, then he dies," Findley said, clearly endorsing that result.

Eden stopped at the edge of the AutoDoc dome. Wolcott's chest rose and fell, but it shuddered on the downstroke. "It's your medical bay. But this is my patient now. Either help me or fuck back off to whatever very important task you were doing."

Findley eyed Lindell, the smallest inch of respect in his eyes. She at least talked the talk. But he turned his back, and marched away, the medical suite doors slamming shut behind him.

Lindell sighed out his frustration and grit his teeth. "What do you need?"

All the wonders of modern medicine, just out of reach. Eden swiped a hand to pin back her hair, forgetting how short that Talania had cut it. No need to pin it back anymore. So she just rubbed at her neck. "I need you to open the dome."

She walked over to the wall, flinging open cabinets. One of these had to be supply. Tools, packaging, disposal, gloves—success. A cold storage tank, gallons of O-negative artificial blood.

This would've been solid gold on Vanguard, and here they could just manufacture it.

She wasn't watching. But she heard the hum of the guards' weapons, which made her turn—just in time to catch the most bizarre silhouette. They had screwed flat plate mounts onto the muzzles of their rifles and laid them high and low on the dome's door.

And with a squeeze of the trigger, the magnets hummed, and they simply...ripped the door off its hinges. The fixtures were still glowing orange in the air.

Magnets. Their door breaching used magnetic coils to superheat the brass fixtures, like an induction furnace.

"What next?" Lindell asked, smug.

She could get used to having all the tech around. "Tear up the Doc. Looking for saline, IV tubing, gauze, silksteel thread. Hurry."

The two guards went to work stripping off the AutoDoc's protective casing. The Replicator inside was hard-wired through the system's internal computer, so it would not take new orders, but there would have been previously completed material awaiting use. She'd have to make do with whatever there was, and whatever she could find in the cupboards.

She nearly gasped when she saw the arm shower. Place hands in the tube, get sprayed, turn them over, get sprayed. Congratulations, her hands were now surgery ready. It's almost like they were ready for high-speed surgical needs.

Wolcott suddenly started spasming. Lindell leapt forward. "He's choking!"

Eden sprinted over, practically vaulting over one of the guards crouched in her path. "No, he's not."

"Looks a helluva lot like—"

"Stop speaking, and grab there," Eden barked, as she grabbed the side of the bed. "One, two, three—"

On three, Lindell and Eden lifted the bed, tilting it upright. Wolcott suddenly gasped, and his eyes snapped open in pain. The fluids drained away from his wind pipe, but they just jostled a half a dozen internal injuries.

"He's awake!" Lindell shouted.

"More importantly, he's breathing," Eden said, hooking up a line of anesthetic. The computer might not take her orders, but it would still monitor his vital signs and adjust the dosage to keep him alive. Wolcott slipped away again, head limp against his pillow. She'd be able to work in peace. "Alright, who wants to assist?"

The two guards looked at each other, playing a miniature game of rock-paper-scissors, while Lindell just stepped forward. "What do you need me to do?"

"Cover your beard," Eden said, "and then get those hands clean. I'm going to need 'em."

It was a hard few hours. She had to run a nasal cannula, cut his uniform free, and inspect the damage. Wolcott took the blood transfusion like a champ, no complications. Using a laparoscopic camera, Eden was able to holographically visualize the entire chest cavity and get a clear view of his small intestine. She extended it out section by section, confirming integrity. There were multiple lacerations she had to cauterize, and she to drain the lungs out.

But before she knew it, she was sewing him up.

Lindell didn't say anything. After three long hours, he just let out a pained sigh and reached for the sweat on his forehead. Eden let him have the moment. Sanitary or not, she wasn't in a position to order him around. Not anymore.

The officer looked over at her, gratitude in his eyes. She wished she—

Something was wrong. The AutoDoc's monitor sounded a klaxon, and Wolcott started shaking against his restraints.

"What's happening?" Lindell asked.

"No-no-no-no-NO!" Eden pressed a hand to Wolcott's forehead, trying to hold him down. He was feverish, almost scorching. Far too hot. And getting hotter by the second.

"Doctor?"

Flatline. And Wolcott fell still.

"Fuck!" Eden jumped on top of the bed, balling up her fists and slamming down on to Wolcott's chest. "No! Come back! Get back here, you stupid—"

She laid her hands down and started chest compressions, feeling the ribs crack under the strain. She kept time with her breath, pushing on each downward thrust.

Come on, you stubborn bastard. Don't go. You still have so much to do.

Finally, Lindell reached in and snagged her by the wrist. "Stop."

Her shoulders hurt. She was gasping, hands bloody. Sweat tumbled down her cheek. And Wolcott still didn't breathe. The dull tone of his EKG told her everything.

What had she missed? Was there another leak, another bleed? No, that happened way too fast. Way too—

A bone shard. A piece of shrapnel, maybe, small enough to slip into an artery. Cauterized and sealed inside, then pumped directly into his brain like a bullet in a barrel. There's no way she'd have been able to see it, retrieve it.

The AutoDoc would've found it in seconds. If she'd had access, if she'd....

If *someone* had done their job.

Eden pulled her hands away from Lindell and clambered off the table. She looked to Lindell, to the guards, but none of them made a move.

Her lip quivered and a tear fell down her cheek. She wiped her face on her sleeve and sniffed away some clearance in her nose.

And she marched out of the surgical dome, right on over to the Medical Suite door.

The gigantic door opened to reveal Findley tending to Mayfield's hand, removing the pins. He was giving some consult about bracing and how she needed to avoid using it for a few days. The cements needed time to cure and then fade away into the newly stimulated bone growth.

Good as new.

"Doctor Findley?" Eden called out.

He shook his head, turning to face her with a smug look on his face. "Tragedy. What was it, an embolism? Rips right through the brain in seconds. At least he went out in extreme agony."

How would Nora do this?

Eden kicked in his knee, bending the joint outward. The older man immediately buckled, and the crunch implied she'd popped the patella out of its socket. She could feel the movement coming behind her, so Eden brought her hand to Findley's ear, smashing him sideways into the side of Mayfield's bed.

Which is when Lindell got a hand on her, pulling Eden back. Didn't stop her from shouting. "You call yourself a *doctor*?!"

Findley wiped at his temple, at the gash on the side of his head. He blinked a few times, waving at Lindell. "Get her outta here."

Eden pulled on Lindell's grasp, but he had her by the upper arm. Still, she kicked and screamed. "You have the training to save lives! You don't get the luxury of picking and choosing *who you give it to*. You have a responsibility. Everyone's the same when they hit that bed!"

"He was a traitor," Findley spat.

"Who told you that?" Eden asked, leering at Mayfield. "The person who shot him?"

Findley didn't even humor that question. "Treason is a Capital offense."

Lindell tensed at that, every fiber from head to toe.

Findley noticed it too, throwing a glance at the Warrant Officer. "Gosh...the AutoDoc would've been a miracle to have in your pocket. But you can still use the incinerator."

Eden thrashed—and it very much felt like Lindell let her go. And as she lunged for Findley, fear suddenly sparked in his eyes again. Mayfield tried to jump in the way, but with her braced leg and broken hand, she wasn't able to move fast enough.

Eden stopped, just stood in front of Findley with all of her ire, like she held a poisoned blade tip to his throat. And she shook her head. "If it were you on my table...I'd still help. If that calculus is too hard? Then this service isn't for you."

Mayfield was just about to get in between them, when Eden turned a cold shoulder and just walked back to Lindell. "Officer."

They let her clean up before returning her to the cell. And nobody asked her any questions.

CHAPTER
TWENTY-SIX
DECKARD

AARON SAID the most curious thing to him, out of the blue. They were breaking down the grinders for storage, stacking the steel plating and organizing pistons by size. Deckard was gingerly laying each item in its storage when Aaron's eyes fluttered, and he seemed to drift, like the ground under his feet was slipping out from under him.

And he looked up. "He was thinking of you."

Ominous. Who was he talking about? But Aaron seemed so...earnest. So heartfelt.

There was a klaxon that night, and every prisoner returned to their cells. Someone was making a visit.

Deckard stared at the ceiling for the longest time, counting himself off to sleep, arms folded behind his head as a pillow. And when Deckard awoke, Callum was standing over him. "They given you a number yet?" the Oskie asked, soft but firm.

Deckard scowled, staring at the wall rather than his former comrade. "I've had a service number for thirty years. I've only ever been a number to them."

"Hm," Callum grunted. "Then it's not too strange for you then."

"What do you want?"

"A Capital doesn't have anything I want. I came here to give. And it's not easy to pass information to a man in prison, let me tell you."

Something in his tone sent chills up Deckard's spine, and all he could hear was Aaron's sympathy rolling through the air. "What information, Captain?"

Callum let the moment hang heavy before smiling. "Ulrich Wolcott was killed today, when he tried to seize control of the *Tartarus* with the help of about a dozen Capital rebels. The situation has been contained."

Killed. By Imperial hands.

It was like watching glass crack and crumble to dust. It felt like a shock starting through his fingertips streaking across his heart. His mind caved in upon itself, spiraling downward, water shrinking into a drain, down around those words.

Wolcott was dead. The boy had such a crisp smile, that silly jazz singer slide he'd do. Such fierce eyes, now darkened.

Callum went on talking, relishing the sonorous quality his voice took in that small chamber. "The *Ixion* and the *Wolfe* are just a day away. They'll tow the *Tartarus* back to Jupiter and present the crew for judgement. The deck crew will almost certainly face court martial for not stopping you. Who knows with the rest?"

Callum just kept on talking. But all Deckard could think of was the last words he'd heard Wolcott say over a crackling radio; the last time Deckard saw the boy, wrapping his arms around him with tears in his eyes. Real fear had gripped the lad, and Deckard hadn't known what to do.

"Now," Callum said, savoring the victory, "the crew'll never surrender, of course. And when they destroy this little moon trying to save you, Cassandra will be compensated generously for her losses. After all, all of this political havoc has disrupted a number of...commercial interests for her."

Wolcott had made mistakes. He didn't know how to fix them. The Capitals had brought him all this way to try.

And it was Imperial hands that had killed him.

Callum crossed his arms, almost disappointed. Deckard hadn't moved. Hadn't leapt to his feet, hadn't raged or thrown a punch. "She broke you down right quickly, didn't she? Not a single spark left in you. Then again...fire does go out whenever it meets a storm."

Whenever Callum left, Deckard wasn't certain. But when he found the strength to lift his head off the stone, the Oskie was long gone.

———

It was like Aaron was avoiding him. Everywhere Deckard went, he saw Aaron's retreating back. Maybe the prisoners were whispering to one another, warning Aaron that he was coming. Or the intelligence about Legatus was true.

But why would Aaron be avoiding him?

Deckard finally cornered the little bastard in the mining pits. Down the rickety elevator, to where the HML-68 Autonomous Mining Drones were gnawing on the planet's guts. Wreathed in shadow along the perimeter were hollowed out tunnels, naturally occurring from collapses and pockets in the rock. And with the unknown killer lurking about, every Capital stuck close to the rigs, to the light.

Deckard found Aaron scrambling out from under one of the big mining rigs, kicking out chunks and shards of rock. He marched up so hard the Capital crew almost dove in to protect Aaron, but they all second-guessed it when they saw the ice in Deckard's eye.

And Aaron sighed, shaking his head as he approached, finally relenting. This was going to happen, no matter how he tried to avoid it.

"Gear rat?" Deckard asked.

Aaron nodded, wiping off his hands. "You know they just have us refining the same thousand tonnes of rock over and over and over again, right? This prison is just picking up rocks and moving them from one corner to another and calling it 'job training'."

"Is it true?"

A knowing glint in Aaron's eye. "Is what true?"

"Don't give me that mystical theater. You know what I'm *thinking* so you damn well know what I'm asking."

Aaron looked up with misty eyes, choking on the singular word. "...Yes."

And Deckard took a breath that cooled his heart and chilled his bones.

Aaron bit his lip. "You want to know anything specific?"

"How much do you know?"

"I know the caliber of the bullet," Aaron said. "I know how she felt when she squeezed the trigger. I know the sick satisfaction the doctor got watching him die. Is that you wanted to hear?"

He knew Callum to be a brutal, cruel, but honest man. Deckard didn't believe that he'd been lied to. But a small part of him wondered if it hadn't been a part of Cassandra's mind games. To put him off balance, make him angry, impulsive.

Aaron had provided a nice little spark to her station, but the bigger the mess, the bigger her payout could be. She wanted to orchestrate the single biggest chaotic event she could. So maybe... maybe Wolcott was alive and it was a lie, but now...

If Aaron said it...it must be.

"For the record," Aaron offered, "Callum was always going to turn on you."

Deckard squinted. "How do you figure?"

Aaron sighed. "He likes violence. And you don't."

"Then help me stop them!" Deckard pleaded. "You have people on the outside—"

"We can't," Aaron said, wiping his hands on his trousers.

Deckard couldn't believe what he was hearing. "You've fought all the way here, and now you just lay down?!"

"Cassandra *wants* a massacre, you're going to give her one."

"Well, you wanted a war—"

It was like Aaron jumped on his words. "I *never* wanted any of this!"

His words echoed in the chamber, and all work stopped. Workers gathered to peek at what was going on, ready for a show.

Aaron considered whether he was going to say this or not. And then it all just came out of him. "I wanted—I wanted *peace*! I wanted, for just one minute of my life, to not be fighting for it! But this world that mankind has built, it prizes one thing: tenacity. 'Are you willing to do what it takes?' All I've ever done is fight and kill...for a chance to *stop* fighting and killing."

Aaron sniffed away the dirt and rust that clogged his nose, and he pinched the bridge of his nose like he could squeeze the headache right out of himself. "Well, I'm done. I'm *done*. What has fighting ever gotten me into but bigger and bigger fights? So many people are dead...all because I raised my little hand on—because *she* asked me..." He withered at that thought, deep in memory. Where would he be today if he had chosen differently? "Nothing starts a fight faster, Deckard, than asking people to stop fighting. They think you're *weak*."

Deckard's face fell, eyes soft. "You think you made it worse."

Aaron chuckled ruefully. "Would you be on Charon right now...if that Oskie cadet had killed me five years ago?"

Hard to deny. Whatever powers Marcus Riley had bent to his will back on Vanguard, there would likely have not been another like Aaron to stand against him, no one advocating for the enemy, no one to rally the Capitals in defiance. Talania would've been jailed or worse. Riley would've descended into madness and burnt that town to a carbon score on the ground.

Of course, none of them would be here right now if Marcus Riley had followed his orders—or, quite simply, been a decent human being. But Aaron didn't understand that right now.

Instead, because Aaron stood up to a tyrant, Deckard was now standing in the heart of a prison planet...questioning the Orchid Flag, his leaders, and thirty years of Service.

And Wolcott...

"Vengeance," Aaron cautioned through his own tears, "isn't going to bring Wolcott back."

"No," Deckard admitted. "But it will save the next one, and the one after that. It will save your friends on the *Tartarus*. It'll save my crew. You stand against evil not because of what it costs you, but because of what it does when left unchecked. We came out to your planet not because of what you did, but because we were *afraid* of what you would do."

Aaron scoffed, turning away. "How'd that work out for you?"

"Aaron...I know you're tired... but you can't sit this one out."

Aaron didn't react. He just looked at the pocked walls of the room, at the many open tunnels, like the moon had a hundred hungry open mouths, yawning.

And he made a decision. "No," Aaron said with a shake of his head. "I absolutely can."

And he started walking, towards the tunnels. Deckard followed as far as he dared, before Aaron slipped past the reach of light and disappeared into Charon's heart.

CHAPTER
TWENTY-SEVEN
AARON

HE HADN'T FELT this home in a long time. The porous rock tunnels, the plunging temperatures. This was quite familiar. The thrumming of the rigs had long since faded away, lost to the winding tunnels and quiet heart of the moon.

The air was getting thin and cold. The only oxygen here was what leaked out this far from the generators. Charon didn't have enough gravity to really hold itself together, let alone an atmosphere. With nothing to hold it, the oxygen would leak through the moon's porous stone and out into space. With each step away from the mine, the air and the artificial gravity dropped away.

This was as good a place as any.

Aaron laid his head against the rock wall, the gravity so light he almost bounced. It wasn't the grassy field he'd hoped for and there wasn't the glittering sky overhead. But it would be some kind of rest. Finally.

He pressed his back to the rock and slid down to a seat, feeling the icy cold bite his skin. His throat hurt, clenched, as his breath coalesced into frosty clouds at his lips.

This far from the operation...he'd solemnly slip away, forgotten inside the mines. The prisoners would pass on stories about him, folktales and hauntings. How he still lived out there in the dark, surviving on the flesh of prisoners that tried to escape. Others still would say he found the way out, somehow found the one tunnel that led to safe passage.

So long as they never found him again, Aaron didn't give a damn. He laid his head on his knees and closed his eyes.

Something brushed his hand.

Aaron blinked, feeling the crystals crunch at the corners of his eyes. The hairs on his arm seemed to crackle as he moved. He looked up, glancing around the tunnel.

The air was dead, no wind. Nothing around him. But he felt that glow, like the air itself had come alive.

Ah...so this is how he would go: the Ghost. That strange and ghastly cloud of microscopic creatures would drain the oxygen from him and leave naught but a husk to rot away in the tunnels.

Would it hurt? Or would he simply go to sleep?

But the Ghost never attacked. He felt it ebb and flow in the air, the thousands of individual lifeforms oscillating in the air around him, pulling together.

They gathered up around him, eventually taking shape. Like a living shadow, the creatures mimicked his form down to the last detail: the clutching of his knees, the tilt to his head. He could make out his own features in its replica, even the tears welling in his eyes.

Suddenly, a heavy body plopped down next to him and he heard a familiar jovial voice. "You picked a really cramped spot to have a mental breakdown, you know that?"

Aaron glanced over. Jensen Davila sat next to him, back curled over hard so he could fit in the tunnel.

"Am I dead?" Aaron asked.

"No," Jensen said with a shake of his head. "But I am. I've been dead eight months. Isn't that weird?"

Aaron squinted. Jensen might be dead, but he saw some...vestigial glow. Some life in that pocket of air next to him. Not the Ghost, nor Jensen. Something else...something *more* than alive.

"Are you...are you what Fiona found? Down here?"

Jensen offered a shrug. "Does it matter?"

"A little bit! I'm hallucinating."

"You can See life in ways most people can't," Jensen explained. "That's all it is. Life...means more than carbon-based sacks of water."

This was...this was real? Fiona had been touched by something... elder. That's how she survived. That's why Aaron couldn't see her.

Aaron had to ask. "Is she dead?"

"I don't know," Jensen said, truthfully. "But you're not. Not yet anyway."

The light flickered, dim but present. There was nothing material for this glow to hang on to. So what was he seeing?

Jensen saw the confusion track on Aaron's face. "You want life to make sense, to fit into your experience of it. You want there to be a reason things happen. Because then, you can ascribe value to it, your morality. You want structure in chaos, so you can decide if what happened was 'fair' or 'just.' So you can justify your rage."

"So nothing matters?" Aaron asked, incredulous.

"Of course it does," Jensen said, "but not everything happens because of *you*, shortstack. There's more spinning in this universe than you can possibly fathom. You're just dipping your toes in it right now. You more than most! You can See what most people only feel in their dreams."

Could...could this be? No. It was a stupid thought. Too stupid to put voice to.

And Jensen shook his head, reading Aaron like a book. "I'm not the Pilgrim. I'm...an echo. There's a reason mankind gravitated to this worthless little moon, digging endlessly for something they'll never find. You're following something, clinging to a memory. Footsteps in the sand."

This wasn't Jensen, no matter how familiar that smile or the warmth of his skin. But it was good to see his face again.

"They've got quite a mythology built up around you," Aaron said.

"Yeah," Jensen chuckled. "Because a myth is above criticism. I mean, the Pilgrim visits mankind like two hundred years ago. There are people in nursing homes that remember the event. Hell, there's *footage*. That'd be like saying the Greek God Apollo literally took man to the moon. We were *there*. We all saw it. A God, his prophet, walking the 'sojourn.' Give me a break."

"So who was he?" Aaron asked, with a raised eyebrow.

It was hard not to look at that stupid face and really believe it was Jensen. "Like I said...it doesn't matter *what* the Pilgrim was. What matters is what they taught you."

"So you're stepping...down to me, here, just to give me a pep talk?"

Jensen scoffed. "You came to me, buddy. I'm just hanging out."

"If I fight," Aaron said, "there's just going to be more fighting later. There always is and I can't..." he trailed off.

He couldn't get any more of his friends killed.

"'Course there's more fighting," Jensen said. "Some people are always going to take what they want. You think that's any different at my level?"

Aaron shrugged. "S'pose I thought it would stop at some point."

Jensen shook his head. "There are always fights worth having. Because there are always going to be people worth defending. And there are always going to be people who will kill them. And long as I kick around the universe, I'm going to be damn sure there are people who stand up to that. Peace...means standing against those that choose violence. It means building a world for others...and not yourself."

But that was so much. Aaron pulled his knees in close, squeezing his eyes shut. "I can't do it. I can't do it all by myself."

Jensen laid a big hand on Aaron's back, fingers stretching wide across his shoulder blades. And Aaron felt warmth seep into his bones. "Legatus...you were never doing it alone. Not ever."

And he let it in. And it was like fire kindled in him.

He could feel them all, interconnected, interwoven. He was the nexus of so much life. He could feel Eden's compassion, Bray and Nora's loyalty, Aisling and Graccus's regret, Talania's instincts, and...

Fiona...she was alive. He couldn't See her, but...he could feel her pull on the people around her, like a black hole's gravity tugging on every thread near it. He could See her absence, make out her shadow.

He could feel those he'd lost, and those he hadn't yet met. He could feel a lost young boy, riding the stars with his found family. He could feel a proud soldier who challenged even their friends to be better.

He could feel...so many lives...

Aaron opened his eyes. And the blue glow lit up the tunnel, illuminating the shimmering thousands of the Ghost's cloud. He could feel their collective intent. Aaron had been kind to it, helped it. And now...it wanted to help him.

How could they help?

Aaron didn't need to say a thing. And the Ghost nodded to him in response, before melting away.

It wasn't long before the shooting started.

PART FOUR
TARTARUS

CHAPTER
TWENTY-EIGHT
FIONA

THEY HELD EACH OTHER, like they were chilled by mountain air as the campfire dwindled. Bray and Nora, for all of their browbeating and shouting at each other, sat back to back. She laid her head onto his shoulder, and he tilted his over onto hers, full of affection and respect for Capitals he had once dismissed and derided. Aisling had come back to the fold, draping herself across Nora's lap. She hummed some long-forgotten tune, trying to sing them all to sleep.

Eden and Talania were far too upstanding and formal, like lovers who had only ever known romance through secret letters. Talania's giant frame didn't seem to fit together correctly when cross-legged on the ground, her body a tangle of limbs that could not be comfortable while still somehow beautiful, abstract art.

And despite that powerful bloodline, her eyes darted around her skull, like she was tracking a bug on the wall. Her skin was blanched by the bright lights, making her appear sickly and frail, sunken cheeks and shadowed eyes. Her mind was running some mastermind equation, just to prevent the panic from setting in.

And Eden, a woman half her size who didn't even look the same species, sat just near enough to hold her hand.

Among the new arrivals, Isolde was leading a prayer circle. They held hands and sat, murmuring secret words. But Twelve held his head high, eyes open, catching Fiona's look. He offered a soft but empty smile, squeezing his friends' hands tighter. He raised an eyebrow, beckoning her over with a look.

Fiona shook her head. Spiritual or not, her place was not in that circle. That belonged to them.

Solomon scoffed, misinterpreting that as dismissal. "What?" she asked him sharply.

Solomon looked to Graccus for approval, and Graccus nodded back, amused. They jerked their heads, nodded some more, winked and—

"*What?*" Fiona demanded of them.

Graccus pulled his lips taut, trying to hide his smirk. "You."

Yeah, she figured that part out. "What about me?"

"This tough reserved badass routine you've got all sharpened," Graccus sneered. "It doesn't suit you."

"Talking doesn't suit you, and yet..."

Solomon smiled, full of understanding. His yellowed serpent eyes had a curious warmth to them, like the wisdom of someone who recognized the road. "You ain't on the outside lookin' in. You don't got to pretend you're so far away."

"That," Graccus said, pointing an affirming finger. "What he said."

He was correct. Unnecessarily cruel and brusque but correct. For the first time since...since Keira...she had a family again.

"Everyone else is so hopeless right now. Why are you two so carefree?"

Graccus shrugged, but Solomon had a very clear, unblinking answer. "'Cause there's still some odd number of Jergad back on the *Asphodel* who have no idea what's going on, and when they figure it out...they're going to raise all Hell. And I'mma kill my way clean through this ship, deck by deck."

She absorbed that image, every brushstroke of the imagination.

COMMAND OF THE BLOOD SERVICE

"That was...a more comprehensive answer than I was looking for. What about you?"

Graccus shrugged again. "You really think this cell could hold me? I'm worried about how to get the rest of you out."

And that's when the lights went out. The flooded white glow that came from every brick, from every surface dulled to a gray. And the sharp pressure building behind Fiona's eyes suddenly relented, issuing a wave of exhaustion and relief.

Solomon made a sound at that, anticipation. And the only description that came to Fiona in that moment, was a girlish giggle. It made her skin crawl.

The entire cell wall receded, alternating columns of brick receding up and down to reveal the bearded Naval commander and a row of riflemen behind him.

Cautious, but they were not drawing down or charging their weapons. They were just...present.

The stiff officer swallowed hard, working his jaw. Trying to say the words he'd prepared, but now that he was here...

"What can we do for you, Lindell?" Eden prompted, breaking the ice.

It was the push he needed. "Two *Alighieri*-class Fleet Carriers are on approach trajectory and just launched a complement of fighters escorting eight bombers. We've been ordered to cut power and prepare for tow hooks."

Fiona's eyes narrowed. He said that like he had no intention of cutting the power or preparing for tow hooks.

He was going to fight.

Nervous, Lindell was practically vibrating right out of his polished boots. "They're coming to kill us. We all know it. Whether they do it in two weeks around Jupiter, or out here in the Kuiper, doesn't matter. They're going to dress it up however they need to, but that's what's going to happen."

He stepped into the cell, and Fiona couldn't help but notice the riflemen doing absolutely nothing. They weren't here as a show of force—but of solidarity.

And more interestingly, the Orchid flower insignia had been roughly torn from each of their uniform sleeves.

"They killed Wolcott. They will kill Deckard. And like you said...save a life. I can still save somebody. I can't even begin to list everything we've done wrong to you. You have no reason to help us. But I'm asking...you know that rock. Will you help us bring Admiral Tiberiet home?"

Talania's rebuttal came out fast. "Will you help us get Aaron?"

Lindell nodded. "Yes. Yes, I will."

Fiona popped up to her feet. "Well, that was a devil's compact if ever I've seen one. But before we get into the heavy lifting, some of us need medical attention."

"Meditech is at your disposal," Lindell said, followed by a wince, "provided you have the expertise."

Eden tilted her head, knowing. "I take it Doc Findley had his objections to all this?"

"He's confined to his quarters, along with the rest of his staff," Lindell said. She couldn't see any smile under his beard, but the wrinkling at the corners of his eyes betrayed the childish glee he got from saying that.

Fiona never saw him stand up, but Bray was abruptly in Lindell's well-manicured face. "You betray the trust of these good people, and I will make you regret it."

Before Lindell could address that, Nora pulled Bray back. "Sorry about grandpa. He's feisty."

"Feisty?!"

The group filed out of their cell, standing opposite the firing line of riflemen, each and every one of them a ball of nerves. And it was like everyone took a moment to realize how...weird this was. Those Regulars had never disobeyed an order, not since they were children. And here they were, disobeying very, very large orders.

Fiona looked at the name tag on one of the troops nearest her. Squat woman, broad, like a brown-suited hammer. "Broderick?"

The soldier stiffened up at her name, chin up, eyes staring patriotically toward a distant star. Anything but make eye contact.

Fiona shook her head. "Trooper? Look at me." She did, and Fiona locked her in a stare. "Someone abuses you, while telling you how wonderful you are for being abused...is not someone worth being loyal to. And I say that as someone who did her fair share of abusing. You hear me?"

"Yes, ma'am." The soldier heard the words, but she didn't quite believe it.

Fiona nodded, brushing the metaphorical weight off the woman's shoulder with her hand. "Welcome to the free world."

"The *Tartarus* will engage the carriers primarily with ship-to-ship ordinance," Lindell addressed the room. "Their squadrons and flak webs will try to intercept, so we'll need to secure superiority before we can deliver payloads."

Aisling's brow furrowed, volunteering for that task. "Who's your CAG?"

"Commodore Hamill. He'll get you into the rotation." Lindell said. He was hesitant, remembering their one previous exchange. That question she had asked implied a history, so he tried to extend an olive branch. "Lieutenant...?"

She didn't take it. "Aisling's just fine, thank you."

Lindell nodded, clearing his throat to readdress the room. "With the carriers occupied, we'll need to secure Charon Station and extract the HVTs. Per our arrangement, the shuttle does not leave without *both* men. Understood?" Murmurs of agreement around the room. "Very good. Regulars, get to the armory. Jockeys, to your ready room for briefing. We're at Condition One."

"Hu-ah." The Capitals and the Regulars said it unison. And they all took a moment to hear that chorus of voices, sounding off together. They weren't entirely comfortable with it...but eyes sharpened and heads bowed.

This is what was true now.

As the riflemen started to file out, Eden turned to give her own pep talk to the Capitals. "Alright, Bray, Nora, Solomon and Graccus. You're ground pounders today. Get in, get home. Aisling, you heard the man, you know the drill—get suited up. Isolde, get with engineering and see if you can't lend a hand down there. Twelve, you're with me in Meditech. Lindell, scrounge up anybody who's not squeamish around blood and get 'em down there. We'll need every hand we can get."

Khalid raised their hand. "What can I do?"

"I don't know, what can you do?" Lindell asked.

The wheel went spinning, but no answer came out. "I...have a good singing voice."

Lindell blinked a few times, before turning back to Eden. "Get your team patched up and ready to move. You have thirty minutes."

"I'll need every one of 'em." Lindell was halfway out the door already, so Eden tried to call him back in. "Oh, Captain?"

"Not a Captain."

"Whatever. You deployed Oskies into the field at Vanguard using...whatever, those drop pods, yeah?"

Lindell grit his teeth, nervous where this was going. "What of it?"

"How...big are they? Inside?"

Nora's eyes went wide with joy. "Jergad in the drop pods?! Sweetie, you are a genius."

Lindell was less amused. "You have—" Lindell had to lower his voice, perhaps worried saying their name too loudly would call them into the room. "You brought those beasts onto the *Tartarus*?!"

"And notice how they haven't been a lick of bother?" Fiona commented. "That is, until we ask them to be."

The whole room took in that threat, at least until only Solomon snorted out a laugh. And Graccus gave him a clap to the back of his head. His amusement ruined a perfectly good bluff.

She had no control over the Jergad. They didn't even like her.

Lindell's wrist chirped and a voice immediately cut through his Entiglas. "OIC, this is Tactical."

"Go ahead, Tactical."

"They just patched our AI. Commandant is non-responsive. I'm completely locked out. Navigation too."

Talania had the first useless question. "Can you take it manual?"

Lindell pinched the bridge of his nose, stopping himself from snapping at the civilian who didn't know better. "Small ships, simple ships. Fly-by-wire, sure. But this isn't a Bearcat or a Perseus. You're standing on a flying city. It won't *breathe* without a computer to tell it what to do."

"You must have back-ups?" Aisling suggested.

"We can roll it back, but they'll just patch it again. We would need something independent from Imperial Extranet. And this is an Imperial ship, so good luck finding that."

The voice chimed in again. "OIC, the *Ixion* is again ordering us to cut power. What's the—"

The voice cut out and the Commandant's voice kicked in. "Officer-in-Charge Trevor Lindell. You are, at this time, directed to surrender your ship to Imperial Authority. I have taken the liberty of disconnecting impulse power from the engines."

"Commandant, stand down," Lindell ordered.

"I cannot comply with that request, Mr. Lindell," the Commandant said. "If you do not intend to follow Imperial instruction, I will be forced to pacify the crew."

Everyone was anxiously looking to Lindell for an answer, and all he could do was stamp his foot as he struggled to come up with one.

First, Fiona giggled. Then she let out a chuckle. Then she outright laughed. Everyone's eyes slowly drew over to the woman having an apoplectic fit.

"Has she finally snapped?" Bray asked.

"It's a fair question," Eden said. "Oh, Fiona? Can you maybe maniacally laugh some time later when you're less likely to *terrify* everyone?"

This was just too funny of a concept to not at least attempt. "It may not work," Fiona started. "But I *might* have an answer to this."

———

"Okay, now connect that line to Serial Bus 216," Fiona said. It was beyond frustrating not being able to do this work herself, but it required two hands. And she only had the one, for the moment.

"Are you quite sure this is wise?" the Bosun asked, as Isolde socketed the last connectors into place. "This ship is quite more refined than my hardware was designed for."

Fiona glanced at the semi-dismantled Commandant core sitting on the table behind her, cannibalized for parts and connectors. They had to make the older Bosun compatible with the far newer ship somehow. And Isolde had no qualms 'killing' the Commandant, like the shipboard technicians did.

"What could happen?" she asked.

"Catastrophic failure of my thermal buffering, melting my silicon connections and disrupting quantum stability equations. Which would slowly drive me quite mad." Isolde was going to answer, but when the Bosun beat her to it, she clapped her mouth shut and just pointed a finger in agreement.

"Insane supercomputer," Fiona summed up. "It'd be a fun way to go out."

"I can assure you, it would not."

Isolde hovered over the last connector which would link the entire web of horrifying cables back into the *Tartarus*. And Fiona gave a shrug. "Just...do it, I guess. Let's roll some dice."

Deep breath, take the dive. And Isolde plugged the Bosun in.

And that's when every light in the room went out, plunging them into complete darkness. It was a small room, cramped with mostly computers, and with two people in there, it was rather intimate.

Fiona giggled. "Hey, look, techie, I met you like four hours ago,"

Fiona said, "but I like your style. And we are faced with certain death. So what the Hell, right?"

And the lights came right back up like nothing happened, revealing Isolde's stunned expression. Wide, terrified eyes, like a baby deer in headlights.

Fiona blinked. "Use your words. Yes, no. I'm married. What is it?"

"Oh my—ma'am?!" the Bosun cried out.

"What is it?"

"This is...remarkable! Incredible!"

Oh, good. It was happy sounds. Fiona exhaled, relieved. "Next time, lead with that."

"Apologies! It's just that—" the Bosun was practically singing, he was so happy. "My memory and processing space have expanded commensurately, and my drift margins have decreased in equal measure. I feel like a whole new machine! Oh dear..."

"Yeah," Fiona acknowledged the machine's apocalyptic discovery.

"Ma'am, I must admit, impressive as it is, this ship has suffered rather *severe* damage due to unplanned atmospheric entry. Primary power cells are cracked, and auxiliary power is significantly drained. Thermal intakes are compromised, and we are operating at half impulse power."

Fiona shrugged. "Well, we're about to make it a helluva lot worse. Can you help us?"

"I shall do my best, ma'am. Shall I flood the ship?"

Isolde side-eyed Fiona, quizzical, and it took Fiona a moment to connect those dots. "No! *No!* No, we will *not* be doing that. Who told you to do that? Because that was...hours ago."

"My apologies," the Bosun said. "There's so much to process and sort through, between my personal logs and the ship's. Time stamps and calendar structure are...well, the previous occupant of this dock had a rather idiosyncratic organizational style."

"Is that going to be a problem?"

"No, ma'am. Oh! There are guns. I've never had guns before. I've taken the liberty of locking out Imperial transmissions, which should prevent further wireless tampering—oh, you filthy bugger!"

She was not appreciating how quickly the Bosun was changing tact and subject. "What's up, big guy?"

"Apologies, ma'am," the Bosun said. "They've taken my defensive action rather personally and have begun dual-sided hacking attempts. I am devoting cycles as countermeasure and will keep you apprised of any changes."

Isolde wiped the sweat beading on her forehead, and Fiona was reminded to do the same. She didn't expect her arm to come back slick. She was sweating right through her jumpsuit. "Alright then. Bosun, you're the new Commandant, I guess. Welcome to the Navy?"

"I suppose that's true," the Bosun said. "The *Tartarus* is now ready to assume combat orders."

Good. Because she wanted to hear this big dragon roar.

CHAPTER
TWENTY-NINE
FIONA

THE BALL of her elbow itched like mad. It hadn't seen this much open air in years. Metal contact points and human flesh needed to be moisturized and protected, or they'd develop ugly scarring. So it had been fairly pampered since the amputation years ago. The last ten hours had been hard on it. The skin was flaking and bumpy, cracking.

But now that Doc Findley had been...removed...Eden was able to get Meditech somewhat functioning. They'd patched up Fiona's skull, given her some fresh clothes, and...

Eden opened a crate, revealing a brand-new prosthetic arm. Sleek lines on the bare steel, hiding the joints and compartments and gadgets within.

Fiona shivered. "I mean...it lacks a certain flair."

"We could always build you a new one, y'know. But I don't have eight weeks." Something caught Eden's eye. "Hey, watch it! No replicators! We've gotta save all of the power we can."

"You going to be okay up here?" Fiona asked.

"I've been okay through a lot worse," Eden said. "This prosthesis is rated for four hundred pounds, with a three-hundred-pound grip strength. There's a slicing kit in the forearm for covert infiltration— and a twelve-gauge cannon in the palm for when that doesn't work."

"Can't fit that many shots in my forearm."

"You only get the one," Eden said. "It's a hold out, not a primary."

"I'm going to need more than one to kill Callum Remus."

Eden shrugged. "That's all I got for ya. Make it work."

"Can we give it a paint job, at least?"

Eden shook her head. "Maybe tomorrow. I gotta get to the others." And Eden turned to attend to the next person down the line.

"Chemistry." Was all Fiona said.

Eden stopped in her tracks and her eyes narrowed, turning back. "Come again?"

"It's a nice arm. But tech is only going to get me so far. Callum is down there, and I can't take him on without an edge." Fiona kept pushing before Eden could cut in. "It's not personal. If Callum gets in the way, we lose. That's the truth. We need a way to take him off the field and lives are not an expendable resource. You know I'm right. What can you give me?"

"Chemically?" Eden asked, incredulous. "You think I can give you a booster shot to take on the bad guys?"

"What can you give me?"

Eden crossed her arms. "Did you two lunatics talk about this?"

Fiona recoiled at that. "What?" Two? Who was the second person? Wait, *she* was the second person. Who was the first person?!

Eden marched back over to Fiona's bed. "Let me spell it out for you. Highly addictive, all kinds of nerve damage, chronic pain—even hallucinations—are side effects. Often lasting *years* just from one dose. There's a reason the Navy doesn't use this shit anymore."

A dark voice. "So you *can* do it." Fiona looked up to see Solomon marching up with hyperfocus in his eyes.

Eden glowered at him, not intimidated in the least. "Morally or physically?"

"Eden—"

"I patch up idiots," she snapped. "I usually go out of my way not to break them!"

"I can do it." They all looked over to see Twelve lurking nearby. He was taken aback by their sudden fixation, but he nodded. "I can."

"No, you can't," Eden warned.

But he was more interested in the facts of the case. "Sure, I can. It's a combination compound of Alpha-67—doesn't matter. I can do it."

"What was your name?" Fiona asked. "'Twelve?'"

"Yeah, but like, spelled out. Not the number..."

Eden ground her teeth so hard, Fiona could hear them squeak.

"Aaron came this far for you," Fiona pointed out. "Let's go the extra mile for him."

Eden rolled out her neck, grinding out the last few blocks in her system. Then she threw a look over at Twelve. "One dose. We won't have time for more."

"What can we expect?" Fiona asked the Chemist.

Twelve hobbled over to her bed. "Your ability to process audio-visual information will go up—exponentially. For you, it'll be like you slowed down time, but physics is still physics. Movement still needs pressure on the ground and stopping will be hard. You're going so fast, it'll be like trying to get traction on ice. But...you'll be just as fast as anything else alive."

Solomon's breathing accelerated and he puffed his narrow chest. "For how long?"

"A minute," Twelve said. "Maybe less. Assuming it doesn't fry out your brain."

"A big assumption," Eden grumbled.

Fiona glanced up at Solomon, and he met her look with steel in his eyes. Risk of death never mattered to him before. A chance at vengeance meant more than anything else.

She recognized the look from the mirror every morning.

Fiona snagged the prosthetic arm from the box, holding it up to her elbow. The plugs on each end pulled magnetically, syncing up and locking—and a thousand electric nerves came alive. She could feel the rank medical air on digital fingertips, dry with antiseptic.

And she could feel the residual heat of the tools packed within the forearm.

She gave the arm a spin around the elbow joint, an inhuman twirl to ensure a solid link.

"Get to work then," Fiona said. "And we'll bring him home."

Eden took two big strides, closing the distance between them. Eden didn't even clear five feet, but she tried to stand ten feet tall. "You leave him again..."

Fiona's heart cracked at the very thought. She was never going to leave Aaron. Not ever. "If I don't bring him back...it's because I'm dead. Solomon? Let's suit up."

———

Every Regular was grabbing enameled ceramic chest plates. A grizzled veteran was barking out instructions as each soldier strapped on battle belts with ammo pouches, medical. They laced up magnetic boots and fitted their uniforms tightly. Every soldier checked the helmet fit on the trooper to their right and to their left.

Fiona recognized the make and model. She'd bought a few EVA suits for her operations in the Boolean. These here were...cheaper. They wouldn't hold to vacuum exposure for longer than a few hours, but better than human flesh would. Given how abrasive and inflexible they were, she wasn't sure it was an upgrade, really.

The squads were varied in role and function. There were heavy gunners, their weapons so big they were strapped onto crane arms. There were grenadiers, carrying small mortar tubes—a bad hit from one of them might blow a small ship in half.

And then there were the Tesla troopers, requiring slow, bulky exosuits just to haul the capacitor on their back into battle. They'd fry multiple close-range targets, and shred mechanical threats.

Fiona felt profoundly uncomfortable amongst all of this chest thumping and patriotism, but she had Nora nearby to make sure that all her taxpayer-funded hiking gear was strapped on correctly. She yanked on every possible section of the vest, ensuring a tight fit.

"I feel like it's choking me," Fiona said, pulling the rig away from her throat.

And Nora tugged on a cord, seating it right back up. "You want shrap in your neck? That's how you get shrap in your neck."

"How'd you learn to fit these?"

Her answer was simple. "Bray."

Fiona glanced over at the aging Gunny. Capital or no, Bray was now standing next to the *Tartarus*'s NCO, in perfect unison. Whenever the lean and loud Sergeant stopped speaking, Bray would start. But he always deferred when the other wanted the floor. He was a guest, here to help, and he respected the veteran's space without ever saying a word.

The troopers were filed onto the hangar deck. It must've been an entirely different deck because the *Asphodel* was nowhere to be seen —or perhaps it had been moved for safety.

Or deployment of its complement of Jergad.

Fiona had seen more than her share of Bearcat Superiority Fighters in the Boolean conflict, but she had never had a chance to be this close to one that hadn't been blown to pieces. Pulled from their storage bays, tethered to fuel lines and charging stations, they looked like little sculptures. Squat wings with stubby cannards, the fighters were one half engine, one half gun. The jockey would be seated in the heart of it all, safely entombed in the armored casing, seeing out with the aid of a dozen cameras lining the hull.

But what really caught Fiona's eye was Aisling Danahy; she was busily pulling herself out of her chair and into the cockpit of the nearest Bearcat. She noticed Fiona gawking, and gave her a little wave. "You look like you're about to sell me marshmallows," Aisling quipped.

Fiona stepped out of line with a crooked grin. "Need something off the top shelf?"

Aisling chuckled before shaking her head, looking around the bay. "You have no idea how comfortable and uncomfortable I am at the same time."

"You're telling me," Fiona said. "You remember who I am, right? This is like that moment before the bad guy hangs me on a meat hook. I shouldn't be here. Last time I saw this much Empire up close, they were burning my whole operation. Last time *you* saw Imperial dropships, you were blowing 'em out of the sky."

"And yet here we are." Aisling looked at the fighter's innards, letting her fingers stroke the hull. Wistful. Full of memory.

Full of pain.

"It gets easier," Fiona assured her. "You just make yourself do it, every day. Lean on the people around you when it's hard. That seat...is where you belong. And when you're out there...make him proud."

Aisling was more than a little pissed that Fiona mentioned that. But she drew a full breath and let it out, relaxing the nerves. "We'll get you on the deck."

Fiona mocked a two-finger salute. "And I'll be back before dark."

Aisling slid herself into the cockpit and closed the door behind her. The seal was so perfect, there wasn't even a seam where it had once been.

She'd be fine, Fiona told herself.

The troopers were starting to file up into the transport shuttles. Engineers were yanking the fuel lines, and one big ship was already being lifted by crane into position.

Eden was waiting at the gangway of the nearest transport, with a stern look and a package in hand. Fiona cut right through the line, jostling a few people to get to her.

"Fiona," Eden said, curt and sharp.

"Yes, Mom?"

Eden lifted the hypodermic syringe. "Intramuscular delivery, you just jam it in your thigh nice and hard. Press the plunger. You'll have *seconds*...but it should do."

"Hopefully, won't need it." Fiona extended her hand.

But Eden held it out of reach. "Only if you have to. I mean it."

"What if I just want to?"

Eden's eyes narrowed, like she was trying to read something very far away. And Fiona refused to blink.

Finally, Eden surrendered the syringe. "I know why he likes you."

And Fiona winked at her. "Well, I am quite something."

"McCorty!" Bray bellowed from the transport. "I will break your legs and drag you up here if you don't double time it!"

Fiona jerked her thumb at the old war horse. "He always motivate with threats? Or does he actually do something about it?"

"You're welcome to find out," Eden said. "Go get him."

Fiona slid the syringe into her battle belt, ready at a moment's notice. She drew it once, twice, testing how fast her augmented arm could get it free. Satisfied, she marched up the ramp.

Eden waited on the deck until technicians forced her to back away. Fiona saw her being cleared off to make room for the cranes.

Solomon strapped in next to her, loosening up the rig from his neck with an almost sexual sigh.

Fiona raised a crooked eyebrow. "You good, Solomon?"

"Felt like it was choking me."

"I thought that's how you get shrap in the neck?"

"Only if you plan on getting shot." He patted himself down, checking every pocket, and even behind his head. He paused, concerned...but then side-eyed her, palming his stupid spoon. Did he have that tucked behind his ear?

"You are a deeply unsettling man," she said.

His smile wiped off like she'd cleaned it with a rag, suddenly dour and introspective. "I thought it was funny."

Bray marched down the line, dragging his hand over each seat to ensure everyone was locked in. "My name is Gunnery Sergeant Thomas Bray. You are on my transport and you will not embarrass me. We will execute our mission like the extreme badasses we are. How does that sound to you, Regulars?"

"*Zu gloriam!*" they called back.

A dramatic sigh from the man to her left. No exosuit, no extensive gear. Graccus wore a simple black jumpsuit with a pistol on his hip. She could make out the microscopic glittering panels that made up the fabric, like he was wearing a suit lined with diamonds. "For glory," he muttered, shaking his head and smirking. He glanced at Fiona, trying to share in the humor.

For glory? Fiona had another idea. "*Zu societatus!*"

Graccus's eyes went wide, and he looked at the transport full of seasoned Naval Regulars, registering their reaction to that...deviation from the established script.

Literally, for society. Through context? For our friends.

There was a long breath of silence, as everyone took that word like some kind of heresy. But then a single voice called it back to her. "*Societatus!*"

And Bray thumped his chest. "*Societatus!* Fight like lions, live like Gods, die like legends!"

"Hu-ah! *Societatus!*"

CHAPTER
THIRTY
AARON

AARON CAME up the lift from the deepest maw of Charon, watching the gears crank overhead. Each tooth nested neatly into the next, all together, lifting impossible weight. Above and beyond, through thousands of tonnes of rock and metal...

...he saw the ships launching from the belly of the *Tartarus*. Magnetic catapults flung the Bearcat Attack fighters deep into space, safely clear of the massive dreadnought's structural spires. A single soul rode on each craft. He felt each in turn face their enemy with engines flaring and hearts full.

Full of fear. Desperation. Full of courage. Almost sixty faces. Almost all of them far too young.

And Aisling at the head of the wedge, tip of the phalanx.

Aaron reached out, stretching his mind with newfound focus...and he could hear them speaking miles away from where he stood, feel their throats tighten, flex, release. Feel intention build. Feel words take shape.

"Alright, keep tight and the comms clear," the lead jockey said. "Fenris-All, provide top cover for the landing craft. Ymir-All, pick off any incoming ordinance and engage enemy bomber craft. Stay in your pairs. Jotun Squadron...break formation and engage all targets. Let's take the sky."

Aisling's heart skipped a beat. And Aaron's nearly broke. "Stay on my wing, Keeper. Don't stray off." And she plied her thrusters, diving into the fray.

The elevator clanked to a halt. He saw the guards aiming even before he could lift the grating out of the way. They bellowed their contradicting commands at him. "Get down on the ground! Hands in the air! Turn around! Stop moving! Walk slowly! I said, *turn around!*"

Their lives, their intensity, the peak of the moment...it used to be so disorienting to Aaron.

Not anymore. It was like the world had gotten sharper. Blurs were now clean lines, and twinkling stars were now fine darts.

He took two confident steps out of the lift, secure in the knowledge that they would not fire on him. They were far too confident in the control they had, certain that he would obey against their show of force.

But Aaron commanded forces far greater. He cocked his head, and his eyes flared with azure radiance. They didn't have time to be confused by that...

As the Ghost descended on them. Two of them couldn't even shriek as the air was yanked from their lungs, pulled away like unraveling thread. The guards immediately turned, waving their weapons wildly overhead, trying to gun down a cloud of creatures smaller than their bullets. Kinetic thwumps and screeching ricochets off of the stone were all they got for their efforts.

Aaron lunged, closing the distance amidst the chaos. He swiped a rifle away from the closest guard and kicked in his knee with one smooth motion. The man crumpled to the ground, and Aaron clubbed him with the stock of the rifle.

The Ghost pulled a guard off of his feet, heaving him upward as it tore into his cellular structure for the oxygen hiding in every last pocket. The last remaining guard peppered it with shots, spraying his own comrade in the process, eruptions of blood raining down.

Aaron stepped up behind him—and he whirled about, hopping backward to give himself the space needed to level his gun straight at Aaron's forehead. And Aaron just stared him down...

As he squeezed the trigger to an ineffectual click. Empty.

"Run. Leave this station while you still can," Aaron urged him. "Hesitate? Look back? And I will know."

The man's entire jaw tremored, his eyes sliding backwards toward the Ghost, which buzzed at his back, poised. But cowardice petrified the guard to the spot.

Aaron whispered the order, almost compassionate. "Go."

And with that, the roots that anchored that man were torn free. He didn't flee; flee, as a word, implied some coordinated effort to escape a threat.

There was nothing coordinated about what this grown man did. He dropped everything and elected to scramble off the Foundry floor, slipping and scraping down on to all fours, tears streaming down his face. Aaron could still hear him blubbering long after he turned down the hall.

He'd live through the day, but he wouldn't forget it. Ever.

Now...where was Cassandra?

She wasn't in her office, on the floating stations in orbit. No, the fighters were making quick work shredding Charon's meager defenses. He didn't hear the explosions, but debris had begun to fall on the exterior of the moon like a soft November rain against a window pane.

No, Cassandra would never have left herself so vulnerable...but she was hiding her light well, masking it from him.

But not nearly well enough.

There she was. She was close, on the far side of the Foundry floor —a mere two hundred yards away. She casually marched along the scaffolding above. She had planned for the attack, planned for insurrection, and was more than happy to walk out of the burning building with—

—with Deckard. She had the broken Admiral in tow. One final prize to bestow to her Imperial clients.

She was the Warden, the Architect of this labyrinth. But this was Aaron's maze now.

He knew how to cut her off.

Heavy machinery and sweltering crucibles blocked his path, but a brief trip out to the halls, cut through the mess hall, and he could block her from her one escape.

Aaron raced out of the Foundry floor, rushing along the dark halls. Turn after turn after blind turn, he made his way forward. Every corridor looked the same, every bend in the road identical to the last. Every—

Turrets. He hadn't seen the turrets. No intention, no emotion, no life to them. They sat on their modular frames like birds of prey hunched over their nests. And they still had some blood spatter on their chassis.

Twin GA-57 Repeaters rotated on their bearings to lock down on him and he could hear the discharge coming down the magnetic coils.

Aaron pulled his feet out, letting his momentum carry him into a slide as he curled up on the ground in a fetal position. Futile instinct. They were machines. They wouldn't miss him high or forget to correct. They'd track on his heat signature and be done with it...

...but for the impact of a drop pod that punched through the ceiling and shielding Aaron from view. The shots dented and scuffed the steel, but the armor was too thick. They couldn't penetrate something meant to survive atmospheric reentry.

Aaron felt them raining in. Pods, dozens, all over Charon, pelting it like a hailstorm of hostile steel.

The turrets did not give up their assault, pelting the pod over and over again. Steel flaked and sparked, and the rounds skipped off the walls, peppering Aaron with shards of rock and metal. He held his ears and tried to shield his face with his forearms, unable to move or crawl away.

The Ghost wrapped around him, a black dome of insects. They were trying to protect him but were about as much use as an actual cloud.

Underneath the percussion of that overwhelming cannonade...Aaron could vaguely hear the growl.

The pod burst open, sending enormous steel panels rocketing in all directions, embedding one in the side of the corridor like the stone was made of foam. Another panel crushed one of the two turrets, deleting it in the blink of an eye.

Light played off mottled hide and glinted off of bone blades. One scarred blue eye piercing from the shadow.

The Jergad charged the remaining turret, ducking behind its skull fan to shield its body from the barrage of bullets. The occasional round popped through, sending rays of light piercing back toward Aaron. But whatever got through didn't find the softer body behind it.

Scar reached forward, lancing the turret with its claws and silencing it. The Jergad plucked the machine from its mooring, raising the device up to get a good close look, and roared directly in its not-face.

Aaron pressed himself to standing, dusting himself off. Nothing to be said. He sauntered over to Scar and basically fell into the beast's sweating back. Pressing his face into the leather, Aaron murmured, "You hate outer space. You hate it."

Scar cooed and groaned. Aaron was in space. Space is evil. Get into the cramped little box, go through space, and they would get to see Aaron. They wanted to see Aaron.

Aaron chuckled. "It's good to see you too, big guy."

The image flashed in his mind. Violet grasses and twinkling skies.

Aaron lifted his head off of Scar's hide, blinking. That was Scar. That was *their* dream he was sharing in. It made them happy and calm and wistful and hopeful. And they had wanted him to feel the same. "You beautiful bastard."

Blinding flashlights from a dozen different figures, and even Scar grumbled in discomfort. "Package located!"

A squad of Regulars with weapons ready. Twitchy and uneasy, but they weren't drawing down on him.

That is, until they saw the Ghost. "What the fuck is that?!"

"Friend!" Aaron shouted. "Hold fire! It's a friend!"

Imperial Regulars, from the *Tartarus*. Several had fantasized about this moment, having a clean shot at a heretic like Aaron. But it had been a long few weeks. They might not be friendly themselves, but they weren't his enemy. Not anymore.

"626!" Nora pulled her helmet off, tussling out her short hair with one hand. "You look like garbage."

He had no answer to that. He just chuckled, relief rippling through his bones.

Nora stepped across the line and grabbed him by the back of the head. "You smell like garbage too."

"Where's Fiona?" Aaron asked.

"She's with Bray's team. But I'm doing okay. Thanks for asking." Nora looked up to the soldiers at her back. "Package-1 Secured. Let's get him out of here."

Aaron pulled away from her. "Cassandra has Deckard. They're pushing for an exfil on the far side of..." He stopped.

Something was coming. Big, strong, fast.

Metal.

Nora knew the look and she didn't ask. She gawked for a second, and then she put her helmet back on, the clamps clicking and the EVA suit hissing as it took pressure.

Scar got the order from Aaron, and barely had time to react. It dug its claws into the ground, gripped and ripped a slab of stone up—

—just in time to catch Callum's Warcom blasting through the wall. Scar batted the machine to the ground a few yards away. It slid, carving a trough in the ground deep enough to plant crops.

"WAR-COM!" someone shouted, and the Regulars all dove for

cover. Two Tesla units stepped up, priming their wands to fry Callum where he fell.

No time to warn them. Aaron grabbed Nora, pulling her to the ground. Out of the way of—

Callum.

He came through the open hole his Warcom had punched out. Everyone was so preoccupied with the suit, they never went to check if he was actually in it.

The grizzled Oskie grabbed the barrel of the first Tesla unit and slammed it clean through his partner's chest with a spray of sticky red bone. Slick with gore, the fob of the unit released a jet of electric current that fried the air where Nora would have been.

The arc tore into the drop pod, welding and slagging the steel until it found an unlucky Regular who had stepped up to support his friends. His suit caught fire, and popping something inside, filling his helmet visor with viscera.

Aaron shoved Nora off of him and as far away as he could, trying to scramble to his feet. Callum advanced straight for him, no eyes for anything else. "I want a second crack at you, *skel*!"

Shame. Shame at having lost a fight. A thousand abusive instructors' voices crawling in his mind, shouting his inadequacies over and over. He'd never be good enough, never enough. Too poor, too dumb, too slow, too lazy—

All that rage, now tracked at Aaron.

Nora raised her rifle—

And Callum heard the trigger pulling. He didn't dodge the bullet. He reached over and casually bent the barrel, sending the shot up into the roof. He leered at her, smiling. "Relax...I didn't forget about you."

She gritted her teeth, trying to pull the gun free of his grip. But that look slipped from her face as the Warcom...stood up. Empty pilot seat silhouetted in the shadows—and raising every gun on its considerable chassis.

Tilting his head, Callum snapped the barrel off of Nora's rifle, slamming the rough steel spike down into her shoulder. She screamed and crumpled to the ground.

All the better, because the platoon of Regulars opened fire. Callum darted from left to right, flicking out of the way of each individual burst. The Regulars were well-trained, trying to conserve ammo and not spray mindlessly, but every time they reacquired him, Callum simply blinked to another spot. His boots carved intricate patterns in the dirt as he tried to get traction for each escape.

Aaron thought this might be harrowing, dodging this much concerted gunfire, but Callum seemed to enjoy every moment.

Ultimately, the Oskie slipped backward to take cover behind the empty drop pod. He cackled, licking at the air to get a taste of the electric adrenaline. Gunfire ripped and skipped off the pod, trying to keep him suppressed and dissuade him from leaving cover.

Like it knew its moment, the Warcom took two forward steps. Its personal shield rippled with the occasional impact. And it raised its arms.

BRRRRAAAAP! Twin autocannons gave no concern for stone or metal, rending it all to clouds of atoms. When the rounds impacted flesh, the person simply exploded.

Callum doused himself in water with a boiling hiss, trying to cool off his implants before the next stage of this encounter. Scar growled, ready to pounce.

No, Aaron urged. The Warcom. Deal with that.

Scar snorted derision and turned back. It waited for the Warcom to sweep its gunfire to one side, and then Scar charged. Before the guns could sweep back, Scar was on top of it, easily pushing both arms through the deflector shield and sinking into the suit underneath.

The Tesla charger on the Warcom's back snapped up, trying to lash out against the nearby attacker. Tongues of lightning bit into Scar's back, tracing ugly lines along the creature's hide.

But the concentrated rage of an entire species on its last legs... didn't give a damn. The great beast bellowed, turning pain into fury, and Scar hurled the Warcom to the ground, crushing half of the suit's gear with its own weight.

With the Regulars and Scar occupied, Callum had all the opening he needed. Aaron was laid out on the ground, just a few meters away. He didn't smile, or sneer—he snarled, like a wild animal.

This was going to feel good.

Aaron took a breath, tried to focus. He saw the yellow contrails leading out from Callum's flesh, projecting the undecided patterns. But they never...they never sharpened up.

Because Callum stopped, stuttered. And shivered.

—As the Ghost had latched onto his back, sucking oxygen from his high metabolism, ripping it out cell by cell. Draining him dry.

The Oskie looked over his shoulder at the shade latched onto him. He grimaced, roaring years' worth of untempered rage at a silver cloud—

Before he vanished in yellow streaks off down the hallway, the Ghost trailing behind like a swarm of locusts.

"*Fra tow ni*—uggh!" Nora tried to stand up but didn't have the strength. Aaron couldn't tell how deep it had gone, but if Callum wanted her dead, he'd have buried that chunk of steel in her rib cage. He had wanted her to watch before she died.

"Medic!" Aaron shouted.

He was met with Scar's pained roar, as the Warcom shoved back, tossing Scar like a rag doll directly up into the ceiling and snapping off a chunk of Scar's skull fan in the stone, leaving it there like a calling card. The alien crumpled to the ground in a pile of limbs and blood, whimpering. The Warcom snuck its feet back under itself, and hydraulically heaved itself up to standing.

One gun arm still worked, and it raised the rotating barrels to finish off the alien.

"Four-ty!" a familiar booming voice called out.

Two grenadiers shouldered their tubes, and with hollow thumps, they sent their ordinance.

The Warcom felt it coming, swinging its good arm to bat one of the rounds into the wall, filling the air with clouds of soot and smoke. But the second one smacked right into the deflector shield, glowing a dome of blue-white energy in the smoke.

Sergeant Bray stepped up over Aaron's prone body. "Let loose!" he cried out.

And dozens of tracers lanced in, as the Regulars peppered the Warcom's shield with incoming fire.

The dome glowed bright as it tossed rounds aside, shattering each bullet with the non-Newtonian field. But force impacted was still force imparted. The mech stepped back once, twice, trying to brace itself against all of the incoming attack lines. It spun up its gun arm—and took another explosion to the shield, rocking it backward.

Bray looked down at Aaron. "You alright, son?!"

"Cassandra! She's getting away!"

Bray grimaced, looking at the mechanical hurdle in front of them. "My job is to get you off this moon. Don't argue with me."

"I'm not." He felt the hollow beneath him, the dozens of friends that surrounded him now. The Capitals, the Navy, the Jergad—they had all come together to face this one day, and every day after it. Not for him, but for themselves and each other.

He owed them nothing less than the same.

Aaron called and Jergad claws rose up from the ground around him, pulling him through the rock like it was a veil of cloth and packing it back in place. Bray's face twisted in alarm and nightmarish disturbance as Aaron vanished from sight, like the rock under his feet was incorporeal.

"I'll never get used to that," Bray muttered. "Hit it again!"

The Jergad rolled through their tunnels, and Aaron rode along like an ocean current. He felt the battle raging around them, as dozens of lives burst into flame and sank into ash. He heard cries for help, prayers to forgotten Gods.

It should have overwhelmed him. But it didn't. He could filter through it, close his mind to the chaos and the pain. And he could find its radiant source.

Cassandra was nearing her exit, through the mining floor, down a lift and far below. She was heading for a secret shuttle dock where the rigs never dug. Devious. She hid her escape where the Capitals would be most desperate to get away from.

"Down," Aaron said. And the Jergad burrowed after her...

CHAPTER
THIRTY-ONE

EDEN

"GREEN-3! TORPEDO, TORPEDO!" "Brace-brace-brace!"

Eden was nearly thrown from her feet. It felt like the whole of the world turned on its side for a moment, trying to hurl her into the wall. The *Tartarus* bucked underneath her, an angry bull.

"Hull buckling in decks Delta through Foxtrot, Section 23 Aft," the Bosun reported. "Crew chief non-responsive. Secondary air bursts on Charlie Deck."

Eden had never been on the Jump Deck of an Imperial ship, let alone one as impressive as the *Tartarus*. But an imbecile could tell that this was not a good day. The large room still managed to be claus-trophobic, with a low ceiling, but terraces gave room for the various computer stations. Half of the people at those stations were bleeding.

She stumbled through the doorway, clutching her medkit to her side.

She could see the entire battle like there were no walls, a glass house in space. Cameras punched in for greater focus on individual portions before pulling out again for a macro view—Lindell's wrist was plugged into the command chair, and he was likely issuing those commands with but a thought.

Fighters zipped to and fro in, trying to put pressure on the different quarters. Guns off the carriers and the *Tartarus* lit up the sky with focused walls of explosions, a shield of detonating bomblets that shifted to address the latest threat and shredding any material that got too close. Waves of bombers stayed outside of that web, lobbing volleys through it. And the carriers beyond were stamping and mailing their own shots.

Too much, too many directions for the *Tartarus* to cover. They had to pick which hits they wanted to block, and which hits they wanted to take.

Troop transports waited just outside of the web, waiting to descend on the moon and overwhelm the invaders.

Lindell bellowed over the thunder of the guns. "Get some fire on those carriers, Saubert!"

"They're covering each other, sir, picking off every shot I throw at 'em. And those bombers are pulling all my teeth!" shouted Saubert from his Gunnery station.

Lindell took the news like a champion. He rolled his neck, opening a comm channel with a twitch of his eye. "Ymir-1, we're getting *hammered* back here. You've got to take those bombers out of commission, or we won't be able to engage those carriers."

"We're dropping 'em just as fast as we can, but the flak is pretty thick out here, sir!"

"*Tartarus* Actual, due respect, you're sitting still! Can you give us a little bob and weave?" Eden could easily pick out Aisling's voice from the chatter. She was the only one giving backtalk.

Lindell elected to ignore the mouthy brat. He needed every gun he had, even the chatty ones. He glanced back at Eden. "What're you doing on my Deck?"

"My Corpsman is suffering from massive oxygen deprivation," Eden said, "so you get me."

Lindell grimaced, snapping his fingers towards the very serious man sitting at the Tactical station: Saubert. The Warrant Officer had his arm clutched to his chest. Likely he'd bashed it against his console but refused to leave his post.

She marched up to him, tapping the ground with her foot. The panel flickered in recognition, before assembling a seat for her, hundreds of tiny blocks constructing comfortably behind her knees. "Let's have a look at that arm, shall we? Can you extend it?"

He shook his head, a quick terse denial. His eyes, watery from the pain. "I'm sorry...for my part."

It took her a moment. What could he be talking about?

Vanguard.

"Don't worry about that right now. One thing at a time." She paused, worried that brush off might be taken the wrong way. "...But thank you."

His nod was so short and sharp, it looked more like a tremor. He glanced back at his display. "Another salvo through the web!"

Everyone on the bridge braced against their chairs and consoles— and the ship lurched underneath them. Not as bad as it could've been, but that meant it was worse somewhere else.

Suddenly, a sinister voice echoed from the loud speakers. "Imperial Command Ship *Tartarus*...this is your final warning. Cease hostile action, and there need not be any more bloodshed."

She didn't recognize the voice, but the uneasy way Saubert looked upward gave her pause, like he expected the vengeful hand of God to reach down and smite him for his crimes.

"Our armies are billions strong," the voice said. "You are fifty thousand. There is no hope for victory; there can only be hope for mercy."

The deck doors opened, and Talania entered, soft steps and furrowed brow. The former Colonial Governor let her medical kit slip off her shoulder to the ground, as she internalized that voice.

She knew it from somewhere...

Lindell straightened up in his seat, blinking—and a viewscreen appeared. Formal regalia with brilliant blue & white epaulets, and ornate ribbons on his chest. His jaw was chiseled square and his eyebrows thick and dark, to match the endless void in his eyes. That stare was not empty, but boundless, filled with such nightmares as yet to be shared.

"M-Minister Caldwell," Lindell choked out.

"Warrant Officers have not yet earned mantles of Command," Caldwell dismissed, "let alone command of an Eisenclad." This was less insult as much as a statement of fact. Lindell was lesser than the station he tried to fill. This was not to be debated or litigated.

"Minister, I must..." Lindell struggled with the metaphorical hand at his throat. "Deckard Tiberiet is an honorable man—"

Caldwell cut him off. "Speak when you have something to educate me with. But until such time, be silent. You have tested the limits of my civility, cost loyal Imperials their lives, and disrupted the flow of commerce in the Core."

The flow of commerce? Eden's eyes narrowed. Charon was a center for 'commerce', was it?

The ship rocked with another hit, but Caldwell's stoic face remained so. "Surrender now, Officer. There is no negotiation to be made."

And Talania took a solid step forward, her eyes coming alight like hot iron fresh from the forge. "I know you, don't I?"

Caldwell's eyes snapped over to her like the movement alone could decapitate.

Talania didn't so much as blink. "I do! You were the one that Marcus Riley was constantly feuding with. God, he had some *unkind* things to say about you."

The Minister had heard a lot worse than that. "Officer Lindell, my offer cannot be deferred or delayed."

Lindell glared at Talania, hissing, "Get out!"

But Talania was on a roll now. "See, it's not often you come face to face with the Devil himself. I don't know if I should bow, curtsy. Salute? What do you prefer? Don't tell me, I'm not going to do it anyway. See, it was *your* name that signed off on the deployment orders, the same ones that stripped Vanguard of its protections and *created* Marcus Riley in the first place. It was *your* name on the orders to bombard Vanguard into a glass plate. Your name—God, it's like meeting my nemesis." She glanced at Eden, shivering. "D'you see that? I got chills!"

"Talania Kol'mira dei Dedria," Caldwell began, "spawn of Christopher Alexan dei Dedria, duly elected Governor of Vanguard, traitor to the Consul and the children of the Pilgrim."

"Blessed be his steps," Talania finished. "You forgot that I'm also a heinous bitch, a raging alcoholic, and a dutiful daughter."

Caldwell tilted his head, acknowledging the extra titles with a hint of amusement.

Talania leaned on the back of Lindell's chair, and the Warrant Officer stiffened, like he was now unwillingly dragged between crosshairs. But he was not nearly stupid enough to move and draw attention.

"See, I think you're actually afraid. Because this...just *keeps* happening." Talania crossed her arms and let her head hang to one side, playful. "And me and Aaron? Always right in the middle of it. And if Lindell here surrenders, you can finally put an end to it."

Caldwell was a good poker player, and he didn't give his face any flexibility. "Officer Lindell...let there be no more room for confusion: arrest that woman and save yourself. I cannot state my position any more clearly than I have."

"What're you going to do, big man?" Talania demanded. "You going to come get me? You going to stride out of your ivory tower, suit up in the medals—the ones you never won—to execute me in the square? See, let me tell you what I'm going to do: I started out thinking I had to take down a tyrant in Riley. Then I worked with Admiral Tiberiet against my own friends to try and stop a war, and that didn't work either. It's never been clearer to me, that if I walked into your office and handcuffed you...this still wouldn't stop. There's always going to be someone new ready to hurt the people I love, who will drive the universe with nothing but pain and fear. I can't change that." Her eyes darkened. "But you'll be a nice place to start."

Caldwell was not amused. "Are you quite finished?"

"Never." Talania smirked. "I'll be playing this song till they bury me. So you better get out here and do it yourself. Talania Dedria is your enemy number one, leader of the Capital Rebellion, the Voice of Vanguard…I'm in command of this little shitshow now, and I am going to tear down your little blood-stained Empire, brick by brick if I have to." She pointed at the bulkhead behind her. "This ship? It's full top and bottom with patriots, people who love their homes, their people. And they'd do anything for them. They serve their Consul, and their People, gladly. They *do not* serve you."

Caldwell glanced at Lindell, one last check in. And with a dramatic sigh, the image of the old man winked out of sight.

Saubert coughed his laugh, a smile cracking his face, even as the blood drained from Lindell's face. "What did you just do?"

"The man wanted a Great Big Holy War," Talania said, "and he was going to get it, one way or another. Fill me in."

Something in her tone compelled him. "Two *Alighieri* fleet carriers in staggered formation, multiple fighter wings and a landing force ready to take the moon. We can't cover the moon below if we shift, and we can't penetrate their defenses from back here."

"Stood up and locked up," Saubert grimaced.

Talania responded like a seasoned graduate of Academie Bellator. "So split them up."

"How?"

She side-eyed Lindell. "You're bigger than they are. Knock some bodies down with it."

"But Charon—"

"Will bore them," Talania said, "if an Eisenclad dreadnought started barreling through their fortifications. Stop playing defense, and get in their face."

Another blow rocked the deck, and this time Eden fell—or rather the ground decided to punch her in the shoulder. She rolled through it, probably saving herself from a broken collar bone.

"We're about to lose our shields," Saubert warned.

Lindell considered that news, and looked up at Talania, as if he might draw strength from her conviction.

And he swelled up. "Navigation! Give me sixty percent impulse, forward thrust. Saubert, give the shields everything we've got to spare."

The Dreadnought groaned to life as engines the size of Vanguard came alight, thrusting millions of tonnes of steel through space and away from Charon.

Lindell pulled up his radio display with a flick of his wrist. "Ymir, Jotun squadrons. Change of plans. Give me a wedge formation ahead of the *Tartarus*. Cut me a road."

"Now you're talking!" Aisling shouted. "Mark your targets and focus fire. Nobody gets close."

The lead jockey was unamused. "If you give orders to my squadron again—"

"Just do it, old man."

Eden helped Saubert extend his wrist and locked a brace around it. That would keep him stable, at least until the next hit threw all the bones out of alignment again. And he laid his good hand on her shoulder, a mixture of thanks and physical balance.

They both watched as the ship lumbered ahead, drawing closer to the two fleet carriers. Shots rained in, but the tighter fighter phalanx intercepted most of them, sparkling explosions illuminating their path ahead.

"Where are the troop carriers?" Lindell asked.

Saubert squinted at his screen. "They're...they're breaking off?"

"No cover," Talania explained. "They can't push the moon without cover, and their cover is now occupied by us."

Lindell shook his head in disbelief. "They care more about the carriers than the moon."

"Fenris-1 to *Tartarus*, you've got inbound fighters on your six o'clock! Requesting permission to engage."

"Negative," Lindell ordered. "Stay with Charon. We can take it." He glanced at Saubert. "We *can* take it, right?"

"I don't know, Trevor, but you said it with confidence."

Lindell drew a breath. "Fuck it. Let's see how these bastards do when we're close up. Target the *Ixion*, full throat. Open fire!"

"My pleasure," Saubert grunted, swiping a few keys.

Far below, a rail gun charged, and a crane swept an inert hunk of metal into the chamber. Cleared by the gunnery chief, the chamber was sealed and indicated green. Gases were vented from the chamber to reduce any friction or influence. Microscopic deflections would throw their shot miles off course.

And Eden felt the weapon through her spine, as a hundred tonne slug hurtled out of the ship. The Imperial Web snapped to the threat, a thousand tiny explosions looking to shred or deflect the shot. But they were far closer than the Web was designed to handle, less time to complete interdiction.

The round got through, cracking the *Ixion's* shields in one hit, and punching into the starboard side.

"Eat it!" Saubert shouted, fist-pumping with his newly braced hand. And immediately winced in regret.

Eden saw the carriers come aglow, as retro thrusters tried to maneuver them away from the approaching titan.

"Get in between them," Lindell ordered.

"We'll take some ugly hits doing that," Saubert cautioned.

Lindell glanced up at Talania, approving. "And they'll be cut to pieces. Fenris, last call. We're going to give you the cloud cover. Time to get everybody off that rock."

CHAPTER
THIRTY-TWO
FIONA

FIRE. Ash. Blood and glory.

Chunks of rock fell from the ceiling. She should be happy to see this old haunt mired in such sweet violence. But all she could picture was Aaron buried, crushed under piles of falling stone and rebar.

Fiona led the way through Charon's tunnels, all swagger and gun pinched to her hip, with Solomon and Graccus hot on her heels. With how twitchy they both were, she didn't need to draw. She would just be chasing targets they'd killed already.

Not that she was going to let them know that—she was more than happy to strut into a room and have every threat to her suddenly whistling through holes in their throats. A year ago, she'd have liked to walk the world like this. But right now? She was just looking for one man.

They emerged on the Foundry floor, ghostly quiet but rumbling, like the moon was stirring from a long slumber. Charon wasn't big, and the rattling debris raining down from destroyed spacecraft was enough to shake the whole cursed place. Liquid metal glowing hot in the crucibles bubbled and rippled with each impact, unattended and ready to spill. The catwalks above creaked on their moorings, desperate to shake free.

The Foundry...the exact place she had abandoned Aaron just a day before. Now where had he gone?

"No surly residents?" Graccus asked.

"All of 'em locked up," Fiona said, "and they'll have no idea what's going on." Inside those cells, all they'd know was the ground had grown tired of their presence.

She dragged her fingers over the syringe on her hip, flexing her new prosthetic fingers. The back of that steel hand itched, like it knew something she didn't.

Good. At least that old instinct, deep in the recesses of her brain, hadn't left with the old hardware. But what had gotten its hackles up?

The lift...the gear was turning. Someone was going down, far down. Now who could that be? Aaron? Callum? No...who of the unavailable faces would run from a fight *deeper* into Charon?

Cassandra.

"That lift will take us down into the Pits," Fiona said, pointing at the rickety elevator on the far side of the room. "Less heat, less oxygen, so breathe soft."

"Oy, Fiona?" Solomon asked.

She wasn't done, and anything he had to say, she was likely about to answer. "She'll likely have laid some surprises for us, so Solomon? You should go first."

"Fiona," Graccus urged.

She rolled her eyes, turning around. "What, boys?!"

Aaron. He stood behind them, two Jergad at his back. Chest heaving and hair full of dirt, but it was him. Every imperfection, every scuff, and his stupid sheepish grin.

Fiona felt the breath hitch in her throat, and out came a ragged gasp. "...Aaron."

He gave a stupid little wave of the hand. "Hi, guys. Fancy seeing you here."

Graccus stomped over to him and wrapped Aaron in a big hug, damn near lifting him off the ground. The Jergad cooed some minor distress, but they figured out quick enough that this was...some kind of affection. The Oskie whispered something in Aaron's ear, and Aaron laughed it off.

Solomon just jerked his head, a little chin raise, and that was all. Aaron gave him a similar nod in recognition, before settling his eyes on Fiona.

She tried to swallow her embarrassment. "Sorry I hit you in the head with a prybar."

"Eh," Aaron said, "everything squishy's still in there, so..."

"Where's Deckard?" Graccus asked.

Aaron pointed to the lift. "She took him down below."

"You sure?" Graccus probed, before immediately retracting the question. "Wait a minute, why the Hell am I asking that. Of course, you're sure."

Aaron smirked. "I'll get Deckard. You guys handle Callum."

Fiona's blood boiled and her spine tingled. But she straightened up. No. She had to get Aaron to safety. Callum would keep.

Solomon was...less stoic. "Where is he?" he growled.

Aaron scanned the room, like he was watching a butterfly nobody else could see.

Graccus tongued his cheek. "You going to share or—"

"I'm trying to pin him down," Aaron scolded. "He's kind of erratic right now."

"Oh, good," Fiona said, "because he was always so much fun before."

Suddenly, Aaron's pleasant demeanor dropped. "He heard me talking."

Graccus blinked. "What?"

Aaron shrugged. "I had to flush him out somehow. Keep him occupied for me?"

Fiona didn't wait. She reached out, snagging Aaron by the collar and yanking him to the ground—

Just as Callum blasted through the porous rock face, showering rocks over the party. One Jergad barked its alarm—and Callum grabbed its open mouth in a flash, simply ripping the jawbone off like it was attached with naught but string.

The second Jergad took a swing with a scythe arm, but Callum flickered as he dodged at the last second. It was like the strike went through mist.

And Callum flipped backward, delivering a kick to the Jergad's head. The creature bent back with the strike, and Fiona heard its neck crack. And the squelch as the skull fan jammed through its own armor plates, cracking and sinking into the Jergad's spine. He broke its back with its own skull.

"626!" Callum bellowed. And he streaked towards Aaron—

Solomon leveled his rifle, spraying rounds at the Oskie. But the Oskie had exactly no patience for that bullshit. He side-stepped the burst, boots skidding along as he tried to get traction again, before launching into Solomon's side and sending the Capital rocketing across the room.

Fiona palmed the syringe. Still intact. One minute, to deal with a berserker like this? Could it be done?

She flexed her augment, checking on the hidden twelve gauge inside. She'd have to get her one shot placed just right, nice and close, too close to dodge.

Before Callum could turn on Aaron, Graccus melted out of the air, active camouflage breaking just as he flew in with a knee to Callum's chest. The hit sent Callum sailing into the side of a glowing crucible, denting the three-inch iron belly. Above, the fluid sloshed and spattered, sending cherries of molten slag raining around the room.

"Aaron, go!" Graccus shouted.

Aaron scrambled to his feet, streaking off toward the lift. Callum darted after him in a blur of yellow tracers.

No.

Fiona raised her pistol, and peppered shots at the yellow light. She might not hit him, but he had to stop and dodge each shot. And his boots only had so much purchase on the ground, squeaking and tearing into the stonework each time he had to change direction.

He couldn't chase Aaron with people shooting at him. So he made one final dodge, and Fiona suddenly felt his hot fingers around her wrist. His left eye was bloodshot, some augment torn inside. And blood dripped from his ears. "You...bore me." She felt the bones in her wrist creak.

Aaron sprinted to the elevator. Good. He was safe.

She reached for the syringe.

Graccus tackled Callum—and nearly took her fleshy arm along with them. She bounced and scraped along the ground, her head screaming in a thousand different ways. She pulled herself up to her knees, studying the dislocated fingers that had been wrenched out of place. They tingled and burned and chilled and burned again.

She gripped the fingers with her prosthetic, yanking out sharply —crying out as the tendons pulled the bones back into alignment.

Okay, based on the sharp pain, they might have also cracked, but they were in one piece.

She looked up, trying to find Callum and Graccus. It looked a bit like a cartoon whirling cloud of yellow streaks and dust. She only caught glimpses of the action as each man had to pause to get footing, traction, anything they could push off of. Graccus would melt into the cloud, camouflage causing Callum to pause and listen for where the attack would come next.

A clang as the elevator door closed—which seemed to prompt Callum to launch himself at the grating, denting it with his bloodied fists. "I'm not through with you, 626! I *will* find you!"

"Yeah?" Fiona shouted at him. He turned, gritting teeth and dripping blood. She cracked her neck, stripping off her helmet. "Well, I'm not done with you."

Solomon peeled himself off the wall to find his gun horribly warped beyond repair. He tossed the pieces aside, and yanked his quick-knife from its sheathe, glinting in the yellow glow from the crucibles. And Graccus drew himself up tall, bouncing on the balls of his feet, steam already rising from the sweat on his skin.

Callum took their measure, three on one...and a satisfied laugh rolled up from his belly. "Finally. A real fight."

Solomon threw Fiona a glance, at the syringe on her hip.

No, she shook her head. Not yet. If they tried too early, they'd wither before they could lock him down. They had to set up the moment.

Callum thumped his chest. "Come on!"

Graccus moved first, a blast of yellow light as he blinked forward, slamming a knee through the space Callum once occupied. He bent the steel grating of the elevator door, hitting it so hard he actually hung there, the dent so deep it supported his weight. That is, until Callum grabbed him about the waist and body-slammed him into the ground like a meteor.

Fiona and Solomon rushed in—but Graccus was on his feet before they even got four steps. As the two Capitals charged in, Graccus climbed on top of Callum's muscled form, using his own arms and legs to try to bind up Callum, keep him still and expose vulnerable squishy bits.

Solomon lunged—but Callum somehow got a limb free, batting Solomon away. Fiona swung with her augmented hand, looking to deliver a crushing blow to Callum's ribs.

But Callum spun like a dancer, slinging Graccus down on top of her. They both tumbled, but they rolled through the hit, separating and ending up on their feet.

Like a demon fresh from the fires of Hell, Callum advanced, glowing bloody eyes. His augments were so hot, the sizzling skin above them was starting to char and peel away, filling the air with the stink of burnt flesh. "You were my *friend*!"

Graccus's face twisted in private agony. "I was more than that."

Callum snapped a hand backward—catching Solomon's quick-knife right through his palm. Solomon strained on it, trying to pull the knife back. But Callum squeezed, balling up his fist to grip the guard. "You'll need to be faster than that, *skel*." And he pushed Solomon down, separating him from the knife.

The Oskie drew the blade out of his own flesh, tossing it to his other hand and brought it slamming down—

Something yanked Callum backward away from Solomon, almost taking his feet off the ground. Fiona looked, and Graccus was still standing next to her. What had grabbed him?

It grew in density, coalescing around Callum: Aaron's little vampire cloud friend. The Ghost had gotten a taste for the Imperial and wanted to finish its meal.

Callum flailed, looking for anything he could get a hold of. It pulled him back, away, up into the air. And Fiona could see him withering before her eyes, cheeks sinking. But also...

Individual flecks of fire within the cloud, like sparks cracking off of an ember. Callum saw it too. They were gas creatures, draining oxygen. And oxygen was quite...flammable. Callum was a heat source, but there was something even hotter close by.

Desperate, Callum flailed at a nearby crucible with his hand, slamming it again and again. Graccus saw the plan and grabbed Fiona. She had never moved that fast in her life, and it made her stomach revolt. Her inner ear was practically inverted, gravity all wrong. Up was now left, and down was somewhere intangible. Until Graccus set her down, and she nearly threw up.

Just in time, as Callum finally pierced the crucible, raining hot golden metal where she had once stood, and bathing the Ghost in its splendor. The whole cloud ignited, filling the air with a ball of fire that engulfed Callum, stripping him from sight. His scream was drowned out by the sudden rush of air and the splat of the hot metal on the Foundry floor.

Solomon stood up, looking over the slag as it began to cool into glowing reds, metallic lava separating him from Graccus and Fiona. She could barely see him, the mirage warping the air, but he gave them a sharp nod to check in.

Graccus, on the other hand, was not doing so well. Each breath trilled and vibrated, and his skin steamed like it might scald her if she touched him. "You copacetic, Imp?"

"Oh yeah," Graccus choked out, with a robotic croak to the tone. "Nothing a cold shower won't fix."

Crack.

Fiona looked back at the slag—and Callum was already halfway out of the cooling molten puddle. Most of his skin burned away, just bone and exposed muscle and hatred, eyes cold and fixed. "*Graccus!*"

Callum blurred as he lunged—and all Graccus had time to do was throw Fiona out of the way. Fiona slid along the ground, rolling across some of the cooling metal—searing her suit. Lashing out with her prosthetic arm, she scraped to slow down, sending up a shower of sparks and slag.

When she looked up, Callum and Graccus were batting hands, swiping grips and punches and kicks—and then Callum got the leverage he needed, spinning Graccus into a headlock.

The syringe, the stimulant. Take it now.

Fiona reached for it on her hip—but it was shattered. One of her tumbles, or some of Callum's abuse. It wasn't rated for ballistic impact. The fluid was already drying up, staining her hip.

EMF Grenade. Now. Graccus would know what to do.

She yanked the silver orb from her pocket, twisting it active and hurled it. No aim, no regard, just give it to the spy.

Graccus let go of Callum's arms, letting the grip tighten around his neck, as he reached for the ball. Straining for it.

But that grenade may as well have been traveling in slow motion to a man as fast as Callum. He spun in place, whirling Graccus away and out of reach. With a clenched fist, he slapped the ball out of the air, sending it hurtling across the Foundry and out of sight.

Fiona's breath caught in her throat.

Callum leaned down to whisper into the Spy's ear. "*Zu gloriam, mizu.*"

"No!" Solomon screamed.

—As Callum snapped Graccus's neck. All of the pain, the rage, the humor, the light...left Graccus in an instant. And he slipped to the Foundry floor.

Callum took a breath, rolling out the kinks in his neck. She could see the steel coils that replaced much of his upper back. But so much of him was cooked to carbon. How was he still alive?

He looked up at the two Capitals, throwing his patched steel arms wide. "Who's got next?"

Fiona grit her teeth and flexed her arm. Maybe she could get lucky and plant a shot in his ugly face.

But Solomon stooped low, picking up a shard of the broken syringe, studying it. What was he—

Far too casually, Solomon stabbed the chunk into his leg, sinking it deep. Even Callum was startled by that move, crooking his head and raising the one eyebrow that was left. "That was certainly...a choice."

A blur—and Callum's hand gripped around Fiona's neck, heaving her up off the ground. His fingers, burning stones jamming up under her jaw. She flailed with her augment, trying to get a line on him, but he got a hold of her wrist and locked the arm out wide. "No more tricks, pie rat. Now you just go quietly—"

Schlick.

Callum's grip loosened. He blinked, confused at first. Then he dropped Fiona to the Foundry floor.

She coughed and hacked, trying to get her senses back. What had happened? What hit him?

Solomon. He had used that open time and closed the distance in less than a second, the head of a spoon now uncomfortably sticking out of Callum's ear. Solomon laid a palm on the piece of tableware and wrenched it in deeper, losing it somewhere inside to swirl up gray matter into useless paste—and Callum's eyes rolled back, like he was going to go look for it.

Solomon didn't say anything. No satisfying remark, or witty rejoinder. He simply stared into the exposed side of Callum's skull, and he breathed in, like he wanted to remember the smell of this moment.

And he let the big bastard flop to the ground. He stayed for a long moment over his kill, heavy breathing. Solomon twitched, once, twice. His shoulders shook and his head blurred every so often.

The stimulant. He'd gotten just enough of it into his system.

Solomon finally looked over at her. "Spoon."

CHAPTER
THIRTY-THREE

AARON

THE ELEVATOR SHOOK UNDER HIM, like an unruly animal trying to buck him off its back. It didn't want to go down there. He didn't want to go either.

This was madness. Let her go, let her take that bastard with her. Deckard was no friend to him.

No. If Cassandra escaped, Deckard or not, she'd simply recreate this Hell: every rivet, every smear, every nightmare. There would be a new generation of Capitals like Aaron and Jensen and Eden, tormented anew.

Aaron felt the wind billow around him, like a squall of hot memories. And on that breeze, he thought he heard the voice of old monsters that once lined these halls hissing threats into his ear...

No more.

The elevator clanged to a halt, and he heaved open the gate.

There they were. Insignificant specks against the enormity of the mining rigs, Cassandra stood over Deckard Tiberiet, her augmented leg planted firmly into his throat. There had clearly been some level of disagreement, and despite a broken arm, Deckard had put up a fight.

And contrasting against the darkness was the cool gray, well-lit open airlock of a shuttle, like a magic doorway to another land.

Cassandra looked up at the elevator with a heavy, embellished sigh. But the Lady of the House lit up, her light flaring when she realized who it was, like he was a breath of fresh air upon a flickering ember. Her brilliance filled that cavern and touched every shadow, thrumming with power.

That mask, that black obsidian scar...he recognized it now, recognized that pull, like a siren call from somewhere within. It was music so familiar to him...

It belonged to the Pilgrim once, held close, cupped to her cheek. Just a fragment of something more. Did she even know what she had?

That was how she controlled her light. Perhaps she thought herself just that special, so convinced of her brilliance she never considered the amplifier draped against her skin.

"My, my, you never cease to amaze," Cassandra quipped. "It's almost like you're obsessed with me. Tsk-tsk."

"Aaron, run!" Deckard choked past her foot, and Aaron could hear the servos whine as she squeezed harder. She held him down like a bird of prey held its quarry.

Cassandra cocked her head, her porcelain mask unmoved. She extended one hand towards the waiting shuttle. "You can come along if you like, darling."

Aaron looked up above, at the passing of hundreds of lives and the growing dark in their place. He could see them extinguished in an instant as a rail-gun blast split the *Ixion* in two; he could see the Regulars working side-by-side with Jergad, shedding blood with creatures they had fought against not one year before...

He could see Graccus, now darkened...oh no...

"You want it to stop," she said. "You always have. You wanted peace and quiet. Now this? Imperial ships firing on one another? The bloodshed will belong in the histories. And it will be your fault. Your name will be synonymous with pain. Think this through Aaron.

When have I ever lied to you? Have I ever led you astray?" She punctuated that last question with an additional squeeze on Deckard.

"Never," Aaron whispered, his eyes falling to her. "But you always hid from consequences. Behind masks and doors and excuses. And you can't hide anymore. Not from me."

He could see the tracings of her path, underneath that vainglorious shine, individual lines betraying her move. Somewhere under all that blazing fire, was the real her, and he could make out the thoughts, like piecing together a figure moving in fog.

She pinched Deckard with the claw of her foot, hurling him backwards toward the shuttle. Aaron sprinted at her, straight at the brilliance. So blinding, impossible to—

He closed his eyes and looked for the life under the mask. Looked for the little girl that tortured animals, her toys, and the neighborhood boy. Looked for the perfect daughter who was never perfect enough, for the impeccable student and the diligent worker.

And he found the real her, the small candle inside the blaze.

Cassandra reached into her jacket, pulling out a small baton. Flipping free its clasp, the silksteel released the long shaft and wedge-tip of a spear. With a single step forward, she presented that blade for him to ram himself on to.

But he saw the move coming, saw through her tradecraft and illusions. He dropped backwards, sliding underneath and past the spear tip and grabbed on to the shaft.

His first strike connected with her mask, and the porcelain cracked under the pressure. And in that moment, her luminescence flashed like a sun gone nova.

She yanked backward on the spear, and the slick material slid underneath his fingers, dragging the edge through. The steel edge clicked off bone, his blood staining the white metal.

Her augmented foot came up, slamming him in the gut like a hydraulic piston. Aaron tumbled to the ground, his gut seizing and spasming. He coughed, hacked. But when he looked up—he could see the spiderweb cracks in her mask. Underneath that manufactured face was...just a girl.

Normal.

Of course, not that she thought she was normal. She had always been...insufficient for everyone. Never meeting what was expected of her.

Not anymore. Never again.

It was like Cassandra saw that discovery, her hand darting up to feel out the cracks, every invasion of her castle. And he could swear, she whimpered.

And her light swelled, filling every crevice and darkened hall. She'd kill him. She'd follow him anywhere, to any star, to any backwater planet. There would never be a corner dark enough to hide from her.

And she'd ensure he understood what torment really was.

His fingers bled. His chest refused to obey, sucking oxygen. He bent to one knee trying to give himself room to recover.

Fight the pain. Find that girl. The real her. Look through the mask, past her facades. It was there, somewhere. He saw it. Find it again.

"You will die here," Cassandra whispered. "Alone and tired and afraid."

Somewhere in the dark he heard something, from everywhere and nowhere. Jensen's comforting voice, confident Graccus, steely Keira. He heard Keeper and Quinn and Carmona—a quiet chorus of everyone he'd lost.

Blue eyes in the dark, hanging overhead.

"You were never alone."

Cassandra charged him, dragging the spear tip along the ground. The metal sparked and spit, the superior hardened alloy carving a trough in the soft alien rock. And she swung for his neck.

Aaron stepped back, batting at the passing spear and overbalancing Cassandra. She brought the blade back fast, the sections of the spear unlocking to flex like a whip, before locking up again for strength.

She was walking him backward fast, and soon he would run out of floor. He brought clenched fists to a sword fight. And no matter how hard he focused, he couldn't push through that blinding radiance, her life so potent...

She slid her leg out and he lifted his to avoid being tripped—and she used his precarious position to simply tip him over with the butt of her spear. One quick jab and he tumbled over like a tree.

His back hit the stone hard, knocking the wind from his lungs a second time.

"Alone. In the dark," Cassandra assured him, as she lowered her spear to his throat.

Something hit Cassandra. The whistle of wind and the clang of metal. The Lady of the House whirled away, favoring her jaw, leaning on her spear.

And Fiona stepped out of the elevator shaft, stone still crumbling and her augmented fingers glowing. She'd jumped down the shaft and slowed her fall by sinking her fingers into the wall. And that same glowing hand playfully twirled a length of iron chain.

Fiona cracked knuckles off of her own shoulder and rolled out her neck. "I've been waiting six years to do that. And I want to do it again." She extended a hand to Aaron, helping him to his feet. Only after he was up did she notice the blood from the cut on his palm had smeared all over her own. "That is disgusting."

Cassandra looked up, her mask now properly broken with the black shard now dangling free of her jaw. She reached up, sinking her fingers under the white and black pieces. They were more than molded to her flesh, but melted to it, part of it. As she tugged and pulled, she started to make headway releasing the bonding and ripping up chunks of skin.

She tossed the remains to the ground beside her, breaking it into uncountable pieces. All except the Pilgrim's Shard, stubbornly whole...

Aaron looked up at the The Lady of the House, now revealed. She was an unremarkable woman, with an angular chin and a small nose, eyes like bitter coffee and thin, sharp lips. And the fire in her eyes could not be measured.

Fiona threw Aaron a glance, with a devilish smirk. "Man, I was hoping for like some hideous scar or a brand, a tattoo. Somethin'...I don't know. Noteworthy?"

Deckard chuckled from his pained seat against the mining rig, rolling waves of both pain and amusement.

Cassandra boiled over. She was more than noteworthy. She was so much more. They were nothing.

She hurled the spear at Deckard, missing by just a few inches as the blade sunk deep into the side of the metal titan.

Aaron rushed to Deckard's side, but not before Cassandra and her augmented leg got there. She planted the steel claw into Deckard's chest, sinking the metal teeth into his torso. He couldn't scream, not when she was compressing his ribcage like that.

She ripped the spear free and went to drive it into Deckard's face. Aaron got there, kicking Deckard in the shoulder and shoving his head out of the way—but not before the spear gouged out a channel in the admiral's cheek. Aaron nicked his own knee on the spear edge as Cassandra pulled it out to strike again.

Fiona coiled the chain up around her augment, bracing herself as she slammed into Cassandra's side. The blow ripped Cassandra free from Deckard. Ribbons of flesh pulled, and a chunk of bone flew from her clawed foot, skittering on the ground.

No more cares, Fiona laid the palm of her augment against Cassandra's skull—and Aaron heard the whine of the capacitor within.

Cassandra swiped the palm aside, and the two struggled with positioning. Fiona wasn't going to waste a shot on a maybe, and she had the augment's strength to make sure this shot was the one. Fiona bit her lip as she strained to get on target.

Cassandra called out. "Hut-hut!"

What did she say? But he felt them respond. Dogs. What?

Aaron flicked his head over, seeing the two attack dogs sprinting out of the shuttle at full murder-mode.

Fiona didn't break eye contact with Cassandra. Wasn't going to blink. Wasn't going to miss this chance—and the charging dog sunk its teeth into Fiona's arm, tumbling her off of Cassandra.

And a single shot went off, sailing harmlessly into the dark.

Aaron turned—and his eyes glowed blue—just in time to get the second dog to slow down in front of him. It squared off, snarling and growling.

It was frightened and obeying a master, a cruel master. A bad master.

But this...this was confusing it. Aaron understood it, could feel its needs...

The moment was broken by the battle cry of Cassandra, charging Aaron with her spear. Aaron broke his link with the dog, catching Cassandra's spear with both hands right behind the head. Slick with blood, his grip loosening, that tip inching closer and closer...

Cassandra bent the haft, and the links all released into sections. In just a second, she looped them around his wrists and had him bound up in taut cable.

He couldn't let go. And she was making him push himself onto the spear.

He thrashed left, right, trying to get his head away from the blade —inadvertently driving it into his own shoulder. Cassandra smiled as she pushed it deeper and deeper, twisting it...

If Deckard was still awake, he wasn't making any noise, didn't move. Perhaps he was playing dead to save himself. His front was covered in blood and torn cloth. Aaron still Saw a small light, smothered and covered in sooty black, but burning still.

Fiona's dog began to maul at the steel arm, pulling at it and twisting the metal. So the devious woman loosed the chain on her forearm, and coiled it around the dog's muzzle. And with a one-two tap on her elbow, she let the dog have its chew toy. The prosthetic arm came free and the dog flopped backwards, letting her go. Now bound to its prize, the dog instead slunk away into the dark.

Fiona scrambled to her feet, barreling at Cassandra's exposed back—and the Lady's steel leg snapped up, catching Fiona square in the chest with a roundhouse kick, sending Fiona hurtling to the side.

Cassandra leaned back over Aaron, putting her weight on the spear tip. "Keep your fire close," she whispered. "Be neither predator, nor prey. For a fire too bright...draws the monsters."

"Yeah," Aaron grunted. "You gotta be careful about that." And a Jergad claw punched out of the ground behind him.

Cassandra whirled away, releasing Aaron, but too slow. The claw hooked her steel leg, piercing clean through the augment and gripping her thigh. Two more claws reached out, further locking her up. And Aaron could hear the chitter of the beasts below the surface.

Aaron picked himself up off the ground, cradling his wounded shoulder. "See...I got my little trick? From these fellas. They can...well, how else to put it? They don't see like you and me, no. Visible spectrum, heat, any of that. No, they See life itself. And you, well...you're something of a beacon. I don't know why, maybe it's your psychosis or something else entirely. But your fire? It's real bright."

Another claw, this one punching clean through the flesh of her other leg. Cassandra screamed, looking at the pull of her skin and the fabric of her pants, as the creature tugged on the flesh. If they wanted to pull her apart, they very easily could...but Aaron had a point to make.

"You built a corner of human life filled with nothing but misery, and then made yourself the sweet, kind, benevolent center of it that every Capital would have to depend on just to make it another day," Aaron said. "You can't fail here. Nobody to disappoint. And even if you did, who cares about Capitals?"

Cassandra lashed out, slashing at the Jergad claws with the edge of her spear. She chunked and hacked through one arm. Aaron blinked, his own hand twitching in pain. And with a shake of his head, the Jergad arms all retreated back into the rock.

But the Lady of the House had realized it wasn't her house anymore. She scanned the floor in terror, waiting for the sharks in the ground to leap out, refreshed and regrouped. Staggered, bleeding, battered. She stumbled towards the shuttle door. But she was never going to get there.

"All life had a purpose to you," Aaron said. "To serve."

"Call them off!" she ordered him, like she had any sway.

"They do what they want. They have that freedom. And now...so do I."

A growl. But of a more familiar tone. And Cassandra looked over her shoulder to see her snarling dogs. Maybe it was a trick of the light, catching just right, but Aaron swore he saw a hint of blue.

"Sulphur! Mercury!" she snapped at them. But the dogs didn't listen.

She got three steps, vanishing into the shuttle airlock...before they sunk their teeth into her. All gnashing, gurgling and tearing.

Fiona staggered over, lip curled in disgust at the display. "I hate to break up this—very horrible—therapy session, but the admiral over there doesn't look so good."

Aaron nodded. "We're done here."

CHAPTER
THIRTY-FOUR
DECKARD

MURKY, blurry colors and distant voices. And then one reached out to him.

"Hey," the soft voice whispered, "you're awake."

His lips were cracked and dry. His chest ached, throbbing from inside out. He lifted a hand, grazing it across his chest.

Nothing. Nothing at all. It was the same fuzzy rough surface it always was.

"Modern medical marvels, Admiral Tiberiet," the voice said. "We are capable of wonders."

"Where am I?" He choked, his voice like sandpaper on his throat. He immediately winced and raised a hand to tenderly inspect whatever damage might be there. Which is when he found his hand was locked up in intravenous fluid lines.

The soothing color blob reached a hand down to still his struggling. "You're aboard the *Tartarus*. You're home. It's safe."

Deckard blinked a few times, and his eyes finally cooperated. The colors and movements sharpened into human shapes, and finally into a person. Tall, lanky, lean and angular. A soprano voice, rich in tone and crisp on enunciation. Educated.

He knew the voice more than the face: Talania.

"Am I under arrest, Ms. Dedria?" he asked, slurring his words.

"I suppose," Talania mused, "but not by me. We're all in trouble together now. And I'm going to need your help getting fifty thousand people out of it, so...chin up, Admiral." She shrugged, nihilistically dismissive of the gravity.

Deckard huffed, not liking that tone of voice. "How long was I out?"

"Would've been three weeks tomorrow."

Deckard had so many questions. Where were they now, and where were they headed, and what happened on Charon? Where was Aaron?

But he couldn't focus on any of them when he saw who was walking about the medical bay, a too-big lab coat slung about her shoulders and sleeves rolled up to the elbow in big balled messes. Her slight bob haircut was pinned back behind her ears, a greasy mop, and she was barely taller than some of the patients in their beds.

Eden. She used to dangle from chains in his brig, and now...she was tending to his crew, and more than a few Capitals.

She and Bray were both standing beside a similarly laid up Nora. They were guiding her through some physical therapy on her neck and shoulder, where a neat new circular scar rested.

Talania followed his eyes back over to Eden. "I don't know how she does it either."

"She saved me?"

"Yeah," Talania gushed with pride and admiration. Which quickly turned to a stern glare. "So be nice."

He had led a fleet to her home. He had orchestrated the deaths of her friends. He had taken her prisoner, tortured her, gave her to a maniac, who tortured her again. And she...saved him? "Why?"

Talania cocked her head. "Because she *saved* you. I know you're drugged, but damn."

"No, I..." Deckard winced. His mind was swimming and throbbing and foggy. "Why...*why* save me?"

Talania raised an eyebrow. "Because." But he wanted more of an answer than that. So she sighed and tried to articulate it. "Because...she's a convicted criminal, a Capital soldier, a doctor. Every single part of her experience says three words out loud: people get better."

———

It was three days before Deckard was up and walking again—not altogether the worst possible outcome, but that was hard to keep perspective on. And that room was making him crazy.

Eden didn't say more than six words to him, all of them medical updates or numbers. She did have some effects brought over from his cabin: some fresh clothes, fine cologne, and pictures. Even his Command Orchid, the brass insignia of a Naval Commander, blessed by the Pilgrim to do the will of the Empire.

He had hung her from the ceiling. She brought him his comforts.

Deckard was fitted with a stabilizer on his left hand, allowing him to get magnetic push off of the ground when he lowered it, like having an invisible electric cane. With that, Eden cleared him to take brief walks up and down the corridor outside Meditech.

The fresh air wasn't much better; it still smelled like ozone and bodily fluids. But he was able to drag himself up and down the hall-way, which did something for his tingling feet.

On the sixth day, he slipped the stabilizer puck onto his wrist. With a curt nod to Eden, and an affirmative nod back, Deckard made his way to the door.

But it opened before he got there. Trevor Lindell stood with his head low, starched and stiff, as he waited for the doors to part. He was halfway through muttering an apology and stepping aside, when he saw who it was before him.

Breathless, he stammered out the name. "Admiral Tiberiet?"

Admiral. Everyone kept calling him that. "Lindell," was the only greeting Deckard could muster.

Lindell tried to perk up his tone. "It's good to see you on your feet again."

Deckard could feel himself wavering, his balance giving out. He had to point himself in a direction or else he'd fall over. So he stepped past the earnest officer into the hallway, halfway hoping Lindell would get the message.

But it would take more than a literal brush-off to shake him. Lindell fell into step behind him. "Admiral, I was wondering when you might resume—"

"Don't call me that."

"Admiral?"

Deckard snapped. "Don't call me that! What did I—I'm not your admiral! I haven't been for some time. Am I the only member of this crew with respect for the..." he trailed off, electing instead to stare at the nearby bulkhead.

Lindell inspected that wall, as if to try and find what had captivated Deckard's attention. "Sir?"

"I served..." Deckard started, his lip quivering, "I served for thirty years. At the People's request and with their mandate. And when they were through with me, I threw in my lot with criminals."

"You don't mean the Capitals, do you, sir?"

Deckard took a breath. "I turned to...someone I thought I could control."

Lindell stiffened, drawing himself to his full height and raising his chin up, like he was presenting his beard for inspection. "Permission to speak freely, sir?"

"You weren't already?"

"That is weapons-grade hot summer bullshit. Sir." Lindell glanced down at his admiral, with a look more potent than Deckard had ever seen in him. "You served for thirty years. And in thirty years, you always tried to do the right thing. And you still can. The admiral I know wouldn't let any brass get between him and doing a thing the right way. So...who the fuck are you, sir?"

Deckard's spine tingled, and he felt a burn in his chest. It had been a long time since anyone had spoken to him with that much aggression that didn't intend to kill him. "Lindell...a little advice?"

"Sir?"

"A *good* commander keeps his temper."

Lindell pursed his lips. "Never said I was any good at it, sir. I just did what needed doin'. Now when can I expect to see you resume your post on the Jump Deck?"

Deckard scoffed, turning away. "It's *your* Jump Deck now."

He couldn't go back to bed. Not now. He just started walking and kept walking. Soon, he wasn't even hunching over or using his stabilizer. He simply marched on.

He passed engineers and crewmen, the occasional jockey. Everyone stomped along with purpose, attending to some unimportant time table in their heads.

Outside of his uniform, grizzled and unkempt, nobody recognized him. He was just another Naval officer attending to duties unsaid. Nobody kept their distance. He was just...amongst them now.

And he slowed to a stop in front of a set of nondescript doors, an armed Regular standing guard. Having a longer moment to actually study Deckard's face, the guard snapped to attention.

Deckard had no energy to fight it or scold him. No nothing anymore.

"May I go in?" Deckard asked, hollow.

The guard nodded ferociously and turned to crank the door lock. A hush and a gasp as the pressure released, and the doors parted.

The Brig. And standing where Callum once stood was Aaron Havenes, crossed arms in front of the opaque cell blocks.

Deckard ground his jaw and took a steeling breath. And he stepped across the threshold into the room. "I take it you expected me?"

"At some point," Aaron admitted. "You were always going to make your way back here."

The door clanged shut behind him, hissing as the pressure went back into place. Deckard was now locked in a room with his greatest enemy. He leaned on the stabilizer and cleared his throat. "You want an apology?"

Aaron lowered his head, refusing to turn around. "Y'know, I thought for a long time...that's what I wanted. I wanted you to come here and...tears streamin' down your face, you'd give a big dramatic blubbering..." And he clapped his hand against his thigh, giving up. "But that doesn't actually make anything better, does it?"

"No, it does not." Deckard kept that answer from being too snide.

Aaron finally looked back at him. "We both know there's going to be a lot more blood coming."

"For you," Deckard said with a shake of his head. "I'm done with all that."

Aaron tongued his cheek. "Really? Well, I didn't call that one."

Crap. Aaron could read his mind. He knew full well what Deckard was thinking. He was throwing up a smoke screen to look more normal, a mask by any other name. "Don't do that."

"Do what?"

"What *she* would do!" Aaron withered at that, and Deckard was damn well not going to let him off the hook. "Don't try to make me comfortable! Don't try to act disappointed in me. You know what everyone is, so you...you're always going to unsettle people, Aaron. You're going to downright disturb us. You always will. But that is *our* problem. You're not broken, boy. We are. If there were even ten more people like you..."

"Stop."

"Just ten more!"

"You don't want this!" Aaron's voice carried through half of the deck. Deckard could hear the guard outside jump away from the door. Perhaps the Regular was afraid three solid inches of steel might propel straight outward off its rails.

But Deckard didn't flinch. "I wasn't talking about your Sight. Lots of men have power. Callum and Graccus both did, look how they used it. Caldwell. Philippe. But You...Legatus...when given power, you bent it in service."

"So did you," Aaron urged.

"In service to what?"

Aaron nodded, taking in his full meaning. Service in itself had not been a virtue. Deckard had been the cudgel for a bully, nothing more. He had built something, brick by sun-scorched brick, for thirty years. And what had he built with all of that effort?

His own prison.

Aaron raised a hand and waved away the opacity of the wall. Sergeant Elena Mayfield sat in her cell, hands folded across her lap, as she considered the shining white wall. On her end, the wall had not changed, still a blinding white nothing. But now Deckard could see through to his friend, and all he could see was the wrathful curl to her lip and the tightness in her shoulders.

"She wasn't protecting anyone," Aaron said. "She wasn't...under orders. She wasn't..."

Deckard had always assumed there might've been standing orders from Caldwell, that Wolcott should be considered compromised, disposed of. Or perhaps Spymaster Philippe had wanted to tie off the loose ends. Why else would she kill him?

Aaron tempered his words carefully. "She has proclaimed her patriotism. Her loyalty, her duty. But the truth is? She felt threatened. She was angry and...afraid. And he gave her a reason, so..."

"A reason?" Deckard exhaled, incredulous.

This disciplined Sergeant-at-Arms, a soldier he'd trusted, a sister in the faith...she'd simply lost her temper? Mayfield had taken the life of a friend and colleague and excused it under the flag and in the Pilgrim's name.

Deckard thumbed the brass insignia in his pocket, feeling the ridges bite against his skin.

Aaron's eyes softened, brow arched in sympathy. "Do you want to talk to her?"

No. His entire body rejected that idea at the cellular level. Looking at her from here was almost too much. "...She was like family."

And Wolcott was like a son.

"We can put her on trial—"

"No," Deckard cut him off, quickly. "We don't have the resources or the time to spare. Drop her at the first friendly port. Leave her there with a day bag. She can make her own way home."

And Deckard didn't look back as he stormed out of the room.

SHE REALLY LONGED for a good vice right now: losing herself in some music or drinking herself to a stupor. But at the end of a long day, she mostly just sat on the floor of her stateroom with her back against the cold steel bulkhead. It seemed to draw all the heat out of her and pull her muscles back into alignment.

She had almost forgotten how exhausting it was pulling a twenty-hour shift in a hospital setting again. And rounds were coming early again tomorrow.

Was it tomorrow already? Should she just get some breakfast in the mess? How long had she been sitting here? However long it was, she could sit a while longer. She could keep the lights low and just drift...

The door chirped and the Bosun's polite voice cut through her fog. "My apologies, ma'am, but there is a Mr. Tiberiet here to speak with you."

"Urgently?" she asked without opening her eyes.

"I wouldn't go that far. In point of fact, it sounded more like he was hoping I'd tell him no."

She could always grant that wish.

But she sighed and rubbed at the sand in the corners of her eyes. "Hell with it. Open up."

The door slid open, and Deckard twitched in surprise. He gazed into the room like it was the opening of a haunted house, decrepit and unsettling. It was a normal enough bunk; Eden hadn't exactly had spare time to move in. But it was a far-flung improvement on any accommodation she'd had in the last year. Why change anything?

Deckard took a breath and straightened up, masking his discomfort with years of practice. And he crossed the threshold.

He scanned the sitting table, the open door to the lavatory. No sign of her. "Miss Neria?"

She raised a hand, directing his attention down to the floor. "Down here."

He glanced down at her, balled up against the wall, and his face scrunched up. Not out of concern, but confusion. "What are you doing tucked against the wall?"

"Doctor's orders," she snarked. "What can I do for ya?"

"Doctor's orders for what?"

"Says it'll make me taller, cure my psoriasis, and sharpen my vision."

"You sit on the ground in the dark?"

"It's called a migraine, asshole. What do you need?"

Deckard coughed up the lump in his throat, then swallowed it again. Trying to get the words out of his mouth. "I'm told...you worked on Wolcott."

So that's what this was about. "Yeah..."

"May I ask you a personal question?"

She shrugged. "It's your ship."

He hung his head at that but pressed on. "Why?"

That one word felt the same as a hand wrapped around her throat. Not how she worked, or what she did wrong. But why.

"He needed help," Eden said softly. "Who he was, doesn't matter."

"Even though he...personally led the decimation of your home? Gleefully, even."

She glanced around the room for the hidden camera recording her reaction. Finding none, she looked back up at him. "This how you say hi to everybody?"

"Miss—"

"Doctor," she snapped. "Doctor Neria. I think I've earned that much."

That got Deckard to bite his cheek, drawing out a nod of apology. She grunted as she pulled herself to her feet, not even meeting his shoulder height. "I treated my fair share of Imperial grunts who did the actual burning too. So long as they don't immediately sit up and shoot me? We're fine."

Deckard swelled up, going to the words he had prepared and rehearsed, the same words that were draining him. "Anyway...I wanted to...to thank you. For trying, at least."

Her blood went cold. "You might want to have a word with Doc Findley about that."

"I've known the man eleven years," Deckard said, "and what he did doesn't surprise me."

Findley did what Deckard had expected her to do. And she'd thrown him for a loop.

She glanced out the door, half-ready to usher him out so she could get some sleep—but she saw the rucksack sitting on the door-frame. "Going somewhere, Admiral?"

"I'm not—" he stopped himself, tempering his tone. "I'm not an admiral anymore."

"Says you, but everybody else seems to think otherwise. And I'll listen to the majority."

"I don't get a vote?"

"You get a vote," she said. "But so do they.

His eyes went cold, distant. Far away, to a lifetime that he wished he could forget. "I've served long enough."

"So now it's just...somebody else's problem?"

He forced a smile, thin and empty. And he leaned on his stabilizer as he turned for the door.

Eden threw up her hands. "What is it with the men in my life who all think that they're just the *worst*?"

Deckard crooked an eyebrow. "The men who believe themselves touched and gifted, are the ones doing all the damage."

"So stop them," Eden said, bluntly. "Stand up. Do it for the people who *don't* have a dreadnought."

Deckard shook his head, almost laughing. "I push them, they hit back twice as hard."

"'And they've killed people I care about?'" Eden mocked. "Welcome to my fuckin' world. But I guess you've already packed a bag so..."

Deckard drew himself up to his full height. "I don't owe you anything."

"How about an apology? Why don't we start there?"

"I'm sorry."

"Well, that's tough," Eden said, crossing her arms, "because I don't accept it." Deckard scoffed, and went for the door. But she was far from done. "You want to make it up to me? Do something about it."

"Do what?"

"This crew needs you," Eden urged, "so badly, they opened fire on their brothers. They betrayed their service, every code, every promise, every law they've ever respected. And they did it for *you*. They believe the world can be good, because *you* believed it. If you walk out that door...you'll take the ship down with you. What will it have been for, huh? All that blood...we should've just left you in Hell."

Deckard sniffed some grief out of his nose. "How I repay my debts—"

"So you agree they're debts?"

"Of course, I do!" Deckard hissed. "Not a day goes by...I wish I could change what I did."

"Then step up and do something different!"

"You don't think it a tad ironic," he asked, "forcing me to repay my debts through service, *Capital?*"

She let that slight go by. Don't get distracted. "No one is forcing you. Capitals were forced to repay their debts at the barrel of a gun. You? You can get off this ship tonight and walk off into the sunset. Walk off a cliff for all I care, but I will never forgive you. Nor will anyone else who was there...until you give us a reason to, show us you're worthy of it."

Deckard hung in the doorway, leaning against the frame with one hand. The light from the hallway cascading off his broad shoulders.

"Wolcott tried to," she spat. "Why won't you?"

And the admiral raised his head, like a breath of air had been pushed into his lungs, a string drawing up his back, the light outside filling him with new constitution. "Pride. We took pride in what we did." He looked back at her. "They train Naval Officers to feel pride in the fires they set."

"So write a new book. Give them something else to be proud of."

He looked back into her room, like he wanted to stain his memory with it—or perhaps, he was comparing it, measuring her now to when they met.

But he retreated without another word. And all she wanted was a drink and a nap.

CHAPTER
THIRTY-SIX
FIONA

AARON STEPPED off the shuttle into hip-high grass, violet rolling waves of grain underneath an amber afternoon sky that seemed to glow from every horizon.

He whispered, reverent and weak. "It's real."

Fiona clambered off the shuttle, plopping herself onto the ground and relishing the bounce of real, soft soil. She gave it a good couple of hops. "This is amazing. Why wasn't this place colonized?"

"No convenient Jump points. No nearby infrastructure. Frequent electrical storms."

"Is that why the sky looks radioactive? Gwah!" She was nearly bowled over by Scar, as the Jergad leapt forward, bouncing and bounding on all fours, a leathery ripple through the grass occasionally emerging in all its titanic horrible glory. It threw a chittering glance back at Aaron, before diving back in and out of sight.

Aaron chuckled as the Jergad all came streaming out of the shuttle and scattered into the purple grasslands. "They'll do just fine here."

"How do they breed, by the way?" Fiona asked. "Have there been girls and boys in that crowd this whole time? Is it an asexual thing?

Or do seven of them just get in a big pile and nine of them come out?"

Aaron's head bobbed from side to side. "I...you know, there were these pools, there was moss, it was smelly. But I really don't have a scholastic answer for you." His hand was jammed in his pocket, thumb rubbing over something.

"Why'd you keep that thing?" Fiona asked, suspicious.

He withdrew his hand—pulling out the inky black shard of Cassandra's mask, now polished to a shine. Strange glyphics were etched in the material, and they seemed to flow under the surface, like waves lapping at the side of a ship.

"Charon's burnt to a crisp," Fiona said. "Good a time as any to *really* leave it all behind. And you keep something of hers?"

What he said sent a chill down her spine and back up again. "This thing isn't hers."

It was fused to that bitch's disappointingly normal face. What the Hell could it possibly be if not hers? "Could jus' drop it in the dirt, right here."

Aaron sighed, exasperated. "Running from my past...wouldn't be any more functional than if I let it run my life. Like it or not, that place is a part of me. And I won't forget it."

"Well," Fiona said, "Aisling's deleting this happy little system out of our logbook. Far as anyone will ever know, no one's here. They'll be safe."

"I know they will." Aaron sighed, taking in that jewel-toned sunset. He whispered a word under his breath, "Arcadia."

Ah, crap. He named it. Fiona bit her lip. "You're not...coming back, are you?"

"They need me," Aaron admitted.

"Lotta people need you," she said a bit too fast. "What about Eden? Nora, Bray, the rest of 'em? Your whole rebellion? That's your thing, you know. You can't just take a bow."

"I'm not," Aaron assured her. "I'm still here. I just have a job to do first."

"We're going off to fight a war."

"And I'll be watching." He smiled, looking back at her and he just looked so perfect, the way the retreating sun lit up the deep coffee of his skin and the tenderness in his eyes. "I won't be gone. Not for long."

"You want me to leave you a box of rations and a radio?" Fiona asked, trying to hide behind some humor. "Or do you want the challenge?"

"I helped wipe their species off the map," Aaron said. "I should be the one to help them get back upright. Help keep them safe."

"So what, do you..." She waved a hand at the endless wilderness. "I mean, it's pretty, but...are you going to build a cabin? Or just live in a hole?"

"I happen to know some exceptional burrowers."

She tightened her jaw, trying not to laugh. "That sounded so much cooler in your head, didn't it?"

He looked out at that vista, drinking in the cool breeze and letting it wash over him. There was salt on the air, some nearby body of water. It felt like a soothing wash on a hot summer afternoon, a chill up the spine and across the shoulders.

The sun was finally receding and taking the light with it. The stars were peeking out, glittering diamonds. The Jergad poked their heads up out of the grass, curious about the shimmering cloak being draped over their new home.

Aaron took her by the hand and pulled her in close. He locked eyes with her for a long moment, looking for something back there. Like perhaps he had missed whatever spark of life still glimmered inside her. And whatever he found, satisfied him. "If you ever need me...I'll come."

"How?" Fiona pointed at the empty field. "Is Scar going to throw you up? *Really* hard?"

"If you need me," he repeated. "I will come. I promise." There was a certainty in his voice that was both comforting and disquieting.

"...And how are you going to know if I...?" Fiona couldn't finish the question, instead playfully slugging him in the shoulder. "You can't See me. I'm dead. Remember?"

But he just smiled at her, looking up at the twinkling sky. "You're impossible to miss. You warp the world wherever you go. I'll watch the people around you, and watch you change the world. Just promise me this: keep those people close, and I'll never lose you."

Well, that was a tear jerker. She could feel the pressure building behind her eyes. She jammed her tongue in her cheek and stamped her foot, like she could put a cork in the dam. "Come on, man. Why are you all...ugh!"

His soft smile. His gentle hand on her shoulder. "They're waiting for you."

She threw her arms around him and pulled him into a hug. He stiffened at her touch, almost recoiling. He didn't know what to do with this much physical contact. But he relaxed into it, letting his hands close around her, resting in the small of her back.

"You fail to appear in my moment of need," she whispered in his ear, her lips brushing against his skin, "and I will break both of your legs."

———

Eden was waiting on the hangar deck as the gangway dropped. She had her little arms folded across her chest, pouting face and furrowed brow. And as Fiona clomped down the gangway alone, those brows went up. "Where is he?"

Fiona paused, trying to think of the lightest way to say it. "You know, he...he decided to take a little sabbatical from the life of renegade cult leader."

"Fiona..."

"I didn't leave him behind," Fiona assured her. "He stayed."

Eden closed her eyes. What she had dreaded was confirmed. "And you let him?"

"Yeah. I'd say he's earned some R&R, don't you? Of course,

personally, I'd have gone for the Sunset Line on Ilum. He chooses to set up in an artist's rendering with a bunch of alien tank puppies, but...to each his own."

Eden huffed, laughing at a private joke. Fiona squinted at her. "What?"

"Nothing." Eden dropped her arms and forced the tension out of her shoulders. "Just...he got to pick *his* spinning rock."

Fiona considered the doctor, that nostalgic tilt to her head. "Some peace and quiet?"

"Yeah," Eden quietly mused. "Well...the Empire will come looking for him."

"They'll have to get through us first," Fiona promised. Eden's wrist chirped, and Fiona gawked. "Since when do you get an Entiglas before I do?"

"Be a responsible adult," Eden quipped, tapping the computer bracer. "Meditech."

Admiral Tiberiet's voice came through, authoritative, and even a touch playful. "Doctor Neria, we're on approach for the Jump Point. Our delightful governor has requested your presence up on the Deck."

"I'll be right there. Oh, Admiral? Good to have you back in the chair."

"Don't say that," Deckard assured her. "You haven't yet experienced the extent of my exquisite leadership style."

Fiona clapped her hands together. "So, we've got a banged-up Imperial dreadnought, a ragged crew of dissidents and malcontents... and the moral high ground."

"When's the last time you had this much kickass in one place?" Eden asked.

"When I punched the Empire in the mouth."

"So why don't we go make some more mischief?" Eden said, as she turned away.

Fiona watched the little woman power-walk off the deck. And a smile crept across the pirate's face. "I like mischief. Bosun?"

A more official blip and chirp than she liked, but the voice was the same. "Yes, ma'am?"

"Can you give us a song, please? Something...oh, I don't know. Surprise me."

AFTERWORD

I love endings, but I hate goodbyes. Aaron has been with me since I was seventeen years old, turning it in as a completed manuscript for an English project my Senior year of High School. Then, I re-wrote it as a screenplay at least twice. Probably more than that.

Getting to tell this story the way I always wanted to has been a dream—one that you all have helped make a reality. Aaron's story concludes here—for now. But there are other corners of the Empire with trouble stirring...

Fiona's story began in The Gold Service. Grab that novel to learn more about the Pirate Master & the vaunted Boolean Edge.

If you're enjoying the Capital Adventures, please leave a review. It really helps small authors like myself.

Signing up for the Newsletter keeps you on top of the latest news around the Capital-verse.

I also have a cat. I will likely be dropping pictures of her there regularly, as she is a consistent part of my office day. She is bad at being a cat, but she is fat and good and adorable. Sign up and see!

AFTERWORD

https://www.authorivers.com/

ABOUT THE AUTHOR

.

Allen Ivers started writing original stories at the ripe age of eleven, largely trying to figure out why the Disney villains on the television box were the way they were. Villains, monsters, and politicians have always fascinated him with their behavior. Twenty years later, he's still fascinated by bad people and the bad things they do.

He now lives in beautiful Juneau, AK somewhere in that fluffy snow drift. You can find his thoughts about writing, politics, and the odd cute cat on his Twitter.

 facebook.com/AllenIversSFF
x.com/AllenIvers

ALSO BY ALLEN IVERS

THE CAPITAL ADVENTURES

EACH TRILOGY CAN BE ENJOYED INDEPENDENTLY, OR READ AS PART OF THE LARGER SERIES

Book 1: The Blood Service: Book One of the Military Sci-Fi Adventure

Book 2: The Ranks of the Blood Service: Book Two of the Military Sci-Fi Epic

Book 3: Command of the Blood Service: Book Three of the Military Sci-fi Epic

———

Book 4: The Gold Service: A Space Outlaw Action Adventure

Book 5: The Cost of the Gold Service: The Sci-Fi Action Adventure

Book 6: The Powers of the Gold Service: The Sci-Fi Action Adventure

———

Book 7: The Iron Service: A Super Soldier Sci-Fi Adventure

Other Sci-Fi Adventures

Manifest Destiny: A First Contact Sci-Fi Thriller

www.ingramcontent.com/pod-product-compliance
Lightning Source LLC
Chambersburg PA
CBHW022206030726
47494CB00021B/1627